Anne Perry is a *New York Times* bestselling author noted for her memorable characters, historical accuracy and exploration of social and ethical issues. Her two series, one featuring Thomas Pitt and one featuring William Monk, have been published in multiple languages. Anne Perry was selected by *The Times* as one of the twentieth century's '100 Masters of Crime'.

Praise for Anne Perry:

'Perry's characters are richly drawn and the plot satisfyingly serpentine'
Booklist

'A deftly plotted mystery. As always, Perry brings Victorian London vividly to life'
Historical Novels Review

'[An] engrossing page-turner . . . There's no one better at using words to paint a scene and then fill it with sounds and smells than Anne Perry'
The Boston Globe

'Her Victorian England pulsates with life and is peopled with wonderfully memorable characters'
Faye Kellerman

'A beauty: brilliantly presented, ingeniously developed and packed with political implications that reverberate on every level of British society . . . delivers Perry's most harrowing insights into the secret lives of the elegant Victorians who have long enchanted and repelled her'
New York Times Book Review

'A complex plot supported by superb storytelling' *Scotland on Sunday*

'With its colourful characters and edge-of-the-seat plotting, this is a rich and compelling read'
Good Book Guide

'Perry brings a wealth of historical detail and accuracy to her bestselling novels . . . A murder mystery made to make you think'
Lancashire Evening Post

'A feeling for atmosphere that would do credit to Dickens and Doyle'
Northern Echo

'Superbly told and richly authentic in its setting'
Peterborough Evening Telegraph

'[P. . . . . ue . . .
Re. . . . . *Bookbag*

D0307687

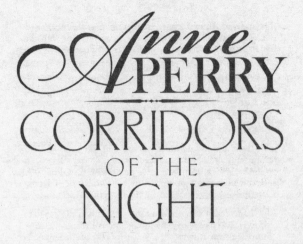

ANNE PERRY

CORRIDORS

OF THE

NIGHT

headline

First published in 2015 by
HEADLINE PUBLISHING GROUP

First published in paperback in 2015 by
HEADLINE PUBLISHING GROUP

1

Cataloguing in Publication Data is available from the British Library

ISBN 978 1 4722 1947 3

Typeset in Plantin by Palimpsest Book Production Limited,
Falkirk, Stirlingshire

Printed and bound in Great Britain by
CPI Group (UK) Ltd, Croydon CR0 4YY

HEADLINE PUBLISHING GROUP
An Hachette UK Company
Carmelite House
50 Victoria Embankment
London EC4Y 0DZ

www.headline.co.uk
www.hachette.co.uk

To my editor at 10/18, Valentin Baillehache, and to
Marie-Laure Pascaud in Publicity.

Chapter One

THE SMALL gas lamps along the walls of the corridor flickered as if there were a draught, but Hester knew that, it being well after midnight, all the doors were closed. Even the windows on the wards would be shut at this hour.

The girl stood motionless. Her eyes were wide, her skin as pale as the nightgown that hung just past her knees. Her legs were matchstick-thin and her feet bare and dusty. She looked terrified.

'Are you lost?' Hester asked her gently. She could not think what the child was doing here. This was an annexe to the Royal Naval Hospital in Greenwich. It backed on to the Thames, well down river from the huge Port of London and the teeming city beyond. Did she belong to one of the other nurses who had sneaked her in rather than leave her alone at home? It was against the rules. Hester would have to make sure no one else found her.

'Please, miss,' the child said in a hoarse whisper. 'Charlie's dying! You gotter come an' 'elp 'im. Please . . .'

There was no other sound in the night, no footsteps on the stone floors. Dr Rand would not be on duty until the morning.

The child's fear vibrated in the air. 'Please . . .'

'Where is he?' Hester asked quietly. 'I'll see what I can do.'

The child gulped and took a deep breath. ''E's this way. I left the door stuck. We can get back, if yer 'urry. Please . . .'

'I'm coming,' Hester agreed. 'You lead the way. What's your name?'

'Maggie.' She turned and started to go quickly, her bare feet soundless on the chill floor.

Hester followed her down the corridor, round a corner, and along another passage even less well lit. She could only just see the small, pale figure ahead of her, glancing backwards every few moments to make sure Hester was still there. They were going away from the wards where sick and badly injured sailors were treated, and further into administrative areas and storerooms. Hester did not know the hospital well. She had volunteered to do temporary night duty as a favour to Jenny Solway, a friend who had sudden illness in her own family. They had served together with Florence Nightingale in the Crimea. That was almost fourteen years ago, but the experiences they had shared on those fearful battlefields like Balaclava, and in the hospital in Sebastopol, forged friendships that lasted for a lifetime, even if they did not meet for years.

Hester caught up with the child and took her small, cold hand.

'Where are we going?' she asked.

'To 'elp Charlie,' Maggie replied without turning her head. She was tugging at Hester now. 'We gotter 'urry. Please . . .'

One more turn in the corridor and they reached a door that was flush with the wall, and appeared to have no handle. A piece of string knotted to make a short rope was wedged to stop the door from closing completely. Maggie let go of Hester's hand, slid her thin fingers under the string and eased the door open.

'Ssh!' she warned. Then she stepped sideways through the crack and beckoned for Hester to follow her. When Hester was through also, she replaced the string and then pushed the door closed again.

Hester went in a step behind Maggie. They were in another

ward, smaller than the ones for the sailors, but holding six cots. The night lamps on the walls showed that there were small forms in all of them, lying still, as if asleep.

'Where are we?' Hester whispered.

'This is our place,' Maggie replied. 'Charlie's over there.' She took Hester's hand again and pulled her towards the furthest bed near the doorway of the ward. It was closed, and Hester had lost her sense of direction to know even which way it faced.

Maggie stopped beside the bed where an ashen-skinned boy about her own size lay propped up against the pillows. He turned towards her very slightly and tried to smile.

'Charlie,' Maggie's voice wobbled a little and there were tears on her cheeks, 'it's going to be all right. I got one o' the nurses ter come. She's gonna make yer better.'

'Yer shouldn't 'a done that,' he whispered. 'Yer'll get into trouble.'

She lifted her chin up a little. 'I don't care!' She looked at Hester. 'Yer gotta do summink.'

Hester's heart sank and she felt a moment of panic. The boy looked desperately ill. Maggie was probably right and he was dying. Was this a quarantine ward? How could she hope to get enough information from a six-year-old to have any idea what was wrong with him, or how to help?

The first thing she needed to do was to reassure him, gain his confidence. She moved forward and stood by the side of the bed.

'Hello, Charlie,' she said very quietly. 'Tell me how you feel. Are you hot? Sick? Shivery? Do you hurt anywhere especially?'

He stared at her for a moment. His face was so pale his skin looked almost translucent, shadows around his eyes like bruises. 'I don't really 'urt,' he whispered. 'Just a bit achy.'

'Have you been sick?' she asked.

3

'Yesterday.'

'Very sick, or just a little?'

'Quite a lot.'

'Have you eaten anything since then?'

He shook his head.

'Drink anything? Water?'

She reached forward and touched her hand to his forehead. He felt hot and dry. She turned to Maggie, who was staring at her, eyes filled with fear.

'Can you go and fetch Charlie a drink of water, please?' Hester asked.

Maggie started to speak, then changed her mind and went off to obey.

'Please, miss, don't tell 'er I'm dyin',' Charlie said almost under his breath. 'She'd be awful upset.'

Hester felt a sudden ache in her throat. She was a nurse – she was used to people dying – but these children alone, with no parent to comfort them, were different. They were so small, and lost. She did not normally lie to patients. She knew that if you did then sooner or later they stopped believing you, and you had lost much of your power to help, and they had lost trust in the one person they needed to believe.

This was different.

'I won't do.' She made too big a promise, without hesitation. 'I don't intend to let you die if I can help it.'

'But will you look after 'er?' he asked. 'An' Mike? Please?'

It was not a time for equivocation. 'Yes I will. Are you the eldest?'

'Yeah. I'm seven. Maggie's only six, although she acts like she's everybody's ma.' He gave a weak smile, a little lop-sided.

'Do you know why you're here in hospital?' It was time to be practical.

'No.' He shook his head a fraction. 'Summink ter do wi' me blood.'

'Are they giving you medicine for it?'

'They keep putting a big needle in me arm. It 'urts a lot.'

'Really? Yes, it would hurt. Does this needle have a glass tube on the other end of it?' She was picturing the major new invention called a syringe, which could transfer liquids into the flesh – or, for that matter, take them out.

He nodded.

'Do you know what was in the glass part?'

He was looking paler and she could hardly hear his voice when he answered, 'Looked red, like blood.'

Maggie came back with a mug full of water. Hester thanked her for it, then took a sip. It smelled and tasted fresh. She put an arm around Charlie. She could feel his bones through his nightshirt. She eased him upright and helped him very slowly to drink a little of the water. When he had taken all he could she laid him back down again, then as carefully as possible, straightened the sheets around him so they were smooth. He was gasping for breath, exhausted. She looked at him and was very afraid Maggie was right.

If he died, how was she going to help Maggie, who looked not much stronger herself? It was probably only fear and the need to believe she was doing something that kept her upright on her feet, albeit swaying a little. Hester would have suggested the child slept for a while, but she knew that if Charlie died when she was not there, the guilt would be with her for ever. It made no sense, but she would believe that she could have done something. In her place Hester would have felt the same.

'How old is Mike?' she asked quietly.

'Four,' Maggie replied. ''E's not so bad. Maybe 'e'll get worse when 'e's older.'

'Maybe not. Do they put the needles into him, too?'

'Yeah,' she nodded.

'And you?'

'Yeah,' she nodded again. 'But mostly Charlie. Can't you do summink, miss?'

Hester still had little idea what was wrong with any of them. A misjudged treatment could be lethal. There was a stage in an illness when there was nothing more anyone could do. A small boy could take only so much 'treatment'.

'What is the doctor doing to help him? Tell me all you know, Maggie. I need to do the right thing for him.'

The tears spilled over and ran down Maggie's cheeks. ''E don't do nothing, miss. 'E comes and puts a needle into Charlie, an' 'e gets sleepy an' sick. 'E just lies there. Can't even speak ter me an' Mike. Please, miss . . .'

Hester knew that Dr Rand went home at night. Everyone had to sleep, but there was a senior nurse on duty all night. Where was she? Sometimes there were emergencies that only a doctor could deal with, and a messenger would have to be sent to waken him. Then the doctor would walk, or even run, the half-mile or so from his home. But this was a hospital for those who were extremely ill, or so badly wounded that often there was nothing that could be done for them, except ease their distress, or at the very least, not leave them to die alone.

That was all too often what military nursing had been during the Crimean War, not so very long ago. Haemorrhage, gangrene, raging fever – these were things Hester had been used to coping with because scores of men, even hundreds, were wounded in battle. There were too few doctors, and usually too little time. That was one of the reasons the two Rand brothers, Dr Magnus Rand and his elder brother, a chemist, Hamilton Rand, had been so pleased to have Hester, another Crimea nurse, fill in for Jenny Solway. Her experience was of great value.

Where on earth was the nurse in charge here? Hester did not dare leave Charlie to go to look for her. Maybe she was ill herself. Or passed out drunk somewhere. It had been known to happen.

'Do you know what his illness is called?' Hester asked Maggie.

Maggie shook her head.

'Do you have the same illness?' Hester persisted.

Maggie nodded.

'What does the doctor do for you?'

There was little time. In the bed beside them Charlie was lying motionless, his face white, and his breathing shallow. But Hester had to find out all that Maggie could tell her before she attempted to help. A mistake would almost certainly be irrevocable.

'Maggie?' she prompted.

''E pricked me wi' the needle, too.' She took a deep breath. 'It hurt something awful.'

'Do you know what was in the little bottle at the end of the needle?' Hester asked. 'What colour was it?'

Maggie shook her head. 'I didn't want ter look, an' 'e told me not ter, but I did, just quick. I think it were blood.'

Hester felt a chill run through her. So Magnus was taking blood. What for? Was Hamilton Rand testing it for something? He was a brilliant chemist, almost visionary in some ways. What was he learning from these children's blood?

Maggie was staring at her, waiting, her eyes full of hope.

'Get me another cup of water,' Hester said to her. 'Please.'

Maggie turned and went immediately. Finally there was something she could do to help.

Hester leaned forward and pushed the sleeve up a little on Charlie's thin arm. She took the skin between her finger and thumb. It lifted away as if there were no flesh over the bone. At least she knew something to start with. 'When did you last go to a bathroom to pee?' she asked.

He seemed a little embarrassed. 'Long time ago.'

'Can you let me look inside your mouth? Please?' He dropped his jaw obediently. She bent and peered inside. His skin was pale and almost dry, even his tongue. Now she knew at least one thing seriously wrong with him. Dehydration bad enough could kill, especially a child as slight as he was. Water might not be all he needed, but it might save him long enough for something further.

Maggie came back, running so quickly she almost tripped, but the glass she carried was full to the brim.

Hester smiled at her, and very gently lifted Charlie up again so he was cradled in her arms and his head was nearly upright. He opened his eyes, but it was Maggie he looked at. He smiled at her hazily, and then seemed to drift off again.

Hester put the glass to his lips. 'Drink a little more, Charlie,' she urged him. 'Just a sip.'

For several moments he did not move, then as he tipped the glass very slightly he took a mouthful. He swallowed it and coughed. After a few seconds he took another.

Maggie was staring at Hester as if she were seeing a miracle. Hester ached with grief for her because this small act was almost certainly useless, but she could not bear to tell her so. Maggie's eyes were bright and she was so intent on Charlie she was hardly remembering to breathe.

It took half an hour, but sip by sip, Charlie drank the whole glassful. Hester felt a sense of triumph as if she had climbed a mountain. She laid Charlie back in the bed and pulled the blanket up over him again. He lay still, as if the effort had exhausted him. Almost straight away he was asleep.

Maggie's smile was so wide it must have hurt her cheeks. She was too full of emotion to speak. She knew it was only the beginning.

Hester stayed with them. Slowly she went around the rest of the ward, checking on each child. There were another six. They were tired and thin, yet still far better than Charlie.

Even Mike, the younger brother, was lying quietly and did not do more than stir and turn over when she touched his brow and then his arm. He looked more like three than four, but she knew that poor or sick children were often small for their ages.

An hour later she woke Charlie and, sip by sip, gave him another glass of water. Maggie helped. She refused to go back to her own bed, even though she was swaying on her feet with exhaustion. She agreed to sit down beside Hester, then at last, somewhere near dawn, she crumpled up and slid on to her lap, sound asleep.

About an hour later Hester laid Maggie gently into her own bed, and then went back to her own ward to tell them where she was and why. She retraced her steps carefully to find the children's ward again, but before going in she looked for the nurse who should have been on duty there.

She tried all the nearby storerooms and cupboards, rooms with sinks, taps, and places for laundry and rubbish, but there was no sign of her. Either she had not come in in the first place, or she had been and gone again almost straight away. Had she been ill, lazy, or on some emergency of her own? Or simply an assignation? It wouldn't be unheard of.

Unhappy and a little worried, Hester went back to the children's ward. She looked carefully at each of them, then, satisfied for the time being, she slept on and off for what was left of the night.

By morning Charlie was sitting up and definitely feeling better. His eyes were still hollow but his skin was less papery, and he could take a cup of water in his hands and drink it himself.

Maggie was elated. She refused to listen to Hester's warning that this was only a temporary respite. She stared at Hester solemn-eyed and said that she understood, but her joy burned in her like a flame and Hester's words meant nothing. Charlie was not dying now, and that was all that mattered. Even Mike, awake and standing beside Maggie, clinging on to her hand, believed her, and regarded Hester as if she were a bright angel.

Hester stopped her struggle with reality and let them enjoy the idea of hope, for however long it might last.

It was still very early. The sky was paling at last and she needed to return to the ward where she was on duty.

'Let Charlie sleep,' she told Maggie. 'And keep on giving him water when he'll take it, but don't waken him specially. And don't forget to drink yourself. If he'll take breakfast, then help him, but don't insist. And all the rest of you must eat as well. Do you understand?'

'Yes, miss,' Maggie said earnestly. 'You'll come back, won't yer?' Now there was fear back in her eyes again.

'Of course,' Hester promised, but wondered how she was going to keep to it. As soon as Dr Magnus arrived she must see him. That meant staying longer than she had meant to, but her own family would simply have to understand.

Nurse O'Neill met her the moment she was through the door of her own ward. She was an imposing woman, young and quite handsome in an individual way. Now she was angry and made no attempt to conceal it.

'What on earth are you thinking of?' she demanded, hands on her hips. Her fairish hair was coming out of its pins and she looked exhausted. Her sleeves were rolled up crookedly and there were stains of blood and spilled water over her white apron front. 'There's only been me and Mary Ann here! They don't pay you to sneak off and find somewhere to go to sleep! I don't care what you did all day; you're meant to be here and on duty all night, just like the rest of us.'

Hester's heart sank. She knew what was the matter with Sherryl O'Neill. She expected to lose patients – this was a ward of desperately ill men – but she still could not bear it. Each death was a defeat and she took it personally.

'We lost Hodgkins,' Hester said quietly, assuming the worst. 'I'm sorry . . .'

'No we didn't!' Sherryl blinked furiously but the tears ran down her cheeks anyway. 'He's still alive. God knows how. No thanks to you.'

Hester waited, confused.

'Wilton,' Sherryl filled in the silence. 'He took a sudden turn for the worse and there was nothing I could do. You should have been here!' Again the accusation was harsh.

Hester understood. Unexpected loss cut especially deep. It made you realise all over again how little control you had. Victory could turn to defeat in an instant. They had all felt certain that Wilton was recovering.

'What happened?' she asked, dreading the answer.

Sherryl's voice was harsh, as if her throat were so tight she could barely force the words out.

'What didn't? He was in awful pain, first in his back, then down his sides, and tops of his legs. He was chilling one minute and feverish the next. His urine was full of blood.' She stared at Hester as if she were still desperate for some kind of help.

'I didn't know what to do,' Sherryl went on. 'He was in agony worse than his wounds, and terrified. I was useless. He was dying and I couldn't think of anything to do for him. He was faint. Some parts of him went absolutely white, as if there were no blood inside him. Others were dark red and, strong man as he was, he wept with the pain of it. God in heaven, that's not a way for anybody to die!' Now the tears ran unashamedly down her cheeks. 'Why the hell weren't you there?' she said furiously.

Hester knew this was anger at helplessness, at pain, and death. They were the tears of exhaustion, and the need not to be alone.

'I'm sorry,' Hester said quietly. 'I was with another patient. A child. I told Mary Ann.'

'She's no damn use!' Sherryl said desperately. 'She thought Wilton was going to live, after Dr Rand took him away for treatment yesterday. He . . . he was so full of hope when he came back.' She stopped abruptly, unable to keep her self-control any longer.

'Did you know there was a children's ward here?' Hester asked, wondering even as she spoke if she was wise to mention it.

Sherryl's eyes widened. 'What are you talking about? Where? There are no children here. It's all soldiers and sailors.' Disbelief was heavy in her face.

'No it isn't,' Hester contradicted her. 'I found a child in one of the corridors, looking for help. She was about six, and her brother was in crisis. I went with her. That's where I was.'

Sherryl's eyes widened again.

'We got him through the night, but I don't know what good it will do. He was very weak.'

'A child too?' Sherryl asked.

'About seven,' Hester replied. 'I couldn't leave her alone to watch him die . . .'

Indecision flickered in Sherryl's face, and then she chose to believe. 'You couldn't have done anything here anyway,' she conceded, turning away after a moment to master her feelings, and wipe her face with the corner of her apron.

Hester was uncertain what to say. She really did understand the sense of helplessness, the going over and over every step, every decision, all the possibilities that could have been tried, and then the agony of watching such a painful, horrible death. Everyone who cared questioned themselves.

Sherryl O'Neill was a difficult person to get to know. Their first real conversation had been when Hester asked about her unusual name, one she had not heard before, and Sherryl had told her of its origins in France. Her parents had been touring the country and had never forgotten its beauty. When their daughter was born the intended name of 'Rose' had been replaced with a version of the French word for 'dear' or 'beloved', and she had been trying to live up to it ever since.

Hester, who had always felt herself to look rather ordinary, understood exactly. It had not started a friendship, but at least rather more than simply an acquaintance.

As soon as Hester knew that Dr Magnus Rand was due in the hospital, and before he could begin any rounds, she went to tell him about Charlie. She found him in his office towards the front of the building. It was an imposing room with an oak desk and a couple of other tables with books, papers and instruments spread out, as if there were always a new work in progress.

Two of the walls were lined with shelves, the books packed in. At a glance they seemed at random. There were no obvious sets of volumes. Once she had had the chance to read the titles and she was impressed with the breadth and variety of his interest, but always in some form of medicine. There were studies dating from the ancient Greeks, through the developing knowledge of the Arabs and Jews, and such giants as Maimonides. Then the herbalists of the Middle Ages, to the modern histories of new discoveries in anatomy and physiology. Harvey, who had discovered the circulation of the blood, was clearly Dr Rand's greatest hero.

He was a mild-seeming man, several years younger than his brother, Hamilton, but his features were not dissimilar, perhaps a little blunter. Unlike Hamilton, his fairish hair was thick and always seemed to have escaped his control.

He looked up as Hester knocked lightly on the open door.

'Ah, come in, Mrs Monk.' His expression appeared mild but his blue eyes were sharp with interest. 'How went the night?'

She stood in front of the desk. Only then did she realise that Hamilton Rand was in the room also. He was visibly the

13

elder of the two. His face was leaner and more deeply lined, his hair thinner. It was difficult to tell what colour his eyes were, but impossible to miss the acute intelligence in them. Now he watched her silently. She was not a social acquaintance so he did not feel it necessary to acknowledge her.

There was no escape. Hester could feel the colour burn up her face. She did not have any doubt that she had done the right thing, but she was by no means certain that either man would see it that way. They would have heard of Wilton's death. To lose a patient was always a kind of failure, and they had not expected this one.

She told them exactly what her own notes had said, until the time she had left to walk along the corridor to fetch more paper for recording patients' progress.

'Wilton was restless.' Magnus affirmed. 'What then?'

'What time was he restless, Mrs Monk?' Hamilton interrupted without looking at his brother. 'Be precise, if you please.'

'Ten minutes past midnight he got tangled in the sheet and started to struggle,' Hester replied. She was used to his manner. He looked for reason in the details and she understood that. He was a man of penetrating intelligence and accustomed to dealing with those who generalised where he required exactness.

'Awake, Mrs Monk? Were his eyes open? Did he focus?'

'His eyes were open but he seemed to focus only now and then. I would say less than half the time,' she replied.

'What did you do for him?' Magnus asked, taking over control of the questions again, but he looked to his brother as he did so, and observed Hamilton's brief nod before he continued. 'And how did he respond?'

'I disentangled him so he would be less distressed,' Hester replied. 'Then I bathed him in cool water to reduce his fever. At first he responded well. He became calmer and spoke quite lucidly for several minutes, perhaps almost ten. He went back to sleep, and I went to see the other patients.'

'Then what?' Hamilton demanded, moving forward a step or two.

'I did much the same for another patient, Latimer. He—'

Hamilton waved a hand sharply. 'He is of no concern in this issue, Mrs Monk. Keep your mind on the subject, if you please . . .'

'You asked her where she went, Hamilton,' Magnus pointed out.

Hester knew he intended it kindly, and yet she found his need to defend her faintly patronising. Or was it that Magnus was so used to his elder brother's manner that he tried to offset it simply out of habit?

Hamilton shrugged irritably. 'I know what I said, Magnus. The woman can take care of herself. For heaven's sake, come to the point. Wilton could have lived!' He swivelled back to Hester. His eyes were fixed on hers intently. 'How did he die? Details, woman!'

Hester drew in her breath. 'I don't know, sir. You will have to ask Miss O'Neill. When I—'

'What?' Hamilton demanded, the colour rising up his cheeks. 'Where the devil were you? I'm not paying you to—'

Magnus put out his hand and gripped his brother's arm. Hester could see his knuckles white and the wrinkles in the sleeve of his suit where he pulled it out of shape. 'Let her tell us, Hamilton. The woman must answer the call of her own nature now and then.'

Hester felt herself blushing, which was absurd.

Hamilton shook off the offending hand, and Magnus let go. He had made his protest.

'Well?' Hamilton demanded, staring at Hester as if he could make the acuteness of his vision bore into her head.

Hester stood a little straighter. She did not avert her eyes.

'When I was returning along the corridor I encountered a small girl, perhaps six or seven years old. She was in extreme distress and said that her brother was dying.'

'What?' Magnus turned to Hamilton, his expression filled with alarm.

Hamilton ignored him, not moving his eyes from Hester's.

'And what did you do, Mrs Monk?' he said, enunciating each word deliberately.

'I went with her to see what I could do to help,' Hester replied. 'It could have been true. As it turns out, I believe it was . . .'

Magnus was ashen. He half rose in his seat.

Hamilton took a deep breath. His voice grated between his teeth. 'What about the nurse, Mrs . . . what's her name? Mrs Gilmore?'

'I don't know,' Hester replied. 'When I had time I looked for her. I never found her.'

Hamilton swore savagely.

'I have come precisely to tell you about this, Mr Rand,' she answered him. 'I discussed Wilton first because Charlie did not die.'

'The boy is still alive?' Magnus asked hurriedly.

'Yes, Dr Rand. He is weak, but I think improving.'

Hamilton leaned forward. 'What did you do for him? Tell me precisely what you did, and how he responded.'

Hester's mind flashed back to her time as an army nurse in the Crimea. She had heard generals give orders to soldiers in just such a tone of voice. Sometimes it had sent them to their deaths. She forced it from her mind. Hamilton Rand would remember every word she said, or omitted to say.

'I asked the girl, Maggie, what she knew of his illness—' she began.

'And what did she tell you?' Hamilton snapped, cutting across her.

'Very little, other than that you used what sounded from her description to be a syringe.'

'Go on! Go on!'

'I touched Charlie,' she replied, refusing to be hurried. Charlie was what mattered, and the other children, not what Hamilton Rand thought of her. 'He was lying still, breathing shallowly and did not appear to be aware of us. I pinched his skin, to see if it came away from his flesh easily, in order to judge if he was lacking moisture. He had vomited recently and had not urinated for a time. He was very seriously lacking moisture. I sent the girl for water. I propped Charlie up and gave him a few sips as often as he would take them. It was four glasses in all, by morning.' She did not look away from him but met his eyes steadily. Now she was not alarmed, only angry that he should have let it come to this point.

Hamilton let out his breath slowly, pursing his lips. He did not look at his brother.

'Indeed,' he said almost without expression. 'You showed some initiative.' At last he looked at Magnus. 'That explains her absence satisfactorily.'

'Of course it does,' Magnus said impatiently. 'Thank you, Mrs Monk. We are obliged to you. We shall take care of the matter now, and get a full report on poor Wilton from Miss O'Neill. We had great hopes that we could save him.' He turned to his brother. 'Hamilton, do you think—'

'No,' Hamilton said instantly. 'Not yet. It would not be wise. I must speak to you further.' He lifted his hand slightly without turning to Hester. 'You may go, Mrs Monk. Thank you.'

Hester wanted to know more, but Hamilton had forgotten her already. He was picking up a bundle of papers off the desk in his part of the office as if she were no longer present. 'Magnus, I think we should consider this. I assume you have read it?'

Magnus turned to respond.

Hester went out of the door, closing it behind her, and walked straight-shouldered, head high, along the corridor to the entrance hall and way out. She was annoyed, but that was personal and of no importance at all. What mattered was the men she nursed . . . and Charlie, and for the moment she had done all she could.

Chapter Two

MONK WAS sitting at his desk at the Thames River Police Station at Wapping. Outside the river sounds were muted: the whisper of water as the tide rose, slurping against the stone steps up to the quayside. Now and again came the voices of lightermen calling to each other, or the clank of metal as a chain was hauled through a winch, and the cry of gulls fighting over food.

Sunlight came in through the open door, pooling in bright patches on the floor, the desk, and catching the pallor in Orme's face. He looked tired, and the white in his hair was more pronounced than it had been even a few months ago.

Orme had served on the River Police all of his working life and he was now nearing seventy. He had been Monk's mentor since his coming here, the one who had taught him without lecturing or criticism, and never in front of the other men. It was Orme who had rescued him from the few serious errors he had made, without ever referring to them again. But he was growing tired. He did not need to tell Monk that he wanted to retire; it was there in the tone of his voice, the stiffness in the way he climbed the steps up from the water's edge to the dock, and the frequency with which he spoke of his daughter and his new grandchild. Quietly, in his own way, he was desperately proud of them.

'Is Laker back yet?' Monk asked.

'Yes, sir,' Orme replied immediately.

'Send him in,' Monk told him.

Orme nodded and went out silently.

A moment later the door opened again and Laker came in, closing it behind him. He was young, just over thirty, and he stood almost to attention, facing Monk impassively. He was totally unlike Monk in appearance. He was fair-skinned with vividly blue eyes and the sort of hair that the sun bleached flaxen blond on the top. He was good-looking by any standard, and he was aware of it.

Monk was both amused and uncomfortable. There was something in the quiet arrogance of Laker that, he gathered, was like he himself had been a few years ago, before the accident that had robbed him of all memory, except occasional, disturbing flashes. People had spoken of him in just the words he would have used to describe Laker. Laker had all the quick wits that Monk had, the self-assurance before the total amnesia had taken away his safety.

He identified with Laker. He was arrogant, often funny, and sometimes right when others who were slower saw only part of the picture.

'Yes, sir?' Laker said politely, but with no deference.

'What did you find in Mr Derby's warehouse?' Monk said, leaning back a little in his chair and looking up at Laker, still standing. 'Any trace of the guns?'

'Yes, sir.' Nothing whatever altered in Laker's attitude. He still stood gracefully, not quite to attention.

'Well?' Monk demanded.

'Just one, sir, but very nice, very smooth. A good marksman could probably hit a man on the other side of the river with no trouble. I tried the action and it was like silk. Not a mark on it. I'd guess it was a sample, sir. But it had definitely been fired. Tried out.'

'Did you see any paperwork?' Monk asked without much

hope. Derby was too clever to leave evidence. He was one of the best smugglers in Europe, but as far as Monk was aware, he was fairly new to the arson trade. Usually he dealt in brandy and tobacco.

'Yes, sir. It read like it was the usual stuff he was supposed to deal in: Spanish steel from Toledo, and exotic woods. So many cases of ebony, so many engraved swords, plates and so on. Probably weighs about the same.'

'Dates, amounts, money?' Monk prompted.

'Yes, sir. And a few other interesting things.' Laker's smile was bright with satisfaction.

'Don't make me pull your teeth, Laker,' Monk said impatiently.

Laker gave a little shrug and his mouth turned down at the corners. 'I think he's got at least one of the Excise men in his pocket, sir.'

Monk felt a chill inside himself. It was one of the ugly pieces of corruption he knew existed and one day he would have to deal with, but it still worried him more than it might another man who was more certain of his own past.

The carriage accident just before he had first met Hester, over a decade ago now, had injured his body, but that had healed quickly. The loss of his memory, however, had never been made up, except in snatches here and there, and as his detection had uncovered things about himself, by no means all pleasant. He did not know who all his friends or enemies were, not by a long way. He had once worked in the regular Metropolitan Police. He knew the docks. Unexpected flashes of familiarity told him that: a corner turned and the scene known to him, a smell that brought back powerful feelings.

The worst fear was that a man he did not know, knew and remembered him. Old debts sometimes waited a long time. Monk had solved a lot of cases. If he could look back on

21

those now, would he still be happy to own the methods he had used in all of them?

He met Laker's eyes. 'I assume you have hard evidence of this, not just whispers in the dark?'

'Yes, sir. Facts and figures, things that don't add up. I'm just not sure which of two or three men it is. I suppose it could be all of them.'

'Good. Write it all down.'

'I'll remember, sir . . .'

'You'll also write it down,' Monk told him levelly. 'I'm not trusting this to any one man's recollection. Thank you. That's all.'

Laker turned to leave.

'Laker!'

'Yes, sir?'

'You'll go up the river, opposite direction, for the next few days.'

'But I might learn something more, sir. I've got—'

'One fact that will be recognised and remembered,' Monk said. 'If you want to remain in the River Police, you'll do as you're told.'

Laker winced. 'Yes, sir.'

Monk went back to his paperwork and completed it before putting it away and going outside into the dock in the late summer afternoon. He was just in time to see Hooper coming up the steps from the water. In the past the matter of the Excise men was something he would have discussed with Orme first, but it was time he allowed Hooper to step forward. When Orme retired, he would have to. Hooper would fight beside him, watch his neck, and risk his own life to save him.

But he would not coddle his superior officer as far as Orme had. His critical judgement was sharper. He would hate doing it, and think less of Monk if he had to be told too often. He had not Orme's gentleness – or perhaps he had, but it was not authorised by age and an awareness of times changing and his own strength slipping away from him. Hooper did not expect a commander who was flawless, but he certainly required one who learned from his mistakes and did not repeat them, and one who never put himself before his men.

One day he would have to tell Hooper about his lost memory, the things in the dark he could not recall. He knew that without Hester's belief in him, when they had just met, he would not have had the courage to fight for his own innocence of the hideous murder of which circumstances had implicated his guilt so powerfully that he had even to accept it himself. It was she who had fought for another answer, not he.

But did Hooper sense the darker self that lay in his past? One day they might talk about it, but not now. The satisfaction, the respect apparent in Hooper's face was something not to be risked yet, unless it became necessary.

'Laker's given a pretty clear report,' Monk said to Hooper, quietly, although there was no one else in earshot. 'Derby has a sample of a particularly good gun. I've looked at the paper that makes it pretty clear he's bringing them upriver soon.'

Hooper studied Monk's face, seeing something in it deeper than these words.

'But he thinks there's someone in Customs and Excise involved. It isn't going to be as simple as we thought.'

Hooper nodded slowly, no surprise in his face. 'Have you told Mr Orme yet, sir?'

'No.' Monk did not know how to explain his reluctance to involve Orme, without robbing him of some of his dignity in Hooper's eyes. 'Not certain yet,' he went on. 'Don't like the thought of someone in Customs tipping them off.'

'You'll have to tell him, sir.' Hooper kept his own voice down, although he was softly spoken anyway. 'He may have some ideas.'

'I know,' Monk admitted. He stared out across the river

where the sun was still bright, although it was late afternoon. It stayed light until nearly ten in the evening this time of the year, especially over the water where everything was reflected back.

'I am going for a walk along the river,' he added. 'South bank. I'll give it some thought. See you tomorrow.'

'Yes, sir,' Hooper replied quietly. 'Good night.'

Scuff was standing on the wharf at Greenwich when Monk's ferry pulled up to the steps and he climbed out. Scuff had grown almost a foot in height in the five years since Monk had adopted him. Or, more accurately, since he had adopted Monk. He had been eleven, or thereabouts, anyway, and felt far too old to need parents!

But Monk himself had been new to his job on the river and really did need somebody who knew the teeming life of the Thames to stop him making the worst mistakes, if he were to succeed, never mind solve any crimes. Scuff had made his own way on the river-bank for several years. It seemed natural that he should keep an eye on Monk, help him now and then, and explain how things worked.

Scuff had always liked Monk. Hester was a different matter. Scuff was too big to need a mother, and anyway, he already had one, but he had left home years ago. There had been no room for him there since he was about seven and his mother had remarried and had more babies.

Scuff had been very wary of Hester. She was an odd one, not like any other woman he knew. At first she seemed so strong she was frightening. She knew things no one else did, about medicine, and government. He was almost ready to admit to himself that he loved her, in some ways even more than he loved Monk. The quality of the feeling was different. There was a kind of peace in it that he did not understand.

He rose to his feet as Monk reached the top of the steps.

Although Monk was smiling, he looked tired, which was a pity because Scuff had things he needed to talk about with him, and he didn't want to have to wait for another opportunity. It had taken all his courage to make up his mind now. He had it worked out and the words were on his tongue, although there were too many for the short walk home. Monk's house was home to Scuff now, just as if he had been born there. Sometimes, however, he woke in the night and just lay still, feeling the space and the cleanness of it, then getting up and touching things to make sure it was all real.

'D'yer wanter walk?' Scuff asked hopefully. 'Dinner in't ready yet.'

Monk hesitated only a second, and then he smiled and agreed.

They started to walk east along the bank, towards the Estuary, which led eventually to the sea. They watched the water, the longest street in London, where the ships made their way past them up towards the Pool, the biggest port on earth.

They stopped to stare as an ocean-going schooner made its way with half-sails set.

'Wonder where it's come from,' Scuff said in awe. His imagination skipped through the possibilities that Monk had taught him: countries on the coasts of Africa, China, Australia, Egypt – names that conjured up visions like a magic incantation.

Monk smiled. 'India?' he suggested, as if he knew it was the one Scuff had not thought of.

'Have you ever been to India?' Scuff asked.

'No,' Monk answered quickly. 'Would you like to go?'

'Not yet,' Scuff said. 'I like it here . . . for now.'

They started to walk again.

'Then what's wrong?' Monk asked quietly.

A string of barges passed, followed by a coastal scow heavy-laden with coal.

Scuff needed to find the right words to tell Monk what he had decided. He was not at all sure what Monk would think; if he would be disappointed, even angry. Scuff glanced at him and felt his heart sink. This was not a good time for him to bring up decisions for the future. Monk clearly had something on his mind already. But he would have to tell him some time soon, and there were always going to be other things that mattered. He drew in his breath to start, right words or not, then he looked at Monk's face again and saw the anxiety in it.

'Summink go wrong?' he asked.

Monk was startled for a moment, and then he smiled ruefully. 'Is it so obvious?'

'Yeah,' Scuff nodded. Then he saw the flicker in Monk's expression and knew that he would rather not be so easily read. Well, he would just have to put up with it. Scuff had always had a pretty good idea of when he was troubled, even if he was quite often wrong as to the cause. This time he made a very well-educated guess. 'Mr Orme going to stop working any more?' he asked.

Monk sighed. 'Yes, I think so.'

Scuff kicked at a small stone and sent it rattling across the path.

'Don't worry. Mr Hooper'll be there.' He said it as comfort, but also with belief and some considerable respect. His mind slipped back to Hooper arriving at the door in Paradise Row, badly injured and needing help because he had gone alone to fight a battle to save Monk. He could close his eyes and see Hooper sitting on the hard-backed chair in the kitchen while Hester stopped the bleeding with all the towels she could find, and then stitched him up. It must have hurt like being stuck with daggers, but Hooper had never moved. It had been a bad time. Scuff didn't really want to remember it, except that if they could all come through that, then they would probably come through anything. And Hooper had been part of it.

'He will!' he said again, with conviction.

'I know,' Monk agreed. His hand casually brushed Scuff's shoulder, just a touch, then gone again.

It was time for Scuff to stop avoiding it. 'I got summink I need ter tell you,' he said.

He glanced at Monk and saw him nod, waiting.

'I've been thinking,' Scuff began. 'I kind of got ter like school. Some of it I don't care about, but most of it's good.' How could he say the next bit? That was what Monk might really mind . . . a lot.

'Good,' Monk said with some surprise. 'When did this happen?'

Now was Scuff's chance to tell him. He drew in his breath, and then his words deserted him. He shrugged.

'I s'pose when I didn't have to work so hard to read. It sort of began to make sense. I looked at the counting and I could see it without thinking.'

'That's how it should be. Reading can be fun.'

'Yeah,' Scuff agreed. He knew this was going to be difficult, but now he was in the middle of it, it was terrible. How would he get over it if Monk was angry, or worse, upset?

They walked in silence for another fifty yards. Below them the tide was rising in the river, covering steps, filling in hollows in the mud and swirling upstream, carrying flotsam and debris with it. A string of barges went by, lightermen balanced with angular grace in the stern, always watching.

'Why are you mentioning it now?' Monk asked him finally.

There was no help for it; Scuff clenched his teeth, drew a deep breath, and said it.

'I want to be in medicine, like Hester. Be a doctor or a

nurse, or something.' He gulped. 'I'm sorry, but I do. It's what I want.'

There was a moment's silence except for the crying of the gulls wheeling and diving above them.

'Are you sure?' Monk said at last. 'It's not easy.' He sounded worried. Scuff could hear it in his voice. He wished he had never spoken, but he couldn't take it back.

'Yeah!'

'Have you told Hester?' Monk asked.

Scuff was caught completely by surprise. Did Monk really think he would tell Hester before saying something to him?

'No!' he said fiercely. ''Course I didn't!'

'Would you like me to?' Monk suggested.

Scuff stopped on the path and turned to stare at him.

'You would?' he said a little breathlessly.

'If you tell me why,' Monk replied.

'Why?'

'Yes. Why do you want to be a doctor?'

Scuff was embarrassed. He was aiming too high.

'I don't think I can be a doctor. I in't the right sort of person for that.'

'Crow's a doctor.' Monk mentioned the doctor for the poor that they both knew. He was not formally qualified, but his skill was high and his dedication total.

'But Crow is . . .' Scuff began, then did not know how to finish. He should never have started this. He was being ridiculous, reaching far too high.

'Crow's a lot like you,' Monk finished for him. 'Perhaps working for Crow would be a good way to start . . . that is, if you really want to, and he'll have you?'

Scuff looked at Monk, then away again. 'D'yer think he would?' Then he wished he had not asked. He really did not want to hear the answer. It hurt when you wanted something really badly.

'Why do you want to be a doctor?' Monk repeated.

Scuff had the answer, he was just afraid that it sounded silly.

'Don't you know?'

'Yes! 'Course I do!'

'Then tell me. I won't be the only person who asks you.'

No, but he was the one who mattered most. Now he had to tell him.

''Cos I like what Hester does, and Crow. They see real bad pain that people can't help themselves, and they get right in there and try to fix it. It's difficult, and sometimes they can't do it, but at the least they stop people being so scared, and feeling alone, and like nobody cares. They treat everyone the same, whoever they are. It . . . it kind of makes us all the same, 'cos take yer clothes off, get washed clean, like, and we all look the same.'

Monk was silent. They were back walking slowly now. He looked very thoughtful.

Scuff felt as if he had to go on. He couldn't bear neither of them saying anything.

'I know it's very difficult, an' yer gotter study a whole lot, an' work very very hard. But yer gotter do that for most things. It's kind of beautiful . . . how it all fits together, and you got somebody live, with hands and feet, an' feelings inside.'

'It is wonderful,' Monk agreed. 'And I think that's a very good reason, in fact the best. Do you want to tell Hester yourself?'

Scuff did not want to tell Hester how he felt. He cared too much, and he felt very foolish even to imagine he could do what she did, or anything like it. But he wanted to so much he would not give up.

'Do you want me to tell her?'

Scuff nodded. 'Yeah . . .'

Monk put out his hand and touched him briefly on the shoulder. 'Then I will,' he promised.

It was over, at least for now. Scuff felt as if he could cry with relief. But that would make him a baby, and he was far too big for that.

Monk waited until the following morning before he told Hester about his conversation with Scuff. She came home from night duty early, and by the sound of her footsteps he could tell that she was unusually tired. He had tried arguing with her before, pointing out that there was no need for her to work such hours. She had answered with a bleak smile that the need was not for herself, it was for the patients. It was temporary. Jenny Solway would probably return soon and that would be the end of it.

Now as he sat up in bed he could hear her moving slowly. He slipped on a jacket over his nightshirt and went downstairs to meet her.

She was standing in the middle of the kitchen. Only the smallest of the gas lamps was lit, leaving the far walls, with their shelves of pots and pans, in shadow. He had left the light for her deliberately.

She turned and saw him, kettle in her hand. Contrition filled her face. 'I'm sorry, I didn't mean to make a noise.' She smiled at him. 'It isn't six yet. You can go back to sleep . . .'

He took the kettle from her and put it on the hob, then bent to open the grate and rake the fire, but it was already beginning to burn up well.

'I did that,' she said quietly. 'It must be what woke you.'

'Hungry?' he asked.

She looked pale and there were bruised-looking shadows around her eyes. He guessed she had lost another patient that night. It would be the second one in two days. He knew the work was as important as anything a person could do, he just wished it were resting on someone else.

'Not really,' she said, trying to be both gentle and truthful at the same time.

He did not argue but went straight to the pantry. He returned with a small wedge of fruitcake. He cut it into two slices, and then as the kettle boiled he made the tea, with cups for both of them. He did not ask how her night had been. Instinctively he already knew, just as she knew when he had had a day filled with tragedy and a feeling of helplessness. He hated adding to it with Scuff's fears, but he had promised that he would tell her, and there would be no other time. He hated seeing so little of her, only moments here and there, and too seldom alone.

Monk waited until Hester had eaten her cake and drunk half of her tea before he filled her cup again, and then told her about his conversation with Scuff.

'Are you sure?' she said with a furrow of anxiety between her brows. 'He's not doing it to please me?'

'There's probably a bit of that in it,' he conceded. 'He wants us to be proud of him.' He smiled. 'And he was terrified I would be upset he didn't want to join the River Police.'

'And are you?' she asked, meeting his eyes frankly.

'No, not at all. I don't want to be in command of him. I would have to lean backwards not to be thought to favour him. I think it would be very difficult. And I would be terrified in case he were hurt . . . or worse.'

She relaxed a little. 'Medicine is very hard. It's difficult and you pay for your mistakes terribly. You . . .' She stopped. 'I'm sorry. You know all that.'

'You should be proud of him,' he said, reaching across the table to touch her hand. 'I'm pretty sure he wants to give something back to the people he left behind when he came to live with us. And he wants to be like you,' he added softly. 'Don't . . . don't put him off.'

Hester was exhausted and grieving, full of the heavy burden of failures and so proud of Scuff and afraid of the pain of such failures ahead for him that the tears spilled down her cheeks.

'I won't,' she promised.

He stood up and came around the table to kneel beside her and hold her in his arms.

After a short rest, when Scuff was on his way to school and Monk had gone down to the river to catch the ferry across to Wapping, Hester went straight to the ferry herself, also to the north bank and then on the omnibus to Portpool Lane. She walked along in the shadow of the brewery to the large, rambling old warren of houses that had once been a thriving brothel. It was now a clinic for many of the same women whose place of business it had been. Added to them were any others without a home and whose illness or injury had rendered them in need.

Hester had no skill in raising money to sustain the clinic, but she had the organisational abilities and the nursing skill and experience that made it seldom necessary to call in a doctor willing and able to lend his greater knowledge without payment.

She went in through the main door. She had no time for more than a brief acknowledgement of the elderly woman who sat at the desk to admit or deny those who came seeking help, a hot meal, or simply somewhere to lie at peace, knowing they would not be molested or thrown out. It was a completely discretionary decision and Hester seldom interfered with it. She had learned over the years to tell a conniver or a malingerer from a genuine case, but she was still far behind Hetty in the skill. Hetty had been a prostitute herself too long for anyone to fool her. She knew every lie and excuse there was and had tried most of them.

Today Hester only wished her good morning, and went straight on into the warren of passages and rooms to find Claudine Burroughs. She would almost certainly be either in the kitchen storeroom or the medicine room at this time of the day. Claudine was a well-to-do woman, unhappily married and without children. She had offered her services in the clinic several years ago now. To begin with she had seen it as a worthy charity, and something of a defiance of the highly conventional part of society to which she belonged. Slowly she had come to care for the people, even the highly dubious and disreputable Squeaky Robinson, who had originally owned and run the brothel, until Oliver Rathbone had tricked him out of it. Squeaky had rebelled, outraged that he, the master trickster, had wound up outsmarted by a gentleman, even if he was a lawyer as well. His choice had been a long term in prison, or to remain with a home in the clinic and work for his keep by managing the finances of the place, strictly in accordance with the law. Grudgingly he had accepted the latter.

Hester reached the medicine room, and saw the door open and the light on inside. She felt a rush of relief when she saw a very small boy, who looked six or seven years old, thin and weedy and with boundless energy. He was throwing pieces of crumpled newspapers around, his crop of thick, unkempt hair bouncing up and down with each movement.

'Good morning, Worm,' Hester said affectionately as she reached him.

He looked up, recognised her, and his face shone with pleasure. 'I'm working,' he announced.

'I can see,' she replied appreciatively. 'Do you think you have enough papers there for a load to take downstairs?'

He regarded them gravely, and then looked back at her. 'Yeah!' he agreed. There were not so very many, but he understood dismissal from overhearing adult conversation. He was stunted by years of half starvation, and he was actually nearly nine, and very definitely a survivor. He picked up the bundle carefully.

'They're for lighting fires,' he told her, just in case she didn't know. He set off down the passageway, not dropping any until he was nearly at the stairs.

Claudine came out of the medicine room to greet Hester. She was a big woman, too broad at the hip for grace, but with her beautiful hair and the intelligence in her eyes she was not without charm, although she would have suspected undue charity in the judgement if anyone had told her so. She smiled with affection as she saw Hester. Then with her quick understanding she recognised that Hester was troubled by something deeper than the ordinary day-to-day concerns of the clinic.

'What is it?' she asked without prevarication. She knew all the social conventions of talking without saying anything of meaning, and despised it. It was not the way to treat a friend.

'I've got to stay at the hospital longer than I'd expected,' Hester answered. 'I can't leave yet, even if Jenny comes back, and I've heard nothing from her. I've discovered children there who are . . .' She gave up trying to skirt around it and, glancing down the passageway to make sure Worm was not within earshot yet, she told Claudine about Charlie, Maggie and Mike, and her whole experience in the hospital. 'There's no one else to care,' she finished. 'I have to stay. Please . . . will you take over everything here, at least for a while?'

'Of course,' Claudine said immediately. For her there was no other answer possible.

Hester looked at her and realised there was something troubling her, and she was annoyed with herself for not even having asked.

'What is it?' she asked now. 'Is it going to be difficult?'

'No,' Claudine said too quickly.

'Yes it is.' Hester knew it immediately.

Claudine would have been appalled if she knew how obviously vulnerable she was. Worm was somebody else's child, an urchin off the river-bank, undersized, completely without education, but in the very few months he had been living at the clinic where he had food every day and a bed every night, she had come to care about him as deeply as a good woman cares for any small, lost creature.

'You're worried about Worm?' Hester asked.

Claudine spoke awkwardly, worried about appearing foolish. 'He . . . he thinks he's no use here . . . accepting charity, and he prefers going off before someone tells him he has to go. I . . .' The distress in her face was obvious. She would not say she loved the child, but the truth of it was naked in her face.

'Find him something to do, even if you work him until he falls asleep on his feet,' Hester said, smiling, then looked again at the door just as Worm reappeared.

'Yer done yet?' he asked hopefully.

'Don't be cheeky!' Claudine reproved him, anxiety sharpening her voice.

Worm looked startled.

Claudine flushed with annoyance at herself. She had reacted too strongly. Deliberately she softened her tone. 'Mrs Monk has told me of a great deal of work that needs to be done. I shall – *we* shall need you to work very hard. There will be no running off to the river to play. In fact I think it would be best if you were to sleep here all the time, so that if we need you we shall know where you are.'

Worm looked at her with wide eyes. 'Wot are we goin' ter do?' There was excitement in his voice, as if he were being given some kind of special treat.

Hester understood with a deep ache inside her. What Worm needed was to belong. If there were work to do, then he was safe from being sent away.

'Do you know how to paint?' Hester suddenly asked.

Worm blinked.

'Not pictures,' Hester added quickly. 'I mean walls. If I gave you a bucket of paint and a big brush, could you paint on to a wall . . . as far as you could reach?'

'Yes,' Worm said immediately, staring at her without blinking. He was lying. She knew it, and she knew why. He wanted to please, especially to please Claudine.

'Good,' Hester said with complete gravity. 'You will be very important to us. Will you please be here all the time, until we have it done?'

'Yes,' Worm said generously, nodding his head. ''Course.'

'Thank you,' Claudine replied with great relief.

'I think I had better make sure Mr Robinson understands exactly what we need.' Hester looked across Worm's head directly at Claudine.

Claudine smiled very slightly, but the colour was back in her face.

'Oh, yes,' she agreed fervently. 'Please do.'

'Paint it!' Squeaky Robinson said, aghast. He was a lean, scrawny man with a cadaverous face, long, stringy, grey-white hair and wildly uneven teeth. He rose to his feet in outrage as he stared across his littered desk at Hester. 'Paint what, for Gawd's sake?'

'Anything,' Hester replied. 'All the door frames to begin with. It can go on from there.'

'Have you any idea how many doors there are in this place?' Squeaky demanded. 'There are dozens!' he went on without waiting for her to reply. 'More than dozens!' he added.

'Good,' Hester said quickly. 'Think what a difference it will make.'

'I am thinking,' Squeaky said incredulously. 'Money! Lots and lots of money. Have you suddenly inherited a fortune you forgot to mention?' He drew in his breath and carried straight on. 'And why paint? Why not something we really need, like medicine, or bandages, or new blankets before the ones we've got fall to bits? Why not even food, for Gawd's sake?'

'We can get those too,' Hester said reasonably, but knowing she was being totally unreasonable. 'But we'll start with paint, one tin at a time.'

Squeaky sat down hard and accidentally scattered half a dozen sheets of paper, sending most of them on to the floor. 'Paint!' he howled. 'And who's going to use it? You?'

'No, of course not,' Hester said sharply.

'That's what I thought!' Squeaky agreed. 'No! Absolutely not. There's no money. No . . . money!'

She knew it was time to give in. 'I know. That isn't the point, Squeaky. I want Worm occupied. He needs to have something to do that'll keep him busy all the time. Claudine is going to stand in for me while I'm busy at the hospital. She hasn't time to worry about Worm . . . and she will do. You know that as well as I do. I'm not having him running off and us all wasting time looking for him, thinking something's happened to him.'

'Oh.' Squeaky stared hard at her. 'Why didn't you say so?'

'I . . .' She looked at him and wondered why she had not told him plainly. He was almost impossible to deceive, and why did she want to save him fear? Did he really care about one more urchin off the river-bank? Perhaps he did, but he would have his teeth pulled out one by one before he admitted it.

'I didn't think you would agree with me,' she finished.

'I don't!' he said savagely. 'But I suppose I'll do it anyway. One tin of paint at a time – no more! I should teach him how to read. Then he'd really be of some damn use!'

'An excellent idea,' Hester agreed. 'But paint the doors

first. Let him help you, not you helping him. He mustn't run away.'

Squeaky stared at her.

'Can you imagine how Claudine will feel if something happens to him?' she added quietly.

Suddenly his face softened. 'We'll keep him busy,' he promised. 'Now get out of my office.'

Hester smiled. 'Thank you.'

Chapter Three

JUST BEFORE she began her evening duty Hester called in at Magnus Rand's office to ask about Charlie. It was barely dusk outside and the room still held the glow of sunset as if the light were trapped in the covers of the books where the leather was polished with use.

Magnus looked worried. The lines were deep between his fair brows and he stared at Hester for a moment before he could recall her name.

'Yes, Mrs Monk? What is it?'

'Charlie,' she answered. 'The boy in the wing with the other children. How is he?' She kept her voice light, but there was insistence in it. She intended to have an answer.

His expression cleared. 'Ah . . . yes. He is much improved. I have recommended beef tea and as much bread and butter as he will take. Thank you for helping him.' He smiled as if that were the conclusion of the interview.

'And Maggie?' she pressed.

'Who?' His frown returned.

'The little girl, his sister.'

'Oh, yes. There is nothing wrong with her. A bit sickly, but she has probably never had enough to eat in her life. Don't worry about her, Mrs Monk. Please return to your regular duties.' He looked down at the page he had been writing on. Hester turned to leave, not satisfied but aware that he would tell her no more. She would have to catch up on individual patients from Sherryl O'Neill.

As she reached the hallway she came almost face to face with a very elegantly dressed young woman of about her own height, but several years younger, perhaps just into her thirties. She was handsome. Her hair was thick and a rich, unusual shade of auburn. Her features were regular, but currently marred by an extreme anxiety.

She made a little exclamation of surprise and gasped an apology.

Hester smiled at her. 'Can I help you?' she offered.

The woman looked at Hester's plain blue-grey dress and the white apron around her waist with its bib extending up to where it was pinned just above her bosom.

'You are a nurse?' she asked, although she had clearly reached her own conclusion.

'Did you wish to speak to Dr Rand?' Hester enquired gently.

'Yes, if you would be so kind,' the woman accepted. 'My name is Adrienne Radnor. It is most urgent that I speak with him.' Her voice cracked under the pressure of her emotion.

'I will take you,' Hester responded. 'Come with me. Is he expecting you?'

'No, but I have to see him.'

'Come,' Hester said again. 'Please . . .'

The woman kept step with her, almost crowding her in her urgency. In a few yards they reached Magnus Rand's door, which was now closed.

Hester knocked on it firmly. When she heard Magnus's voice, even though she did not hear what he said, she turned the handle and went in, ushering Adrienne Radnor to come in beside her.

At the intrusion Magnus Rand looked up from his desk, a flush of anger darkening his face. Then he saw Adrienne Radnor and instinctively recognised her desperation.

'Dr Rand?' she said shakily. Her voice was husky, uncertain, but there was a quality of hysteria in it that impelled her forward, regardless of what he would say. She took a step towards his desk, ignoring Hester. 'Dr Rand, my father, Bryson Radnor, is terribly ill. Indeed he is dying.' Her voice trembled and it took all her self-mastery to continue. 'He has the "white blood disease" you have written about. You are our last hope . . .'

Hester looked from Magnus to Adrienne and back again. She saw an extraordinary change come over him. The irritation was smoothed away like creases under a hot iron. It was replaced by an intense pity; then that too vanished as a sudden energy filled him.

'Tell me more, Miss Radnor. When did you first recognise the illness in him? Be as precise as you can. I'm sorry, please sit down.' He rose hastily from his chair and hurried around the desk to pull forward a seat for her, completely ignoring Hester.

Adrienne barely took time to arrange her fashionable, autumnal-shaded skirts, which so complemented her colouring. She sat a trifle awkwardly, leaning forward towards him. 'I can remember the day very well. It was two months ago. Papa had been growing weaker for a period of time. At first the doctors thought it was just weariness. My father is over sixty and he insists on behaving as if he were a young man.' She gave a slight smile but it vanished in an instant. 'He travelled extensively. He was always very vigorous in his pursuits, climbing mountains, riding for days on horseback. He attended the opera and the theatre, visited Paris, Rome, Madrid.' There was pride in her voice. 'It was not foolish to wonder if perhaps a long rest would do him good.'

'And did it?' Magnus enquired with interest. His eyes were intent upon hers, and his expression very grave.

She lowered her gaze and her answer was almost a whisper.

'At first it seemed to, but I fear now that we saw only what we wished to see. He is failing very rapidly. Unless you are willing to help him, I think he has only weeks left.'

'I must consult my brother,' Magnus said with unusual gentleness.

Adrienne leaned even further forward. 'My father is a man of very considerable means, Dr Rand. He would be well able to recompense you for your skill, and to meet any expenses you might incur in treating him. Surely that is worth something?'

Hester winced at the words, and yet in the young woman's place she might have said the same thing, clumsy as it was.

Magnus brushed it aside.

'I will not take your money, Miss Radnor, unless I am certain that we have some chance of helping your father. I must still consult my brother. He is a chemist of more than skill – of brilliance – and it is his experiments that give us hope that we can cure this, and perhaps many other diseases.'

'Then call him!' she begged. 'Call anyone, only please do not delay.'

Magnus looked up at Hester. 'Mrs Monk, you have heard Miss Radnor's plight, and that of her father. Please inform my brother of the situation and ask him if he will be good enough to lay aside whatever he is doing at present and come to my office so he can ask whatever he needs to of Miss Radnor, and reach some decision.'

'Yes, Dr Rand,' Hester said willingly, and turned to leave.

She was not accustomed to going to Hamilton Rand's laboratory. It was closed to the hospital staff for excellent reasons. It was full of chemicals that were highly likely to be harmful if touched, mixed or spilled, and of experiments that could be ruined if disturbed. Hester believed it was also because Hamilton Rand did not wish his work to be interrupted for anything short of the building being on fire. But now she had no choice.

She walked quickly, without distraction. She hurried past other nurses barely acknowledging them. She did not even glance at storerooms, other wards, even operating theatres. When she reached the laboratory door she knocked on it firmly and loudly.

There was no answer.

She knocked again, harder.

Still there was no response.

Hamilton Rand spent most of his time here, not only all day but frequently most of the evening. He had been known to work all night, which had earned him both fear and respect.

Hester was moved not so much by concern for Magnus as pity for Adrienne Radnor. She understood painfully well her deep love for her father and the desire to save him at almost any cost. The guilt still ached within Hester for her own father whom she had not been there to save. She had been fighting her own battles for independence and purpose as an army nurse in the Crimea when her father had been dishonoured by a brutal trick, and had taken his own life. If she had come home even a month or two earlier she might have prevented the tragedy that had driven him to such a thing. That would have spared the whole family. For her mother, the loss of a son in battle, followed by financial ruin and then the death of her husband had been too much. Her health could take no more. James, Hester's younger brother, had done all he could, but it was beyond his power to help.

Hester had no option but to override good manners. She turned the handle and opened the door. The laboratory was a very large room, as large as a ward, but there were no beds in it. Shelves and cupboards lined all the walls. In the centre were benches with sinks and racks of all manner of scientific instruments: glass tubes, bottles, retorts, individual gas burners and other contraptions whose use she could only guess.

Hamilton Rand was only about eight feet from the door.

He stood rigid, his face like a wedge of ice, his white cotton coat splashed with chemicals and what looked to be blood.

'What do you imagine you are doing here, woman?' he demanded. 'How dare you barge in and interrupt me? Get out!'

Hester straightened her shoulders and stared back at him. Doctors did not frighten her, chemists still less.

'I came to deliver a message to you from Dr Rand,' she replied levelly. 'He requests your presence in his office to consult a young woman whose father is dying of the white blood disease. He is desperate, and has the financial means to pay you for any cure you are willing to try. Dr Rand does not wish to take the decision without consulting you.' She said it with some satisfaction in telling him because she knew he would not resist the temptation. Even in the short time she had been here, his devotion to science had become clear to her. He spared neither himself nor others in the search for healing.

He put the dish he was holding down on the nearside bench. 'Then move out of the way, woman!' he ordered. 'We must see this patient at once.'

He looked her up and down. He was not a tall man, and she was close to his height.

'What are you?' he asked, frowning at her. He had seen her before only a day ago, but had instantly forgotten.

'A nurse,' she replied equally stiffly.

'Ah!' There was light in his eyes. 'Yes. Now I remember Magnus telling me about you. Come with me. Don't stand here wasting time!' He brushed past her and she stepped aside out of his way to avoid being knocked down. She swivelled round and followed him briskly back down the long corridors all the way to Magnus's office.

He flung the door open without asking. Adrienne Radnor was still sitting in the chair and she had the composure not to rise as he came in, announcing himself brusquely.

Magnus introduced her and she answered as calmly as she could, but Hester heard the tremor in her voice. For her Hamilton Rand was far more than a brilliant and ill-mannered chemist. He represented the hope of life for the father she clearly loved profoundly.

Hamilton turned to Hester. 'You wait there,' he ordered her. 'And close the door, for God's sake! Do you expect this young woman to tell me all her father's symptoms with the whole world listening in?'

'Mrs Monk,' Magnus interrupted, 'you may return to your regular duties. Thank you.'

'No, you may not!' Hamilton snapped. 'Stay where you are, and listen.' He completely ignored his brother but turned more gently to Adrienne. 'I have asked Mrs Monk to remain because she was an army nurse. That means she has great experience in treating men who have been badly injured and lost much blood. She thinks quickly and does not panic. If we take your case, she will nurse your father. Now tell me everything I need to know. And the truth, if you please. The exact truth as much as you know it. Our ability to help him depends upon it.'

Adrienne obeyed without hesitation, and Magnus only occasionally interrupted. As Hamilton asked questions and made brief notes Hester listened with professional interest and intense personal compassion.

'My mother died eleven years ago,' Adrienne said quietly in answer to Hamilton's question. 'She had been failing for a little while, then she caught pneumonia and within days she was gone.' There was no expression to her voice. The loss was old and she was only remembering how she had felt.

'Your father's health?' Hamilton returned her to the only subject that interested him.

'Oh, it was excellent,' she said with a quick smile, which vanished even more rapidly. 'We supported each other. I went

45

with him on some of his travels.' Her voice thickened with unshed tears. 'It was marvellous. He was interested in everything. He showed me so much . . .' She blinked quickly several times, and went on before Hamilton could prompt her. 'He did not become ill until three years ago, and at first it seemed to pass after a short rest. He always had so much energy . . .'

Hamilton was busy making notes. He looked up, waiting.

'Then he began to tire more easily. He tried to hide it, but I noticed.' She went on to describe his gradual decline, pain naked in her face.

Hester listened as she described the pain, the unexplained bleeding he tried at first to conceal, then her horror when at last it was too much to hide from her.

'He had once been so strong,' she said. 'So vibrant and passionate a man, a force few would dare to challenge. Now he is scarcely able even to feed himself, let alone fight the final battle without me by his side. I try to make myself hope, but I am beginning to fail in that. I don't know how much longer I can pretend to believe he will recover.'

Hester could imagine it so clearly it was as if she had been in the room with them. What treatment had they tried? No doubt Rand would ask Miss Radnor all of that.

She went on listening as arrangements were made for Bryson Radnor to be brought to the hospital the following day. Hester watched Adrienne rise a little shakily, express her thanks yet again, and walk with dignity out of the office and down the corridor towards the way out. Refusing to accept the task of giving whatever assistance she could did not even enter Hester's mind. It would still mean very long hours for her, but daytime rather than night. They would have people around to cover the nights, until Jenny Solway returned.

She went back to the ward and encountered Sherryl O'Neill at the door.

'Where've you been?' Sherryl demanded. 'Angus McLeod's

much improved. I wanted to tell you. He's asking for you. Sitting up!' Her face shone with her pleasure at the news. McLeod had lost a leg and the wound had bled badly. For a while it had seemed beyond their ability to save his life.

'He's still pretty weak,' Sherryl warned, falling in step with Hester as they moved between the beds, 'but he's full of hope.' They exchanged glances, and Hester understood all that the other woman was not saying, as well. Nursing was moment to moment. One accepted the good and learned from it but took very little for granted.

'I won't be here tomorrow night,' she said quietly. 'There's a new patient coming in. By the time I've finished with him, I think Jenny will be back. Thank you for your companionship.'

Sherryl looked startled, and then put out her hand with sudden warmth. 'It was a pleasure. Some of your stories of the army made me realise how lucky I am to be here at peace, and yet I also feel as if I missed something.'

'Don't worry,' Hester said with a lop-sided smile. 'You'll get plenty of other tasks.'

Hester went home immediately and tried to go to bed, since it was now early evening. But she had prepared herself to be on duty all night, and sleep was elusive. She lay still only so she would not disturb Monk beside her. She had not told him the reason for her change of duty. He had more than enough to worry about with the rearrangements necessary when Orme finally retired. He was pleased that she was working the same sort of hours as he was. At least they were together all night, a warmth and a sweetness that he valued more than he was willing to admit.

In the morning Hester was in Magnus Rand's office when Adrienne Radnor arrived with her father. Hester looked at Radnor with intense interest and a pity she found it difficult to conceal. Nature had designed him to be a big man, physically imposing, but now he was gaunt. His broad shoulders and deep chest were painfully bony, his arms limp by his sides where he lay on the palet on which he had been carried. His powerful face, with its aquiline nose and wide, thin-lipped mouth, registered rage at this present dependence upon others for his mere ability to move from one place to another. He must have been magnificent in the days of his health.

Adrienne was at his side, far more soberly dressed than the day before. Her skirt was of a brown so dark as to be almost black and she wore a very plain blouse, which looked drab in the bright August sun that streamed through the office windows. But nothing would dull the burning colour of her hair.

The porters who had carried Radnor set him down on a long couch in the office frequently used for patients who were too unwell to walk. At a nod from Magnus they left, closing the door behind them.

'Help me up!' Radnor said to Adrienne, not even glancing at anyone else.

Hester was startled at his tone. It was an order, not a request.

Adrienne moved forward instantly. With a practised gesture she slipped her arm around his shoulders and eased him up.

Hester passed her two pillows to prop his body at a comfortable angle and stepped back. With a smile of tenderness Adrienne smoothed his hair, which was white but still thick.

He did not thank her. It was as natural and accepted as if he had done it himself.

Adrienne stayed beside him, but allowed Radnor to speak to Magnus without her appearing to be between them. Let no one imagine that Bryson Radnor was not still in charge.

Hester understood. She might have done the same. No one

else would know what gratitude he might express when he and his daughter were alone, what private passion or despair she might be a silent witness to, what indignities she would pretend not to observe, yet he would always be conscious that she knew. The very ill have little privacy, even for the most intimate of things.

Radnor studied Magnus for several moments and seemed to be satisfied with what he saw. Magnus was an unassuming man. He had none of the arrogance of his elder brother, but he had the confidence of both education and practical success. And unlike Hamilton, he had patience.

Radnor nodded and inclined his head towards Hester. 'Who is she?' he asked, his question clearly still directed at Magnus.

'One of Florence Nightingale's nurses,' Magnus replied without hesitation. 'She was standing in for a friend, on night duty, but we have asked her to remain and look after you. We will find someone else to replace her in the ward.'

Radnor regarded Hester for only a moment longer, then nodded. 'Good. You may begin.'

Before he would do anything further, Magnus had Hester make all the usual measurements and assessments of pulse, temperature, history of eating, drinking, digestion and elimination, patterns of sleep or lack of it, and such treatments as they had attempted, and their results.

Radnor told her grudgingly, and twice Adrienne stepped in to answer in his behalf. Hester accepted this, because it was not uncommon for people to find it awkward to answer such things to people they did not know, or more often in the presence of those they knew very well.

She assessed the answers with her own private marks on the notes to indicate where she doubted the truthfulness of them. She would explain later to Magnus what they meant. Dependence can make people hate those they depend upon. It could be a complex and exhausting relationship. Often it was better to be nursed by someone whose opinion does not matter to you.

Finally Radnor was in the room he would occupy for the next days, perhaps weeks, possibly even in which he would die. Hester suggested that Adrienne wait until he was settled, and then come to wish him goodbye, for the time being.

'Oh, no,' Adrienne said immediately. 'I must come with him. I will make sure that everything is as he likes it.'

Hester stood in front of her on the threshold, and spoke quietly but firmly. 'It was not a suggestion, Miss Radnor.' She spoke very softly and with her back to Bryson Radnor. 'We will look after him, and start treatment as soon as we can. You will be in the way. Please don't argue. Time is important.'

Adrienne hesitated. The fear in her eyes was momentarily undisguised.

'But he needs me!' Her voice trembled. 'You don't understand . . .'

Hester was blunt. 'Dr Rand will not proceed until all other people are out of the room. How long do you wish to hold him up?'

Adrienne let out a sigh. Then she took a step backwards.

Hester touched her gently on the arm. 'We will do everything we can for him. Don't lose hope.'

Adrienne nodded, the tears spilling over on to her cheeks.

'Go home,' Hester advised her. 'It will be a while. We will send a message if there should be anything urgent.'

'Can't I wait . . . somewhere?'

'Yes. But it is uncomfortable and you will be both tired and hungry.'

'I don't care!'

'We do,' Hester told her. 'If Mr Radnor recovers, he will need you to be well and strong in order to nurse him back to full health. He will be in no position to look after you. This is a time to be strong.'

Very slowly Adrienne acquiesced. She turned and walked away, a stiff-shouldered solitary figure moving all the way down the hall until she was just a silhouette against the daylight, and finally disappeared.

Hester followed Radnor and Magnus Rand into the room that was to serve both as treatment theatre and bedroom as long as he needed it. The bed was ready and beside it was a large contraption, the top of it shoulder high. It was constructed largely of bottles and tubes held in exact place with clamps, springs and hinged metal arms.

Radnor stared at it, but if it alarmed him he hid the fact superbly. He made no comment as the porters lifted him on to the bed and then, on being told by Magnus that they were not needed any further, they excused themselves and left.

Magnus busied himself with the contraption.

Hester assisted Radnor out of his clothes and into a long, white nightshirt. She had done such a thing countless times before, usually to soldiers who were either very seriously wounded, or exhausted from debilitating disease such as typhus or cholera. She was used to bodily functions both natural and those produced by disease. She had seen men naked and in terrible distress. She had watched people die when there was no time to mourn. She knew that action could protect against the utter helplessness, and keep panic or despair at bay.

Bryson Radnor had never been assisted by a woman he did not know since he had left childhood behind. It embarrassed him, which made him angry, and yet he could not lift his own limbs to dress himself without her help.

She would like to have told him that he should feel no self-consciousness. She had no personal interest in him whatever. But that would have been unprofessional, especially in front of Dr Rand. Very possibly it was all an alternative to showing the fear that must be flooding his every thought at the moment. She was alive and well. He was dying. Those were the only facts that mattered.

She was gentle with him, averting her eyes where practically possible. When he was ready and the sheets pulled up to his chest, only his shoulders and arms above them, she stepped back and made room for Magnus to begin.

Hester looked at Radnor. His face was totally calm and he stared back at her coldly, almost contemptuously. Only his almost skeletal hands on the sheet in front of him gave him away. They were locked rigidly, the rope-like blue veins standing out.

'I will begin in a moment,' Magnus told him. 'I have to take a small amount of blood from you. I will look at it, then as soon as I am certain, I will prepare. It must all be fresh, and absolutely clean, you understand? Do not move.' He did not wait for Radnor to reply, but turned away from him to Hester. 'Mrs Monk, the syringe, if you please.'

Hester passed him the long, thin needle with its tiny clear glass tube on the end. She was familiar with it only as it was used to give medicine directly into the bloodstream, or as had proved so tragically fatal, opium in its most virulent form.

Very carefully Magnus took Radnor's arm, bent it at the elbow and then felt for the vein. It took him several moments to find it to his satisfaction. He sank the needle into it.

Radnor winced, but the movement was so slight Hester, watching his face, barely saw it.

Magnus pulled the handle of the syringe back very slowly. The glass tube filled with blood so lacking in the dark red of health that he needed no more than half the instrument full to satisfy his need for knowledge. The last shred of doubt vanished. Bryson Radnor was dying of the white blood disease.

Magnus removed the needle and pressed a piece of surgical lint over the mark. 'Mrs Monk, will you come and assist me to prepare the equipment?'

Hester followed him out of the room and into the next one from it. She stared at the pale blood in the glass tube that Magnus had drawn from Radnor, the knot inside her stomach clenched tight.

'I want you to go back and explain to Radnor what I am going to do,' Magnus said gravely, as if he had not noticed her emotion. 'I will put another needle into his arm. It will remain there for the best part of an hour, or possibly even longer. He must keep calm, and on no account remove the needle. You will watch his progress closely. See that his temperature is steady, and his heart rate. If he becomes feverish, nauseous, clammy, or has difficulty in breathing then we will stop immediately. It will mean that the treatment will not succeed. Have I explained myself clearly, Mrs Monk? Do you understand your duty?'

She hesitated. She wanted to argue, tell him that she did not know what the treatment was, but she knew that she had no right to know. It was experimental, but Radnor had little to lose. Untreated, the disease would kill him within weeks.

'Are you going to explain it to Miss Radnor?' she asked.

Magnus turned away and concentrated on what he was doing. His powerful short-fingered hands were absolutely steady. 'The scientific side is my concern, Mrs Monk. I find people . . . difficult. I rely on you to take care of his fears, or . . . or apprehension. And there may be a great deal. Some patients have a feeling that amounts to dread. It is a symptom that the treatment is failing.'

'I can't explain what I don't understand,' she said with rising alarm.

'You don't need to,' he replied, trying to sound reasonable, but his impatience showed through the thin veneer of courtesy. 'Just keep him calm. I've watched you. You are good at it. You like people. To me they are –' he shook his hand as if to brush away flies – 'cases! I am trying to heal them. I have

53

to look at their bodies, think rationally, disregard fear or pain, except as they are symptoms of their disease. Pity is natural, but it is of no use to me. Just do your job, Mrs Monk. Keep the man calm, steady, as unafraid as possible. If you do not do that, I cannot help him. Do you understand?' He stared at her for a moment, his hands still, the contraption, the jars and bottles forgotten.

'Yes, Dr Rand, of course,' she said quietly, as she would have to a child, someone else's child whom she did not much like.

She found Bryson Radnor lying motionless with his eyes closed. She stood beside him and wondered if he were praying. Would it be for help? Or to make some peace with his Maker, and deal with life's regrets; all the things not said, not done?

He became aware of her and opened his eyes. The instant she saw them, the idea that he had been praying vanished.

'Come to comfort me?' he said sarcastically. 'Tell me God loves me, or some such tripe?'

'I have no idea what God thinks of you,' she snapped back at him. The words were out before she gave them consideration.

To her surprise he smiled. 'Of course you haven't. But I'm surprised you have the nerve to say so. What are you supposed to do for me? You must have a purpose. God knows, you're not here as an ornament.'

'I imagine you buy ornaments,' she replied. 'If you want them. If they break, you replace them. I am here to help you behave appropriately, so the treatment has a chance to work.'

'I have never in my life had any woman tell me how to behave!' he said witheringly, his eyes sharp in spite of his distress.

'So I assumed,' Hester answered coolly. 'Certainly no one made much of a job of it.'

He grunted. 'Were you really in the Crimea?'

'Yes.'

'Why? God-awful place. Totally pointless war.'

'I didn't go to fight,' she told him. 'I went to nurse the wounded.'

'Very noble.' The sarcastic edge was back in his voice again. 'Found yourself a husband, did you?' He was watching her closely, his eyes searching for emotion in her face, perhaps for the vulnerability he could probe. Was that resentment of life, because he could feel it slipping out of his hands?

She wanted to tell him that she could see his fear, even understand it. But that was not what she was here for. She should have been able to pity him, but so far he had made her dislike him too much for that. He was frightened, so he was trying to transfer the pain out of himself and into her.

'No,' she answered the original question. 'My father died, and that drove out all other concerns. I can imagine very easily how your daughter feels now.'

A look came across his face that was too complex for her to read. There was intense emotion in it, but a mixture of pleasure and pain, a slow relish of something sweet, and a loathing as well.

Then it vanished.

'I don't need your sympathy, woman,' he sneered at her. 'Just do your job, whatever that is.'

'Just as well,' she said before she thought. 'Because you don't have it. And my job is to distract you now, and to keep you from ripping the needle out when Dr Rand puts it in your arm. If you do pull it out, you will lose what little precious blood you have.'

He stared at her. 'Got a tongue like a butcher's knife, haven't you?'

She smiled at him as if she liked him, and saw the confusion in his eyes.

'Like a surgeon's scalpel,' she corrected him. 'Far more precise and sharper. If I have the need.'

Magnus came in and grasped hold of the contraption, wheeling it over the slightly uneven boards of the floor. He stopped it very close to the side of the bed. Hester glanced at the bottle hanging from it, with the soft rubber tubes trailing like tentacles. The light did not pass through the bottle. It was full of something.

'Please be still, Mr Radnor,' Magnus said politely. 'If you fear you might pull away, I can have you strapped down. But the pain will be slight. I cannot answer for a degree of discomfort.'

'I can hold still,' Radnor said through clenched teeth. 'Stop treating me like a child, man. Do what you have to.'

Magnus did not argue with him. He turned to the contraption, and checked all the connections once again, in case the journey across the floor had jarred anything loose. Satisfied, he took a small cloth that smelled strongly of surgical spirit, and wiped the skin on the inside of Radnor's arm. Then without warning he jabbed the needle into the vein and held it hard.

Radnor gasped and his face turned even whiter than before.

Hester was not surprised. There was something about the shining point of a heavy needle sinking into one's own flesh that would make anyone shudder, however much they steeled themselves against it. It was far darker than the delicate stitching of the skin a surgeon would do to a wound.

Magnus glanced at Radnor, just to assure himself that he was steady enough, and then he began to adjust the dials and pressures on the contraption.

The glass above the needle this time was dark brown. Hester could not tell from looking at it what it might be. She watched Magnus's face, his intense concentration, and then she turned back to Radnor. He was lying motionless, but there was a beading of perspiration on his forehead. She decided not to disturb him by wiping it away. To him it would seem like fussing.

The seconds ticked by.

Magnus looked at the contraption, then at Radnor. He fiddled with the rubber tubing to make sure it was still working.

Hester put her hand gently on Radnor's forehead.

He opened his eyes and glared at her. She saw the fear in him and felt a moment's pity. She could tell him that his temperature was holding steady, but no doubt he knew that. There was nothing feverish about him. She did not do so because she did not want to provoke him to respond. Instead she told Magnus.

'Quite steady, Dr Rand,' she said quietly. She moved her cool finger down to Radnor's wrist. The pulse was light, but no faster or more uneven than before.

More minutes slipped by.

Magnus told Hester to take Radnor's temperature properly, with the thermometer. She did so, and his pulse with a stop watch.

'His temperature is up a degree,' she told him. 'Pulse is the same as before, but a little stronger.'

'Good. Good, so far,' Rand said with relief. 'We will continue.' He did not ask Radnor. This was medicine, an experiment. All that mattered was the result. Radnor as an individual meant nothing.

Carefully, with Hester's help, Magnus unhooked the dark brown bottle and then attached another, seemingly identical. It was only then that Hester saw the rime of blood on it, and knew beyond doubt what it was that Magnus and Hamilton were doing. It was human blood that they had taken from the children, and were putting drop by drop, into Bryson Radnor. They were replacing his sick, white blood, empty of life, with that of Charlie, Maggie, and whoever else they had in that ward full of children.

It was terrifying, barbaric – and brilliant, if it worked! She had enough knowledge of medical history to know that it had been tried before. As far back as the 1600s doctors had tried to give healthy blood to save sick people. On rare occasions it had worked, for a while. Usually it killed the recipient, most unpleasantly, as if the new blood, which had kept someone else alive, were poison to the one who received it. Nobody knew why.

One great difficulty was that blood clotted – if it did not, then any cut would cause the victim to bleed to death – but you could not put clotted blood into another person. How had Hamilton overcome that? What had he added to the blood he had taken so that it ran liquid and easily through those brown rubber tubes? How much of it was exactly right to keep the blood liquid, and yet so that it still clotted when it had mixed with the recipient's own blood?

Did Bryson Radnor know what was happening to him?

She looked at him closely as Magnus tied up the second bottle and began its slow, steady drip into the glass vial and the needle at the end of it. Did Radnor even wonder whose blood it was? Maybe he thought it was from some animal. Or a convict destined to die anyway.

She took his temperature and pulse again. The temperature was still normal. His pulse was markedly stronger. The skin of his face had lost some of its grey look.

As she was staring at him he opened his eyes. They were a strange, golden brown colour, brighter than before.

It's working! His pale lips formed the words. They were silent, but she could hear the ring of victory in them as if he had shouted loud enough to fill the bare hospital room with the sound.

By late in the afternoon Radnor was lying back against his pillows drinking beef tea and requesting more food than he had eaten in the entire previous week. His colour had returned, his temperature was close to normal, his pulse steady.

Magnus was pleased, but he did what he could to contain his elation.

'We've had such success before,' he said warily, when he and Hester were alone in his office. He took a deep breath and let it out with a sigh. 'Sometimes we succeed for a few days, even a few weeks. Then when they are ill again, we treat them again . . . and they die.' He closed his eyes and leaned back in his chair. 'Horribly.'

'And you don't know why?' she said with a sudden chill taking away her moment of victory. That was what it was about – not making it work just the once. She thought of Wilton, and Sherryl's description of how he had died, and thrust it out of her mind.

She saw in her mind's eye soldiers lying on battlefields, limbs torn off, riddled with bullets. With current medical knowledge they could be saved, but only for a while. Even with the best care in field hospitals, they died of shock and loss of blood.

And not only soldiers, other people, in street accidents, industrial disasters, women dying in childbirth from bleeding no one could control.

But the blood had to come from somebody. Somebody like Charlie, Maggie, even little Mike. One pint of blood from a child that age – undersized anyway, malnourished, alone and frightened – could be enough to weaken him so the first infection he caught killed him.

There was no way out.

But that also meant no way forward!

All the men who had died here from war injuries – could blood have saved any of them? Hester couldn't know. It was all too late now. For Wilton, anyway. What about the next one? All the men in this hospital, other hospitals, all the future?

Did this potentially life-saving treatment always come at this sort of price?

Chapter Four

HESTER WAS fully occupied with her duties caring for Bryson Radnor. He was very sick indeed, and although his daughter, Adrienne, was as much help as she could be, there were still certain things that Hester needed to do, as much for observation as skill in the execution of them.

She found him a disagreeable man, but quite often the very ill were frightened and in pain. Many resented being dependent upon other people for even the most simple things, some of which it was instinctive to keep private.

'For goodness' sake stop fussing, woman!' he snapped at her late on the second day. Adrienne was out of the room.

Hester was making the bed so it would be more comfortable for him. She was keeping her temper with difficulty.

'If you prefer the sheets wrinkled, Mr Radnor, all you have to do is say so,' she told him.

He gave what was intended to be a wave of dismissal, but he was too weak to make it effective.

'Where's Adrienne?' he demanded.

'Asleep,' Hester answered. 'She was with you all night. Everyone needs to rest at some time.'

He turned his head and stared at her, moving his eyes slowly down from her face to her body. He did not bother to be discreet about it. She found it unpleasant, almost prurient, as if he were trying to reduce her to the physical necessities as much as he felt she was to him in his dependence.

She wanted to snap at him, tell him how childish and offensive he was, but she knew better than to allow any patient to provoke her like that. And it would give him the satisfaction of knowing he was dictating the relationship between them. Instead she forced herself to smile at him, gently, almost sweetly, as if she were nanny to a rather objectionable child.

He looked away. That was a battle she had won, but she knew there would be more.

She finished tidying the bed and the rest of the room, opened the window to let in the warm fresh air, and went out into the corridor.

She all but bumped into Adrienne, who looked exhausted. Her plain, dark dress was crumpled; her hair was pinned up too hastily and was pulled tight in places. But it was her face that most affected Hester. Her skin was pale and looked like that of a much older woman. There was no bloom to it; she looked almost bruised around her eyes.

'How is he?' she asked immediately, her voice sharp with fear.

Hester put out her hand and laid it on Adrienne's arm, holding her, feeling the strength with which she pulled away.

'He's resting,' she answered firmly. 'And he has taken some beef tea with a little tonic in it. Dr Rand is hoping to begin the treatment soon.'

Adrienne was still pulling away, as if she would not believe anything until she saw it for herself.

Hester kept hold of her.

'You must take more care of yourself,' she said gently. 'Once treatment begins, we will need your help. You need to be well, in order to look after him.'

Adrienne stared at her. She was exhausted, frightened and

desperately in need of belief that the long battle could be won.

'Come and have a cup of tea,' Hester asked. 'I need to tell you certain things about caring for him that you need to know.'

Adrienne hesitated.

'You have done an excellent job so far.' Hester could see the doubt in the other woman's eyes, the hunger to check for herself that Radnor was indeed all right. As soon as she was in the room he would ask her to do one small task after another, all of them unnecessary, and she would obey. Hester had already seen how he needed to feel the power of ordering her around, and she never refused him anything. Whether it was love, fear of losing him, or guilt that he had imbued her with over the years, she could not tell. And it made no difference. He was drawing the strength out of her, and what Hester had told her about how she would be needed later on was perfectly true, even if that was not the reason she said so now.

'I've tried.' Adrienne smiled very slightly, searching Hester's face to see if she were telling the truth, or just trying to be kind.

'I doubt he would still be alive if you had been any less diligent.' Hester meant that. Radnor might well have survived out of sheer will to feed on the relationship. 'Please come so I can tell you more of what will happen,' she added.

Adrienne yielded and followed Hester along the corridor to the small room where nurses could take the necessary breaks now and then. There was a small burner where a kettle could be boiled and Hester immediately lit it and began to prepare the teapot and two cups.

There was nothing of real importance to tell Adrienne, but she could make it up easily enough. What she really wanted was to persuade her of the necessity of getting several hours of sleep herself. Tired people made mistakes. Every fear was larger when the emotional strength was worn out. Whatever they did, Radnor would die someday. Adrienne needed to be free of the guilt for living on, being younger, stronger, most of her life still ahead.

She made the tea, piping hot, and they sat together sipping it, along with some excellent biscuits, and she was glad to see that Adrienne ate until the plate was empty. She wondered when Adrienne had last eaten a full meal.

Adrienne had finished her tea. She leaned forward a little as if to stand up.

'Your father has told me about some of his adventures,' Hester said quickly. 'He has seen so many things most of us don't ever imagine, and he describes them so vividly.'

Adrienne smiled and relaxed back again. 'Oh, yes. He will live more fully in one year than most men do in their whole lives.' Her face was bright with admiration.

Radnor had spoken only of himself. Was that self-obsession, or did he assume Hester would take it for granted that Adrienne had been on at least some of his adventures?

'I have been only to the Crimea, and to America once, at the very start of their civil war,' Hester said.

'That doesn't sound very pleasant.' Adrienne looked at her with interest, perhaps even a touch of compassion. 'I've been to Paris. It's a wonderful city, so beautiful, so . . .special. There's a magic in the air. Does that sound silly?'

'Not at all. Tell me something about it.'

'My father took me,' Adrienne began. 'It was a little while ago now, but I shall remember it as long as I live.'

Hester listened for half an hour, reboiled the kettle and drank more tea as Adrienne told her about Paris, how her father knew it so well, his passion for the beauty of it, the history, and the little out-of-the-way corners most people never found.

Her face was animated; her eyes bright, her voice lifted

with enthusiasm, and admiration, not for the city so much as the man so passionately alive who had shown it to her.

She mentioned nowhere else. Radnor had spoken of a dozen places. Was Paris the only one to which he had taken her?

When at last Adrienne left, still determined to check on her father, Hester finally escaped Magnus Rand's attention and hurried back to the children's ward to see Maggie and Charlie. She wanted to know for herself how they were, even though Magnus had assured her that they were doing well. More than that, she had questions to ask them.

She found all three of them sitting on Charlie's bed, playing cat's cradle with long pieces of string tied into loops. Until they noticed her, they were all concentrating on weaving patterns with their fingers.

Then some movement caught Maggie's eye and she looked up. Her face filled with delight and she dropped the thread of string, ran over to Hester and threw her arms around her.

Hester hugged her back before she gave a thought to the impropriety of it, or not.

'Yer come back!' Maggie said with delight. 'Look at Charlie! Yer saved 'im!' She broke free and turned to point at Charlie, sitting up in bed, still pale and thin, but with a little more colour in his cheeks and definitely very wide awake. Mike, beside him, no longer looked frightened.

'I think we both saved him,' Hester answered. She did not want any of them to see her as a miracle worker. 'I've come to see how you are,' she went on. 'And to ask you about yourselves. I'd like to know.'

She walked over to the bed and Mike shifted closer to Charlie to make room for her.

First she touched the foreheads of each of them, and then felt their pulses. She was satisfied that the new nurse who had replaced Mrs Gilmore was doing her job well, and she felt the knots of tension ease inside her.

'You're doing fine,' she said with a smile. 'How did you find this hospital? Do you live near here?'

'I dunno where we are,' Maggie admitted. She looked at Charlie, and he shook his head.

'Greenwich,' Hester told them. This was not a good start.

'That's the other side of the river,' Charlie told her, shaking his head. 'An' down a bit,' he added.

So they came from the north bank, and upriver a bit, not far from Wapping.

'Limehouse?' she asked. 'Or the Isle of Dogs?'

'The 'igh Street,' Charlie told her.

Every neighbourhood had its High Street, so that was some help, but not a lot.

'Do you remember coming here?' she asked, looking at each of them in turn.

They all shook their heads.

'Were you asleep?'

'Must 'a been,' Charlie agreed.

'Did your ma and pa come with you?'

They shook their heads again.

'Do you remember saying goodbye to them?' She did not like the picture this was beginning to paint, but perhaps she should not have been surprised. 'What's the last thing you do remember, before being here?'

'Is summink wrong?' Maggie's eyes clouded over. 'Summink 'appened ter me?'

'I don't think so. But if you tell me what your mother's name is, and where she lives, I'll go and find out,' Hester promised. What she certainly would find out was why these three children were here alone, and no one had come to see them. There were many possibilities, and the ones she dreaded the most were either kidnapping, or the deliberate sale of children that a poor family could no longer feed. Of course, they might have been abandoned – perhaps their mother had died – but it was unlikely they would then have come here.

Maggie looked puzzled. Maybe she knew her mother only as 'Ma'? The idea of another name might be extraordinary to her.

'What's your last name?' Hester asked Charlie. 'Charlie what?'

'Charlie Roberts,' he replied.

'Tell me something about the street where you live. What are the shops you remember? Can you see the river from the street? Can you tell me what are the nearest steps to a ferry . . .?'

It was later in the afternoon than Hester would like it to have been when she got home. Dinner would have to wait, or even be no more than a cold meat sandwich. As soon as Scuff was through the door she told him her plans. Ten minutes later she propped a note on the kitchen table for Monk, and she and Scuff were on the road down to the ferry.

Scuff was deeply nervous. He kept fidgeting once they were on the water, and staring both backwards towards the Greenwich steps, and forward to Wapping.

Hester understood. He had been filled with a mixture of anxiety, fear and excitement for a few days now. He wanted to be a doctor so much he was terrified that he would not be accepted, would not be able even to understand what people were talking about, once it came to the theoretical part rather than the practical. He wanted Crow's help, and was afraid he would refuse it or, worse than that, Scuff would disappoint him. Perhaps worst of all was the dread that he would let Hester and Monk down, when they had trusted in him and believed he could succeed.

She thought of saying that they would back him whatever he chose to do, but she knew that would make no difference. Nothing would matter until he himself believed he could succeed.

At the far side of the river she paid the ferryman. Then they went up the steps and turned east, down the river from Wapping, and caught an omnibus on the High Street. Crow now rented space in a new building much larger than the old clinic he used to run. There was someone at the door and a room where patients could wait, almost like a regular doctor's office. Except that many of these patients couldn't pay. Old and young, some were abnormally ill, some acutely. There was even a dog with what looked like a jagged cut, neatly stitched up and now almost healed.

At first Hester was dismayed to find so many people here. She had judged the time badly. Then she realised that it probably would not matter what time she came, it might still be like this.

She gave her name to the woman at the front and asked that Crow might be told she was here, it was urgent, and she would not take up much of his time.

Ten minutes later Hester and Scuff were shown into his rooms.

Crow was well named. He was of indeterminate age, perhaps close to forty. He was tall, lanky and with jet-black hair, which had not recently been cut, and a huge smile showing very white teeth. He was clearly delighted to see her.

She knew better than to waste precious time with chatter. After the briefest of greetings she told him exactly what she wished for.

'I have three small children in the Greenwich hospital, aged four, six and seven. I need to find their parents and learn exactly why they're there. The family name is Roberts, and they live on a High Street, possibly in Limehouse, close to some river steps and behind a butcher's shop.'

'I know a couple of possibilities,' Crow said after a minute or two. 'But it's a rough area. You shouldn't go alone. Does Monk know about this?'

'Not yet. And there's another reason.' This time she hesitated. That was foolish. Crow had no time for dithering; she of all people should know that. She went straight on. 'Scuff would like to study medicine. I would be very grateful for any help or advice you could give us.'

Beside her Scuff was blushing scarlet and shifting from foot to foot, wishing he were anywhere else.

Crow regarded him with interest, waiting.

'Well, you're going to have to want it a lot more than that,' Crow said after a few more seconds of silence. 'Help me with the patients we've got waiting now, and when they're clear we'll go and find Mr and Mrs Roberts. Are you on?'

Scuff looked up at him, eyes wide. 'Yes . . . sir!'

It was a very long hour and a half for Hester. She helped as well, of course, but all the time part of her mind was worrying about how Scuff was getting on with Crow, and real patients, real medicine.

He had watched her many times, and helped when Monk was ill, and when Hooper had been badly injured. But holding things, passing them when asked, was very different from actually doing anything yourself. Was this not too hasty a way to introduce him to the practice of dealing with people who were frightened and very likely in pain?

Or perhaps Crow was seeing immediately, the hardest way possible, if Scuff had the obedience and the courage even to undertake such a course.

She had to force herself to turn her mind totally to the people she was working with. That was another lesson – from the time you were treating a patient, your own difficulties did not exist.

It was almost sundown, the colour was brilliant across the western sky, when they finally left Crow's clinic and started to walk together to the first butcher's shop on the High Street that Crow thought likely to be near the home of the

Roberts family, whose three children were in Greenwich Hospital.

Hester was longing to ask Crow how Scuff had fared, what he thought, if he would really help or not, but she could not do so in front of Scuff. What could she say to comfort him if the answer was 'no'? How could she protect him from the bitterness of the disappointment, and the humiliation?

She couldn't. If she protected him from this one, then how would he be armed or prepared for the next, or the one after that? Without pain how would he learn compassion? If it were easy, what value was it?

Scuff was a little behind them crossing the road.

'He'll do,' Crow said quietly, satisfaction in his voice. Then he flashed his wide smile at her. 'Get him to come Saturdays. If he isn't keen enough to come, then you know it's not for him.'

Ridiculously she felt a momentary sting in her throat, as if she were going to cry, and she had trouble getting the words out.

'Thank you.'

He shrugged, brushing it off lightly. 'I asked one or two people about the Roberts family. They should be around about the next corner.'

They found two butcher's shops. The first denied all knowledge of a Roberts family, but the second grudgingly gave them directions to a small, shabby house wedged between the back of the butcher's yard and a pawn shop facing on to an alley.

Crow knocked on the door. He was lifting his hand to knock again when it was opened by a large man, his untidy shirt tucked into his trousers, his face pale and bloated.

'Mr Roberts?' Crow enquired.

''Oo's askin'?' the man said anxiously.

'They call me Crow. I'm a doctor—'

'Gawd! Wot's 'appened?' the man said with a sudden burst of anger. 'It weren't my fault!'

Crow must have heard the fear in him. Hester could all but smell it in his breath and the stale sweat of his clothes. Both knew they would learn nothing of use if they made themselves enemies.

'I'm not investigating anything wrong,' Crow said quietly. 'At least I don't think so.'

'I din't see nothing,' the man said, still defensive.

'Are you Mr Roberts?'

'What if I am? Not that I'm saying so, mind.'

Crow kept his voice level. 'Well, supposing it is you, do you have three children?'

Roberts froze. His whole body stiffened and the little colour there was drained out of his skin.

Hester felt a pity for him she could not afford to indulge. Was it fear of authority or hatred of it the reason he had not reported his children missing, if indeed they were?

Then she saw a movement behind Roberts and realised that his wife was standing close to him, listening. There was fear in her face too, and indecision, but most of all there was grief.

'May we come in?' Crow asked.

Roberts said 'no', and his wife said 'yes' at the same moment.

Crow waited, Hester beside him and Scuff a few feet behind them both.

'Please, Alfred?' Mrs Roberts said quietly, choking her voice back.

Another moment's silence, then Roberts backed away, leaving her to pull the door open.

Hester followed Crow into the small front room, which obviously served for dining and any relaxation they might have. Scuff waited outside. The room was sparsely furnished, but tidy and surprisingly clean. Hester looked around. There were no toys in sight, no books except one, which was thin, with its binding glued back together a trifle crookedly. A child's book.

Mrs Roberts was bony and her hair lank, but her features were good and she could have been in her early thirties. Poverty and child-bearing had extinguished the light in her.

Crow sat down as if he intended to stay. He indicated one of the other chairs to Mrs Roberts to sit also.

'You have three children?' he asked her gently.

Hester waited quietly, watching.

'Six,' Mrs Roberts answered, and then when she saw his confusion she added, 'Eldest's gone her own way. Youngest are still babes. Thank 'eaven.' The tears welled in her eyes and she spoke with difficulty. 'It's Maggie, Charlie and Mike 'as gone.'

'Did they all go at once?'

She nodded and the tears spilled down her cheeks. 'They're good kids, mister. Maggie specially.' She gulped. 'Wot's 'appened to 'em?'

'I don't know yet.' Crow evaded the answer. 'But I'll find out.'

'Tell me the details, Mrs Roberts,' Hester asked gently. 'When did you last see them? What time of day? When did you realise they were gone?'

'What good does it do now?' Mr Roberts moved closer to his wife, snarling at Crow, ignoring Hester. 'You're not gonna do your doctor thing ter make yourself important over our grief! They're gone.'

''E's only tryin' ter 'elp, Alfred,' Mrs Roberts said desperately. 'Mebbe they in't gone for good! Mebbe 'e can find 'em!' Her voice wavered. She looked from Crow to her husband and back again.

'Don't accuse me!' Roberts said furiously. There was rage in his face, and something else Hester took a moment to recognise. It was a wild, unquenchable pain, and only after staring at him and seeing the dull flush on his skin did she realise it was also guilt. He had not reported the children's disappearance because he had something to do with it.

He had a wife and five children to feed, and he was in financial desperation. Maybe he had sold the children, possibly even to someone who had promised to feed them. She had seen it before. It was a terrible answer, but perhaps all he had. Sell some, to save the others? It was better than losing them all.

She looked at the woman's face again and saw the haunted misery in it. She was in such pain she could hardly bear it, and she knew there was no escape.

There was no escape for Hester or Crow either.

'Mr Roberts,' Crow turned to the man. 'I have no interest in trying to prosecute you for whatever you may have done with your children. Their lives now are what matter . . . which you are accountable for! Tell me to whom you sold them, for how much, and what they told you they were going to do with them.'

Mrs Roberts did not even look at her husband. Guilt for the silence was consuming her also, even though she might have said nothing so as to protect him, and therefore the remaining infants.

Slowly and painfully Roberts described the man who had approached him and offered to buy the children, feed and care for all of them, so they could be companions for an elderly lady in hospital, who had no children or grandchildren of her own.

'And you believed him?' Crow raised his black eyebrows.

Roberts avoided his wife's eye and totally disregarded Hester.

''Course I did. 'E were a gentleman. Said they'd be fed the best food, regular, and sleep in proper beds. I can't give 'em that!'

There was no point in arguing. The truth was only too

bitterly obvious. Was it a crime? Perhaps. Who would do differently, given such a choice?

Crow stood up slowly. He seemed to be considering saying something more, then changed his mind. He looked beyond Roberts and spoke to his wife.

'What are their names?'

'Charlie, Maggie and Mike,' she replied, staring at him with desperation in her eyes.

'They're all right, for now,' he said. 'We'll try to see that they stay that way.'

They went outside into the darkening evening. Neither of them spoke, but Crow touched his hand to Hester's shoulder for a moment.

Scuff moved into step behind them.

At the same time that Hester, Scuff and Crow were walking along the High Street in the Isle of Dogs, Monk and Orme were rowing easily, smoothly over the water towards the Customs and Excise office in the Pool of London. The evening air was soft, filled with the sounds and smells of incoming tide, salt and tar, river mud, fish.

Around them the hulls of ocean-going ships loomed up in the sunset haze, sails furled and lashed to the spars.

'Dawn is the only other time as good as this,' Orme said with a slow smile. 'Good as it is at home, quiet; long, flat marshes with birds flying over, thousands of them, black against the sky. Sometimes you can hear the creak of their wings, you know?'

'Yes, I do,' Monk agreed. 'It's a good sound.'

'I'll still miss these,' Orme said ruefully, gazing at the huge hulls resting almost motionless on the flat tide. 'They've been round the world, and back. And my dreams with them.'

'You can always come up here if you want to,' Monk reminded him.

'I'll think about it,' Orme replied. 'That's what Devon used to say. Seems like a long time ago, doesn't it?'

Monk thought back. He could see Devon's face vividly that last time they met, before Devon took the step down the river with all that terrible death in the hold, and set fire to it, sacrificing himself so they would all be safe.

He had left a request that Monk should replace him in command. Orme had honoured that, and supported Monk through all his early, stumbling leadership trials. Now Orme deserved to step down with honour, and the gratitude of the River Police, and sit by the riverside with his daughter and his new grandchild.

'I'll miss you,' Monk said.

'For a while,' Orme agreed with some satisfaction. 'Hooper's a good man. But he won't watch for you the way I did. He'll push you. Maybe you're ready for that, now.'

'I'd better be,' Monk agreed, but with a sudden chill of loneliness. He could not tell Orme how much he would miss him; it would not be fair to cast that shadow over his retirement.

He dragged the oar a little and Orme lengthened his stroke to pull the boat up to the steps. Monk stepped ashore and looped the rope around the bollard. Orme followed after him.

The plan was already made. They needed only McNab's co-operation to keep the raid secret from the rest of the Customs and Excise. There was no need for them to confer again.

They walked up the path, across the road and into the Customs office. Monk stated their names and ranks.

'Yes, sir,' the man at the desk replied. 'That'll be the second door on the right, one floor up, sir.'

Monk and Orme followed the man's directions up the stairs and knocked on the door with McNab's name on it. Perhaps that should have told him something. He had never bothered to have a plate on his own door. Everyone who mattered knew where to find him.

McNab obliged him to wait several moments before he answered. He was a stocky man, a little less than Monk's height, but with a powerful body that strained his uniform into awkward shapes across the shoulders. His hair was thinning and he had it carefully combed.

There seemed for an instant something familiar about him, then Monk dismissed it as being merely that he resembled many others, a type often found in the police, or the army.

Monk introduced himself again, and then Orme.

'I know who you are,' McNab replied. There was no pleasure in his voice, no sense of an old colleague met with again. Usually it was Orme who made this connection with the senior Excise officer. Their relationship was not comfortable, but it was easy with use. And yet Monk must surely have met him in the past, in all his years in the Metropolitan Police.

Monk felt a twinge of warning, and ignored it. He could not afford to quarrel with this man. On the river, in particular, they had too many cases in common. He drew in his breath to state his reason for having come.

McNab pre-empted him.

'I know all about your gunrunning ship,' he said aggressively. 'Should by rights be our case. Smuggling is Customs and Excise, as you well know! But this one'll hit the news, if it's done right.' A slight touch of amusement was in his face. 'Or wrong. They'll make a meal of that, too.'

It was a long time since Monk had met an old enemy who knew him, but of whom he had no recollection. What was it with McNab? Had they been rivals? Enemies? Had Monk wronged him in some way? He knew enough to know he was not proud of everything in his past, and there were so many ghosts whose faces he did not see clearly, just an impression here and there, a familiar turn of phrase, a reference that struck a chord, and then was lost again.

He was right back in that open, vulnerable place he had

been when he first started trying to make his way, blindly;
with a past he did not know.

'Then we had better get it right,' Monk replied, keeping
his temper with difficulty. 'I am informing you of our plans,
as a professional courtesy, and hoping that you will be able
to assist us with another boat, and just three or four armed
men. These gunrunners have a lot to lose and if they have a
good watch out, the battle could be fierce.'

Now McNab's smile was overly hard.

'Indeed it could, Mr Monk,' he agreed. 'You'd better tell
me exactly what you have planned, or we could end up shooting
each other! And wouldn't that be a sad end to such an . . .
interesting career.' He met Monk's eyes with a brittle smile.

Now Monk had no doubt that he and McNab had known
each other before his accident, and perhaps McNab's dislike of
him was founded in genuine wrongs. That was unalterable now,
but what must be faced was the possibility that McNab would
take out his dislike of Monk on his men as well. It looked very
much as if this was his chance for a long-delayed revenge.

Monk would not let his men pay for offences they were no
part of, if indeed they existed. And this was far too important
and potentially dangerous an operation to allow room for
anyone's personal feelings, justified or not.

'Then let's make damn sure it works, Mr McNab,' Monk
said softly. 'I can't think you want those guns on the street
any more than I do.'

McNab evaded a reply. 'So let me have the details, if you
please?' He looked at Orme.

Stiffly, Orme obliged.

When Monk got home that night it was far later than he had
intended, and he was so tired he had difficulty concentrating.
He had partial memories of McNab, but he could not deter-
mine if they were recent or not. It was just McNab's face,

angry, his eyes filled with loathing. Had that been real? Or was it tricks of the shadows, and half-recalled emotion?

Hester and Scuff had already eaten, and Monk had bought a ham sandwich from a pedlar along the river-bank. Hester made him a cup of tea and he ate a slice of cake with it. She started to say something to him, but she stopped again, just smiling at him and touching him lightly on the cheek.

'Go to bed,' she said gently. 'It can wait.'

Chapter Five

MONK WAS on the river early, well before dawn the next morning. A clear sky was just paling in the east and the shadows were still long melting into one another. At a glance the boat where he sat would have seemed like any other returning from a long night's patrol, until one noticed that there were three men in it, not the usual two, one for each oar, and another crouched in the stern. They were closely followed by a second heavy, two-man boat also with a third man in the stern. They were picking their way towards the three-masted schooner anchored out in the stream. It was one of the many still laden with cargo, waiting its turn to off-load at one of the docks.

It was Orme who sat in the stern of the first boat, facing Monk, his grizzled face turned downstream, watching the distance close between them and their quarry. The riding lights of the schooner marked its position clearly, but as the darkness faded in the east its masts were black against the horizon and its fat, wide-bellied shape was easy to see.

Monk and Bathurst moved in comfortable unison, guiding the boat through the quickly running tide. The other boat slid just as easily twenty yards away, Laker and Hooper at the oars. If all went according to plan, they would board just as the light was breaking and the dock was visible. They were coming from the west, in the last of the night shadows. If McNab were right, she was carrying smuggled cargo. If it had been brandy or tobacco, Monk would have been happy to leave it to McNab and the rest of the Excise men, but this was a gunrunner, a different thing altogether. A thousand rifles like the one he had seen in the Wapping Station, with ammunition, could start a small war on the streets of London. They could even provoke street battles for their possession the moment they landed.

The River Police were almost in the lee of the schooner now. Monk could feel the difference in the drag on the oar as they were sheltered from the swifter-moving current. He nodded at Bathurst and saw him shorten his stroke so the boat would not swing round.

Monk raised his arm in signal. Orme stood, his balance perfect; the rock of the boat, the movement of wind and tide were second nature to him. He swung the grappling iron and let it fly. It landed, caught the rail, and he pulled it taut.

At the bow of the other boat, Laker did the same and secured the rope.

Bathurst sat back. Monk had given him his orders, no argument. He had to wait with the boats.

Without hesitation, Orme went straight up the rope, pulling himself up the ship's side and over the railing, grasping at it and heaving himself over.

At the bow rope, Monk could see Hooper's long figure going up, but more cautiously, hesitating before he swung over.

Monk glanced back, expecting to see Orme at the top, but there was nothing. What had he missed? He peered upwards. Still nothing.

With one movement Bathurst was standing beside him, staring at the unbroken line of the deck.

'Please, sir?'

'No,' Monk replied. 'We need someone to stay with the boat.'

But there was something wrong. Orme should have been at the rail. Monk looked along at Hooper. He saw an arm flailing and Hooper lurch forward. On the water below, Laker looked confused, uncertain what to do. He reached for the bottom of the rope.

Monk grasped the line Orme had left.

'Stay here,' he ordered Bathurst. He went up the rope himself as fast as he could, faster than was safe, but he had to know what had happened on the deck. They had come up quietly, without any warning, climbed up in the shadow on the lee side of the ship. It should have been safe.

He was almost at the top. His fingers were chafed, his muscles crying out at holding his weight. He heard a thud and a muffled cry. He stopped with his head just below the vision of anyone on deck.

There was a sound like the clash of steel on metal, and a cry. Laker was almost to the top also. Monk used all his strength to heave himself up and roll over on to the deck. He rose to his feet instantly, hand on his pistol.

Ahead of him on the deck, now clear in the broadening light, Orme was facing a man with a cutlass in his hand. Orme was motionless, his pistol still in his belt.

At the far end of the deck Laker was over the edge and on to the deck, creeping forward, his pistol drawn. If he fired he would save Orme's life but the noise would bring the rest of the crew up on to the deck, armed. There would be a pistol fight and they might all end up wounded or dead.

Then Monk saw a movement out of the corner of his eye. He turned slightly to see a hand come over the far edge of the deck, and then a head. Suddenly he realised what was happening. The ship was being boarded by a rival gunrunner, from the windward side! How could that happen? Were they wrong in their guess about the rogue Excise man, and it was McNab after all and now he was betraying Monk and his men?

Hooper must have seen the intruder the instant later. He waved an arm and pointed along at the hatch, making a chopping motion in the air.

Monk nodded.

Hooper closed the hatch and locked it shut just as Laker raised his gun to shoot the boarder.

Then Orme moved, lunging forward at the man so suddenly he had no time to react. Orme caught him in the belly with his shoulder and they both went down hard. Monk had a clear shot at the other boarder on the windward side. He ran forward, keeping low, but instead of firing at him, he hit him as hard as he could over the side of the head. He might have killed him with the weight he had put behind the blow, but it was silent, nothing more than a splash in the swift river. No one below could have heard him fall.

Monk had no idea how many more of them there were. Still on his hands and knees he moved to the edge and glanced down. There were two longboats in the water. Perhaps eight men and still leaving room for the guns they must have come to steal. There were four more crawling up the nets hanging over the sides.

He swivelled around to see how Orme was faring with the man who had the cutlass. Monk needed that blade.

It lasted only seconds, but the moment was caught like a photograph image on Monk's mind: Laker frozen, not certain what to do; Orme on his hands and knees, the man with the cutlass sprawled on the deck, beginning to get up again.

There were shouts and crashes from the deck below as the crew realised someone had battened them in and they were prisoners on their own ship. Would they go for the guns? Presumably they had ammunition as well as the actual weapons in the cargo? How long would it take them to think of that, break open the boxes and come back to shoot their way out of the hold? Then they would mow down everyone on the deck, police and pirates alike. They had the perfect cover to do it. They would kill Monk and all his men, and claim they never saw them. Sink their boats, and possibly their bodies as well. They could blame the gun robbers, leave on the tide, and sell their merchandise elsewhere. There was always a market.

Monk hurled himself across the deck and smashed the butt of his pistol on the wrist of the man with the cutlass. He felt the bone break before the man screamed. He snatched the cutlass and went back to the edge of the deck. The light was strengthening now. It caught the swirls in the current and the dark shapes of flotsam.

The men climbing up on the far side were nearly at the top. Monk lifted the cutlass and brought it down as hard as he could on the ropes, cutting one, two and the third. The whole web fell away, dragged loose by the men's weight, tying them in it as it crashed into the water, carrying them all down, burying them in the tide.

Hooper was at the other end of the deck. There were different ropes there, a different web. Monk threw the cutlass to him and Hooper caught it just as it touched the deck. He grabbed the hilt and slashed at the ropes as the first man put his hand over. Hooper winced, and then kicked the man in the side of the jaw. He toppled backwards, taking the ropes with him. The second man peeled away and crashed into the water, tangled in the net, his arms and legs thrashing.

Laker was beside Orme, trussing the watchman in ropes, jamming a wad of rags in his mouth.

Monk went back to the side where they had boarded and saw Bathurst, ashen-faced, still obediently in the stern of the boat. He signalled that all was well, and for Bathurst to stay there, and then he went back to the deck.

The first shot came through the wood of the hatch and sending splinters into the air. A second followed straight after.

Monk glanced at his men. They were all motionless, waiting. Hooper had a pistol and the cutlass. Orme and Laker both had pistols.

'Don't waste your shot,' Monk said quietly. He indicated where each man was to stand near the hatch, far enough from it not to get caught by stray bullets.

'Watch the side, Laker,' he ordered. 'If anyone comes up out of the water, or from one of their boats, fire a warning shot, then the next one to kill. If they come up behind us we're dead.'

'Yes, sir.' Laker did not argue. His face was pale in the dawn, his eyes steady. He moved slightly so he had a clear view of the whole east-facing deck.

Another shot came through the hatch, splintering wood.

No one moved.

The butt end of a musket smashed the already weakened centre of the hatch. The next moment a gun barrel came out and fired at a sharp, low angle. The bullet hit no one and went off over the water, passing close to Bathurst.

Monk held up his hand to prevent any of his men from responding.

It was so quiet they could hear the slurp of the water against the hull, and the dull thump of a piece of driftwood hitting the beams.

Then there was another bump, louder, as of a weight brushing against the hull.

Laker stiffened, squaring his shoulders, holding his gun towards the source of the sound.

There was a noise of men moving below the hatch.

Laker fired, the shot sounding like a cannon in the silence.

Someone burst through the shattered hatch, firing blindly. At the same moment, Laker shot at the man boarding up over the side. He fell with a scream. A moment later they heard the smack as he hit the water below, and the splash as the water subsided.

Monk wanted to tell Bathurst to go, get out of the way. He had no idea how many of the gunrunners there were in the hold, or of the pirates boarding from the east. One man alone at the oars would have no chance.

Monk swung around, making for the west side of the deck. His instinct was to shout a warning. Bathurst wouldn't know the shots were fired at boarders on the far side. But if Monk shouted down to him, he would warn everyone he was there, and leave Bathurst undefended.

He turned back and saw a huge, bearded man scramble out of the hatch and roll sideways on to the deck, a pistol in his hands. Hooper had his back to him, aiming his own gun at another boarder who was climbing hand over hand up the mizzen rigging. If he got high enough, he would have a bird's-eye view of the entire deck and every man on it.

Hooper shot at him and missed. The wind was rising and the ship rolled just enough to take the man a yard to the left as the mast swayed.

The bearded man on deck raised his pistol and aimed at Hooper.

Laker, a dozen yards forward of them all, raised his gun, fired, and sent the man sprawling back, blood gushing from his throat. It was a brilliant shot, or a lucky one. His gun fell to the deck. Orme lunged forward and kicked it away, far out of his reach.

Without hesitating Hooper adjusted his aim and shot at the man on the rigging. This time he caught the man's shoulder and for an instant he swung wide, holding on by one arm, then he crashed into the sea, sending up a huge spray of water.

Another man was away up the rigging. He held the ropes with one hand and his gun with the other.

A second man was coming out of the smashed open hatchway, straight at Laker.

Laker saw him and froze.

The second man on the rigging also aimed at him.

Monk lowered his gun because he could not fire at the man in the hatchway without hitting Laker.

The ship was beginning to roll a little with the freshening wind.

The man in the hatch straightened up, lifting the barrel of his gun. The man on the rigging looked at Monk, half-sheltered from him by one of the yards, and turned back to the deck.

Orme seized a coiled rope and flung it across the deck.

It caught Laker in the middle of his body just as the man in the hatchway fired, and the deck erupted in splinters where Laker had been. Hooper took one of the men on the rigging, and Monk took the other. One of them got caught in the ropes and swung grotesquely by one leg. The other crashed to the deck and lay motionless, blood spreading around him.

Laker swung round and fired at the hatch, then stared in horror as the man toppled out of it, gushing blood, but still clinging on to his gun, jerking the trigger again and again, firing randomly.

Laker winced and shot him again.

More men were coming out of the hatch now, armed with rifles. They must have broken open the cargo and loaded at least three of the guns. They had enough ammunition to hold a siege. They emerged three together, facing in different directions.

There were more men coming up over the rails, too. Hooper was picking them off, but taking heavy fire himself. There was a widening patch of blood on his left shoulder.

Monk saw a man climbing the rigging of the mizzen mast, right above the hatch. His view would be perfect. And if Monk could pick him off, he would fall right into the hatch, blocking all of the men there. But he needed the man to be higher, at least another ten feet.

The man stopped, ready to take aim at Hooper.

Monk fired first, below him.

The man shot back, without aiming, and scrambled higher. Another fifteen feet and it would be too late; he would be shrouded by the rigging.

Orme was cornered between the hatch and the gunwale.

There was no time to warn Bathurst. Monk fired below the man on the mast, then as he was about to reach up to the crow's nest, he took more careful aim and shot him in the chest. The man let go and plummeted down, crashing into the edge of the hatch and scattering the men there, one falling on to the splinters of the broken wood. His scream was short and terrible.

Suddenly there was gunfire everywhere.

Orme was at the gunwale, shouting and waving his arms.

Hooper was on one knee; his gun aimed carefully, the blood on his shoulder widening.

Laker was aiming steadily, picking off the remaining men at the hatch. He was close to them, dangerously close.

Monk shouted at him, but he took no notice.

Hooper was on his knees, watching the gunwale in case any more raiders came up over on to the deck.

There was more gunfire from the water. It seemed to be all around them. It was Orme who charged across the deck and caught Hooper on the chest with his shoulder so they both fell sideways just as the hatch erupted in flames.

'Over the side!' Monk yelled at the top of his voice, waving at the gunwale over which they had boarded and, please heaven, Bathurst and the other boat were still waiting. None of them would last long in the filthy water and the swift, treacherous tide. He had no idea how much ammunition the ship was carrying, but if the fire reached it the whole deck would be sprayed with bullets.

Monk scrambled across the few yards of deck to Hooper,

who was trying to get to his feet, swaying dangerously. Now his left arm was red with blood and there was more on his leg.

Monk caught hold of him and for a moment felt his weight. Then Hooper made a surprising effort and straightened up just as Laker came to take his other side.

Orme was at the far side, but now he came forward, gun at the ready.

'Bathurst's there,' he shouted over the increasing roar of the flames and the sharp crack of bullets exploding in the hold. He could not see the other boat. The fire had clearly reached the ammunition. If they had gunpowder too it would all go up.

Hooper half turned, looking to the east where the raiders' boats lay. None of them had any idea how many more of them there were.

'I'll hold them!' Orme shouted, and then swung around to face the boarders, visible now in the strengthening light.

There was no time to argue. Monk and Laker half carried Hooper across the deck. The hatch was burning fiercely now, smoke pouring out of it in grey billows.

At the far side they eased Hooper over, and he clung on to the ropes with his good hand.

Bathurst was yards away, standing well off from the ship, so he could have escaped if one of the raiders had come round from the east side. He was their one connection with help, and he had to know that.

As soon as he saw Monk he grasped both the oars and threw his weight into turning the boat, sending it back to within a yard of the ship's side. By the time Monk and Laker had lowered Hooper, Bathurst was there to catch him and ease him down.

'Go,' Monk ordered Laker.

'Can't leave you here, sir,' Laker replied stolidly, and

although his voice shook on the last word, his eyes were steady.

'You'll do as you're damn well told to!' Monk shouted back at him. 'Bathurst can't outrun that lot alone, and Hooper's not fit to.'

'Then you go, sir,' Laker replied, 'and I'll cover Orme.'

Monk hesitated an instant, and then knew what he should do. He nodded at Laker, then climbed over the gunwale and dropped down into the boat. He was sick to leave Orme behind, but he knew he had to go. But after this Orme would only be filling in time until his notice was finished. He had seen and done enough. He had stayed on only to see Monk master his job.

'Shore,' Monk told Bathurst. 'Get Hooper to a doctor.'

Hooper tried to protest. 'We can wait—' he began.

'For what?' Monk asked him. 'The rest of the raiders to come round from the other side and cut us off? If Orme and Laker can hold out till we get ashore, we'll send enough boats out to finish that lot off and arrest any still living. Now be still.' He moved awkwardly past Hooper and took the other oar. He had by now learned to row expertly, swiftly, and in perfect unison with anyone else.

They reached the nearest steps in minutes and were met by eager hands half lifting Hooper out of the boat. He protested but no one listened.

'More men coming, sir,' one of the constables told Monk. 'Armed. Some gone already round the far side, in your other boat.'

Monk looked around. He could see no one. Out in the water the schooner was still burning. From the shore it looked like only a few flames, but already other ships were pulling up anchor and raising sail to move clear of her. She might not even be armed, but no one was taking the risk.

With amazement Monk realised that the whole boarding

and fight had taken less than fifteen minutes. So quickly did victory or loss take place, and everything was changed.

'Another boat!' he called out. 'Anything you can get out into the river! Our men will be in the water in minutes, if they're still alive. Hurry!'

A ferryman came forward, his face pale and grim.

'I'll 'elp yer. Got no gun, like . . .'

'Thank you,' Monk accepted. 'Take Bathurst here and go and pick up our men if they're in the water. He'll know them.' He glared at Bathurst, daring him to argue. He looked at one of the constables. 'You're taking Hooper's gun and you're coming with me. Right!'

He watched the ferryman, followed reluctantly by Bathurst, go down the steps and pull away. The dawn was clear now and everything had a cold, watery light. Smoke was billowing up from the schooner and the fire seemed to be dying. Possibly it was just less visible against the broadening light and the silver reflection off the water. If there was gunpowder it could still blow any second.

Silently the other men obeyed. His own men knew Monk well enough not to waste time in a pointless argument. The constable either knew him by repute, or understood well enough what he saw.

They went down the steps to the boat Monk had just left. They each took an oar. The constable was accustomed to the system of rowing one man in front of the other, each with an oar. It took only two or three strokes for them to catch the rhythm and begin to pull away back towards the burning schooner, but this time around the far side. The constable was not armed usually, just as no other police were, but he understood his role as an officer of the law, and he expected to fight if the occasion demanded it. Hooper's gun lay on the floorboards beside his feet. He was ready for action at close quarters, if need be.

When they rounded the stern of the schooner, to windward of the smoke still pouring out of her, Monk saw three boats in the water, one listing badly, and apparently abandoned. The other two were close to the hull and there were four men clambering down the sides of the schooner, carrying what arms they could salvage from the cargo. Each boat had only one man in it, keeping it close and steady. Any minute they would be ready for a battle Monk and the constable could not win.

Monk had no idea if either Laker or Orme were still alive and whether they were on the schooner or in the water. He shipped the oar and told the constable to do the same. They had only moments.

The constable bent and picked up Hooper's gun. He had no idea how much ammunition was left in it.

Monk aimed carefully at the man nearest the boat. He would be the first to be able to fire back. He felt relief, then a wave of nausea as his bullet hit its mark and the man fell like a stone into the water.

One of the men standing in the boats whirled around, his face a mask of horror. The other, with more presence of mind, raised his pistol.

Steady-handed, the constable fired Hooper's gun. The man swayed for a moment, then collapsed into the bottom of the boat, setting it rocking so violently that the man hanging on the rope and ready to drop in, had to wait. It was long enough for Monk to fire at him also.

Now more police boats were coming from the shore. The battle was over. Monk was suddenly tired, his body aching from the tension, the climbing up and down ropes, and most of all from the anxiety over his men.

As soon as he was certain that those in the new boats had taken over the salvaging of what was left, he turned to row back to the lee side of the schooner, going wide around it, since there was still a danger that it would explode.

As they turned, both he and the constable saw nothing to break the surface of the slightly choppy water except a few tangled knots of debris that could have been anything. There was no one struggling to stay afloat, no bodies.

Please God, Orme and Laker were not still up on the deck! He did not want to risk the constable's life by going up into the burning ship, but he could not get either man down by himself, let alone both. It really needed three men: one to stay in the boat and two to board. But there was no time.

Monk turned on the oar without noticing that he had not told the constable what he intended. He saw the shock in the man's face for an instant, and then he realised, and turned the other oar as well.

Where the hell were Bathurst and the ferryman? Still searching the water? Following the current searching for anyone swept away in it? Or had they been shot from the deck, and the boat gone with the tide? The thought made him feel sick. He dug the oar in hard and sent water splaying across the surface.

The constable hesitated, missing a stroke so the boat righted itself again. Within moments they were alongside.

'Hold it here,' Monk ordered. Without waiting for a reply, he climbed painfully back up the side, hand over hand. At the top he hesitated, listening, then rolled over the gunwale and instantly got to his hands and knees.

Laker was sitting a few yards away, a length of cloth tied roughly around his thigh, much of it dark with blood. Orme lay half across him, face up but not moving.

'What kept you?' Laker said with a twisted smile. The words were mumbled, his throat almost too dry to speak.

'Bloody pirates,' Monk replied, as if it were all a trivial matter, like being late for dinner. 'Can you stand?' He forced himself to look down at Orme. He was pale but there was a slight rise and fall to his chest. At least Monk thought there was.

'Yes, I think so,' Laker nodded. 'But I can't carry him. He's heavier than I thought.' He blinked. 'Where's Hooper? He all right?'

Monk looked at him and, for an instant, before he masked it, he saw the boy in Laker, the uncertain one who could so easily be hurt.

'With the doctor by now, I hope,' he answered, easing Orme off Laker's thighs and laying him gently on the deck. 'Bathurst and a ferryman came to look for you . . .' He reached out his hand to haul Laker to his feet. As he swayed for a moment, he felt his weight lurch, and gripped him more firmly.

Laker steadied himself, and then held out his other arm. 'You can't carry him alone,' he pointed out.

'Well, you're damn all use,' Monk snapped back. 'Go over the side and try not to fall into the water. Send the constable up here to help me with Orme.'

Laker hesitated.

'Now!' Monk shouted at him, hearing the raw edge in his own voice. He could feel the heat coming up through the deck. The ship was still burning below them.

Laker turned round and went awkwardly over the gunwale, hanging on with his hands until the last minute, then falling away.

Monk strained his ears, but he heard no splash, only the bump and slurp of water as the boat rode against the timbers of the ship.

It seemed an age before Monk saw the constable clamber over the gunwale and come quickly across the deck towards him. Together they lifted Orme, who was barely conscious and unable to help himself. They cut a length of rope from the rigging and tied it around his chest, under his arms, and did their best to lower him as gently as possible to where Laker was keeping the boat steady.

Ten minutes later they were at last at the dockside where

willing hands half hauled them up. A doctor was waiting. Someone passed brandy around, and Bathurst came limping across the wharf, his face flooded with relief. He looked at Monk, then at Laker and Orme.

Monk wanted to say something. This was the time when he should reassure the men, but what was there to say? Everything he could think of sounded obvious, and they deserved the truth.

He just nodded, an acknowledgement, not an affirmation of anything.

Orme was carried into a waiting ambulance.

Monk went with him to the hospital, riding in the wagon while the doctor did what he could to stanch the bleeding.

Orme lay still now, drifting in and out of consciousness.

Monk spoke to him all the time, willing him to stay awake, stay alive. He wished Hester were here. She might have known what to do; at the very least just her presence would have reminded him of love and life, honour, gentleness, all the things that were the beauty of existence, that demanded to be believed in, however black the night.

The journey seemed to take for ever. The traffic was growing heavier as people made their way to offices, shops and factories.

Monk looked at Orme's face. He still had some colour, but it was sunburn, not health, and he looked so much smaller than he really was. The sunken-eyed hollowness of death seemed to rest on him. It was two hours since they set out on to the river, and everything had changed.

The doctor was tense; his hands steady but there was sweat on his face.

'Can't I help?' Monk asked. He knew as he said it that the question was ridiculous, but he needed to speak, to feel as if he was part of the effort. What he wanted was for the doctor to tell him he could save Orme, but Monk was afraid to ask.

What could the man say, except that he didn't know? He was trying everything he could.

Monk rode the rest of the way in silence, looking at Orme, every now and then touching his hand so that if he were conscious at all, he would know he was not alone. When they arrived he helped to carry Orme out on a stretcher, and into the hospital.

Orme was taken to a room where they dealt with emergencies. Monk was allowed to wait. Even the doctors had no idea what to do for him, once the bleeding was stopped. They bound the wounds in his arms and legs, but the one that mattered was in his side, the bullet breaking ribs and ricocheting off. Once they were certain it was not still inside him, they bound the wound as they could, cutting off his clothes, now stiff with blood.

He was growing weaker by the minute.

'Can't you do something?' Monk asked the doctor desperately.

It was a question not really worth asking. Of course he couldn't, or he would have done it already.

'Can I stay with him?' he asked a moment after.

'Yes, of course,' the doctor answered, smiling for an instant, then his attention was back on those he could help. He excused himself, leaving Monk alone.

He looked at Orme, and thought of all the times they had shared, all the myriad things that Orme had taught him, by example, very seldom indeed in words. He was a quiet man, resolute, at first glance seeming even grim.

But he was always softly spoken, slow to judge, even though Monk had exasperated him often. They had shared food in companionable silence. He remembered standing beside the brazier, shivering with cold in the February wind slicing up from the river, and Orme paying the chestnut man extra. Neither of them spoke of it. He could picture Orme in his mind's eye, smiling and unconsciously tapping his foot in time to the band playing on one of the docksides. It was a dancing tune. He wondered with whom Orme had danced to that particular tune. His wife, long since dead?

He reached out his hand and put it over Orme's. He began to talk to him about all the things he recalled, good things and bad, many of them funny, confidences, jokes, and memories.

Orme stirred and opened his eyes once, looking at Monk with a moment's hesitation, not certain if he knew him or not. Then he smiled.

The moment disappeared and it was as if he had left the room. Monk knew Orme would not speak to him again; nevertheless, he went on talking quietly, reminiscing.

It occurred to him that perhaps he should have sent a message to Orme's daughter, but he did not recall her address, only that she lived a considerable way down the river. The information was in his office, not his mind.

Someone at the office would have a messenger take her a letter. But Monk knew that Orme was dying, perhaps already deep into unconsciousness. The poor woman could not get here in time. And someone you did not know, carrying a letter, was not the way to find out that your father was dead.

It was Monk's duty to tell her, one he dreaded, but it was inescapable. He would do it, when he was not needed here. Orme might never waken again, but if he did, he would find Monk here with him.

The doctor returned some time later – Monk had lost track of how long – and it did not matter.

'I'm sorry,' the doctor said quietly. 'He'd lost too much blood. It's shock . . . the body can't make it up . . .' He shook his head, the energy that had driven him all night gone in defeat. 'Did you know him well?'

'Yes,' Monk answered. 'But perhaps not as well as he

knew me.' He stood up stiffly. His whole body ached. 'Thank you . . .'

He went back to the police station at Wapping. It was almost deserted, only a few men keeping watch. He called in only to tell them of Orme's death, to find out if the injured were all right, and to pick up Orme's daughter's address.

He was so tired his whole body ached, and he was longing to see Hester, but this must be done first. He must get a ferry to take him down river, wait for him, then bring him back. This was going to be the worst duty of the day, but it was inescapable, and it was his to do. He owed Orme that, and far more.

Hester had put in a long day nursing Radnor. He was not an easy patient and his illness was extremely serious. Her excitement at the possibility of a cure was deeply shadowed by Hamilton Rand's means of treating him.

She was so tired her whole body ached, but she must confront him before she went home, and it must be done privately. It was not an issue that should be referred to at all in front of other staff, and least of all in front of Radnor himself, or his daughter.

She looked first in his office, not really expecting to find him there, and then went to the laboratory.

He was bent over a microscope, studying whatever it was on the glass slide. A look of annoyance at the interruption crossed his face, until he recognised her.

'What is it, Mrs Monk? Has his condition changed?'

She closed the door behind her. She did not want even the slightest chance of being overheard.

'Only for the better,' she replied, walking past the jars and bottles, the burners and vials. She stopped close enough to him to see that it was a smear of blood he was examining.

'Then why are you interrupting me?' he asked.

'The children are getting weaker,' she said slowly and clearly. 'You can't go on taking blood from them at this rate. It's too much.'

He straightened up slowly, staring at her as if she were a specimen he had just recognised. His eyes were both intimate and strange. 'Exactly what are you proposing, Mrs Monk?' he said softly.

She felt a chill, her mouth dry, but she had to speak.

'That you delay the treatment, or find other donors as well.'

'And if I refuse?' he whispered.

She swallowed. 'Then you risk their dying, and I will not let you do that.'

'I see. You know, Mrs Monk, I believe you.' He turned and walked a couple of yards towards a cupboard, opened it and took out a bottle and a cloth. He was between her and the door.

He looked up, smiling with a strange expression of regret. Then he moved swiftly. She felt her arms held. It was painful. There was a pungent smell, something over her nose and mouth. She tried to fight him, but the darkness closed over her and she plunged forward into nothingness.

When Monk got home there was no sign of Hester. He guessed that she had been kept at the hospital. Maybe the patient she had been nursing had reached a critical point and she could not leave him.

Scuff left a note, saying that he was working with Crow and had no idea when he would be back.

Monk went to bed alone, restless and unhappy. He had wanted intensely to tell Hester about the schooner, and all that had happened, the suspense and the pain, his fear for his men, and how they had shown such startling care for each other when the dangers were worst. He was proud of them, and he had wanted to tell her so, and see her pleasure. He realised with a touch of self-mockery how much he wanted to see her face, her eyes, when he told her. Out of all of it, the way in which they had survived was what mattered to him.

And, of course, there was the question of McNab, whose men had never shown up. Was that mischance, misunderstanding, carelessness – or deliberate betrayal as revenge for something Monk could not even recall?

He wanted more than anything else to tell her about Orme, and the grief he felt, how deep was his sense of loss. He wished to tell her about Laker, of all people, who had tried so desperately hard to save him. Laker had wept when he knew that Orme was dead. She would have understood.

Sharing all this with her mattered intensely to him. It would have eased his own pain and been the beginning of healing.

He woke in the morning stiff and still tired, but he got up straight away, shaved and dressed. He went downstairs and found Scuff in the kitchen.

'She isn't home yet,' he said, looking Monk up and down. 'Wot 'appened? You been in a fight?' He did not give words to his anxiety, but it was clear in his face.

'She must have been detained,' Monk answered, going over to the stove, which had been carefully banked all night so it was still burning. Scuff had already opened it, cleaned out the old ash and put more coal on it. The kettle was hot. Everything was set for breakfast, it was only Hester that was absent. But for both of them, this left the room incomplete.

Scuff helped Monk make breakfast and they ate together in companionable silence. Scuff left for school and Monk went down to the ferry and across to Wapping.

But by that evening there was still no word from Hester, and Monk could take it no longer. He put on his coat again and went to find out where she was.

When he reached the hospital, he went immediately to the

annexe wing where Hester worked for Dr Rand. He found that, in spite of his aching muscles, his step quickened at the thought of seeing her in moments, even if she could not return home with him. Just to see her, hear her voice would unravel the knots that were so painful inside him.

Inside, he enquired for Magnus Rand's office and went along the corridor past all protest. At the door he knocked abruptly.

'Come,' a voice replied from inside.

Monk opened the door and went in. He closed it behind him and looked at the rather harassed man seated behind the desk littered with papers. He barely noticed the rest of the room, the bookshelves or mementoes.

'Dr Rand?' he asked.

'Yes, sir? Who are you, and what may I do for you?' Magnus Rand asked.

'I am William Monk, Commander of the Thames River Police,' Monk replied. 'I have come to see my wife, Hester Monk. I am concerned about her. She has not been home in two days. Where is she?'

The colour drained from Rand's face. It was seconds before he found his voice to reply.

'I'm sorry, Mrs Monk is not here,' he said a little huskily. 'She left today, without giving me a reason. It was only a temporary post anyway. She was filling in for a friend who had to take leave.'

Monk was stunned.

Chapter Six

HESTER WOKE up with a headache. She opened her eyes to sunlight so bright it blinded her, and she closed them again quickly. She had recognised nothing in the room. She was not at home. Was she still in the hospital? A room she did not know? Why?

She licked her lips and tried to swallow, but her mouth was too dry. Her tongue tasted like a piece of old blanket. Her body ached as if she had been involved in a fight, and yet she could not remember anything like that. In fact, the last thing she could remember was standing in Hamilton Rand's laboratory. He had said something. She had argued. She struggled to remember what it had been about, but it eluded her.

She moved slightly. She was lying on something soft. If she had not ached so much, it would have been comfortable.

She opened her eyes again, narrowly. It was less bright. She took a deep breath and made herself focus. She was lying on a bed with carved wooden bedposts at the foot. She was in a small room with dark, reddish-pink wallpaper. The ceiling was low. Bright sunlight came in through the small, latticed window, falling in a pool around her. It looked like a cottage bedroom.

She sat up slowly. Nothing impeded her, no ropes or ties. She had a sudden memory of the smell of ether. It had been over her face. That was what had happened to her! Rand had put ether over her nose and mouth. Now the sense of panic returned of a wild moment when she could not get her breath. She was choking, trying not to take in the fumes. Then darkness.

This was not good enough. Slowly she put her legs over the side of the bed and then stood up. She was still a little dizzy, her head hurt, and her stomach was queasy, but she was not injured. She walked with increasing firmness over to the window. It was low, a cottage window as if under the eaves. She peered out. She was right: the roof was thatched; she could see the ends of straw poking out at the upper edge of the window – old straw, dark and slowly pulling apart.

She looked down. She was one floor above the ground. There was an unkempt garden below her; the flowers gone wild, self-seeded all over the place. Beyond was what seemed to be an orchard of apple and pear trees heavy with fruit. Something disturbed a flight of birds, sending them soaring up into the air. A man was passing through the long grass. He was tall, long-legged, and he carried a shotgun casually over his shoulder.

Where on earth was she?

She racked her brain to remember what had happened before the ether was put on her face. She seemed unhurt, and she was still wearing her usual blue-grey nursing dress and white apron. She touched her hair. It was a mess, half-unravelled from its pins. Then she realised that her arms were tender. She rolled up her sleeves and saw the bruises beginning to show. She had struggled.

With whom? Magnus Rand? Surely not the man with the gun, who had now disappeared into the orchard.

She was fully dressed except for her shoes. There was nothing else in the room that belonged to her. She walked over to the door and touched the handle. It barely moved. It was stuck. She rattled it until common sense told her it was locked.

'Where are you?' she shouted. 'Let me out of here!'

There was no answer. She strained her ears to hear if there were any movement below her, or beyond the door.

Perhaps it was stupid calling. If they wanted her to be free, they would not have locked the door. And the window – that was latched too.

Who was it? Where had she been before the ether? What was she doing? Helping Magnus with Bryson Radnor. Radnor had been very weak and tired but unable to sleep. Ill-tempered, but then he often was. He was frightened. She could not blame him for that. He had made no terms with death. It was not uncommon. He was not old, little over sixty.

Then what had happened? Was she kidnapped, or was she just moved out of the way? For ransom? Revenge? What?

'Let me out of here!' she shouted again, her voice louder, higher pitched. She could hear the rising panic in it.

The door opened almost immediately and a man stood on the other side. It was Hamilton Rand, his long, scholarly face showing only slight disapproval.

'You are making an unnecessary noise, Mrs Monk,' he said irritably. 'Pull yourself together and get ready to do your job. You look somewhat disorderly. I shall provide you with a comb and a looking-glass. Tidiness gives a patient confidence in you.'

'Really?' she said sarcastically. 'And being rendered unconscious by force, and brought here against one's will and then locked in a strange room – is that intended to give confidence also?'

'There is nothing strange about the room,' he replied levelly. 'It is quite pleasant and perfectly ordinary. It is clean, and you will keep it so. As for the unconscious part, you brought that upon yourself. Had you kept your duty in mind rather than your personal comfort, you would have come willingly. It is your duty not only to your patient, but to medicine itself. It disappoints me that it is necessary to remind you of this.'

She started to protest.

'As for your confidence in me, Mrs Monk,' he snapped, 'that you apparently lack it is disappointing, but irrelevant. None of this is about you. It is about the survival of Bryson Radnor, and a discovery in medicine that will save tens of thousands of lives.' His face was bleak. 'Now please stop behaving like a child and prepare yourself to care for your patient.'

'Who is caring for him now?' she demanded. 'I don't even know where we are, or how long we have been here.'

'Where you are is also irrelevant,' he dismissed the subject. 'We have been here a little over an hour. It is however, far longer than that since we left the hospital, and your skills are needed. Control your pettishness, tidy your appearance, and come to attend him. I shall wait for you.'

'I shall come. You should not leave him alone,' she replied. 'If he is ill, he will have little care for my appearance.'

His eyes flared in a moment's temper.

'You will do as you are told, Mrs Monk. Let that be understood from the outset. I do not wish to treat you like a prisoner who must be bribed to behave well, and punished if you do not. But do not delude yourself that I won't, should you make it necessary.'

'Give me the comb. I can manage without the looking-glass,' she responded. She could think of no arguments he might listen to at the moment.

He pulled a small comb out of his pocket and handed it to her. He also appeared to consider speaking, and then changed his mind.

She pulled the remaining pins out of her hair, ran the comb through it, then expertly recoiled it and replaced the pins. She handed him back the comb.

He took it without comment. 'Miss Radnor is with him,' he told her as he turned to lead the way across the landing and down a very narrow staircase to the ground floor. 'She is adequate, and diligent, but she has neither your experience nor your skills. You are a very good nurse, Mrs Monk, far too good to indulge your own temperament at the expense of a patient. I will overlook it on this occasion. We have a great deal of work to do. This could be the greatest leap forward in medicine since Harvey's discovery of the circulation of blood.'

Without thinking she answered immediately. 'Since ether,' she argued. 'The ability to operate while a patient is unaware of it makes all kinds of things possible that were not before. The next thing we need is to stop infection.'

A look of surprise and indeed faint satisfaction crossed his face, as if he were pleased at her knowledge. 'The infection is irrelevant when the patient has died from blood loss,' he retorted. 'And no operation is going to cure the white blood disease. But I am glad you are interested in such things.' The anger was gone from his voice and the enthusiasm was there again. 'You cannot help yourself, Mrs Monk. You are going to participate in one of the great moments in medicine, a discovery that will save lives when the soldiers and statesmen of the world are forgotten. Come!' He waved his hand forward impatiently, urging her to keep up with him.

He came to a door off what had once been used as a sitting room, but now was devoid of most of its furniture. The aspect was sunny and would have been pleasant in other circumstances. He opened the door without knocking and held it briefly until Hester came through.

The room was spacious, and the central place was taken up by a large bed with iron head and foot pieces. Bryson Radnor lay propped up on pillows, sheets and blankets drawn up to cover all of him but the top of his chest and shoulders, although the room was warm.

His skin was damp and pale, and there were marked shadows around his eyes, blue, like bruises.

Adrienne Radnor stood beside him, a glass of water in her hands and a small towel over her arm, and she wore a white apron half-covering her plain brown dress. She was tense and did not hide her distress. She ignored Hester. There was neither surprise to see her nor recognition in her face. She looked straight at Rand.

'Come!' Rand jerked his arm to have Hester follow him to Radnor's bed.

'Can you hear me, Mr Radnor?' she asked clearly, standing beside the sick man and looking intently at his face. 'I am going to take your pulse, and then your temperature.'

He half-opened his eyes. 'Are you asking my damn permission, woman? Do what you need to.' His voice was weak and even anger could not return its timbre.

'No, I'm not asking your permission,' she answered, taking his wrist in her hand and feeling for the beat of blood in the veins close to the skin. They were blue, a little ropey and very easy to see – even more so across the back of his hand.

His flesh was cold and clammy to the touch. His pulse was weak, but regular. She felt it for another minute, but it did not change. She put her hand to his brow.

'Do something!' Adrienne's voice was sharp with panic.

'Not until I know what to do,' Hester replied more calmly than she felt.

'Not you!' Adrienne snapped. 'Mr Rand! Help him . . . please.'

It was only then that Hester remembered with a surge of fear that Hamilton Rand was a brilliant chemist, possibly even a genius, but he was not a doctor of medicine. He understood chemicals rather than living people, while she knew plenty of medicine. This gave her an immense power, and he did not know that she would not use it to bargain for her freedom. She was not a doctor, but it was certainly not the first time she had been alone with a patient with no one else to turn to, and no time for indecision.

'When did you last give him anything more than water?' she asked.

Adrienne was silent.

Hester turned round to look at her. 'Don't just stand there! When did you last give him anything better than water? If you want me to do something, then tell me the truth.'

'I gave him a little beef tea, about an hour ago,' Adrienne told her.

'And before that? Do you even know how long we've been here? Or how long since he left the hospital?'

'About three hours, I think.' Adrienne's voice was strained as if her throat were tight with fear. 'And an hour here. Was it too soon for him to have some nourishment? He was asking for it.'

'Possibly not soon enough,' Hester replied. She had no idea if she was right, but both Adrienne and Radnor himself needed to believe in her. Hope was sometimes the only medicine that kept people alive between one moment of crisis and then relief the next. 'What have you been eating?'

'I haven't . . . just . . . a little bread. But he can't take that . . . can he?'

'Probably not. But you must eat too. You are no use to him if you start fainting. Do we have a cook here?'

'No, just the gardener. Please, Mrs Monk . . .'

Hester felt a twist of sorrow for the other woman. She understood her fear, her grief, even her sense of guilt that she was healthy herself and could do nothing but watch as her father's life slipped out of his grasp. It had driven her to collude in what amounted to a kidnap. Did she even think about what price that could cost her in the future?

'Then you must be the cook,' Hester said far more gently. 'Just work carefully. Everything must be cooked lightly, with very little salt, no pepper, no mustard or any other sharp seasoning. Keep the goodness in it. Vegetable soup, a little light chicken, or beef broth. Do the best you can, and do it quickly. If there's anything you can bring up straight away, then get it now. Even tea with a little sugar would be good.'

Adrienne hesitated only a moment, reluctant to leave her father, then she accepted the inevitability of it and was gone.

Hester turned to Rand. 'It's only temporary,' she said very quietly. 'You shouldn't have left the hospital. The blood transfusion was working!'

'I know it was,' Rand agreed. 'And it will again.'

'Can you store the blood? How? Blood clots if you leave it, even for a short time.' She knew that from the countless men she had seen bleed. The clothes soaked in the blood of the dead went stiff quite soon.

Rand's eyes were shining. 'Lemon juice,' he answered in a whisper so quiet she read his lips rather than heard it. 'And potash . . . it is just as simple as that. The trick is to get exactly the right proportions, and have the nerve to carry it through.'

She stared at him, beginning for the first time to feel the force of his will, the power of the intelligence behind those strange eyes that changed colour in the light.

'You brought blood with you?' Then she was suddenly sick with the thought of what he had done to the children in order to get that amount of blood. She dare not show the horror she felt, or the grief. How could she hide it? She wanted to take one of the bottles on the small rigid table and hit him with it until his intense, smiling face was broken.

'Don't be ridiculous,' he said smoothly, as if no ugly thought had crossed his mind. There was no outrage in him at all. 'I have no idea how much we shall need, or for how long. I have bought the children themselves. You keep missing the point. Really, you mystify me. Sometimes you seem so capable, so imaginative, fired with the love of knowledge. Then at others I marvel that you can be so stupid!'

He shook his head and went on talking, meticulously, as if he had been lecturing a student. 'The purpose is to find the cure for bad blood – white blood – and the insufficiency of blood because of major injury and shock to the system. Radnor is merely the first of many. We will save him, and from that we shall gain great knowledge, and so support from others who will fund further research.' He looked in her face to see her grasp of the magnitude of what he was saying. It was not vanity or praise he wished for. She knew that. He wanted companionship in his quest.

She was ashamed of herself because for an instant she could see what the implications could be. She forgot the taking of the blood and its terrible cost; like Rand, she saw the marvellous results. Within her own immediate knowledge were hundreds of men who could have been saved. Beyond them were countless women who had bled to death in difficult childbirth. The people to be saved stretched into the future without end.

Then she remembered again the cost to Charlie, Maggie and Mike. Not to mention their parents!

'The children are here?' she said. It was one question she could ask without raising his anger or suspicion.

His eyes widened, so that for an instant she saw the hazel gold in them.

'Of course. That is the other part of your duty. You will look after them, see that they are healthy. The better they are, the more settled, the better chance we have of saving Radnor.'

She stared at him. He was both human and monstrous.

A very slight smile curled the corners of his characterless

mouth. 'In case you had at any time thought of running away from here, Mrs Monk, remember that you do not know where you are. And if I fail then Bryson Radnor will die, and he is your patient. But possibly of far more emotional importance to you, the three children may well die without you.' The smile vanished from his lips. 'And if Radnor dies then I will have no more use for those children whom I cannot care for myself, and who might well cause trouble for me. I hope you do not require me to make myself any plainer?'

Hester understood, and she believed him. He was a chemist – it was Magnus who was a doctor – but for Hamilton, medical discovery overrode everything else. He would sacrifice the children and not even see harm in it. If he had ever had doubts, any comprehension of pity or regret, he had overcome them.

'No, Mr Rand, you don't.'

'Then please continue with your care for our patient by seeing that the children are fed and in as good health as is possible.' He looked her up and down. 'I imagine you can cook. I do not wish to leave it to Miss Radnor. I think she has little understanding of the art, and still less desire. She will care for her father and keep his room clean and attend to the laundry.'

'Where are the children?' Hester asked, using a softer tone with difficulty. For their sakes she could not afford to antagonise him. Until she could find a weapon against him, she must keep his trust.

'I shall take you,' he responded. 'They are in the old coach house. It is perfectly adequate for them, clean and warm. They are locked in, of course. It would not do for them to be wandering around. They could get hurt, or even lost.' He was leading her through the large, stone-floored kitchen area. Adrienne glanced at them as they passed, turned to pour boiling water into a large teapot then bent to her chopping board again and the vegetables she was dicing.

109

Outside in the sunlit yard Rand pulled a key from his pocket.

'This is for the outer door,' he remarked. 'I shall give it to you. I think you have sufficient intelligence to deduce for yourself what will happen to the children if you do not care for them to the utmost of your ability.'

'Mr Rand!' Hester spoke so huskily that he stopped and turned to look at her, his eyebrows raised. 'I understand you,' she said, trying to keep her voice steady. 'You do not need to keep reminding me.'

'Good.' He nodded. 'Like it or not, we shall work well together.' He handed her the key, turned on his heel and walked briskly back across the yard and into the kitchen.

Hester opened the door to the coach house and closed it behind her before she looked at the single, large room. There was little furniture in it: just one cupboard with a few drawers beneath, and three small beds. There was a large knotted rag mat on the wooden floor, and a single door leading to another room, presumably toilet facilities, possibly even a bath. Rand understood the dangers of contamination from uncleanliness.

Maggie was sitting up in one of the beds. She was pale and her whole attitude listless, until she recognised Hester and her face lit with joy. She slid off the bed and ran across the floor, throwing herself at Hester and clinging on to her with surprising strength.

'Yer come fer us! I told 'em yer'd come!' She buried her head in Hester's waist, holding on to her as if she were drowning.

Hester put her own arms around Maggie and hugged her back as she looked at Charlie, who was sitting up on one of the other beds with Mike beside him. They were both pale also, but she had seen them worse in the hospital in Greenwich. She felt her pulse steady as she realised Rand had understood that he must keep them well, at least as long as he needed them. After Radnor was recovered, or believed that he was, it would be different. But until then she had time to think, and to plan. They must get away, because this was only a breathing space; it would not last.

'We must be careful,' she said to Maggie, letting her go and looking across at the boys.

'I thought yer'd come,' Charlie said with an uncertain smile, his wide eyes meeting hers, looking for a promise she longed to be able to make.

'Me, too,' Mike added, smiling as well.

Her heart lurched as she looked at him. He was little more than a baby still, his milk teeth even and white, his hair curling and in need of a cut.

She sat on the bed and regarded them very gravely.

'We are going to be so good that nobody has any reason to be angry with any of us, or think we are planning something they wouldn't like. Agreed?'

They all nodded.

'We will look after each other, and one day quite soon we will be able to go home. Either we will find a way out ourselves, or someone will come and help us.' It was a wild thing to say. She had no idea where they were, or how anyone would find them here, if anybody were even looking. Rand could have told Monk anything. He knew she cared about the children. He might have been told she was nursing them, so would relax in the assumption that she would simply return home when they were well.

Fear took hold of her for a moment and overwhelmed her. This was not good enough. She could feel the pressure of Maggie's fingers still tight on hers. Maggie would know she was afraid.

'Right!' she said briskly. 'To begin. Are you hungry?'

'Yeah,' they all said in unison.

'Good. Then I will go and see what I can find in the kitchen.

You must stay here. I shall lock the door so no one else can get in and disturb you.'

'D'yer 'ave ter go?' Maggie asked.

'I can't cook dinner in here,' Hester said reasonably.

'But yer will come back?' Charlie looked at her doubtfully.

'Yer will?' Mike echoed.

'Of course I will,' she promised. 'We're in this together.'

Hester went out into the kitchen garden to see what was growing, even if it had run a little wild. It had been originally laid out in plots with narrow paths between them, to make for easy gathering of herbs, but they were now overgrown.

She walked along the paths between all the beds, looking for something more substantial, possibly potatoes or carrots. Perhaps it was a little late for beans. Those fit to eat would have been harvested already.

It was not as well kept as she had expected, having seen the gardener from the window. Did he have other tasks so that caring for the vegetable patch was not a priority?

She found the potato bed, but they had already been lifted and there were a few weeds taken root. There were no carrots. She thought it likely the soil was too heavy. The only cabbages left had gone to seed.

They would have to make do with whatever was in the kitchen or the scullery.

Nevertheless, she made out a good clump of chives. There was mint all over the place, but mint was like that. Its roots ran under the surface to spring up in a dozen different places. There seemed to be both spearmint and apple mint. There was also some rather ragged parsley, a large bush of rosemary, and flowering sage, which gave off a very pleasant aroma when she disturbed it. There was also highly pungent lemon thyme, as well as the usual more ordinary sort. She would certainly make use of such a good crop. The herbs were both appetising and medicinal.

She picked some of the parsley, cropping the dead pieces as she went.

The kitchen door was unlocked. It was only as she was turning the handle to open it that she noticed the shadow of the gardener as he came around the corner, the large-barrelled gun still swinging easily on its rope over his shoulder. He stopped abruptly and watched her go in, before crossing the yard behind her and disappearing. Seeing him gave her a cold, miserable reminder that she was a prisoner.

Inside the kitchen was warm and pleasantly aromatic. She could smell soup in the big pan on the stove, and hear it bubbling. There were many strings of onions hanging from the rafter beams, and what looked like shallots. She hoped Adrienne had put some in the soup. She should have asked her to.

Adrienne was standing in front of the stove, a wooden spoon in her hand. Her hair was falling out of its pins and curling in the steam. Her face was creased with anxiety. Clearly cooking for seven people was a challenge she did not enjoy. At home she would merely give orders to the servants. She might never have even been into the kitchen herself.

As Hester passed she gave her a glance, but did not speak. Their relationship was changed utterly from when they had been in the hospital, as equals with a purpose in common. Now Hester was a prisoner and Adrienne was part of the force that held her so – even if in effect she was as much a prisoner of circumstance herself.

Hester understood Adrienne far more than the younger woman would have believed. The fear of a parent's death was far behind her, but the guilt of not having been there still lingered.

She held up the parsley. 'I found this in the garden,' she

said as she offered it. 'Almost all soups look more appetising with a little chopped and sprinkled on top. And it is very good for the digestion.'

Adrienne accepted it, but did not meet Hester's eyes. 'Thank you.'

Hester remained and helped finish off the vegetables that Adrienne had found in the storeroom, then took a generous portion to the children.

She returned in time to chop the parsley and sprinkle it over the soup, and then together they took it upstairs to Radnor's room. Hester held the door open and Adrienne walked in, carrying it in a soup bowl, on a neatly set tray.

Radnor was sitting propped up in bed. He looked tired and ill, and he made no effort to hide it until he saw Hester behind Adrienne. Then he pushed his hair back off his brow. It was still thick, although there was little colour left in it.

'Papa, we have brought you some soup,' Adrienne told him gently. 'I've made it the best I can and it should do you some good.'

Radnor regarded her with a strange mixture of emotion in his face. There was pride quite openly, but a flash of anger as well, and a fierce regret that was almost as visible as the ravages of his illness.

Seeing it, Hester felt very much an intruder who was not meant to witness such an intimate relationship. She thought of excusing herself, but it was part of her duty to make certain Radnor ate as much as he could, and to help if it should cause him any distress. Her discomfort was irrelevant.

She merely asked Radnor if she could help him to sit more comfortably in order to eat, then realised with anger at herself that that would make her sound like a servant. She was a nurse, not his parlour-maid. And she was here under duress! Briefly, as she helped him lean forward while she restacked the pillows behind him, she wondered what he knew of the circumstances of her being here. Did he realise she had been rendered unconscious by ether, and brought here against her will? That she was now actually a prisoner, with the children as surety for her good behaviour?

Would he care if he did?

She met his cold, clear eyes for an instant as she laid him back again, and it was she who looked away. There was something far too perceptive in him, too probing into her thoughts.

Adrienne insisted in feeding him herself. He was too unsteady to hold the spoon without spilling the soup, which angered him. Hester could see it in the lines of his face and hear it in his grunts as he swallowed. If Adrienne noticed, she affected not to.

He was also getting breathless. The effort it cost him was apparent to all of them and it humiliated him.

'Perhaps we should stop for a few moments,' Hester suggested. 'It won't get cold.'

Adrienne hesitated.

'Do as you're told!' Radnor snapped at her, and then choked as he caught his breath.

'Papa, I'm sorry!' she said quickly. She looked at Hester desperately. 'Do something! He's choking!'

Hester had a strong suspicion that it was largely affected. She had seen him manipulate his daughter's feelings before; this time she was even more suspicious.

'Help him!' Adrienne commanded.

Radnor looked at her, and coughed again.

This time Hester was quite certain. 'Perhaps we had better not give him any more,' she said coolly. 'He is not as well as I thought. It's a pity. But it won't be wasted.'

Radnor glared at her with chilling malevolence. 'If you want soup, woman, make your own. This is mine. My daughter made it for me.'

Hester smiled sweetly at him. 'Indeed she did. I am glad you are well enough to appreciate that.' She turned to Adrienne. 'I think after all he is perfectly well enough to finish it.' She turned and walked out of the room, before Radnor should see the disgust in her face.

Radnor seemed stronger when he had eaten. Even an hour or two after the soup he rallied, and insisted Adrienne should remain with him during the night. She would only call Hester, or Rand, if he seemed to be in distress.

Hester watched Adrienne try to settle him. She must have done it countless times before in the long months of his illness and deterioration, but she still seemed nervous. He was helpless to do the most ordinary things for himself, and, like many people she had seen before, he resented it. He felt robbed of dignity, which was easily understandable. But it was in no way Adrienne's fault.

Hester watched with embarrassment for them both as Adrienne tried to assist him to the bathroom so he could relieve himself. She held his arm to help him keep balance on his enfeebled legs, without appearing actually to support his weight. He was bent over, and his nightshirt was thus made too long at the front. He was in danger of tripping on it and falling.

'For God's sake, stand up straight, girl! I'm ill, not an idiot!' he snarled.

It was totally unfair. She was obviously doing her best, but she did not complain, nor even try to defend herself.

He swayed, and Adrienne panicked. She swung around to Hester, her eyes wide.

'Pull yourself together!' Radnor said to her furiously. 'Don't let me fall, damn you! Can't you do anything right?'

'I'm sorry, Papa. Lean on me more. I won't leave you!'

Hester could see Adrienne was frightened and losing control.

She moved forward quickly and took hold of Radnor by the other side, steadying him firmly. She felt his muscles tighten as he pulled away from her. Was it deliberate?

'Mr Radnor!' she said curtly. 'Lean on me, and let Adrienne open the bathroom door for us.'

He half turned to glare at her. He had more strength left than she had expected. 'Think you're coming in here to watch me relieve myself, woman?'

'Someone needs to hold your nightshirt up for you,' she retorted. 'If you try it you'll fall over. You might even spend the night on the floor, or worse than that, break a hip. Or both.'

Adrienne stifled a sob and shot a glance at Hester filled with both loathing and despair. 'I'll help you,' she whispered to her father, then to Hester: 'Please go. You leave him no dignity at all! How can you be so . . . cruel?'

Hester lost her patience, not with frailty or the fear of indignity, but with the mixture of love, hate and dependence that each of them seemed to have for the other.

'There is no indignity in being human,' she said, anger at the stupidity of it making her voice sharp. 'We are all born naked and screaming. We all function essentially the same way. We all need each other from time to time, dressed in robes and bleeding inside, or naked and weeping. Nobody takes your dignity away. Either you keep it, or you give it up yourself by behaving like a fool.' She turned to Radnor. 'You are no different from any other man. For goodness' sake stop making such a performance out of relieving yourself. Nobody cares!'

Adrienne gasped.

Radnor seemed to consider for a moment whether he would retaliate or not, and decided against it.

Five minutes later he was back in bed, ready for the night. Adrienne, exhausted, was sitting by his side with a book in her hands, quietly reading to him while he appeared to be falling asleep.

Hester awoke in the morning with a moment of fear. As she remembered where she was, a sense of loss overcame her. She lay still, thinking of Monk, and of Scuff. Did they know yet what had happened to her? What had Magnus Rand said to them?

Then she heard sounds below her, footsteps. What she felt was unimportant. What mattered were the three children and the promises she had made them.

She swung her legs out of bed and stood up. She was stiff, and still tired, but there was nothing wrong with her. She had a battle to fight every hour, every minute. If Radnor could be saved, well and good, but she must keep the children alive until she could find a way for all of them to escape.

She washed and dressed in the same clothes as before. She had nothing else to wear. Then she went down to the kitchen. It was dark outside still, with just a paling in the east to say that dawn was coming. Then she realised what the sound was that she had heard. The gardener was cleaning out the kitchen grate and rebuilding the fire. He snapped the front of it shut and stood up slowly, facing her, half a foot taller than she, and powerful, even without his gun.

'You'd best not even think of it,' he said quietly as she glanced at the back door. 'I could bring you down in a moment, and then what would those little ones do, eh? Miss Radnor in't going to look after 'em. She's too busy with 'er father.' He gave a twisted half-smile. 'Cooker'll be hot in five minutes. There's oatmeal in the wooden bin over there, and plenty o' good milk. An' there's eggs.'

Hester looked at his bony face and his big knuckled hands. He'd probably killed chickens and rabbits with them, with a quick twist, and thought nothing of it. He would do whatever

Rand told him to. There was no imagination in his eyes, and no pity.

'A good idea,' she agreed. 'Thank you for getting the fire going.'

He grunted and turned away. He had been prepared for anger, or pleading. Agreement caught him off balance.

She made plenty of porridge, sufficient for all of them, including Rand himself. Then she left it simmering while she went to get the children up, washed and dressed, and then brought them back to the kitchen.

She served them porridge with plenty of milk. They were all sitting at the wooden table eating when Rand came in.

'And what do you think you are doing in here?' he demanded when he saw them. 'You eat in your own place! Mrs Monk, I will not have this . . .'

She stared straight back at him. 'If you do not allow them fresh air and as much food as they need, what you will have is sick children whose blood is no use to you,' she answered him tartly. 'I presume you have not gone this far in order to fail over such an obvious detail?'

For an instant there was surprise in his face, and something that could even have been appreciation. Then it vanished. 'See that they are finished and in their room in one hour. I shall require you to assist in taking their blood. Radnor is still failing.'

She stared at him, at his clever eyes whose colour she could never be sure of, then back at his precise mouth, which seemed to have no curves in it, no passion.

She found herself agreeing obediently. She could not afford his anger.

The porridge had lost its flavour, but she finished it anyway, and took the children back to their room, locking the door behind her as she left. Her mind was racing all the time, seeking ways of escape, and finding nothing.

Rand came back when he had said he would. He was exact in everything. He never made an unnecessary gesture, never mind an ill-thought act.

'We will begin, Mrs Monk,' he told her. 'Watch me and do exactly as I tell you. You are an intelligent woman and a very good nurse. Please do not waste both our time by pretending not to understand.' He met her eyes for a moment, as if making certain he had her attention. 'We are going to draw blood from the older two children, about three-quarters of a pint from each,' he continued. 'I shall mix the lemon juice and the potash with it in exact proportions, and you will observe. Please do not be stupid enough to affect displays of emotion. If you do, I shall be obliged to hurt you. If harm comes to the children it will be the result of your stupidity.'

He looked at her steadily and there was a degree of respect in his face. 'I know something about you, Mrs Monk. I did not choose you at random among the nurses. You have seen surgical operations; indeed, you have performed some yourself when there was no one else. You do not lack either skill or nerve. Do not fritter away these people's lives with moral histrionics. Do you understand me?'

She understood him perfectly. He saw it in her face and turned away without waiting for a verbal answer.

First she watched him make a mixture of lemon juice squeezed and refined until it was absolutely clear, then mixed with potash, to exact measurements. He put it in a small glass jar and sealed it.

Next she followed him to collect Maggie and bring her back to the room upstairs where they would draw three-quarters of a pint of her blood.

Hester inserted the needle herself because she knew she would be gentler than Rand. His chemical knowledge was superb, his measurements precise to the minutest drop, but

he had no concept of gentleness, nor did he seem to understand fear.

At least that was what she thought, until it was Charlie's
turn. This time Rand seemed to find it difficult to watch, not
because he had another task, but she heard his slight indrawn
breath as she touched the point of the coarse, hollow needle
to the vein in Charlie's thin arm. It was barely healed from
the last time.

Hester spoke to Charlie quietly, apologising for what she
was doing, but telling him what a marvellous gift he was
giving to other people, to the science of medicine, and to
knowledge in general. All this time she heard her own voice
she was wondering if she should be telling him such a thing.
She did not want him to think she liked this or thought it
right, but she needed Rand to think she believed it.

She was intensely aware of Rand only a foot away from
her, standing so close to make certain she did nothing whatever except exactly what he had told her to. Whatever she
said or did, he would never trust her. Nor should he, except
not to cause unnecessary pain.

She drew the plunger back gently and watched the scarlet
liquid fill the glass tube. It revolted her that she could be part
of such a procedure, but at least she would hurt Charlie less
than Rand would. His smooth young face was white as he
watched too.

Hester could feel the warmth of Rand's body almost touching
her, and the very slight hiss of his breath.

When she had finished she passed the vial of blood to him,
and he took it without looking at Charlie, or thanking him.
Either Rand was concentrating so intensely that he was already
oblivious of other people, or he was in the grip of some
emotions that required all the self-mastery he could call upon.
For a moment Hester thought it was the latter, and then she
changed her mind. Why did she think Rand even had emotions?

She smiled at Charlie and touched him gently. 'Thank you,' she said. Then she added, 'Come and lie down for a while. Look after each other. There's plenty of water, so please drink it. I'll try to find something special for lunch.'

He gave her the best smile he could manage.

When she returned from taking Charlie back to his bed, she found Rand waiting for her impatiently.

'Time is of the essence, Mrs Monk. I thought you knew that.'

'So is the health of our . . . providers of blood!' she snapped back at him. 'If they don't do well, neither does Mr Radnor, and more importantly, neither does the experiment.'

'I am glad you appreciate that it is all one effort.' He sounded slightly mollified. 'Please help Adrienne finish preparing Mr Radnor. I will show you exactly what is necessary with the blood another time. It is good that you should understand.'

She had not said that she cared in the least about how he treated the blood. But she noted that he seemed to want her interest – or was it merely that he had noticed it already? She was annoyed with herself for feeling interested, and then for being careless enough to let him know. Morally it repelled her, and yet the possibilities of the good it could do fired her imagination. Thousands, soldiers, ghosts from the past thronged her mind.

'Yes, Mr Rand,' she said obediently, and turned away so he would not see her face. He saw too much, too easily, and she could not read him in return.

She found Radnor propped up on several pillows. There was definitely more colour in his face today and even a spark of interest in his eyes. Adrienne was beside him, watching every movement, listening to each word as always. Was it comforting to him, or did it irritate his patience? Could it be possible that it was both?

Radnor looked Hester up and down with a bright, assessing eye.

'What makes you nurse, Mrs Monk?' he said curiously. 'Have you no family of your own to look after, no man to keep you? You're not bad-looking but you've a sharp tongue and men can get very tired of that.'

Hester looked at him with surprise. He was definitely feeling better, and yet somewhere beyond the desire to provoke her, even hurt her, she saw a dark fear. He wanted to live. More than that, he resented that she, whom he considered a lesser being, was healthy where he was not.

She smiled slowly. 'During the Crimean War it was a desire to be of use, and a deep respect for the courage of many of the men. Anger at the foolishness of others, I suppose.' She met his eyes squarely, staring back just as hard as he. 'Now I am filling in for a friend, temporarily. When she returns I shall go back to my usual occupation. If I survive, of course. I am here under duress, as you perfectly well know. But I admit Mr Rand's experiments are interesting. There is much to be learned.'

Radnor nodded very slowly. 'You like to learn. So do I. Learn all you can. Knowledge is the wealth of the world, beauty is its joy. See the beauty in everything! Learn all you can, sit up all night under the stars and discuss everything there in all the sublime possibilities of the mind.' He smiled as if in memory he were tasting it now. 'Eat the fruit of life till the juice of it runs down your chin. Laugh at the absurd until your sides ache and you can't get your breath. Grasp it! Hold on, till they have to prise your fingers off it when you're dead. Wear colours, woman! Not that damn blue-grey.' He looked her up and down again, his lip curling with contempt.

'Perhaps I'll wear scarlet, like a soldier's uniform,' she replied, still without looking away from him. 'So the blood doesn't show.'

He nodded and smiled at her slowly, but the fear was back in his eyes. 'I'm dying, but at least I was alive. Have you ever been alive, woman? Really alive? You with your skinny body and prim dress, your back stiff as a ramrod! Ever loved a man, except from a safe distance? Eh?'

'Yes. And I may love tomorrow, and many tomorrows after that. You won't. When you get up, pay attention and get prepared to take more blood,' she told him with a faint, chill smile.

'How dare you speak to my father like that?' Adrienne said firmly, jerking forward in her chair and rising to her feet. 'Remember who you are, and your position here!'

Hester stared back at her. 'I am a prisoner here because you need my skills in order to have some chance of saving your father's life. I remember that. I think it is you who seem to have forgotten it.'

Radnor brought his hands together in a faint dry rubbing of skin, but it was intended as applause. 'Not your match,' he said to Adrienne. There was a smirk of malicious satisfaction on his lips. 'In fact, you are nowhere near as much fun!'

Adrienne winced, but she remained standing. She did not look back at him, or answer. She insisted on helping Hester prepare his arm by sterilising his skin with surgical spirit, then make him as comfortable as possible so he would not find it difficult to remain perfectly still.

Rand came back. The apparatus was wheeled into place and the procedure began. The needle was inserted into Radnor's arm. Hester knew that it hurt, but he refused to register it, even in his eyes. Only his breathing altered for a moment, then returned to normal. She respected his courage, though little else. His will to live was almost tangible in the room, like the energy in the air when a storm is building. She understood how Adrienne would be desolate if he died, and yet guilty because part of her would also be relieved. Like a great tree, he sheltered those close to him at the same time as he took the sunlight, and also sucked the soil dry of its goodness.

Adrienne stood a little back from his side, but never took her eyes from him. Did she really imagine that she might do something to help? Or was it only a mixture of habit and fear, and of possession of him, her ownership as his daughter?

As the moments ticked by, Hester checked that the blood was flowing easily and that Radnor's temperature and pulse remained steady. His eyes were closed, but she knew he was awake, feeling the life in his veins strengthening with Charlie's fresh, bright red blood inside him.

What was it in the blood of these children that gave life, yet of so many others brought illness and then death? Rand was a chemist; did he know? She would ask him some time, when they were alone. Why was their blood different? Was there some tiny thing in the procedure that was different, a timing, a balance of ingredients, something about the patient receiving it?

Adrienne's face was tense. She was ignoring Hester as if she were part of the apparatus, with its tubes and bottles, its frame, clamps and wires to hold everything in place.

The colour was returning to Radnor's face. Hester knew that Adrienne saw it too. She leaned forward a little. The muscles in her neck were rigid with tension, her eyes wide. What was she seeing – life returning to the old pattern, her father with his vigour and all his old energy? Hester could not tell whether the passion in her face was love or dread. She had not heard Adrienne speak of her own life, except in terms of her father's dependency on her. Was she as much a captive as Hester was in this house? Except that while Mr Radnor lived, there was no end in sight.

But if he died, then the end for Hester was very much in sight. Rand could not afford to let her leave here with the knowledge of what had happened. She would testify against him; she would have no moral choice. And – a thought that was even uglier to her – Charlie, Maggie and Mike would be killed as well. The older two at least would speak up. Rand would not risk that.

She must do better. She must find a way to get all of them out.

There was only one person who might help. How long did she have before she was not necessary to Rand? If the treatment succeeded, by the time he was sure, it would be too late for Hester to act.

Rand knew that. He would be watching Radnor's progress, every rally, every setback, and he knew that she would too. Would he act first to kill her? Or would he miss the moment, and she would escape? Or fail, and be caught, making it all infinitely worse? She was cold at the thought, the small hairs standing up on her arms, as if someone had let in an icy draught. One mistake would be one too many.

She looked across and found Adrienne watching her. Their eyes met in a moment when they seemed to have a complete understanding of each other. And then it was gone again, and they were the strangers they had been before.

Chapter Seven

THE NEW blood made a conspicuous difference to Radnor's recovery. The day after the procedure he was sitting up in bed and welcomed a good breakfast. Hester brought it to him with conflicting emotions. Her profession and her will were to heal. She was trained to disregard the personality of an invalid; and the oath and promise of all healers was always to do their best, without judgement. All patients must receive the best effort you could call up, regardless of whether you are tired, discouraged, frightened or ill yourself.

The treatment was working. That was a victory, a new and major one.

On the other hand the closer Radnor was to complete recovery, the less purchase did Hester have on her own life – less time to think.

He was watching her now.

She set the tray in front of him and saw with both pleasure and revulsion how he picked up the knife and fork and began on two soft-poached eggs on crisp, brown toast. She had baked it herself, as it was a skill Adrienne did not have. He ate slowly, with relish, savouring every mouthful, quite aware that she was seeing and noting. In fact, it appeared to amuse him, as if her awareness gave an extra dimension to his enjoyment.

She took away the empty tray and set it on the landing,

then returned to check his pulse and temperature again. She took his wrist and held it, counting. The blood beat strongly, as if she could touch the life in him.

'Well?' he asked when she had completed the count. 'Satisfied, Mrs Monk?'

'You are progressing, Mr Radnor,' she replied, letting go of his hand as soon as she could. 'And your temperature is almost normal.'

He smiled. 'Have you ever had fun, woman? Ever laughed at something ridiculous, seen the hilarious absurdity of life? Do you always do what you're told to, or do you look in your masters' eyes and tell them to go to hell? Perhaps you have less red blood in you than I have.' He gave a jerky little laugh. 'What does Mr Monk do that he chose a woman like you, eh?' His expression was curious, almost prurient, as he looked her body up and down.

'He is Commander of the Thames River Police, Mr Radnor,' she replied with a smile just as hard as his. She saw the look in his eyes, and he knew that she had seen it. It annoyed him. 'And yes, I have done all the things you say,' she continued. 'Especially telling them to go to hell, which is not easy in the army. And I have done them with good people. Has anybody ever loved you that you didn't buy first, Mr Radnor?' The minute the words were out of her mouth she regretted them. She had allowed him to provoke her, and that was a tactical error as well as one of morality between patient and nurse. His moment of surprise before he recovered his composure was her only reward.

His smile widened, showing his teeth again. He was satisfied that he had provoked her, and she had not resisted.

She spent the middle of the day with Maggie, Charlie and Mike. For a while she cleaned and tidied the room. That was important. They would be highly vulnerable to infection.

Mike seemed to be as well as before, but he was frightened, and very young to be without either of his parents. Usually Maggie took care of him, but today she was listless. She looked very pale, and every so often she fell asleep. Mike went to her and stood beside the chair where she was curled up. He wanted to talk to her, but she was too sleepy to pay attention.

He went over to Charlie, who was staring out of the window. There was nothing to see except the wind in the trees and the cloud shadows over the hills in the distance.

Mike leaned up against him. Charlie put his arm around him, but he did not say anything.

Hester went to the small pantry and came back with a tray of glasses and a jug of milk. Mike ran over to her and threw his arms around her hips. She thought at first that he was thirsty for the milk, but after she had poured it and persuaded Maggie to have a small amount, she realised Mike was frightened. He just did not have the words to say so.

She wanted to hold him close, soothe away the hurt inside him, but he was not her child. She had no right to that intimacy and she was nervous of intruding, creating a bond she would have to break when they were returned home. She wondered how she could give them some respite from the uncertainty of what would happen to them, even if they would get home. Did they know that Rand was drawing away their lives in order to save Radnor, and solve by experiment the healing mystery of their blood?

She racked her mind for stories she could tell to children their ages, but she could not remember what tales she had heard so far back in her own childhood. And of course by Maggie's age she could read on her own.

Nothing came to mind but bits and pieces of stories. She could remember *Cinderella*, but what would these children make of princes and glass slippers? What about history? That was full of stories. Or legend?

The first to her mind was King Alfred and the Viking invasion. At least she could describe the great Norse ships, and how Alfred was beaten, and then began to fight back.

'Shall I tell you a story?' Hester asked, sitting down in the other chair. 'A true story, of how a brave king gathered all his men together and fought a great battle?'

Charlie looked at her gravely. 'Did he win?'

'Oh, yes, in the end,' she assured him. 'He was very brave, and he never gave up, no matter how bad it was. In fact we still call him Alfred the Great!'

'Yes . . . please,' Charlie agreed.

Mike looked at her steadily for a long moment, then he took a handful of her skirt in his grasp and slowly climbed up on to her lap. He settled himself and waited.

'A very long time ago,' she began, 'not so very far from here, there was a man called Alfred. He wasn't specially big, or strong, but he was very specially brave . . .'

An hour later Mike was asleep, still on her lap, and she was surprised how heavy he was. He seemed to be all elbows and knees and she had to move him gently in order to be at all comfortable herself. Maggie was curled up in the chair. Charlie was still listening, and every time she stopped he prompted her to go on.

In the late afternoon Rand came in. He stood near the doorway, watching for several moments before he demanded her attention.

She stood up, carrying Mike over to place him near Maggie, and then followed Rand out of the room. She was acutely aware of Charlie's eyes in her back as she closed the door.

Rand's bland, scholarly face was marred with irritation.

'You are losing your professionalism, Mrs Monk,' he said coldly. 'You are not here to entertain those children. You are a part of this experiment. You would be very foolish to forget that.'

This time caution controlled the response that rose to her lips. 'Only a part,' she agreed. 'I am replaceable, but not easily or conveniently at the moment. The same is true of them. Their blood works. You have no one else's that does. It is practical that we keep them as well and as calm as possible. Is that not true, Mr Rand?'

He met her gaze for a long, silent moment. He was disconcerted by her remarks, and yet oddly pleased that she understood not just calmly, but with passion. He turned and led the way down the stairs, across the hallway and into the room where he did most of his work of measuring and refining. It was here that he examined things under the beautifully wrought microscope on its stand near the window.

He turned to face her as he closed the door, so there was no chance Adrienne would overhear them.

'What person of honour would refuse to give a little of his own blood to save another's life?' he demanded.

'None,' she answered. 'I have never doubted the purpose, Mr Rand, only the means you use to attain it.'

'And what means would you have me use, Mrs Monk?' he asked. 'How long do I wait? Until I find another family of children whose blood heals everyone? As you have pointed out, I don't even know where to look, or how to recognise it if I do – except by trial and error.'

Was that emotion in his voice, or did she imagine it?

'How many more people lose limbs and die of shock and blood loss?' His voice grew rough-edged, as if something in his memory all but choked him. 'How many men waste away with the white blood disease?' He moved so that she could not see his face except in profile. 'Sometimes the many are saved by the sacrifice of the few. It is not my way, it is nature's.' He stopped abruptly and stood in silence. Then he straightened up and reached for a small square of glass that he used to smear blood upon to look at it under the microscope.

'I need your assistance,' he said sharply. 'We cannot waste time in emotional indulgence.'

'Seeing that the children survive is not an emotional indulgence, Mr Rand,' Hester said bitterly. 'When you save someone completely, you need to know why their blood – and no one else's so far – is good. There are surely many things that could be the cause, aren't there? Is it something in their parents? Their lives, their heritage, their environment? Is it something they eat, or even that they do not eat and others do?'

She stared at his stiff body, his square, rigid shoulders.

'Finding that it works, and Bryson Radnor will live, is only the beginning,' she continued. 'Do you want to announce to the world, "Yes I did it, but I don't know how, so I can't do it again"?'

He turned to face her very slowly. He seemed pale, but his eyes were suddenly bright.

'How perceptive of you, Mrs Monk. I was wrong to be disappointed in you. Of course I must know what it is that heals so remarkably in this particular blood, and that is different from other people's. But if I succeed with Radnor, then there will be more money available to fund research. People will be clamouring to have a part in it.' His very slight smile was bleak. 'I will have many new "friends" among those who now have no interest at all.'

Hester caught the grief under the bitterness. She had not thought him capable of personal hurt, but perhaps she was wrong. It was more than a tactic towards her own survival and the children's that pushed her to ask him. She knew not to be devious; he would sense it immediately, and resent it.

'It is personal for you, isn't it? You really are not after glory.'

'Glory!' he said the word as if it were an obscenity. 'Is that what you think medical science is? A pursuit of self-aggrandisement?' Her face was pinched with disappointment, and a sort of disgust with himself for having hoped far more.

She knew she had made a mistake and tried to correct it.

'Perhaps I should have said a pure search for knowledge, for its own sake, rather than for its practical application. That is not something to be despised.'

He was momentarily confused by her grasp of the issue he had thought beyond her. He was forced to think again.

'Why do you care, Mrs Monk? Do you think I am unaware that you keep reminding me of the value of these children because you have developed a sentimental attachment to them?'

'Now you are wrong again!' she said, her anger surging back. 'You imply something maudlin and basically selfish. That is unworthy of either of us. I care for them because they are sweet and brave people, and should grow up to have as much of a chance at life as fate will give them. That is not sentimental, it is basically decent, that's all! If you don't care about individuals then you are lying when you say you aren't after glory. Without a purpose beyond yourself, then you *are* after glory, praise, reward. Don't deceive yourself.'

He winced as sharply as if she had struck him.

'How quick you are to judge,' he accused her. 'I want the cure for white blood disease so no one ever dies of it again: man or child.' His voice was intense, shaking as if it were beyond him to control it. 'I watched my own brother die of it, and he was barely older than Charlie. He was the most beautiful child I ever knew: brighter, gentler, more visionary than I am.' His mouth twisted into a grimace of anger. 'Magnus is all he can be, but he will never make up for Edward.' He drew in a deep, shaky breath. 'Neither will I. But perhaps I will save someone in the future who will achieve greatness, beauty of the mind and the soul.'

'Maybe Charlie,' Hester said softly, this time without criticism. 'One cannot know. Or the children he will have one day.'

He looked at her. For a moment there was no pretence at indifference in him at all, only memory and grief.

'Damn you!' he said quietly. 'I want you to nurse these children and keep them alive so I can use their blood until I can save Radnor, and find out how I am doing it! What is it about them? Why does their blood always work, and other people's does sometimes, and it kills other times?'

'Would you have used Edward, if some other person had caused you to work at this?' She knew she was taking a risk, but she would never have a better chance than this.

'I can't use Edward,' he said savagely.

'Magnus?' She would not let it go.

'I need him alive! He's a doctor, a good one. I need his skills. That should be within your grasp to understand.' A shadow passed over his face. 'Anyway, we tried transfusing Magnus's blood. It didn't work. Nor does mine. Tried it twice with mine. All the patients died.' He turned away from her. 'Now will you please stop badgering me with your questions and attend to your work? We may need more blood tomorrow.'

'You can't!' she said, all her fear returning. 'You'll kill them! Then Radnor will certainly die. You will have failed. You can't keep on taking blood so often. Apart from anything else, their blood will be depleted of all goodness. For heaven's sake, can't you see that?'

He stood motionless with his back to her.

'Why on earth are you here doing this anyway?' she demanded. 'You may be brilliant, but you're a chemist! Magnus is the doctor – why isn't he here?'

'I know enough medicine to manage,' Rand replied, still facing away from her. 'And you have the experience. You'll hold your nerve.'

'That is not an answer,' she said. She kept as calm as she could, but felt a different kind of panic welling up inside her. 'Does Magnus even know what you're doing?'

Now he wheeled round, his eyes glittering. 'Of course he knows what I'm doing! He has the doctor's qualification, but I know almost as much medicine as he does. But if we fail, he has the more to lose.'

She was stunned. Was Hamilton Rand really taking the responsibility to save his brother, if it all went disastrously wrong?

He saw her face and understood her thoughts as if she had spoken them aloud. He raised his eyebrows high. 'You don't think I would do that? You know nothing! You look at us, see little, a very little, and jump to conclusions. Who do you think brought Magnus up, helped him study, encouraged him, paid for his medical schooling?'

She swallowed. Her mouth was dry. 'Your father . . .' As soon as she said it she knew she was wrong. 'You?'

'I gave up medical school when my father died. I went to work to earn money to keep the family. Then Mother died as well. It was after Edward . . .' he breathed in and out to steady himself, '. . . after Edward died. There were only Magnus and me left. I was determined one of us would make it. Magnus had the chance. He's going to be a success now.'

Hester could think of nothing to say. Her feelings were torn in so many different directions it was like a physical pain inside her. She could barely imagine the loss, Hamilton's willing sacrifice, the burden of gratitude weighing on Magnus. And every time Hamilton said 'Edward', she could see Charlie's face, pale, losing his grip on life as his blood was drained away.

'Nothing to say, Mrs Monk?' Rand asked her bitterly. 'No judgements?'

She shook her head. 'I think it's time to finish this, and for

135

me to go and make dinner. Adrienne is probably looking after her father. And frankly, I'd rather scrape a used saucepan than feed him.'

Rand smiled with a downward twist of his lips. 'You don't have to like him, Mrs Monk. Just keep him alive.'

'I know, Mr Rand,' she answered him, this time meeting his eyes. 'It is entirely in my own interest to do so. I won't forget that, I assure you.'

In the early evening, Hester went back up the stairs to see Radnor again. With the new transfusion of blood he had seemed to rally considerably and Adrienne had felt well able to care for him without assistance for a couple of hours.

She met Hester at the bedroom door.

'We do not need you, Mrs Monk,' she said coolly. 'My father is gaining strength every day. Dr Rand is a genius. I think he will make medical history.' She said it with pride. Perhaps it was a safer emotion than hope so fragile. She had been very afraid, and she must now be uncomfortably aware that Hester had witnessed her fear almost intimately, much too close to forget.

'I'm very pleased to hear it,' Hester smiled back at her. It was easy to be honest, for many reasons. 'I will still go in and check his pulse and temperature.'

Adrienne stood in front of the door, blocking it. They faced each other for a few seconds in silence. Finally Hester spoke.

'Is there something you do not wish me to see, Miss Radnor?' she said levelly.

A shadow crossed Adrienne's brow. 'Of course not. I just don't want you to disturb him. Your manner is discourteous, sometimes even quarrelsome; as I am sure you are aware. He needs to rest. Go and look after the children. I think you care more about them than you do about him anyway, even though it is he who is ill.'

'The children are ill also, Miss Radnor, and they have no one else to care for them,' Hester replied with surprise. She had been aware that Adrienne did not have any affection for them. In fact, she showed no outward compunction about the fact that Rand was regularly taking their blood for her father. Perhaps she was so desperate for him that she had not even given it consideration. Her fear that Radnor could die obscured everything else.

Hester thought for the first time that since Adrienne was in her early thirties, perhaps she had devoted so much care to companionship with her father that she had missed some opportunities for marriage, and might not have many more. Then she would have no children of her own. Did that cause her pain?

One never knew what wounds other people carried where no one saw them. She spoke more gently.

'I simply want to make the usual checks, Miss Radnor. I will not disturb him. Then I shall report to Mr Rand, after which, if he has no more for us to do, I will make sure the children are also well.'

Adrienne stepped aside without speaking, but she indicated that Hester go through the door. She did not open it for her.

Radnor was awake, sitting almost upright against the pillows, a book lying open in front of him. However, he was watching the door. Hester was certain from the expression of interest on his face that he had heard at least part of the conversation just outside.

'I am glad you are feeling well enough to read,' Hester said with a slight smile as she closed the door behind her.

He held up the book for a moment, and then closed it. 'It's good,' he observed. 'But no substitute for life. Do you miss the army, Mrs Monk? Don't you want to pit your wits against something more than extending some old man's life by a couple of years?'

She stared back at him. 'Yes, Mr Radnor. Right now I would much rather be at home, but unfortunately I don't have that choice. There are lots of things I like to do, and this isn't one of them.'

He smiled. 'Honesty at last! But you would like to see Rand succeed, wouldn't you? You'd like to be part of it. Are you going to lie to me about that?' He looked as if he would enjoy that, savour his superiority in at least acknowledging the truth within himself.

'Yes, I would like to,' she admitted. 'That doesn't mean that I will.'

'You mean escape?' he asked with satisfaction. 'You haven't the fire, or the intelligence. You'll always stay in the safe bounds of doing your duty.'

'You are definitely much better.' She reached for his wrist to take his pulse. She touched his forehead with the back of her other hand. It felt warm, but with the warmth of life, not of fever.

'You won't go, will you?' he challenged. 'You'll stay, always hoping for mercy from Rand – until he kills you!'

Hester finished counting his pulse. It was a fraction fast, but well within normal.

She ignored his comment. 'You are much better, but you have had a brush with death, and I think you know that.'

'God in heaven, of course I know that. It is my body that is ill, not my mind. Stop talking to me as if I were senile! I'm still young enough to take you, with passion you've never even imagined. I could leave you breathless and gasping for more.'

'Which I doubt you would be able to give,' she responded with a touch of cold amusement, although in fact she felt peculiarly vulnerable. She was used to fairly uncontrolled remarks from soldiers. Life and death are very close at times.

He glared at her. Then she recognised something other

than fury in him, and she knew exactly what it was. It was terror, the all-consuming terror of annihilation, of becoming nothing, not even a hole in the darkness. He was well enough now not to long for the peace of death as an end of pain, but as an irrevocable step into oblivion.

There were no words that would make a difference, and she was afraid he would see the understanding in her face.

'With luck, you will have a good night, and feel like breakfast in the morning,' she said blandly. She hated the sound of her own voice, as trite as if she had seen and understood nothing. It was insulting to her own intelligence. And yet it was still better than acknowledging the truth.

She made the bed tidy and comfortable, leaving a small night candle burning so Radnor was not in the dark. The country dark was absolute on a moonless night, nothing like the city where there was always a lamp lit somewhere, however faint, and usually the sounds of traffic, hoofs, wheels, and the rattle of harnesses, the reminder that there were other living beings in the world.

This would be complete – as he might envision death to be.

As Hester left the room, she saw Adrienne waiting, watching. Hester suggested that she sleep in the chair beside him, uncomfortable as that was.

'Of course!' Adrienne said sharply. 'What did you think I was going to do – go to my own room and forget about him? I'm not a paid nurse.' She said the words as if they were obscene.

Hester did not remind her that she was not either, but a prisoner kept under threat of death.

'If you were a nurse, Miss Radnor,' she said quite gently, 'you would know that we never ignore or abandon a patient, any more than a doctor would, whatever our conditions of service, paid or not.'

Adrienne stared at her for several more seconds, then moved her position with a gesture of discomfort. 'No,' she said at last. 'I suppose you can't, can you?'

'Adrienne!' Hester said quickly.

Adrienne looked back. 'Yes?'

'I want him to live, for a lot of reasons, but this is a dangerous and controversial experiment. I think you know that, but you are prepared to take the risks in order to save your father's life.'

'Of course I am!'

'Hamilton Rand cares only about it succeeding, and the innumerable people it could save in the future. But in doing this he has imprisoned three children and is risking their lives by taking blood from them.'

'How else could he do it?' Adrienne protested.

'Probably no other way,' Hester said honestly. 'And if he succeeds he'll go down in history as one of medicine's greatest heroes. But have you thought what will happen if he fails?'

Adrienne was close to tears. Her face looked almost blood-less.

'We can't let it fail.'

'But if it does, have you thought of what Rand and the gardener will do with us?' Hester hated saying it, but she might never have another chance.

Adrienne stared at her, her eyes dark with horror as the understanding sank into her mind.

'You hadn't,' Hester said. 'Maybe you don't care if he kills me. And he will have to. He has kidnapped me. He can't afford to trust that I won't tell the police. My husband is a policeman! And the three children – he'll have to kill them as well. Or maybe he'll have the gardener do it—'

'Stop it!' Adrienne sobbed.

'And you,' Hester went on. 'Do you think he'll let you live? Risk you going out into the world and telling everyone what happened?'

'But I wouldn't tell.'

Hester smiled bitterly. 'Maybe not this year . . . or next. But if you're dead too, then you won't ever tell.'

'What . . . what do you want me to do?' Adrienne whispered.

'If the experiment fails, then we must escape – with the children.'

'Then why are you trying to save him? Why not just let him die and make your escape now?'

'Because I couldn't live with it – could you?'

For a long moment Adrienne stared at Hester and there was understanding in her eyes, and respect. Then she turned and went into Radnor's room, closing the door firmly.

Hester was woken in the night by the sound of the lock in her bedroom door turning and then Rand's voice, sharp-edged.

'Get dressed, Mrs Monk, and then come downstairs immediately. Radnor is having some kind of a crisis. Now, Mrs Monk. Right now.'

Old memories came back in a flood: being woken in the night for battle-wounded coming in. It was as if the years between had vanished. In less than two minutes she had dressed warmly, since the fires had been banked for the night. She wound her hair up into a coil and secured it with pins so it would not fall across her face. Another few seconds and her boots were fastened.

Rand had left her bedroom door open. She went straight across the landing and down the stairs as fast as was safe. She could hear in her memory the voice of Florence Nightingale telling her not to hurry so much that she was careless. Care – always do things properly. Never panic, absolutely never. Apart from being pointless, it frightened other people.

Now she pushed open the door to Radnor's room calmly, still tying her apron with a bow, and went in.

Adrienne was standing by the bed, ashen-faced, her hair disarranged, half pinned up, the other half wild and fallen as if she had torn at it in anguish. Now her hands were knotted together in front of her, white-knuckled.

'Where have you been?' she demanded as soon as she saw Hester. 'Why weren't you here?'

'She has to sleep sometime,' Rand said quietly. 'Mrs Monk, do what you can.' He looked at her, and then back at the prostrate form of Radnor lying on the bed. His arms were flung wide in the tangle of sheets, and his eyes were closed. His colour was terrible: grey-white around the eyes and fever-red on his cheeks. He seemed to be unaware of them, as if already falling into a coma.

Hester walked over to him, brushing past Adrienne and obliging her to move out of the way. She looked at Radnor more closely, and then touched her hand to his forehead. He was damp and burning hot. His nightshirt was so soaked with sweat she could almost have wrung it out. Even the sheets were damp.

'Get clean sheets if you have them,' she said, mainly to Adrienne. 'If you don't then we'll make do with blankets.'

'You can't put him in blankets,' Adrienne protested. 'They're rough and scratchy.'

Hester turned to her and looked into her eyes. 'Do as I tell you,' she said firmly. 'These sheets are soiled and wet. Bring back at least two towels and a bowl of water. Now do it!'

Adrienne looked as if she had been struck.

'Do it!' Rand snapped.

This time she obeyed, turning on her heel and clattering out of the room clumsily, bumping into the doorpost in her agitation.

Hester looked at Radnor and felt the panic surge up inside her. Her mouth was dry and her heart was beating violently as though it might burst. If Radnor died, then Rand would have to hide what he had done. He would have no more use for Hester, or for Charlie, Maggie and Mike. He could not afford to let them live, and risk their telling anyone what had happened here.

She looked at Radnor again. She must clear her mind of everything else. His fever was raging. She had no idea why, or even if it was connected to the latest blood transfusion. It could be something else, a simple germ that a healthy person could have fought. That was the best hope, and probably the only thing she could do to help.

She turned to Rand. 'We must try to reduce his temperature. If the fever gets any worse it will kill him. Before we change the bedding we will give him a cool bath. We'll use wet towels, and then the evaporation will cool him further. Bring as many towels as you have.'

'We haven't many . . .' he began.

'Clothes will do, clean or used,' she replied. 'We have to begin as soon as Miss Radnor returns with a bowl of water.'

He went as far as the door before she spoke again.

'Mr Rand!'

He turned, eyes wide.

'If we need to put him in a cool bath, have the gardener fill the tub: cool, not cold. He may have to help us carry him. I assume he will do whatever you tell him to?'

'Yes, yes of course.' Nodding with a small gesture, Rand hurried off to obey.

Adrienne returned with a bowl of water and two towels. 'What are you doing?' she demanded. 'Haven't you got medicine to give him? Why are you just standing there? I know you hate him, but you can't let him die! That's murder!' Her voice rose dangerously near hysteria.

Hester needed her under some self-control.

'Miss Radnor, I require your help,' she said calmly. 'This is not an appropriate time to let your feelings overwhelm your judgement. I am going to do what I can to save your father. I don't know what has happened to him to bring on this fever, and I have no way to find out. Put the bowl down and pass me one of those small towels. Now!'

Reluctantly Adrienne obeyed, giving Hester a hand towel.

Hester took it. 'Now help me. We are going to wash him down gently with the water . . .'

'It's cold!' Adrienne gulped. 'And what does it matter if he's clean? You stupid creature, he's dying!' Her voice rose to the edge of a scream.

'I'm not washing him,' Hester snapped at her. 'The water is not cold, it's cool! I'm trying to reduce his fever, before it stops his heart. Now do as you're told. Hold that bowl steady and pull the sheet back from his body, down to the waist.'

Adrienne obeyed, but unwillingly, distress clear in her face.

Hester wrung out the towel and laid it gently on Radnor's pallid flesh. She did it again, and again. Then she laid it on his brow and smoothed it over his cheeks, softly, as if she cared for him.

Adrienne watched, resentfully at first, then slowly with degrees of understanding.

'I'll get fresh water,' she offered after the sixth time.

'Cooler,' Hester told her.

When Adrienne came back she continued. Radnor's pulse was still racing and weaker, but his temperature was lower.

'Put the bowl down and take one of the other towels,' Hester told her. 'And do the same to his legs, as high up as you can.'

Adrienne looked startled. 'I can't! It's—'

Hester tried to be patient. 'Do you want him alive or dead? His legs aren't any different from any other man's.'

'He's my father!'

Hester met Adrienne's gaze, and saw the terror in her, the embarrassment, the fear of loneliness.

'Adrienne,' Hester said more gently, 'this is necessary if we are to save him. If you prefer to, you continue with the upper part of his body, just as I was doing, and I will take his legs. It is beginning to work.' Please heaven that was true. 'But we must keep going. If the fever breaks then we will be all right . . . at least for the time being.'

'Will he?' Adrienne's voice was hoarse. 'Are you sure?'

What should she say? It was all they could do. There was no other way she knew of to bring the fever down before it killed him. Perhaps all their lives depended on it.

'Keep cooling him down with the water,' Hester told her. 'Gently! If we can lower the fever it will save him.'

The tears spilled over and ran down Adrienne's face. 'Thank you.' She took a deep, shuddering breath.

They worked all night. Rand came back with tea for both of them and a mixture of spirits and cordial to offer to Radnor if he should regain consciousness and be able to swallow.

As the very first light showed palely in the east, so that black branches of the trees were outlined against the sky, Radnor opened his eyes.

'Papa!' Adrienne was overwhelmed with relief. She grasped his hand and held it to her face, kissing it again and again.

Hamilton Rand looked at Hester and very slowly smiled.

'Thank you, Mrs Monk. You were true to your highest calling.'

Hester looked at Radnor and met his eyes. In them she saw arrogance and victory, and the second after, his knowledge that she had seen it and knew it for what it was.

She felt as if ice had touched her heart.

Chapter Eight

MONK SEARCHED every avenue he could to find Hester. He spoke with all his own contacts along the river, including Crow, who told him of his visit with Hester to the Roberts family, where they had learned that the children had been taken to the hospital with their father's consent, albeit also with payment. Monk spoke privately with Sherryl O'Neill, the nurse with whom Hester had worked most closely, but Sherryl knew even less than Monk did. She was distressed herself about Hester's disappearance, but could offer no suggestions. She was also afraid of endangering Hester by making a fuss, which Monk noted with a chill to his heart. And she confirmed that the children were no longer in the hospital.

He informed all his own men, up and down the river, of Hamilton Rand's disappearance, but that in itself was not a crime, as Dr Magnus Rand reminded him.

Radnor and his daughter had no doubt gone willingly. But where?

It did not take long to find out where Radnor lived. His butler watched while Monk conducted a thorough search of the entire beautiful house with all its paintings, ornaments and mementoes, but they turned up nothing that indicated where Radnor had gone. It was more than possible that he had not known in advance.

Similarly there was no sign of Adrienne. Her maid said that

none of her clothes was missing, except the dress she had worn the last day she had been at home. The woman had no idea where her mistress might be. In fact she was concerned that Radnor had died, and that Adrienne was so frantic with grief that she was out of her mind, wandering somewhere alone and unable to face reality.

For once Monk could think of nothing to say except to suggest she consult whatever legal or financial counsellor whose name she could find in Mr Radnor's papers. The one thing he learned was the name and whereabouts of Radnor's lawyer, and he determined to send Hooper to interview the man. Not that he expected much from that. Radnor had the right to come and go as he pleased, and no obligation to inform anyone. He had committed no offence whatever.

Monk left with his mind whirling. He walked down the quiet street in the sun and felt neither its brightness nor its warmth.

Hamilton Rand had taken Hester for the obvious reason that he needed her skills. He was a chemist, not a doctor, and he had no practical experience of nursing, let alone caring for a man dying of white blood disease, and either the victim or the instigator of an experiment.

Rand would keep Hester alive as long as she was more help than trouble to him. Did she realise that? Hester was a fighter – one to fight first and think of the cost afterwards. Not this time! Not if she wanted to live as badly as Monk wanted her to. It was terrifying how much of his happiness was tied to her presence, her love, her belief in him. He wondered if he would even have had the will to carry on when he had no memory, no knowledge of who he was if she had not believed he was worth fighting for.

He had become a better man in order to live up to what she saw in him, and he could not see in himself.

That was a chill thought. What might he have been if they

had never met, or if she had abandoned him in the darkest days of his awakening after the accident? He had in a sense been given a new life, a chance to recreate himself in a better mould.

Without being aware of it he had increased his speed. He hailed a hansom and gave the driver the Wapping Police Station address. He had no idea what to do next to find Hester. He had made enquiries as to any other property Radnor might own, asking all Radnor's known associates, business or social, though he had few friends. No one knew of anywhere.

Hooper looked up the moment Monk came in. He was still pale and moved with the occasional wince of pain. Monk would like to have given him leave to recover, but he could not do without him. He thought with deep loss of how often Orme had run the station in the early days while Monk was learning the ways of the river, getting to know the men and they to trust him.

Orme's death had moved them all deeply. There was grief in each man's face in unguarded moments. They would have missed him cheerfully were he at home down the river, fishing, swapping gossip with his neighbours, tending his garden. They would all intend to drop by some day and see how he was, share a cup of tea, or a mug of ale at the tavern. Even if they never did it, the possibility was there.

They would have cursed his absence, but with a smile. Now it was irrevocable.

Monk missed not only Orme's skill and all the quiet managing he did without speaking of it, but more than that, he was aware as never before of his own loneliness in command. There was no one to catch his omissions, smooth out the occasional roughness he created with his manner, his still imperfect knowledge of the water and its customs. Most of all he missed the warmth of feeling Orme had created with his trust in eventual good. He had never spoken of faith, but something of it was there beneath his words.

'Morning, Hooper,' Monk said with as much cheer as he could manage. 'Been to Radnor's house. Searched the place but found nothing useful, except the name of his lawyer. The man's not obliged to tell us anything. Radnor's not wanted by us, even as a witness.' He realised how futile it sounded. 'But if he has property somewhere else it could be where they've gone to.'

Hooper took the piece of paper Monk handed him, but it was clear from his expression that he did not believe it would be useful any more than Monk did.

'Anything gained?' Monk asked.

'No, sir. But Laker's following up on McNab. He's got a few connections in Customs. I think the bastard left us in the wind on purpose.'

Monk agreed with him, but with the added misery of believing that it was in repayment for some old wrong he felt Monk had committed against him. He had lain awake struggling to remember what it was, but nothing whatever came to him.

Hooper was watching him, waiting for a response.

'I think it's personal to me,' Monk said quietly. It was difficult to admit. All of his men were now paying for whatever it was, and he couldn't even tell them because he didn't know himself. It might be better than his imagination conjured up . . . or worse.

He must give Hooper some reply. Should it be the truth – that he could not recall anything but vague shadows and snatches from before his carriage accident? How could he expect his men to have confidence in him, knowing that?

But Hester trusted him. John Devon had, even Runcorn had learned to. Was the real issue that he did not trust Hooper? What would he make of it, on top of the death of Orme?

What was he thinking now? That Monk was evasive at best, at worst a liar.

'Come into my office,' he said at last, then turned and led the way.

Once in the room he closed the door and remained standing, Hooper facing him, now looking even graver than before.

'McNab,' he said awkwardly. He hated having to do this, but he had trusted Hooper with his life many times before now. Perhaps it was unfair not to have trusted him with this earlier. But when was the right time to tell anyone such a thing.

Hooper was waiting silently, his eyes steady on Monk's face.

'It may be my fault. I don't know, because after the end of the Crimean War I had a very bad traffic accident. When I woke up in hospital I couldn't remember anything. I mean not anything at all. Not my name, what I looked like, where I lived. I learned a lot about myself from others, from deduction. I never told anyone at that time except one colleague. I didn't dare, because I was totally vulnerable.'

He saw the amazement and the compassion in Hooper's eyes.

'I could remember most of my skills, bit by bit. Perhaps they are part of my nature. And I gradually and often painfully learned who liked me and who didn't, but not always why. I never got any memory back. I learned how to function without it. Hester believed in me, more than I did in myself.'

He saw the quick flash of understanding in Hooper's face. He knew Hester and could not be surprised.

'I don't know if McNab has a grudge against me, but it looks like it. I have no idea what it is, or whether it is based on a genuine wrong or not.' The next thing was the hardest to say, but he had to acknowledge it. 'But I wish Orme had not paid my debt. If it's real, it should have been me.'

'Real or not, McNab shouldn't have collected, sir,' Hooper replied. 'If we collect from everyone we think owes us, we may not have enough to pay all that we owe, when others come collecting.'

Monk smiled in spite of himself. 'Thank you, Hooper.'

'Do the other men know, sir?'

'No. ' He did not want to go into explanations; they would sound like he was trying to excuse himself.

'Right, sir. I'll leave Laker on it, if you don't mind while I'm busy with looking for Mrs Monk. I want to get this bastard. We all do. A good man died because we were double-crossed. We'll be prepared for McNab next time.'

'Yes . . . thank you.'

Mornings and evenings were the worst. Monk went home to what for him was even more painful than an empty house. Scuff was always waiting for him. The look of hope in his face evidently took a greater effort to summon each time and it twisted like a knife in Monk's gut. Scuff never gave words to his feelings. Monk did not know if he even had the words to say how much he hurt, or whether he felt it too private a thing to speak of at all. Or maybe he was afraid of causing Monk too deep a sorrow. What do you say to someone who fears the worst loss of their lives, one they could see nothing beyond?

Sometimes Monk wished he would speak, and then they both could talk about their fears for Hester's safety. They were too busy tiptoeing around each other, as if not sharing their fears made them less real.

The worst of all for Monk was the sinking into sleep when he was too exhausted to stay awake any longer, the blessing of oblivion, then the waking up in the morning when it all flooded back again, sharp, powerful with the strength of new pain.

The evening after he'd searched Radnor's house he walked the last few steps up Paradise Row and opened the door. Scuff was standing in the hall waiting. He must have been listening for Monk's step.

Monk took a deep breath and tried to smile in recognition, not because of good news. Actually it would not have mattered what he had said. Failure was in his eyes and Scuff read it.

'I'm glad you're 'ome. I made dinner. It in't much good, but it's 'ot, an' it's ready.' His grammar had slipped since Hester had gone, even in those few days, as if he were willing time to go backwards.

'Thank you,' Monk said absently. He did not want to eat. Then he looked at Scuff's pale face and realised how much time and effort it must have taken him. He hated domestic chores. They were women's work! It was the best way he could show Monk that he loved him, and he cared intensely that he had done it well enough.

Monk made the effort. 'I'll just wash my hands. I'll be at the table in a few minutes.' He turned his back so Scuff would not see the emotion in his face. It was ridiculous. He could feel the tears sting his eyes. Scuff needed more from him than this.

He went upstairs. The water he dashed on his skin was clean, and sharply cold, enough to make him wince. Then he roughly dried himself on the towel he liked most, put a comb through his hair, and went downstairs again.

The meal was set out on the kitchen table as Hester would have done it. It was simple fare: potatoes boiled and mashed, then fried with a little onion. The sausages had already been fried before and were a bit overdone, so bursting out of their skins, but smelled inviting.

Monk took another deep breath, and sat down. 'Didn't think I was hungry,' he remarked, almost in his usual voice. 'But this changes my mind.' He started to eat, slowly, concentrating on what he was doing. It really was not bad.

Perhaps Scuff's own relish for food had taught him a thing or two.

He ate every last mouthful, aware of Scuff's eyes on him all the time.

Afterwards they sat opposite each other in the sitting room with a cup of tea each and a slice of cake that Scuff had bought from the local baker. Scuff asked him about the day. Very carefully Monk skirted around the subject of Hester, as too painful a wound to touch. It was like discussing the weather while the ship sinks beneath you.

'Mr 'Ooper getting better?' Scuff asked.

'I think he hurts pretty badly,' Monk replied, 'but he's improving. He should be taking time off, but he won't.'

''Course 'e won't,' Scuff said immediately, his eyes wide. 'Nobody's gonna do that, less they can't stand up!'

Monk smiled in spite of himself. 'Laker can hardly stand up, but he's in there doing paperwork, which he hates.'

Scuff was impressed. He hated paperwork too. His face reflected his respect for Laker's sacrifice.

'Have you see Worm?' Monk asked, largely for something to say. 'Is he all right? And Mrs Burroughs?'

Scuff shrugged and put his cake down on his plate. 'Yer really wanna know? Worm's awful! 'E's dyin' ter get out an' do summink useful, summink ter 'elp. Mrs Burroughs is working like someone's got a whip at 'er back. And Mr Robinson's got a face like a rotten egg and a temper ter match. I reckon 'e'd like ter kill someone, 'e just don't know who.' He looked at Monk. 'I told 'im we'd find 'er and get 'er back, and I thought 'e were gonna hit me. Then 'e stormed out the door an' slammed it behind 'im. 'E looked like I feel when I want ter cry, but I don't want nobody ter know, 'cos I in't a little kid no more.'

'It isn't only little kids that cry,' Monk told him.

'I know that!' Scuff replied, picking up his cake again. 'But we in't gonna cry, 'cos we're gonna get 'er back. They won't 'urt 'er 'cos they need 'er. We just gotter be quick, in case that old bastard dies on them.' He took a bite out of the cake and went on with his mouth full, 'We gotter think who else cares as much as we do, and then trust them a little. I bin thinking about that. If them little kids die, they'll 'ang the man wot took 'em, won't they?'

'I hope so,' Monk replied. 'In fact I'll see to it!'

'That's what I thought,' Scuff said soberly. 'D'yer reckon as 'is brother would get real upset about that?'

Monk stared at him, a sudden new thought taking shape in his mind until in seconds it was fully formed.

'Yes,' he said decisively. 'Yes, I do. And since he is part of the whole plan and could be charged with it as well, he will care very much.'

Scuff frowned. 'Yer said yer asked him already.'

'He says he doesn't know where they are, but I'll take him back over every step of their lives, every place they've ever lived, visited or known anyone.'

'Yer did that before . . .'

'Either he knows where they are, or if he doesn't then he'll be as worried as we are, even if for different reasons. If he hasn't heard from Hamilton he'll be terrified by now. His own reputation rests on it, too. I need to remind him of that.'

'Squeaky'd help,' Scuff said eagerly. ''E can clean up real good! Look like a lawyer, an' all! And 'e can write papers wot looks real.'

'Yes . . .'

'And—' Scuff started again.

Monk smiled: suddenly it was less difficult. 'I will. I'll go to the clinic tomorrow morning and see Squeaky.'

Scuff smiled back, a little shyly. 'You better be careful. If yer use dodgy paper on anyone, like wot's bin made by someone like Squeaky, yer can get inter awful trouble. The p'lice'll get yer . . .'

'I know.'

'Specially you,' Scuff was not going to be stopped. 'The River P'lice thinks yer flamin' walk on water, but the reg'lar p'lice don't like yer much.'

'I know that too,' Monk agreed. 'I'll be careful. Now I'll clear up the kitchen, and you go and do your homework.'

Scuff had wisely kept very quiet on the entire subject of homework – indeed, school altogether – and Monk, this once, did not ask.

Monk went to the clinic in Portpool Lane early the next morning. As always, it was busy whatever the hour. He had barely got past the entrance hall when Claudine appeared. For an instant so short it could even have been an illusion, there was hope in her face. Then she knew from Monk's eyes and from the way he stood, the tension in him, that there was no news.

She came forward, trying desperately to look as if everything were normal.

He saved her from having to think of something to say by speaking first.

'I've got a further idea about searching for them, but I'd like to speak to Squeaky first.'

She relaxed a fraction, with just an easing of her shoulders. She looked him up and down. 'He's in his office. I'll send you in a pot of tea. How about some cake as well? You don't look as if you had breakfast yet.' She nodded and turned away without waiting for his answer. She was not going to accept a refusal anyway.

'Thank you,' he said with a faint smile. He did not need taking to Squeaky's office. He had been there countless times before, and he knew that Squeaky lived on the premises.

He knocked on the office door sharply, and then opened it. He caught Squeaky unaware. At any other time it would have raised his always-volatile temper. Now it caught his vulnerability. He looked up from his writing, angry. Then when he recognised Monk, there was that same instant of hope as had been in Claudine's face. The second it was gone it was overtaken with rage, because he would not let anyone else see his disappointment.

'What do you want?' he snapped. 'You think I haven't got enough to do?'

Monk wanted to shout at him, even to swear so violently it would ease his own suffocating emotions. But far more important than relieving any anger of his own, he wanted Squeaky's help.

'Help,' Monk answered. 'Perhaps you could recommend a good forger, if I need one. Good, discreet and cheap. And one who will work for me, in spite of the fact that I am police.'

Squeaky's face went through a range of incredulity, fury, outraged pride, and ended with hope.

'You got something particular in mind?' he asked.

'Not yet,' Monk admitted. 'But I am going back to see Magnus Rand again, and this time I am not going to be asking for help. I intend to make it very clear to him that his brother will be charged with kidnap and murder if any of his prisoners die before we rescue them. It would ruin Magnus's professional reputation. I think that might matter to him very much indeed.'

'About bleedin' time!' Squeaky said fiercely. 'What d'you want from me? I can do it all, and you bleedin' know that! How about a really nice, short and savage newspaper draft showing what would happen to him, eh? "Today disgraced doctor, Hamilton Rand, was hanged at Newgate for his hideous murder of innocent children, who he bled to death in his terrible experiments".' He looked at Monk with his eyebrows raised. 'Should make him think again.'

Monk noticed that Squeaky would not say the words that Rand killed Hester, even to emphasise his point. Monk did not say anything. He would have done the same.

'It's a good idea,' he agreed. 'Make it as good as you can, but quickly. It doesn't have to be perfect, just to look good enough to make him understand what would happen. It will be far more powerful than simply telling him and leaving him to imagine it. Thank you.'

'I'll have it in half an hour,' Squeaky promised. 'Now let's think exactly what to say.'

There was a knock on the door.

'Come in,' Squeaky said loudly. 'But you'd better have a good reason.'

The handle turned slowly and the door swung open to reveal Worm. There was a small tray with a teapot, milk jug and a plate and cup sitting on the ground. He could not hold it and knock at the same time. He bent to pick it up, and carried it a little unsteadily across the room to put it on the desk in front of Monk.

'I s'pose that's a good reason,' Squeaky said grudgingly.

Worm was used to him and took no notice at all. Instead he looked hopefully at Monk.

'Thank you,' Monk said to him, also ignoring Squeaky. 'We are planning how to get Hester back. I hope you are staying here all the time so you can look after Claudine?' He fixed Worm with a steady gaze.

Worm nodded gravely. 'Yeah, I am. All the time.'

'Thank you,' Monk accepted. 'And thank you for the tea.'

'She says ter drink it while it's 'ot,' Worm added. 'Cold tea don't do no good.' He looked at the plate. 'Cake's good any time.'

Monk looked at the piece of fruitcake. He broke it into halves and offered one piece to Worm.

Worm gulped. 'It's yours.'

'You may have half of it,' Monk told him.

Worm was a little boy – he had resisted once; that was enough. He took the cake and ate it in two mouthfuls.

Monk watched him go out of the door, and ate the rest himself. Then he sipped the tea. It was certainly still very hot.

'Let's begin,' he said to Squeaky.

Once he had the article in his hand, Monk left the clinic and caught a hansom directly to the river, then he took a ferry to the Greenwich wharf. By then he had the article he and Squeaky had compiled so clearly in his mind he could have recited it. It was short, vivid, even garish, but the relish in the fall of Hamilton Rand and his execution by the rope was realistic, and brutal. Such newspapers as *The Times* would not have printed such a thing – they would have been far more restrained, even philosophical – but even so, it would be read by the people whose opinions both Magnus and Hamilton Rand cared about. It would be published by the papers that caught the eye in the street, quoted on billboards, and seen by one's neighbours, whether they wished to or not.

Monk paid the ferryman, then climbed the steps and walked the short distance to the hospital. The warm sun shone at his back, the light was brilliant on the water, and the sound of distant voices came to him on the breeze. This bank was his home. If he looked up the hill he could see some of the trees, billowing like green clouds, that he could see from the windows of his own house. He had been happier here than any other place in his life.

Actually, considering that more than half his life was lost in amnesia that was a rash statement. Yet he had no doubt whatever that it was true. If he had lived anywhere else as he lived here, then surely some echo of it would remain? Small things would remind him: the perfume of grass, the sound of a woman's laughter, a familiar footstep, the curve of a cheek, or throat, the colour of her hair . . .

He would do whatever was necessary to make Magnus Rand tell him where his brother was. He would dredge up any memory, ignite any fear . . .

He marched up to the hospital entrance and went in, looking neither to left or right. Someone called out to him and he ignored them. He knew where Rand's office was and he would either find him there, or wait for him. This was not to be done in public, for many reasons. If he did it in front of Rand's colleagues who respected him, possibly even liked him, certainly owed him some duty of loyalty, then they would all side with him, maybe even to forcibly removing Monk.

Also, if they were in front of those about whose opinion he cared, Rand would have an almost insuperable reason not to yield any information at all.

Magnus was standing staring at the bookcase, obviously searching for a particular title. He swung around as Monk came in. He did not bother to hide his annoyance.

'I have already told you, Mr Monk, I have no idea where my brother is. Not that I would necessarily tell you if I did. Your wife is an excellent nurse. She has rare experience in certain areas that are useful to us, and if she chose to go with him, and has not informed you, then that is her own concern. Such things happen. And finally, Mr Monk, I do not know you very well, but if you are as overbearing with her as you are with me, then I could understand her choice.' He looked across at Monk with defiance in his face, as if he had won some kind of victory within himself.

For an instant Monk was furious, then a wave of incredulity swept over him. That was so unlike Hester. But did every man think that he knew his wife so well he could understand everything about her, when actually he knew only the thinnest of outer layers, and all the hurt of her was hidden? Perhaps because he did not wish to see it? Might it reveal more of him than he wished to know?

Did Magnus Rand really believe what he was saying to Monk? Or was it a prepared defence?

Monk smiled thinly. 'Of course, if that were so, Dr Rand, I might be the last one to realise it. But your brother also took with him three children who are not old enough to make any decisions as to where they wish to go. The youngest is barely four years old. That is kidnap, Dr Rand.'

Rand smiled without warmth, but there was still that sense that he was comfortable in himself, a belief of having the perfect defence.

'Unwanted children, Mr Monk. Tragically, the river-banks are littered with them. Homeless, hungry, desperately vulnerable to unspeakable forms of abuse . . .'

'Exactly,' Monk agreed. 'Even to being taken and kept so they can be drained of their blood to perform medical experiments on sick old men who want to live, no matter what cost to others.'

Rand was a little paler. 'That is the way you see it, Mr Monk, because it would give you the right to come in here and demand information that would justify going after your wife. The law would see it as rescuing abandoned children from starvation and sleeping in the streets, and giving them good food, clean beds and safety from attack by predators who might molest them sexually, or force them into manual labour. The medical side they would see as treating their malnutrition, and taking blood occasionally in the performance of an experiment that might save countless lives in the future. My brother will go down in history as one of the great innovators in the science of medicine.' There was a faint flush of pride in his face as he said it, and deep satisfaction.

Monk put his hands in his pockets and felt the paper that Squeaky had prepared. He was reluctant to use it, but if he did, he had one chance before it lost its power. He must lay the foundation carefully. If he wasted it he had nothing else left.

'The children were not homeless,' he said levelly. 'Their parents were desperate, and sold them to you in order to have money to feed the youngest ones. They had no idea what you were going to do with them.' He saw the sudden doubt in Rand's face. 'Do you care so much about your brother's fame in history?' He could hear his own heart beating as he waited for the answer.

This time Rand hesitated. He seemed to have retreated within himself and to be remembering, or weighing some decision.

Monk longed to interrupt him and press home his advantage, but this was too important to make the slightest error. Hester's life could hang on the balance of his judgement now. Almost certainly it did! His throat was so tight that when he swallowed he all but choked.

'Yes,' Rand said at last. 'Of course I care that he succeeds, and that he is recognised for the brilliance and dedication he has given his life to. How could I not? You have no idea what it has cost him, or you wouldn't ask.'

'What did it cost him more than most people?' Monk asked.

Rand put his elbows on the desk and leaned his head forward into his hands, scraping his hair back with his fingers.

'Hamilton was the best of us,' he said quietly. 'At least intellectually, perhaps in all ways. I never really knew Edward. He died while I was still an infant. All I can remember was the dim room, the curtains always half drawn to keep in the warmth in the winter, and the bright sun out in the summer. He was five years older than I was, but he always looked small, very thin, and very pale. He smiled at me, but he didn't speak very much.'

Monk drew in his breath to ask who Edward was, then

changed his mind. He decided to let Rand tell the story, rather than break the thread of memory and the sensation of pain by interruption.

'Of course I had no idea how ill he was,' Rand went on. 'But Hamilton knew. He was older, ten years older than I. Edward was about eight when he died. I can remember the grief. It was summer, but it was as if the whole house was permanently in a cold, grey cloud. No one laughed for a long time. It can't have been years, but it seemed like it.

'My mother died shortly after that,' Rand went on. 'My father walked around like a ghost. Time went by. Hamilton did superbly well at school. He was going to go on to university and become a doctor. It was what he dreamed of.'

Monk could imagine it easily: a boy steeping himself in the study of medicine to lose his sense of grief, and perhaps to learn the one skill whose practitioners had failed his family.

'I wanted the same,' Rand went on. 'But I was a long way behind Hamilton – in years, of course, but neither had I the brilliance of intellect he had. Then our father died, and there was no money. Hamilton gave up his studies and found a job. It wasn't one that he liked, but he earned sufficient to keep us both, and eventually to pay for my place at university. I became the doctor he had always wanted to be.'

In spite of himself, Monk felt a deep pity for them both. It was easy to imagine the brothers, the loyalty and sacrifice between them, the duty to live a life for both of them, and perhaps even for Edward as well.

He looked at Rand, waiting for him to continue.

Rand sighed. 'At last I was earning enough to support us both. Hamilton could give up the job he had come to hate, and take up his studies again. He felt it was too late, and too expensive for him to qualify in medicine. But he was brilliant in many directions. It was not hard for him to qualify in chemistry, at which he excelled.'

'What did Edward die of?' Monk asked, almost certain what the answer would be.

'White blood disease,' Rand said softly. 'Did you not realise that?'

'I supposed,' Monk answered. 'And yes, Hamilton paid a very high and selfless price for his medical skill. But he chose to. These children did not choose to die for it, and they might well do. Which I think you know.'

Rand looked tired, his thick hair tousled.

'I have already told you, Mr Monk, I do not know where they have gone. I imagine Hamilton did not tell me precisely because he knew you would come asking.'

Monk raised his eyebrows. 'And he didn't trust you not to tell me?'

'Of course he did!' Rand was hurt. 'He knows my loyalty. He is protecting me so I cannot be to blame.' He looked angry, belligerent.

'To blame for what?' Monk asked, keeping his voice soft. 'For the deaths of the children? Or my wife?'

Rand's skin blanched. 'What are you talking about? He's not taking your wife's blood. Don't you understand anything? It's only the children's blood that is any good. It works on anyone, everyone! We just don't know why yet. Without knowing why, we can't tell who else's blood will work. It's only a fortunate experiment, not a system. For God's sake, man, think what it would mean!' He leaned forward across the desk. 'Think of the lives it would save! We have to know—'

'I know you're not taking her blood,' Monk cut across him. 'But if this doesn't work, if Radnor dies, then you won't need her any more. Do you imagine he will let her walk away?'

Rand looked haggard. 'She helped! She can't say anything. In exchange for the children's lives . . . he'll . . .'

Monk looked at him witheringly. 'Reality, Dr Rand. That is a chance he won't take. Once she is gone, with the children safe, why would he trust her to remain silent? Or the children either, for that matter?'

'You're speaking as if he's a monster!' Rand almost choked on his own words. 'He's not! He's a brilliant man, brave enough to take the risks one has to, to discover new cures, new procedures to save uncountable lives in the future. Can't you see that? It's like . . . it's like setting sail alone across the ocean and finding a new continent.' The wonder in his eyes was momentarily like that of the child he must have been when Edward died, and Hamilton gave up his dreams to care for his family.

Monk put his hand in his pocket again and pulled out Squeaky's mock newspaper article.

'I don't think they'll see him as the discoverer of a new continent,' he said gravely, looking at Rand. 'I think it will be more like this.' He put the paper down on the desk and smoothed it out.

Rand saw it and frowned. 'What the devil is this?' he demanded.

'How I think the future will see your brother,' Monk replied. 'Read it.'

Rand read it slowly, and every vestige of blood drained from his face. For seconds he was too stunned to speak, too appalled.

'It's time to face reality,' Monk said more gently. 'Hamilton cannot afford to let them go. Whether Radnor lives or dies, he will be exposed if they live. As soon as he doesn't need Hester, he'll kill her. The children he may save for longer, or if not them, at least their blood. He'll keep them imprisoned as long as they survive. It's likely none of them will attempt to escape because they'd have to leave the smallest one behind. He's only four. He wouldn't make it.'

Rand started to shake his head, to deny it all, but his whole body was trembling.

'And that alone will hang your brother,' Monk continued. He loathed what he was doing but Hester's life depended on it, as well as those of the three children, and the happiness, perhaps even the sanity of their mother.

'Is that his legacy to the future, Dr Rand? A man who bleeds children to death for his experiments, and murders the nurse who tries to save them? Tried and hanged, by common consent of the public . . .'

Rand jerked to his feet. 'Stop it!' he shouted furiously, his voice blurred with pain. 'That's not who he is. You're wrong – terribly wrong. He's a great man.'

'Then you have no need to conceal him,' Monk replied, standing up as well. 'Where is he? Please God it is not already too late.'

'I've told you, I don't know! He didn't tell me!' Rand was close to losing all control of his emotions. He was ash-pale and swaying on his feet.

'Sit down and think,' Monk commanded him. 'You've known him all your life. Where would he go? Where have you gone in the past? Does he know anyone with property he could use?'

Rand put his hands over his face.

'Stop it! I can't think . . .'

'Yes you can,' Monk insisted. 'You have the intelligence and the self-command. You don't faint at the sight of blood. You don't panic when people are injured and need you. Now use your mind, your memory. Have you friends with a house in the country? We've looked and can find nothing under your name. But that means little. Where do you have relatives? Take holidays? Where does your family come from?'

Rand stared at Monk as if he had risen out of the ground in a stench of sulphur.

'My aunt Betty had a cottage on the Estuary. She left it to us—'

'Where exactly? Kent side, or Essex?'

'Kent. Little village called Redditch. It's outside the centre. It used to be a farm.'

'Name of the farm?'

'Long Meadow,' Rand replied so softly it was almost inaudible. 'Don't hurt him . . .'

Monk took a deep breath and let it out in a sigh. 'Not willingly,' he answered, hoping it was a promise he could keep. If Hamilton Rand had hurt Hester, he would kill him.

Chapter Nine

'WE NEED to get a cart of some kind that doesn't look like we come from the city,' Scuff said thoughtfully. 'One o' them they take stuff in to the market.'

They were in the sitting room in Paradise Row: Monk, Scuff, and Hooper, who was still aching from his recent injury. As the summer faded it was getting dark earlier every day. Monk looked at Scuff with surprise that he should imagine he was coming on this mission.

'It could be rough,' he told him quietly. 'I don't know how many people Rand will have there, and they may be armed.'

Scuff stared straight back at him without flinching. 'Yer tellin' me yer could get shot? Killed, even?'

'Anybody could,' Monk answered honestly. To lie about it would help nothing, and only make Scuff feel even more excluded.

Scuff's gaze did not waver. 'Then yer no different from me,' he pointed out. 'I can do things.'

Monk was momentarily at a loss for an answer. He wanted to protect Scuff, make sure that in this tragedy at least he was unhurt. Hester would never stop grieving if Scuff came to harm in rescuing her.

'I'm coming.' Scuff did not wait for him. 'We're going for Hester, and kids that were just like I was. I'll be useful. An' Mr 'Ooper's still hurt. Yer need me. We got ter do this.'

'Yes, I do,' Monk agreed. 'But you have to do as you're told!'

'I will,' Scuff promised, nodding his head.

Monk did not believe him, but it was not the time to argue.

'He's right,' Hooper observed. 'We need a farm cart of some sort. Something that won't draw attention on a country road. We've no chance of taking them if we don't get them by surprise. I'll see if anyone knows of someone who has a dray we can use.'

'Squeaky would,' Scuff said eagerly. 'He can get anything if 'e wants it bad enough.' He did not add that for Hester he would, but Monk knew it was in his mind. 'I can go tell him.'

Monk glanced at Hooper, then back at Scuff. 'Good. Go and ask him. We need it before sunrise tomorrow morning. We've no time to lose. I'd go now, except we have to wait for light. We can't do it in strange lanes at night.'

'I gotter tell him what for,' Scuff pointed out.

'Of course,' Monk agreed reluctantly. 'There's no help for that. Tell him as much as you need to so he understands, and that it can't wait. Tell him I'll pay whatever I need to.'

Scuff gave a brief smile, and then picked his jacket off the coat stand where it hung beside Monk's, and a moment later he was outside and they heard the door close.

Monk and Hooper bent to study the maps they had of the area where Magnus Rand had said the cottage was. They could see the main roads, but there would be many lanes and by-roads unmarked. There was much planning needed, with variations to cover the unforeseen that might happen.

Scuff set out at a run on his errand to Squeaky Robinson. The light was hazy across the water already and the colour deepening in the west. He caught the first ferry he could, jammed on the seat next to a fat man with a bowler hat that was too large for him and resting on his ears. Scuff paid his fare before they pulled out into the current, and he leaped ashore as soon as they touched against the stone steps on the further side.

Normally he would wait for an omnibus, and change as many times as necessary to get at least as far as Gray's Inn Road. Now he ran out into the traffic and hailed a hansom. He was surprised that the driver did not question his ability to pay. Perhaps at least he looked like a young man, not the boy he felt inside.

'As fast as yer can,' he asked. 'I want ter go to the clinic in Portpool Lane, opposite the brewery.'

'You sick?' the cabby looked at him dubiously.

Scuff stretched the truth a little, or perhaps rather a lot.

'No. My mother's the doctor there. Please 'urry.'

The cabby looked dubious, but when Scuff put two shillings in his hand, he stopped discussing the matter and urged his horse forward.

Scuff knew he had given the cabby ample to cover the journey, so as soon as the cab swung in towards the kerb in Portpool Lane he leaped out and ran across the narrow pavement and in through the door.

The woman sitting at the desk looked up immediately, expecting an emergency. Then she recognised Scuff and it ceased to be medical and became personal. She rose from her seat and hurried towards him, her freckled face both eager and frightened.

'Hello, Ruby,' he said hastily. 'I need ter see Mr Robinson, very quick. Is 'e in 'is office?'

'I expect,' she replied. 'D'yer want me ter—'

'No, thanks.' He brushed past her, ran along the narrow corridor and swung round at Squeaky's door. He knocked, then opened it and went in anyway, closing it hard behind him.

Squeaky opened his mouth to give him a piece of his mind

about such manners. Then he saw Scuff's face and for once held his tongue.

'We know where she is.' Scuff leaned forward over the desk scattered with the usual papers, letters and scraps of calculation. 'We got ter go, tomorrow, and rescue 'er. We've got ter creep up on 'em, like, so they don't know it's us. There could be guns. It's in the country. Yer've got to 'elp, please!'

Squeaky stared at him, his over-long hair wild, his gaunt face filled with outrage. 'You suggesting as maybe I wouldn't? Watch your tongue, boy! I'll box your ears for you, after we done this. Where is she? What does Monk say? He sent you, or you come on your own? Guns, eh?'

Scuff took a deep breath and steadied himself. 'It's a farm cottage we got ter get to as early as we can, but it's all lanes and tracks, so we can't do it in the dark. They can't know 'oo we are . . . even think it!'

'Slow down! Slow down!' Squeaky said, gesturing with his hands. 'Who's "we"?'

'Monk and Mr 'Ooper an' me,' Scuff replied. He changed his weight from one foot to the other in his impatience. 'Yer can find a cart fer us, if yer want to! Yer can find anything at all, if yer want to enough.'

Squeaky stood up. 'Of course I can,' he agreed. 'How many people has this cart got to carry? That's what I need to know.'

Scuff swallowed. 'Us three, and Hester and the three children 'e took fer their blood.'

'God Almighty! Took for their blood! What d'yer mean, boy?'

''E's making experiments . . .'

'How d'you know that?' Squeaky narrowed his eyes. 'You listening in to wot you shouldn't, eh?'

'Only a bit! Are yer goin' ter get us a cart or not?'

''Course I am!'

'I'll come with yer. I . . . I s'pose I got ter drive it.' That was a frightening thought. He knew the river, but horses were a completely different matter. However, he couldn't afford to let anyone see that he was afraid.

Squeaky looked him up and down and there was something in his eyes that could have been respect.

'Come on, then,' he said abruptly, as if Scuff had kept him waiting. 'We'll go and find a horse and cart.'

Scuff straightened up instantly. 'Yes, sir!' he said, before realising he had actually called Squeaky 'sir', and it was too late to take it back.

The errand took longer than expected. There seemed too often to be reason or an excuse. The cart was too large, too small, one wheel was broken, the horse was lame, or the price was ridiculous. The last Scuff would have given in to, and paid whatever was asked, but Squeaky hushed him sharply, and walked away. The lamps were lit and it was completely dark by the time they had found a very good cart and bought a load of hay to go along with it for authenticity.

'And to hide anything we might want to,' Squeaky added. 'Best that people don't know what they don't have to.'

Scuff understood. This must succeed. Anything that would make it better, safer, was good. He even agreed to go home quietly and trust Squeaky to arrive at four o'clock in the morning, with the horse and cart, so they could set out from Paradise Row just before dawn. That way they would be well out of the area where they were known before other people were on the roads.

'By the time we're passing people who are up, they'll be farmers,' Squeaky pointed out. 'Best we be invisible. An' that means Mr Monk's gotter get out of his clothes that fit him like he had a tailor cut 'em for him special. Which I dare say he does! Better not to look like a waterman neither, not as far from the river as we'd be going.'

'We?' Scuff asked, and then wished he hadn't, but it was too late.

Squeaky turned to look at him. 'You gonner tell me you can drive a horse all that way, and back again? You don't just tell horses, you know. They got minds o' their own, like anybody else. You've got to go an' rescue Miss Hester, an' them kids, never no mind arguing with a horse what doesn't understand you anyway.'

Scuff nearly asked him if the horse understood him, but he didn't really want the answer. He broke all his natural instincts and agreed without argument.

He even repeated it very firmly when he arrived home at Paradise Row to tell Monk that he had succeeded.

Monk thanked him, gave him a thick, cold meat sandwich and told him to go to bed. He would be wakened at half-past three to get ready, in the assumption that Squeaky would keep his word and be there by four.

Hooper was coming with them. He would sleep in the sitting room, and be ready also.

'That all?' Scuff asked nervously. 'Just us?'

'You can change your mind,' Monk said, his voice suddenly gentle. 'We don't know how many there are of them, possibly just Rand and whatever staff he has. But Laker has to run the station. He isn't fit for this yet, and we can't all leave. The other men have their regular duties. I can't take them off police work.'

Scuff swallowed. 'I'm coming.'

Monk nodded, frowning a little. 'I know. But you must do as you're told. You are part of a team. Any man disobeys, he endangers the rest of us. Understand?'

'Yes, I do,' Scuff said decisively. 'I'll do it exactly. I promise.'

It did not prove to be as difficult to keep his word as Scuff had thought, at least not at first. He would have promised anything at all rather than be left behind.

Squeaky arrived exactly when he had said he would. He was unrecognisable at first. He appeared out of the shadows at the end of the street, seeming to dissolve into the darkness between one streetlamp and the next, taking form again as he passed under the brief light. He was bent forward over the reins, his gnarled hands half-hidden by fingerless gloves. There was an ancient, dented top hat on his head and his long, grey hair straggled out of it on either side. He wore what was either a cape or a ragged coat; it was impossible to tell which. But all that mattered to Scuff was that he chose a large wagon piled with loose hay, a pitchfork skewered into the largest heap. The whole was pulled by a powerful horse, too good for the contraption it was yoked to.

Monk and Hooper were waiting at the kerb.

'Excellent,' Monk said, sizing it up at a glance. 'Thank you.' Even without Squeaky being able to see his face, Monk's gratitude was evident.

Squeaky held on to the reins. 'Get in and let's be going.'

Monk looked at Squeaky and then at the horse. 'Thank you,' he said again, and climbed up into the cart, swinging his leg over the side, and sitting down in the hay.

Hooper gave Scuff a hoist up, and then followed him.

They travelled in silence, apart from the steady sound of the horse's hoofs on the road, and the creak of the cart. No one spoke, each alone with his thoughts. Scuff looked sideways at Monk a few times, wondering if he was planning what they would do, or if he were merely remembering better times, thinking of when they were all three of them together at home, worried perhaps, but safe. He thought he saw anxiety in Monk's face, but even in the broadening dawn, there was still mostly just shadow.

Did Monk know what they were going to find when they got to this place? Would there be lots of people there, and they would have to fight? Scuff half hoped they would. He

173

wanted to hurt the people who had taken Hester. He was pretty good at the sort of snapping that happened at school now and then. But this would be different. The men might have knives, even guns. What if Hester had been injured? She would have fought when they took her. That thought was so painful he forced it out of his mind. He found his throat tight and his mouth dry.

He started to watch the hedges and the road instead. As the sun rose, he distinguished fields on either side of them, copses of trees in many, and cattle slowly stirring. Most of them were standing up; he wondered if that was how they slept.

Still no one spoke.

Hooper glanced at him once or twice, as if to make sure he was all right. Scuff liked Hooper. There was something in the way Hooper looked at him that made him feel good.

There seemed to be an awful lot of countryside, miles and miles of it, all wide open, as if there were no other cities. Then Scuff realised that they were avoiding the villages, except the smallest ones, and he felt silly for not having understood that they would do that.

He was very glad when they stopped for a late breakfast. The horse needed a break and a drink as well, although Squeaky was very careful not to let it have too much.

'Why do you do that?' Scuff asked as they were standing in the yard of the inn, early sunlight splashing pale gold on the cobblestones. ''E's thirsty. E's bin pulling us all this way.'

'He's a she,' Squeaky corrected him. 'And horses can drink too much, and then get sick. I got a couple o' carrots for her. D'yer want to give them to her?'

Scuff thought about it for a moment. Now he was standing on the ground, the horse seemed very large. Then he saw Squeaky's smile.

''Course I do!' he said abruptly. 'Gimme the carrots, then!'

Squeaky handed them over. 'Hold your hand flat, like this. You don't want her to take your fingers as well. Fingers aren't good for her.'

Scuff gave him a dark look and took the carrots. He walked over to the horse and held them out on the palm of his hand, trying to appear as if he fed horses every day.

The horse took them delicately, blowing warm breath at him. He watched her face as she chewed them and then searched him hopefully for more.

'I in't got no more,' he told her. 'Yer not got to eat too much, or it'll make yer sick. Don't yer know that?'

The horse nudged him again, harder. That was the moment when he saw movement in the hay on the cart. It was just a slight fidget, as if there was something alive inside it.

He did not like rats at all, but he was used to them – or he had been, when he lived on the river edges. He would far rather find it when he was standing on the ground than if he were sitting in the hay next to it. He seized a handful of the hay and pulled it. He found Worm, crunched back as far as he could get, staring at him with wide eyes.

He was about to demand what the hell Worm was doing here, but the answer was obvious. He wanted to help too.

'Wot the 'ell do you think Miss Claudine is going to do when she finds yer gone?' he shouted. 'She'll go crazy! She'll take the clinic apart looking for you.'

Worm crept a few inches forward. 'No she won't,' he hissed, trying to keep his voice down. 'I left 'er a note tellin' 'er.'

'Yer can't write, yer stupid little article!' Scuff said desperately. 'And we 'aven't got time ter take yer back now.'

Worm wriggled another foot forward. 'Ruby wrote it for me,' he answered. 'An' yer can't blame 'er. She just wrote it for a message, an' I put me name after. I can write me name. She showed me that, an' all!'

Scuff used a few choice words he thought he had forgotten,

but Worm understood them perfectly, and did not even blink.

Scuff felt a heavy hand on his shoulder and jumped.

'Yer shouldn't oughter use words like that,' Worm said sententiously, but looking beyond Scuff at Squeaky standing behind him.

'And you shouldn't ought to be here,' Squeaky said sternly. 'I told you that before.'

Worm said nothing.

Scuff turned round and saw Monk and Hooper approaching them, Monk's face dark with anger as he saw Worm.

Worm looked frightened, but he didn't move.

It was Squeaky who spoke.

'Got a stowaway,' he said casually. 'Wants to help. We'll make the little beggar work for it. One thing about him is that no one will take any notice of him.' He looked steadily at Monk, barely even blinking.

'Did you know he was there?' Monk demanded.

'No,' Squeaky replied.

From the expression on his face Monk had no idea whether to believe him or not.

Scuff did not, but he said nothing.

Monk looked at Worm. 'You'd better do exactly . . . exactly what you're told. We're going after men who will kill children. Do you understand?'

Worm nodded.

'I suppose you're hungry?' Monk added.

Again Worm nodded.

With a sigh Monk broke his thick slice of bread in half and offered one piece to Worm.

Watching Monk's face all the time, Worm reached out and took it. He ate it in thirty seconds.

They travelled steadily, according to the directions Monk had wrung out of Magnus Rand. The doctor had been reluctant, but by then deeply afraid that his brother would be disgraced, and if any of the children died, even hanged.

By late morning they were in the right general area. After a few errors and a couple of enquiries, they found an unnamed outlying farm close to Redditch. It answered Rand's description almost exactly.

'Looks right,' Hooper said, staring at it from the road. It was an old farmhouse, a hundred and fifty yards away along a dirt track. The thatch on the roof was in need of repair, but it was surrounded by fertile land. There were several fields close by. Looking to be within its boundaries was an orchard with thirty or more apple and pear trees, and a group of outhouses huddled nearby, seemingly well maintained. A kitchen garden, even seen from a distance, looked neat and weeded, as if receiving constant attention.

'If this is it,' Monk said guardedly, 'then Rand has someone here all the time. Weeds grow pretty fast in good earth like this.'

'Gardener?' Hooper suggested, his eyes searching all of the land he could see.

'Maybe. Could be more staff than that.' Monk followed Hooper's gaze. There were a score of places where a man could be unseen from the road.

Squeaky said nothing.

'I'll go and look,' Scuff offered, his mouth was so dry he stumbled over the words.

'Send Worm,' Squeaky interrupted. 'They'll take no notice of 'im.' Without waiting for Monk's approval, he turned to Worm, who was standing a few feet away. 'You go just as far as that bend – see?' He pointed to the cart track. 'Look at what you can see from there, then come back and tell us. Right?'

'Yeah. Right,' Worm agreed, and started off at a brisk walk. Monk made a lunge to grab him back, but Worm eluded him as easily as an eel in the river, and scampered off towards the bend in the track. Monk swung back to face Squeaky, and the argument died on his lips. They had no time to waste on reconnaissance, and they all knew it.

They stood close together in the sharp, early light. Monk, Squeaky, Hooper and Scuff watched the small figure of Worm as he reached the corner, looked around him carefully, and then went on towards the front door.

Monk swore under his breath.

Hooper put a hand hard on his shoulder. 'Don't stop him, sir. We've no time to lose if this isn't the place.'

'And how is Worm going to know if it is or not?' Monk said savagely.

No one answered him.

Worm had disappeared out of sight. The seconds ticked by, dragging out until time seemed endless. There was no sound but the wind in the trees, a ticking of insects in the long grass at the sides of the road, and the occasional snap as a seed head burst in the strengthening heat of the sun. A bee wound its way lazily through the hedgerow flowers. Sheep bleated in the distance.

It was almost unbearable.

Scuff did not dare to look at Monk.

Then at last they saw Worm coming back along the dirt track, not quite at a run, but moving quickly. He arrived breathless, and it was only then that Scuff noticed he was barefoot.

'Well?' Monk could not help himself asking.

Worm nodded vigorously. His face was flushed. 'There was two women in the kitchen. I'm almost sure one of them were Miss Hester. There was sheets on the laundry line, an' a nightshirt, big.' He stretched his arms wide without ever taking his eyes off Monk's face. 'An' there's a big man, like 'im.' He jerked his hand at Hooper. 'But 'e's got a long gun, an' 'e walks around the garden all the time. But 'is 'ands is dirty, like 'e digs in the ground a lot. 'E told me ter get out of it, an' if I come back 'e'd shoot me, like a rabbit.' He swallowed hard, still staring hopefully at Monk, longing for his approval.

'Two women in the kitchen?' Monk asked him.

'Yeah,' he nodded.

'How much did one of them look like Miss Hester? A lot, or a little bit?'

'A lot. 'Ceptin' 'er 'air were all screwed back like she didn't care. Not . . . pretty, like.'

'And the gardener carried a gun?' Monk pressed.

Worm gulped and nodded.

Monk glanced at Hooper.

'Then we must take the gardener first.' Monk made the decision. They would get no better information than this. He touched Worm lightly on the shoulder. 'Thank you. You did very well. From now on you will do what you are told, or I will have to tie you to the wagon. You promise?'

Worm nodded, but he was smiling, flushed with the praise. He had helped.

They studied what they could see of the landscape for a few more minutes, and then began to lay plans as to how they could flush the gardener out of the immediate surrounds of the house so that they could ambush him and take his gun. It was finally agreed that Worm would lure him out, from a distance.

'I can do that,' Scuff said immediately.

'No, you can't,' Monk told him grimly. 'You're getting too big. At a distance he'll take you for a man. We have to let Worm do it again. Your job will be to attract his attention later.' He bent and drew a rough diagram in the dust at the side of the road. 'I will be here, Squeaky there. Hooper will come this way and when Worm gets to here, Scuff will go this way and get Worm out of there. Do you understand? We must give him too many targets to be certain which way to shoot. Hooper, when he turns this way, please God before he can shoot me, hit him as hard as you can with the pitch fork.'

'Yes, sir.' Hooper already had the fork from the hay in his hands.

'Right,' Monk accepted. 'Nothing to wait for. Everyone clear?'

They agreed as one. Hooper set off to the right, Squeaky to the left with Scuff on his heels.

Worm set off down the middle of the track again with Monk close to the hedges, moving then stopping, keeping ten yards behind at least. He felt guilty for using Worm, even more because of the child's eagerness to please and to belong, even at this risk. He had racked his brains for another way, and found nothing. Now he needed to think, to watch, to be ready for anything.

He saw the gardener before Worm did. He was standing half concealed by a dense bush, watching the boy.

Worm walked on. From what Monk could see, he had no idea that the gardener was only feet away from him, and still with that gun. It was a shotgun. He could hardly miss with it.

Should Monk shout? It would distract the gardener for a moment, but it would also distract Worm, perhaps long enough for the man to level the gun and fire it. Or even to lunge out from behind the bush and seize Worm, even kill him accidentally with his sheer weight.

Monk bent, and picked up the largest stone he could find and hurled it at the gardener. He did not believe he could hit him, but he could certainly distract him long enough to give Worm a head start. Please heaven he ran back towards Monk, or sideways towards Hooper! Squeaky was out to the left, but he was an old man and unfit, used to forging papers and deceiving tax men, not physical fights.

The stone struck the bush, shaking the branches and landing heavily.

The gardener swung round, fearing attack.

Worm took to his heels, running this way and that, like an eel through river weed.

The gardener ran after him, waving the gun. His legs were far longer, his stride three of Worm's, but the gun hampered him and he was slow at changing direction. Nevertheless, he was gaining ground. The distance between them closed.

Then suddenly the gardener hurtled through the air and crashed face down on the earth, arms thrashing, legs jerking and twisting as if tied together.

Squeaky bent and picked up the fallen gun. Holding it by the barrel, he swung it back and crashed it into the gardener's head. The man went utterly limp, as if he were dead.

Monk sprinted down the slight incline towards them and arrived just as Squeaky patted Worm on the head. 'Well done, boy,' he said calmly. 'Got yer wits about you.'

Worm's eyes were full of tears, but he refused to cry.

Monk looked down at the gardener, at the blood on the side of his head, at his chest heaving as he struggled to breathe, and at his legs, which were loosely tied together with a length of very thin rope, one end of which was knotted around a heavy spanner.

Squeaky shrugged. 'Pity to waste a good length o' rope,' he said with a very slight smile. 'Most folk chasing don't look so careful where they put their feet.'

'You threw it out around him?' Monk said incredulously. 'Where did you learn that?'

'Timing,' Squeaky answered, his smile wide, showing his crooked teeth. 'Good thing, timing.'

'I'll take the gun.' Monk held out his hand and Squeaky passed it over.

Hooper appeared, glancing at the gun in Monk's hand and

the gardener on the ground. Then he saw Squeaky's face, and Worm, who was still very pale, and worked out what must have happened. He picked up the length of rope and tested its strength. He moved to tie the man's hands together.

'Before you do that,' Monk said quickly. 'Take his jacket off. His hat's over there. I'll put them on and go in. Hooper, take the gun and go around the front, in case Rand tries to escape that way. Squeaky, you stand guard over the gardener, when we've finished tying him up. Hit him again if you have to. There's a good strong stake in the ground over there, holding that young tree up. Lash him to that. Scuff?'

'Yes?' Scuff stepped forward eagerly.

'Go and fetch the horse and wagon. Drive it down here carefully and wait. We'll need it close by if we've got sick people to carry out. Squeaky'll help you turn it around so we can go straight out, maybe in a hurry.' He glanced at Hooper busy tying up the gardener, who was beginning to stir into consciousness again. 'Don't use more rope than you have to,' he warned. 'We may have more people needing it. Rand won't come easily. Maybe Miss Radnor won't either.'

'Got plenty, sir,' Hooper said cheerfully, giving the end of the rope a hard jerk to tighten the knot. That brought the gardener back to full consciousness, and he started to howl in pain.

'Quiet!' Hooper told him sharply.

The gardener glared at him, met his eyes, and was silent.

Hooper checked the gun to make certain it was loaded and the action smooth. Then he moved slowly towards the side of the house and the front door.

Scuff and Worm went reluctantly up the lane towards the horse and wagon.

Squeaky glared at the gardener then gave Monk a nod, almost a salute, as he moved quickly and quietly towards the back of the house and the kitchen door.

Worm had said he had seen two women in the kitchen,

and he was almost sure that one of them was Hester, which meant that the other would be Adrienne Radnor. Had they become friends, or deeper enemies? What was Monk about to walk into?

One mistake now and it could still end in tragedy. If Adrienne had a kitchen knife in her hand and panicked, she might do anything.

He pulled the gardener's cap further forward over his face. Did the gardener usually knock before he went in? Was he an ally of Rand's? An employee? A servant? A debtor over some past help? Even a relative? Or another experiment?

He had shown a streak of violence when he had seen Worm a second time. What kind of man goes after a seven-year-old child with a loaded shotgun?

A frightened one, with something very dangerous to hide.

Monk knocked on the door and immediately opened it. He was in the back entrance to a large, farmhouse kitchen. Across the stone-paved floor, about ten feet away in the middle of the room, Adrienne Radnor was standing with a large-bladed vegetable knife in her hand, chopping carrots on a wooden board. For an instant she took no notice of Monk. Then she realised he was not the gardener and her eyes widened. Her hands clenched the handle of the knife and she came towards him, eyes narrowed and the blade held at the ready, low, as if she would jab with it.

Monk moved over towards the huge, black cooking range. It was hot. There were pans on it with stew coming to the boil, and a bubbling pot in another of the sort in which you cook puddings. There was enough food to satisfy eight or ten people.

The rack on which the empty pans stood was a foot away from his right hand.

She was moving forwards, closer to him with the knife blade pointing at his stomach.

He seized one of the smaller, copper saucepans and hit her on the arm with it as hard as he could. He felt it jar on bone, and the knife clattered to the floor. Adrienne gasped with pain and the blood drained from her face. She sank to her knees on the floor, her arm hanging uselessly.

For a moment there was silence.

She drew in her breath to scream.

Monk picked another of the saucepans. 'Don't,' he said quietly. 'That arm won't mend if I hit it again. Sit down on that chair and stay there. I don't want to have to tie you, but I can't leave you loose.'

He kicked the knife out of the way, far enough so she could not reach it, then helped her up and on to the chair. There was enough strong kitchen twine to lash her to it beyond her ability to get free. He was surprised how many nautical knots came to him from some recesses of his memory.

Monk left her there and went silently through the door into the hall, listening for any sound of human presence. It was several moments before he was able to hear the murmur of voices.

He tiptoed to the door and listened again. He heard a man's voice, then another different male voice, then finally a woman's. He could not make out the words but he knew Hester's tone, the music of it, whatever she said.

He put his fingers around the handle and turned. It gave at his touch, and he threw it open.

Inside the room was a large bed. Propped upon pillows lay an elderly man, his face gaunt as with illness, but powerful, vividly alive. His arm was strapped around the upper part and a needle held into his skin, piercing it, attached to a glass tube filled with red. It could only be blood. The tube led to a bottle, which was suspended from a metal, wire and cord contraption next to the bed.

Hester stood to the left of it, still dressed in her blue-grey nurse's working clothes. They were crumpled and soiled with blood, as if she had worn them for days. But the joy that flooded her face when she saw Monk made her as beautiful as any woman alive.

Rand, white with fury, his eyes glittering, was just beyond her. Quick as a cat he seized a scalpel from an instrument case and reached out to take her by the shoulder.

In a sickening instant Monk knew what he intended to do. He would cut her throat if Monk did not retreat. She was, above all, what she had always been to Rand: a hostage to be used.

Hester reached forward as if to plead with Monk. Then she yanked her arm back again, hard, driving her elbow into Rand's stomach, in exactly the vulnerable place at the curve where his ribs met.

He gasped and bent over, retching. She hit him again, this time in the face, on his top lip just under the nose, which spurted blood.

Monk grasped Rand's arm and twisted it so that the scalpel fell, just as Hooper came into the room from the hallway.

Thirty minutes later it was almost over. Scuff had brought the horse and wagon closer and made soft beds in the hay for Charlie, Maggie and Mike. Radnor, protesting bitterly, was helped up to lie on the other side of the hay. Adrienne was still bound although Hester did what she could to set her broken arm and support it in a sling.

They were ready to begin the long ride home. They left the gardener where the local police would set him free, and lock up the house until the investigation could be completed. Hooper remained with him to see that everything was done legally and in order.

Squeaky drove the wagon home with Scuff to relieve him every so often. Worm sat beside them on the box, watching everything.

Hester and Monk sat side by side in the hay, occasionally ministering to the angry, hurt and reluctant prisoners. Largely they ignored them, even Radnor, who appeared to be the least disconcerted of them all.

Chapter Ten

OLIVER RATHBONE arrived home in London with an intense degree of pleasure, although he had enjoyed his stay in Edinburgh. It was a handsome and cultured city, but Scottish law was different from English, and always had been, and he found testifying – albeit as an expert witness on an old case – to be somewhat testing of both his skill and his memory.

He had taken a short holiday afterwards in the beautiful Trossach hills, and perhaps that was what had really troubled him. Their wild, almost haunting loveliness had increased his awareness of being alone. He had longed to turn to someone and say, 'Isn't that exquisite? How the light falls on the water! How the trees crowd together against the sky with such grace.' And there was no one. No degree of kindness from strangers made up for the understanding of a friend; nothing at all for the absence of love.

He did not miss Margaret, the wife who had left him after his disbarment. No, that was not true; she had left in heart long before that. It was simply the excuse that exonerated her and made it easy. He missed what he had believed they had, what he had hoped that with time it could become.

He had telegraphed ahead the hour he expected to be home, and his manservant, Dover, met him at the door before he could turn his key.

'Good evening, Sir Oliver,' he said, bowing very slightly,

satisfaction in his voice. 'It is very nice to have you home again, sir. Very much has occurred in your absence, which I am sure you will wish to know. May I bring you a light supper, sir? A cold beef sandwich, perhaps, and a glass of claret?'

Rathbone felt a warmth of familiarity wrap around him. This was a new apartment since his separation from Margaret. There had been no purpose in keeping the house. It was too large, but above all, it was the empty shell of a dream that had died. This place was elegant and almost sparse in its furnishings, and quite large enough to cater for all that really pleased him. There was no ostentation, only quality. And Dover made it seem like home. His loyalty was proven, his opinion given only when asked for.

'That would be perfect,' Oliver replied, walking ahead into the sitting room with its familiar extremely comfortable chairs. It was pleasantly warm without a fire, and there were late roses in the vase on the side table.

'Yes, sir,' Dover said quietly. 'Would you like the newspaper, sir? I have kept *The Times* from while you were away, and there is rather a large stack of them.' He frowned, as if that fact displeased him. 'It might not be the pleasantest way for you to learn the news, sir, if I may say so.'

His tone warned Rathbone that he had missed something important. He felt a chill, even in the warm room. He turned to look at the man.

'What is it that I will so dislike reading? Perhaps you had better tell me.'

'I will fetch the sandwich, Sir Oliver, and the claret.'

'No, Dover, you will tell me now!' Rathbone felt the sharpness of anxiety rich inside him.

'It is a long story, sir, and somewhat complicated. But I assure you the end is satisfactory, at least so far. What the final result will be, of course I cannot say.'

'I'll go upstairs and wash,' Rathbone replied. 'Trains always make me feel grubby. Then you will tell me whatever it is. Is . . .' He found his mouth dry. 'Is Sir Ingram York dead?'

'No, sir, not so far as I am aware.'

Rathbone felt a faint stirring of disappointment. Ingram York was the judge who had inveigled Rathbone into the case that had caused his ruin. No, that was not true. York had dug the pit for him, but Rathbone himself had stepped into it, in the arrogant belief that he could bring about justice in spite of the law, and without paying the price for it.

Ingram York was also the now mentally broken husband of Beata, whom Rathbone had learned to love in spite of all his best judgement. Best judgement! What an inappropriate term to use for his recent decisions, personal and professional.

And yet it was Beata he had wanted to turn to and share the aching, melancholy beauty of the Trossachs, of Loch Lomond with its rocky shore and glimpses of light on the water.

He returned downstairs, cleaner and no longer in his travelling clothes, but in an old smoking jacket instead. Dover had the sandwiches on the table and a glass of deep ruby-red claret warmed to room temperature, breathing its fragrance into the air.

'So what is the news?' Rathbone asked as he sat in the armchair and picked up the first sandwich.

Dover remained standing, as was his custom. He considered it the way of a good manservant to conduct himself. It was part of his identity.

'First of all, sir, I would like you to know that Mrs Monk is quite well and safe at home . . .'

Rathbone found himself suddenly almost unable to breathe.

'What do you mean, Dover? Why would she not be? What has happened? What about Monk himself?'

'Quite well, sir, but he was never in danger. It was Mrs

Monk who was kidnapped, along with three small children, apparently from the river-bank.'

Rathbone stared at him. 'Three children? Who? And for God's sake, Dover, why? Tell me the story properly, man!' He knew he was being unreasonable but he could not help himself. He was now sitting up rigidly and his sandwich and claret were forgotten.

'Mrs Monk was working at the Royal Naval Hospital at a special annexe there, mostly at nights, to stand in for a friend from her army days, who was sick herself,' Dover said steadily. 'Somehow she discovered that the doctor and chemist brothers who run that part of the place were conducting experiments on sick people, and injured ones, and using the blood of children they had picked up on the river-bank.'

Rathbone shut his eyes as if doing that would somehow close out the pictures in his imagination.

'When they realised that she knew what they were doing,' Dover continued, 'they took her and the children, along with their current patient, and went off into the countryside with them. Had them locked up in some farmhouse, both to keep them quiet and to use them for this thing they were doing. Of course, Mr Monk found out where they were, and he went and rescued them. Took the chemist brother prisoner, and the daughter of the patient they were trying to cure. They'll be coming up for trial soon. It's going to be all over the newspapers, so I thought you should know before you read it, sir.'

'Yes,' Rathbone said slowly, his mind still reeling. 'Yes, of course. You are quite right. Thank you, Dover.'

'Sir.' Dover inclined his head and turned towards the door.

'Dover?' Rathbone said quickly.

He turned back. 'Yes, sir?'

'What happened to the children?'

'Wasn't reported, sir, except that they're being taken care

of somewhere safe. Best that way, if you'll pardon my saying so, sir.'

Rathbone did not argue, but his mind was racing. He determined to find Hester the following day, and make certain for himself that she was really unhurt, and not actually far more distressed than she was allowing anyone else to know. Perhaps there was something he could do to help.

As it turned out in the morning, he was forestalled in his intentions before he had even finished his breakfast. He was still tired from the long train journey. There was no urgency to rise, since his disbarment over the case where he had so signally taken the law into his own hands. He had been permitted recently to take second chair, a mere assistant to the lawyer conducting the case. It was a position he was unused to, and in which he was uncomfortable. It was many years since he had accepted small cases: petty theft, public nuisance or minor affray. It was a long fall from where he had been before, as probably the finest criminal lawyer in the country, and then a newly acclaimed judge on the bench. The slow climb back was bitter; even at best, it was difficult.

But sleep often eluded him, and lying in bed wide awake was the most debilitating of all to the spirits. He needed to find something worthwhile to do, a cause that would stir his blood again.

He ate reasonably early. Dover was always awake and ready. Rathbone should show more appreciation of his loyalty. He had poured his second cup of tea from a fresh pot when Dover came in looking fairly smug.

'Mr Ardal Juster is here to see you, sir. He apologises for the earliness of the call, but he says it is important. Shall I bring another cup, sir? The tea is quite fresh.'

In spite of himself Rathbone felt a stir of interest, even excitement. Ardal Juster was the lawyer who had defended him in his own case, and since then had quite often asked his advice on other matters.

'Yes, by all means,' he agreed without hesitation. 'And do bring a cup for him. Ask him if he has eaten, and if he would care for something more?'

Dover disappeared and a moment later Ardal Juster came in. He was several years younger than Rathbone, in his mid-thirties, slender and dark. He was almost handsome, but the quality that took the attention most was the keenness of his face, the vitality in him.

'Good morning, Sir Oliver,' he said, holding out his hand as Rathbone rose to greet him. 'Sorry to interrupt your break-fast, but a case has arisen in your absence that I have accepted to prosecute, and I am certain will interest you, both profes-sionally and personally. I would consider your counsel inval-uable, and would actually seek more than that: your actual help in court, if you are willing?'

Rathbone gestured for Juster to take the other chair at the table. As Dover returned with a clean cup and saucer, he offered him tea, and poured it as soon as Juster inclined his head.

Dover went off to make fresh toast and Juster began imme-diately, leaning forward across the table in his eagerness.

'Are you aware yet of the kidnap of Hester Monk and the three Roberts children? All safely rescued, and Hamilton Rand taken into custody, along with Adrienne Radnor, the daughter of the patient on whom the experiments were conducted.'

'I have heard a little,' Rathbone answered, watching Juster's face, trying to assess the nature of his emotional interest. Was it outrage at the crime, fascination with the legal aspects, hunger to try his skills against powerful interests ranged in the defence? He hoped it was something better than the consid-erable fee and the chance of appearing in a highly publicised case. 'But please tell me exactly who Rand is, and what is the charge, as the law sees it,' he added.

'It is complicated.' Juster sat back a little and took a sip of his tea, but his eyes did not leave Rathbone's face. 'Hamilton Rand is a chemist of very great skill, possibly even genius, and a little madness. His brother, Magnus Rand, is a fine doctor, but not charged with him, although he may very well be an accomplice.' He was clearly weighing what he said, trying to keep emotion out of the words he chose, as well as his tone. 'They have been experimenting with the transfusion of blood from one human being to another, in order to prevent death from loss of blood in those seriously injured, and to treat illnesses such as white blood disease.' He looked enquiringly at Rathbone, waiting for him to comment.

Rathbone nodded, ignoring his own tea. A tiny worm of fear stirred inside him. 'Go on.'

'It is not a new idea,' Juster continued. 'In fact, it has been tried with varying degrees of failure for more than two centuries. If it succeeded it would be one of the greatest leaps forward in the history of medicine.'

'The point?' Rathbone prompted him.

'Hamilton Rand appears to have had some success. One of his patients is still alive, miraculously so. Or at least he was, until a couple of weeks ago. He has disappeared, but there is no reason to suppose he is dead, or even ill. His name is Bryson Radnor. It was in order to continue his treatment that Rand kidnapped the three small children whose blood seemed miraculously always to work. I gather that is highly unusual, although no one seems to know why. He also took Mrs Hester Monk, who was nursing Radnor.'

The chill inside Rathbone grew.

As if he had seen it, Juster answered the question. 'Mrs Monk was taken against her will, and remained only under duress, and in order to look after the three children, who

193

were becoming weaker and weaker as they were bled regularly, and too much—'

'But they are alive?' Rathbone interrupted. The idea of this madman, genius or not, bleeding children to death, was hideous.

'Oh, yes,' Juster assured him. 'But too young to testify. The oldest is only about seven.'

'The case is against Hamilton Rand? Kidnap?'

'Yes. And against Adrienne Radnor, the daughter of the patient, a woman in her early thirties. She was entirely complicit in the kidnap, both of the children and of Hester Monk.'

'I see.' Rathbone drank the rest of his tea. Dover came in with fresh toast and both men ate in silence while Rathbone considered the facts and Juster waited.

'The charge is kidnap,' Rathbone continued after a few moments. 'Why does the case interest you so much? Clearly it does.'

Juster smiled. 'Lots of things, Sir Oliver. Kidnap of a nurse, who cannot even attempt to escape because of the children she would leave behind; indeed, who cannot leave her patient because she is the only one skilled enough to care for him. And yet if he dies, her life may be hostage. Rand dare not let her go, alive. She must hate Radnor, but she is sworn to help any sick person, however vile, and in whatever circumstances.'

Rathbone felt his whole body chill.

'Rand is not a doctor, he is a chemist,' Juster warned him. 'He has sworn no oath to medicine. The Hippocratic oath says, "First, do no harm"! Yet how can you discover new medicine if you make no experiment that might end badly?' His face was keen with the magnitude of the thought. 'Who is to take the chances to step forward into the unknown where no one can evaluate the risks? Clearly what he did to Mrs Monk, and to the children, is wrong! But is he entirely wrong? What is the law? And what should it be?'

Rathbone nodded slowly, seeing the quagmire of Juster's argument. 'And what about Miss Radnor?' he asked. 'How much is she to blame really? And what will the law say about her?'

'Exactly,' Juster agreed, the ghost of a smile on his lips. 'And yet they must be prosecuted. If they are not, then anybody can justify anything with the defence that they were seeking new medical insights.' His voice became more urgent. 'Help me with this, Sir Oliver. Mrs Monk was deeply wronged, and I seriously believe that if Commander Monk and his men had not rescued her, then both she and the Roberts children would have paid for this with their lives. Fortunately she was not injured, as it turns out – at least not physically. But fear and imprisonment are a torture to the mind, and that also is a crime whose damage we may never be able to quantify.'

'Why me?' Rathbone asked. He was not seeking any kind of praise, not even affirmation. He could see no reason why he was suited for this case, and he knew Juster well enough to understand his ambition.

Juster smiled. 'Because you have known and cared for Mrs Monk for many years. You will fight hard, but fairly for her. You'll not try to trip her on the witness stand. And if the defence does, you'll attack them hard and mercilessly. I know your reputation with other lawyers is mixed. You are not yet fully restored to the place you want to hold. I don't know if you ever will be. But you are the best, whether it is acknowledged or not. And the public knows it, even if their Lordships of the Bar do not.' He smiled very slightly, but there was a warmth in it. 'And you never give up.'

'And you very diplomatically did not mention that I have a debt of honour to you,' Rathbone added. 'You defended me brilliantly, when no one else would, and at some risk to yourself.'

Juster's smile widened, showing white teeth. 'Really? I had forgotten that.'

Rathbone grunted. 'Indeed. Only because you are sure that I have not. Yes, I will consider the case very carefully and do all I can to be of assistance. It is, as you say, extremely interesting. Thank you. Will you have more tea . . .?'

After Juster had gone, Rathbone very carefully weighed what he had been told. He asked Dover to bring in the newspapers that had written of the incident, and he studied them all. He was perfectly aware that what newspapers wrote, even the best of them, was not necessarily the truth. It was not facts he was looking for, it was how it was reported, as that was what would form most of the public opinion.

Just after luncheon he took a hansom. He crossed the river and went along the south bank up the slight hill to Paradise Row.

'Oliver!' Hester greeted him with surprise and great pleasure. 'How good to see you! Are you well?' She regarded him carefully, as if she wanted more than the politeness of a usual answer, which was always in the affirmative.

He smiled at her. It still filled him with a strange mixture of happiness and regret to see her. He had once asked her to marry him, and he never totally forgot it, even though he acknowledged it was Monk she truly loved, and that would always be so.

'Don't talk nonsense, Hester,' he said quite gently. 'I have read the newspapers and Ardal Juster came to see me before I had even finished my breakfast. He has asked me to help him prosecute Hamilton Rand and, of course, Adrienne Radnor. I am very well. Now tell me how you are, with no polite evasions.'

'Then come inside,' she invited him. 'The sun is nice at the back and we can sit with the garden doors open and drink lemonade. I think I even have some cake.' She turned and led the way inside.

He followed her, without mentioning that it was half-past two in the afternoon, and far too early for cake.

As it happened, Scuff had eaten the cake anyway, but the lemonade was excellent. Its sweet sharp taste seemed peculiarly appropriate. The roses would last another month or two, but there was autumn in the air.

'What is it you wish to know?' Hester asked a little guardedly.

He remembered, not without pain, the time he had humiliated her in the witness stand in a case several years ago, because he had believed passionately in the cause he was fighting. She understood why he had done it, but the memory of it was in her eyes also, the lack of trust. She had made it plain she did not blame him. She would have despised him if he had served friendship before justice. She would not have placed sentiment before medicine.

He reminded her of that now.

She smiled ruefully. 'You are right,' she admitted. 'We should speak honestly now, but it isn't easy.'

'Isn't it?' Did you go with Rand willingly?'

Her eyes widened. 'No! Of course not!'

'Hester, I need to know what the defence will ask you that you may find it hard to answer. We must be prepared with the truth now, not when it is too late.'

She smiled very faintly, and her face was a little paler. 'I did not go willingly. Actually I was unconscious. I think, from the lingering smell, that they used ether. When I came around I was in an upstairs room in the cottage Rand and his brother inherited, somewhere in the country. All I could see from the window was a stretch of garden, and then the fields and slopes of hillside beyond. I had no idea where I was.'

'Who else was there?'

'Hamilton Rand, Bryson Radnor – he was the patient – his daughter, Adrienne, and the three children, Charlie, Maggie and Mike. And the gardener. He seemed to patrol the grounds most of the time. He carried a gun.'

'Do you know what kind of a gun? What did it look like? Can you describe it?'

'A double-barrelled shotgun. I'm an army nurse, Oliver; I've seen guns before. Probably thousands of them.'

'Yes, I'm sorry. I forgot.'

'And I really am all right,' she added. 'Please stop talking to me as if I were about to faint.'

'Hester, I . . .' he began, then stopped. What could he say that would not embarrass her and make her more conscious of the fact that he had once loved her so deeply? He was here now as a friend, and as a lawyer who wanted to trust her on the case so she would not be caught out on the stand when the defence would do everything they could to discredit her.

'Hester, no one is dead,' he said gravely. 'The charge is kidnap. If the defence can make it appear that you went willingly, then the case against Rand depends on the testimony of three small children, who are very young, and who can probably neither read nor write. We can't call them to the stand. The judge wouldn't believe them and the defence would tie them in knots! It rests on you, and on Monk and whoever else was with him when they found you. They are all Monk's men and the defence will most certainly point that out.'

Hester frowned, the first shadows of real anxiety in her eyes.

Rathbone leaned forward a little. 'Hester, they'll say that Monk stormed the place, and they had no idea who he was. Very naturally they fought back! Who wouldn't? If they can make it look as if you were a willing part of the experiment, then we have no case. Adrienne Radnor will very probably lie and say that you went as willingly as she did. If you did not tell your husband where you were, that is a domestic issue, and not their fault.'

She looked stunned, a little dizzy, as if he had slapped her.

'I'm sorry,' he said gently, putting his hand over hers and feeling her fingers cool and stiff, as if she were afraid of him.

'Rand would have killed me if Radnor had died,' she said. 'And worse than that, he would have bled those children to death, too, if it would have saved Radnor. He actually told me, when I argued for taking better care of them, that he didn't need all of them alive.'

'I'm not talking about the reality,' Rathbone said. 'I need what we can prove. And that has to be not what is believable, but what is beyond reasonable doubt. Any doubt at all that offers another explanation, and the jury will have to acquit both of them.'

She blinked back sudden tears. 'How can I prove that I stayed because I couldn't leave the children alone there? Maybe there'll be a juror who would have? They'll all be men, won't they!' Jurors were always men.

'Many will be married, and with children,' he replied, hating himself for doing this, although with every evasion he would feel the greater and greater need. It was almost something he could taste, like the sharpness of the lemons in the drink. 'They'll know that their wives would never leave children to be bled to death like that, frightened, alone and unloved or comforted. We may have to rely quite heavily on character witnesses.'

'For me?' she said, forcing a slight smile of self-mockery. 'I run a clinic for prostitutes,' she reminded him. 'You might be better off not raising that one.'

'An army nurse now looking after the fallen in a different war,' he said drily.

Her smile widened in spite of herself. 'What about the children? That can't be acceptable. You only have to see them to know how small and vulnerable they are. And Maggie could testify. She'd fight anyone if they threatened her brothers. No lawyer will look good if he bullies a six-year-old little girl who's been bled half to death for an experiment!'

'We can't prove that,' Rathbone said grimly. 'But it doesn't matter, because the judge won't allow the testimony of a child that age. The defence will fight tooth and nail to keep all of them off the stand.'

'But they were there!' she protested. 'That's a fact.'

'Rand will simply say he paid the family for their participation in a medical experiment. Even if it didn't work, could Rand have been close to success? Is it possible that he believed it could? Please . . . be very careful how you answer.'

Hester sat still for so long he thought she was not going to speak. Then she straightened up and faced him. 'Yes, I think he was very close indeed. And if I am asked on the stand what I thought of his medicine, I would have to say that if he succeeded, it would be one of the greatest steps forward in saving lives that I have ever heard of. It wouldn't just be people with white blood disease, it would be women bleeding to death in childbirth, anyone injured and dying from the shock of blood loss, soldiers, sailors, people in accidents of any sort – in the street, industrial – anything! It would stretch into the future beyond imagination. Think of having an operation, and not fearing the bleeding, knowing that what you lost would be replaced! There is no counting the people who would not die . . . if that could be made to work.'

He looked at her, searching her face, and he saw the wonder in her eyes.

'Will you say that on the stand?' he asked, realising that their case was vanishing in front of him.

'If I'm asked, I have to. Do we need to punish him more than we need to save all those people in the future? Anyway, it's the truth. If he succeeds, or anyone does, it would be like a miracle.'

'And whose children do we bleed?' he asked.

The colour bleached out of her face, leaving her haggard. 'We don't,' she said hoarsely. 'We find another way. That's the problem he didn't solve. Why was those children's blood all right, while other people's works sometimes and other times it doesn't? And if the blood is wrong, it's a hard and miserable way to die.'

'So his success is partial?'

'Yes. It's a step along the path, that's all. But I think it's the best step anyone has made so far. We can't say if it would have worked if he'd been able to continue.' A sudden, dark shadow filled her eyes. 'And of course if he is found not guilty, then who can even guess how many other people will try something similar?'

Rathbone had not even thought of that. He felt as if the air had suddenly turned ten degrees colder.

'Then we must be a great deal more certain of success if we prosecute,' he said quietly. 'A victory would also be validation.' He hesitated a moment, hating to ask her, afraid of the answer. 'If you are asked on the stand what you think of his work, what will you say?'

She bit her lip. 'That he was wrong to kidnap me, and deeply wrong to take the children and bleed them. But he could be on the brink of solving the problem of using willingly given human blood from one person to save the life of another. Especially if one could take a little from each of several people, adults, and given voluntarily.' She shook her head. 'I'm sorry, Oliver, but that is the truth. I can't lie about it. He's a loathsome man, but that has nothing to do with the lives that his work could save.'

'I understand. I put the law before individual people I care about, if they are wrong. I expect you to put medicine before them as well, in the same way. We must. And if we don't, then everything else is also lost, sooner or later.'

She nodded, too full of emotion to look for words that were unnecessary anyway.

Rathbone drank the last of his lemonade and stood up to leave. His mind too was crowded with conflicting thoughts and emotions. He had told Ardal Juster that he would accept the case and work beside him on it. Now he was beginning to see that the complexity of it was deeper and far more tangled than he had imagined.

Rathbone went that evening to visit Beata York. It was an impulsive idea and perhaps not very wise, but his longing to see her overrode his judgement. He realised just how much it had done so when he stood on the doorstep and had already pulled the bell rope. It was too late to leave. If he did, he would look like a naughty child who played practical jokes because he was too young to understand how silly it was, and what a nuisance to servants who had better things to do.

The butler received him with not only courtesy but charm, as if he still felt guilty over Ingram York's appalling behaviour, which was now some time ago.

'Good evening, Sir Oliver,' he said graciously. 'If you will come into the morning room I will inform Lady York that you are here.'

Still feeling self-conscious, Rathbone accepted, following the man across the now-familiar hall and into the morning room. It was still as austere as when York himself had lived here. That was before the awful night when he had completely lost his temper and attacked Rathbone with his cane, finally collapsing to the floor in some kind of seizure. Every time Rathbone came into this room since then, the horror had come back to him. It was not from fear of injury, it was shock and then desperate embarrassment at York's sudden headlong fall from what had seemed to be merely eccentric into a state of complete insanity. He had disliked the man too much for pity, and yet in spite of himself, he felt something very close to it, if one can feel pity and revulsion at the same moment.

The butler returned and conducted him into the withdrawing room where Beata awaited him.

Rathbone felt a sudden lurch of emotion as he saw her again. It has been over three weeks, and some of the sharpness of memory had faded. There were small things about her that seemed new: a softness of the light on her hair, the way her eyebrows arched, the very direct way she looked at him, yet without challenge. He knew that would change if he said something she felt to be cruel, or unworthy. The loss of the warmth in her would be the most devastating thing he could imagine at this moment.

'I thought you would be back when you heard about what had happened to Hester Monk,' she said gently. 'Isn't it a sad commentary on our public interests when the trial of a doctor for medical horror is more worthy of news than the kidnap of a nurse and three small children?' She looked past him at the butler, then back at Rathbone. 'Have you eaten recently?'

'Sufficiently,' he replied. 'It seems almost an irrelevance at the moment.' She had indicated a chair on the opposite side of the fireplace from her own. He had a strange, sharp feeling that it had been Ingram York's, before his collapse. In fact he could remember him sitting in it. How totally even a small time could change everything! It was not so long ago that he had first come here, honoured to be invited. And yet since then he had been a judge himself, and in that office lost even his right to practise law in court.

She had asked the butler to bring cold ham and egg pie and a pot of tea, and he had barely heard her. He murmured his thanks.

'Are you going to accept the case?' she asked.

'Only to assist,' he answered. 'Ardal Juster is prosecuting.'

'I know the legalities,' she chided him with a tiny smile. 'Whatever he thinks, you will lead. He is not a fool. He will be out to win, and he knows very well the value of your experience, and your judgement.'

'My judgement?' he said incredulously. 'If he has any wits at all, he'll not listen to that!' He allowed himself to smile at her. It had its own kind of absurdity, and he did not want her to hear bitterness in his voice. There was little less attractive than self-pity, and he cared fiercely what she thought of him, far more than it was safe to admit.

She smiled back, this time ruefully, aware of her own weaknesses.

'You were right in your moral judgement, my dear, just wrong in the law as to how you went about it. But there was no right way. Is there a right way in this? From the little I have read in the newspapers, it is far from a simple issue, but the press always exaggerate so! Competition is good for some businesses – it makes everyone do their best – but seeing who can shout the loudest only ends in deafening us all.'

He felt the knots ease out of his muscles, as if there were warmth in the room that unlocked the old tensions.

'I only read *The Times* . . .' he began.

'But of course,' she agreed with a hint of laughter. 'I cannot imagine you reading the penny dreadfuls.'

'It might be where the story belongs,' he said ruefully. 'Hamilton Rand is a brilliant chemist, but he's not a doctor. According to Hester, and she doesn't exaggerate, Rand kidnapped her, and the three children whose blood he was taking, and held them in a cottage in the countryside in Kent. Going willingly was Bryson Radnor, a wealthy man suffering from white blood disease, and his adult daughter, Adrienne, who helped to look after him, and with the household chores.'

Beata listened without interrupting him.

'The difficulty lies in the fact that Radnor and his daughter were entirely willing. She is being charged along with Rand . . .'

'And not Radnor himself?' she said with surprise.

'He is claiming to have been ill and barely conscious when he made the journey from the hospital to the cottage.'

'Really? How gallant of him!' There was stinging sarcasm in her voice.

'It could be true, and the jury could well believe him.'

'What does the daughter say?'

'Nothing, so far. She seems very dependent upon him.'

'Financially, socially, emotionally?' she queried.

'Probably all of those.'

'Oh dear. Then it all rests upon what Hester says, apart from the three children.'

'They are too young to testify. And their parents accepted money to provide food for the youngest child still at home.' He said it with a degree of bitterness he did not even try to hide. 'How much can you blame parents who convince themselves that an older child will be all right if they sell him or her to someone who will pay enough money to feed and save the babies left behind, crying with hunger?'

She looked away, her eyes filling with tears.

'I'm sorry!' He wished profoundly he had thought before he gave words to something she should not have had to know. 'Beata . . . I'm sorry . . .'

She swivelled back to face him, her eyes blazing through the tears. 'Don't you dare protect me from the truths of life as if I were a child, Oliver! I don't deserve that!'

He was stunned. 'I'm . . . sorry. Was I doing that?' He was truly appalled at his own clumsiness.

'Yes, you were. Please don't do it again. I have seen my share of cruelty, injustice and grief. I do not need to be treated like some flower that will bruise if you touch it.'

For the first time he considered what she must have felt when Ingram York said some of the things that he had. What private, intimate cruelties had she suffered that she could tell no one, ever? What shame did she feel on his behalf that she could not speak? What dreams of hers might he have crushed, like a slowly tightening screw?

He knew how his own disillusion with Margaret had hurt him, though perhaps it was a good deal his own fault. He had chosen to believe she was different from how she really was. Awakening had cost him not only the future but the past, taking the meaning and the heart out of what he had thought it to be.

What had Beata lost that she would be humiliated to give name to? He would never ask and, please heaven, never be clumsy enough to assume again. But another apology would only make the issue bigger than it already was.

'Medical ethics are so complicated,' he said. 'Experimentation is fraught with the chances of failure, and pain or even death. Yet without it we learn nothing. No new cures are found and ignorance has destroyed progress. It depends so much on whose view you have. If someone I loved were ill, I would probably consider any price payable to save them. If I were ill myself, I don't know. I might be too tired and in too much pain to want to struggle any more. If I were starving anyway, who knows what I would do? I might go willingly, but what idea would I have of the pain I would suffer? Even the changes, perhaps irreversible, that would happen to my body, or my mind.'

'Are you going to say that in court?' Now she was watching him with interest, no anger left, no thought of herself at all. 'Are you going to point out that consent cannot be informed if it is from a person with no medical understanding of what the experiment means?'

He did not bother to say again that it would be Ardal Juster that was speaking, not he. 'Yes,' he answered thoughtfully.

'And I will sound as if I am standing in the path of all progress.'

'Rand could have used someone else's blood,' she pointed out. 'An adult more able to understand and willing to take the chance.'

'That's the thing,' Rathbone said ruefully. 'There is something in the blood of these three children that works every time. He has already tried others, and failed.'

'Oh . . .'

'There is not only the question of life, but of the quality of life,' he continued. 'Perhaps Radnor is more a victim of this than he realises. I have a lot of studying to do before I advise Juster what to do.'

'Expert witnesses? Other doctors?' she said thoughtfully. 'Don't forget professional rivalry, Oliver. The defence will have experts, too. People perjure themselves for many reasons; some don't even realise they are doing it. You are safer to stick to the emotional facts. Hester was taken against her will, and kept prisoner. Is there any way you can make the jury realise that if she had not been rescued, and Radnor had died, that Rand would have killed her?'

'I don't know,' he admitted. 'But I believe it . . . and that is a good deal of the way there.'

'You have let your tea go cold. Let me send for a fresh pot, and eat your pie. Cook really is very good.'

He relaxed back into the chair. 'Thank you.'

They spoke of other things, long into the evening. By the time he left he could think of little to do with the case, only how intensely he cared for Beata. How long would Ingram York cling on to his raging, damaged life, locked up in the asylum, half paralysed in a world of nightmares and silence? Surely it was also mercy to hope for his release?

Rathbone spent the rest of the week speaking to other doctors who were experts on diseases of the blood, or death from the shock of injury, and the consequent loss of blood. At Hester's suggestion he also spoke to midwives who had delivered healthy babies, only to lose a mother from bleeding that took too long to stop.

The more he learned the more he understood the desperate need to find a solution to giving blood that a healthy person could easily spare, and which would restore life to someone who would otherwise die.

He even asked himself what risks he would take, if the dying person were Beata. Could he watch her fade away, suffering, if the gift of someone else's blood could save her?

What was the great terror? Death? Annihilation? Being alone for ever? Being guilty of some irreversible sin? Or cowardice? The eternal blame of those you ignored, or of those your courage could have saved?

On Friday evening he went to see Ardal Juster in his home. It was considerably later than good manners would have permitted calling, especially upon someone you did not know well. He still went.

Juster was surprised, but he realised immediately that the matter was grave. As soon as they were in his comfortable, overcrowded study he closed the door and faced Rathbone.

'What is it?'

'I don't believe we should prosecute,' Rathbone said gravely. 'I think we may end up losing, and making Rand seem a hero . . .'

'For God's sake, man!' Juster said incredulously. 'He kidnapped a woman whom you know well, and care for. If Radnor had died, or even one of the children, he would have had to kill her. She would never have kept silent over it. I know that, you know it, and Rand as sure as hellfire knew it.'

'But it didn't happen, Juster,' Rathbone pointed out. 'She's alive. You can't prosecute someone for what you believe they would have done in circumstances that did not happen. You know that as well as I know it. The defence will say that the children's parents took money . . .'

'But they didn't know what was going to happen to the children,' Juster said hotly, his voice rising.

'But what if Rand said he had told them in the beginning?'

'He didn't!' But Juster's voice wavered.

'Of course he damned well didn't,' Rathbone agreed. 'But can you prove that, if Rand swears he did?'

Juster stared at him.

'You can only charge him with kidnapping Hester, and hope that her testimony stands up to the defence, because they'll attack her any way they can think of.'

'Is that really why you're withdrawing?' Juster asked, but his voice was softer, without blame.

'No . . . no, I don't think so. In fact I'm not withdrawing. I would rather be there to sit beside you and give you whatever counsel I can when the time comes, which it will. If you go ahead . . .?'

'If I don't, they'll find someone else,' Juster pointed out. 'They've already told me as much.'

'Then we are in for a battle,' Rathbone answered him. 'We had better prepare.'

Chapter Eleven

RATHBONE WAS filled with an extraordinary sense of both exhilaration and fear as he entered the courtroom at the Old Bailey, London's famous Central Criminal Court. This was the opening of the case against Hamilton Rand and Adrienne Radnor, for the abduction of Hester Monk.

He was afraid for Hester, because she was the only witness against either of the accused during the major commission of the crime. If the defence could cast doubt on her word, either by fact or by the assassination of her character, then there was no case to answer.

Of course, Hooper would be called. Charles Colbert, taking the defence, could very simply raise questions as to Monk's impartiality, as Hester's husband, his judgement, and the need now to defend his very violent action. He could even call the surly gardener to attest to his injuries, incurred in very properly protecting his master from the intrusion of men about whom he knew nothing. They were the attackers, not he, and it was he who had received the injuries.

It would be better to call Hooper, although even his testimony could be brought into doubt. After all, Monk was his superior. Apart from loyalty, there was also the question of his future employment. It was far too easy a weapon for Colbert not to use it.

Squeaky and Scuff were equally vulnerable. Worm was not

even to be considered, although, having met him, Rathbone thought he would hold his own very well. Anyone who bullied him would look brutal and earn the jury's contempt, and even worse, their dislike. Of course, Colbert would not let it get so far. He would have him eliminated unseen, on the grounds of his age and total lack of education.

It was going to be a very difficult case. Rathbone looked across the long familiar courtroom with its magnificent carved judge's bench, its double row of jurors' seats. Above them, isolated from the body of the court, was the dock where the accused would sit, guarded by gaolers. He sat at his table beside Ardal Juster before the empty space like an arena, in which was the witness box, with its own little spiral stair. Charles Colbert for the defence was sitting, ostentatiously comfortable, at the other side. It was a well-learned art. He was not a comfortable man. He was lean, a little hollow-chested, with very long legs. He reminded Rathbone of a studious stork, physically ill-balanced, but when you met his eyes or heard his knife-edged tongue, you realised his intellectual brilliance.

This was Rathbone's first appearance since being legally reinstated after his disgrace. He was second to Juster, but he was permitted to question witnesses. They had already agreed that he would not question Hester. Their history, both private and professional, was too open to innuendo.

The court was brought to order, presided over by Lord Justice Patterson, a judge Rathbone was not familiar with. Perhaps that was an advantage.

The preliminaries were the same as always. The jury took their places. They were all respectable men in their middle years, men who owned substantial property, and of course had no known blemishes on their reputations. That they were peers of the accused was seldom true, but in this instance it was. Except, of course, for Adrienne Radnor, sitting beside

Hamilton Rand in the dock. Women did not meet the requirements of the law, and were not considered suitable intellectually or emotionally for such a task.

Juster rose to his feet and gave a very brief introduction to his case. He said only that it concerned an issue that some of the jury might not have had occasion to consider. The evidence would be deeply disturbing, and their responsibility would be heavy and complex, but he trusted them completely. To fail in this case would be to fail honesty not only here in the present, but far into the future as well.

Rathbone had agreed to this when they discussed it earlier. Seeing the jury's faces now, he felt even more strongly that it was the right tactic.

Hester was the first witness called. This was the most risky tactic because in the end the case depended upon her. If she impressed them well, then the other witnesses would be believed; if not, then nothing else would work.

Rathbone sat stiff-backed, his fingers laced together, white knuckles in his lap beneath the table where they could not be seen.

Hester climbed the steps of the witness stand and stood at the top, her hands by her sides, her face calm. She was wearing a blue dress, which was softly draped and flattering. It was the colour of her nurse's dress, but without the white apron.

Juster began. He and Rathbone had planned this in detail.

'Mrs Monk, in August of this year, where were you working?'

'At the annexe to the Royal Naval Hospital in Greenwich,' she replied. Her voice was calm and steady, but she looked pale. Rathbone hated it that she had to endure this again and he was afraid for her. She could so easily be hurt.

'In what capacity?' Juster's voice was gentle, but it carried to every corner of the gallery behind him as well as to the jury in their carved seats, and the judge before them all.

'As a nurse, mostly on night duty,' she answered.

'Had you been there long?' Again he asked innocently, as if he had little idea what her answer would be.

'About three weeks.'

'So the job was new to you?' Now he looked surprised.

'The hospital was new to me,' she answered. 'I have been a nurse on and off since the Crimean War.'

He affected surprise. 'The Crimean War! Were you in Sebastopol then, with Florence Nightingale?' He pitched his voice so that no man or woman in the court could have failed to hear him, or the name of perhaps the most famous nurse in the world, a heroine to any soldier.

'Yes,' she acknowledged.

'And you are still nursing?'

She lifted her chin a little. 'I did so for some time after returning to England, then I married. I went back to nursing temporarily because a friend from those days was taken ill. She asked me to fill in for her, until she was better. She did not know how long that would be. It was a hospital treating mostly men from the navy, with injuries not unlike those I was used to treating before. I did not feel I could refuse her.'

'So you took her place, mostly at nights?'

'Yes.'

'Were you working for Mr Hamilton Rand?'

'No. I was on general nursing duties, and I answered to Dr Magnus Rand.'

The interest in the gallery was beginning to wane. Rathbone was aware of people fidgeting, occasionally changing position. Juster should move on.

As if he had heard Rathbone's thoughts, Juster changed the subject. 'Were you on night duty when you discovered the ward for children, Mrs Monk?'

The attention was total again. No one stirred.

'Yes. I saw a child, a girl who appeared to be about six years old, alone in the corridor in the middle of the night.'

Hester's voice wavered a little with her own emotion. 'She was white-faced and terrified. She told me her brother was dying.'

Now, one could have heard a pin drop.

Colbert moved as if to interrupt, and at least a dozen people glared at him.

Hester continued without being prompted. 'I went with her. She led me down a passage I had not seen before and into a ward where there were six beds, all occupied by children looking to be between three years old and ten or eleven.'

'And was one of them her brother?'

Again Colbert took a deep breath, and then changed his mind.

'Two of them said they were,' Hester answered. 'The older, Charlie, was very ill indeed. The younger, Mike, was frightened but not seriously ill. He was about three or four. I remained all night and together we managed to keep Charlie alive. By morning he was returned to consciousness, and seemed to be recovering.'

'What was the matter with him?' Juster asked innocently, glancing at Colbert, and then back again at Hester.

Rathbone relaxed a fraction, stopping his fingernails from digging into his palms. Colbert was waiting for the slip, the assumption, the statement of a skill Hester did not have.

'I didn't know,' Hester replied. 'He seemed to be suffering from lack of fluids . . .'

This time Colbert could not resist. He rose to his feet.

'My lord, Mr Juster has perhaps forgotten that he has not given us any background of Mrs Monk's medical training for such a diagnosis. Nor has he asked her why on earth she did not call the doctor!'

One or two jurors looked puzzled, turning from Colbert to the judge, and back again.

Juster smiled. He looked to Hester. 'How do you know

this, Mrs Monk? And why did you not call the doctor, if Charlie was as ill as you say?'

'It was the middle of the night,' she replied. Her voice was perfectly level, but thick with emotion. 'Dr Rand does not sleep on the premises. And it is a nursing job to know if someone has lost too much fluid and not replaced it. However, the nurse on duty was absent. There are several ways to know if someone is dehydrated.'

She held out her arm and gently pinched the flesh of it between the finger and thumb of her other hand. 'When it is firm, you are all right. When the skin comes away, as Charlie's did, then there is not sufficient fluid. One can feel dizzy, headachy, a little sick, and very tired. The inside of the mouth becomes very dry, even painful. You pass water very little. It is easy to let this happen, especially if you have lost a lot of fluid as with vomiting, or having diarrhoea. I simply encouraged Charlie to drink as much as possible. Later we made beef tea, so there would be some nourishment in it for him.'

Out of the corner of his eye Rathbone could see one or two women towards the front of the gallery nodding their heads.

Colbert had fired his first volley, and conspicuously missed the mark.

'Thank you, Mrs Monk,' Juster said, barely hiding his smile. 'I think perhaps many of us here are not certain what is a doctor's job and what is a nurse's. It seems clear now that you used your experience in nursing the very ill to save this boy's life.'

Colbert rose to his feet. 'My lord, my learned friend is testifying. I understand his eagerness, but he knows better. At least I believe he does!'

'I apologise,' Juster said quickly, before the judge could intervene. He turned again to Hester. 'When Charlie seemed better in the morning, did you then report the situation to Dr Rand?'

'The matter was taken out of my hands,' she replied. 'Dr Rand heard that I had been in that ward and he asked me to help with the treatment of one of his patients who had white blood disease.'

Colbert looked sharply at Juster.

Juster smiled. 'How did you know that that was his illness, Mrs Monk?'

'I don't,' she replied. 'I know that was what he said, and I had no reason to doubt him.'

There was a slight titter of amusement around the room.

'And did you consent?' Juster resumed.

'Of course.'

'Why?'

She looked slightly taken aback by the question. 'I would never refuse to treat a patient, whatever the illness. And it is not contagious, so there was no question of quarantine.'

'Exactly so,' Juster agreed. 'In what way did you assist in this treatment? Can you tell the court something about the patient?'

Hester described Bryson Radnor briefly, concentrating on his state of health and his symptoms, mentioning that his daughter, Adrienne accompanied him.

'She was of great assistance,' she continued. 'She had been caring for him for over a year in his illness and could describe the course of it clearly for Dr Rand. She also assisted in nursing him, which was helpful to the hospital.'

'What was the treatment you gave him, Mrs Monk?'

'Transfusion of human blood,' she said quietly.

There was a gasp around the room. Someone in the gallery stifled a cry. Two of the jurors leaned forward as if they were uncertain if they had heard correctly.

Lord Justice Patterson frowned. 'Did you say transfusion of human blood, Mrs Monk?'

'Yes, my lord,' Hester answered levelly. 'It has been tried many times before, going back two hundred years or more. It has never been done with any permanent success. Often the failure is immediate. The patient suffers distress, nausea, faintness, eventually death.'

'And Mr Radnor?' Patterson asked.

'He rallied,' Hester replied. 'Sometimes it was for several hours, sometimes longer. Then he would grow faint again and need the treatment to be repeated.'

Patterson stared at Juster. 'Have you any other witness to this remarkable story, Mr Juster?'

'Yes, my lord. If you will allow me to continue?'

Patterson nodded and sat back in his great carved seat.

Juster continued to question Hester and draw from her piece by piece a vivid description of the blood transfusion machine. She began with how blood was drawn from Charlie and Maggie, but it was added to so that it would not clot and coagulate.

'What was added?' he asked.

'I think it ill advised to tell you,' she answered, 'in case anyone might attempt such a thing themselves. It is highly skilled.'

'I see,' he nodded agreement. 'Can you tell the court how it was administered?'

She described Radnor's treatment, his recovery, and then relapse. Juster questioned her about her abduction from the hospital and finally how she was rescued by Monk and his men.

No one interrupted her. The court was so quiet that the faintest of movement was audible: the rustle of fabric on wood, the creak of a chair as someone moved their weight.

'And did you attempt to escape during this time?' Juster said at last.

'No. I could not leave the children behind,' she answered.

'And your patient?'

She hesitated.

'Mrs Monk?'

'I don't know,' she said at last. 'He had one bad crisis, and I don't think Miss Radnor could have dealt with it.'

'Did you think of escaping?' Juster insisted. Rathbone had warned him that Colbert would press the issue. He could not afford to ignore it.

'Yes, I thought of it,' Hester said very softly. 'But the children were growing weaker. He took too much blood from them. They are very small, very thin . . .' Her voice wavered.

Colbert looked up sharply and started to rise.

Juster turned towards him. 'Your witness, Mr Colbert.'

Rathbone immediately thought that Juster had let Colbert take over too soon. There were other things he could have asked Hester, let the jury see her courage and dedication more clearly.

It was too late. Colbert rose to his feet, walked out into the body of the court to stand below the witness box and stared up at Hester.

Rathbone lost his certainty. It was too long since he had been in the courtroom. His judgement was blunted. He was too personally involved.

'You have been very specific, Mrs Monk,' Colbert said with a slight smile. 'We are grateful to you. Most of us here are laymen when it comes to medical details such as you describe. Help us, please. Do I understand you correctly that Dr Rand was taking an amount of blood from two of these children and then placing it, through a very fine needle and a machine that he had created, into the veins of his sick patient? And after this treatment, the patient showed considerable recovery? Is that a fair description of what you assisted him to do?'

'It is incomplete,' Hester replied, her voice perfectly level. 'But it is not inaccurate as far as it goes.'

'What did I miss?' Colbert looked puzzled.

'Mr Radnor did not have insufficient blood,' she explained. 'His blood was diseased. Dr Rand had tried once some time ago to perform this transfusion with other patients, and other donors. Apparently these three children, the youngest as well, had blood that worked on all upon whom he used it. No one seems to know why that is. But the children are young, very small and increasingly weak.'

'You mentioned that,' Colbert was still polite. 'But it did work, did it not? Mr Radnor was alive and apparently gaining strength when Mr Monk and his men broke in and forcibly stopped the treatment. They arrested Mr Rand and Miss Radnor, and brought all of you forcibly back to the city? Yes or no will do, Mrs Monk.'

Rathbone stiffened. Whatever way she answered he would trip her up. If she said 'yes' then she was admitting that Monk had effectively damaged Radnor's chances of recovery. If she said 'no' she would be suggesting that she knew more than Rand did about his disease and recovery.

'I don't know,' Hester said with the shadow of a smile. 'I could tell you his pulse rate, temperature, whether he was eating or not, and sleeping. What that meant with regard to his recovery, and whether it was temporary or permanent, I do not know.'

Colbert masked a slight irritation, but Rathbone saw it.

'Do you always refer to a doctor, Mrs Monk? Surely in your heroic experience in the battlefield you had to take major decisions yourself when a man was critically injured? My research into your career tells me that at times you performed surgery right there on the grass. You even amputated limbs from dying men, and saved their lives!' He invested his tone with intense awe, drawing the emotions of the court with him. 'You were less circumspect then, far less timid.'

Hester was pale. 'Seconds of delay can allow a man to bleed to death when he has lost a limb, Mr Colbert,' she said a little harshly. 'There may be no doctor there to ask. And by the time you find one it would be too late. With Mr Radnor I did all I could to preserve his life. He was suffering from a disease that is usually fatal, but not in a matter of minutes. I had plenty of time to ask Mr Rand's counsel and then act according to his instructions.'

'And yet you do not know if he was recovering or not?' Colbert said with disbelief.

'The treatment was experimental,' she explained again carefully. 'The essence of that is that no one knows whether it will work or not.'

'Your answers are very considered, Mrs Monk, very well thought out. You sound as if you are picking and choosing your words to protect yourself from accusations of complicity in this . . . experiment. Did you believe it would fail?'

Rathbone looked across at Juster and saw the anxiety flicker for an instant in his face. Had the jury seen that? Was it the same fear that he felt gnawing inside himself? Hester was sometimes painfully honest. Where would her first loyalty lie now? Towards justice, safety for the children she had come to know and protect? Even to love. It could be anger at what had been done to them, but he doubted it would be as simple as revenge. Might her loyalty be to medicine itself, to all the future lives that could be saved if Rand succeeded, or even if someone else picked up the knowledge so far and went forward with it?

How would her conscience drive her to answer? She must not hesitate too long, or it would look contrived. Colbert would press on that. More importantly, the jury would see her indecision as lies.

Rathbone looked at Juster again. Perhaps he should object, say that Colbert was asking her to give the very speculation he had claimed she was medically untrained to offer. It would be legally correct, but it would also quite clearly be an evasion. The question had been asked. It must be answered, or the jury would provide their own answer. Colbert was a great deal less mild than he looked.

'Mrs Monk?' Colbert said with a lift of curiosity in his voice.

Hester smiled. 'As you have said, sir, I am not medically qualified to give such an opinion. But since you have opened the door by asking me, I can say that I was deeply impressed by Mr Rand's means of keeping freshly taken blood from coagulating, which would make it unusable to give to another person. His equipment was well designed and seemed to work efficiently . . .'

'Mrs Monk—' he interrupted, frowning his annoyance.

She ignored him as if she had not heard, and continued, '. . . to carry out the function of giving the blood to the patient. Occasionally Mr Radnor's reaction was not good, but with nursing he recovered. I think it is impossible to say if in time he would have recovered from his illness, or if he would have continued to need blood regularly. Nor did Mr Rand ever learn why the blood of these children always worked, and with other people sometimes it did, but more often it did not. That is a series of experiments one cannot make. More often than not they failed and the patient died, not always could one say from exactly what cause – whether the transfusion killed them, or merely failed to save them.'

Colbert knew when to leave a subject alone. He thanked her and dismissed her.

Juster decided not to question her again. He too knew a winning hand when he had played it.

The next witness he called was Hooper. As soon as he was

sworn and stated his name and occupation, Juster moved forward into the open space, and stood gracefully and at ease looking up at him on the stand. He was confident Hooper could take care of himself, and that certainty was in every angle of his body as he began.

'When did you know that Mrs Monk had been kidnapped by Mr Rand?'

Hooper smiled very slightly. 'When we found her in his cottage near Redditch, and he was standing there with a surgeon's knife in his hand, the blade at her throat, threatening to kill her, sir.'

It was not the answer Juster had expected, but the response in the courtroom more than satisfied him. There was a gasp around the gallery and a rustling of clothes as if a wind had passed through a great tree in full leaf. The jury stiffened, some staring at Hooper, others at Hester, who was now seated in the gallery herself.

Mr Justice Patterson bit his lip, and still failed to conceal a smile.

Colbert was on his feet. 'My lord!' he protested.

Patterson raised his hand. 'It was a fair question, Mr Colbert, and a fair answer.' He looked at Hooper. 'Do I take it, sir, that until that time you did not know what had happened?'

'I believed it, my lord,' Hooper said soberly. 'But until that time I did not know. It was just what seemed most likely from the evidence, and evidence can be wrong.'

'Indeed it can, Mr Hooper,' Patterson agreed. 'Please continue, Mr Juster. I imagine you have other questions?'

'Yes, my lord,' Juster bowed his head very slightly, mostly to conceal his smile. Rathbone knew that, because he was doing the same. But they were a long way from victory yet. The defence had not even begun.

'Mr Hooper,' Juster continued, 'Mr Monk is your immediate superior, is that correct?'

'Yes, sir.'

'Did he order you to join him in this journey to look for Mrs Monk?'

'No, sir. He didn't order me to do anything apart from my usual River Police duties. We're kind of short-handed after several of us were wounded in a battle on a gunrunning ship.' His voice dropped. 'And one of us bled to death. I'm officially still on sick leave, sir.'

Rathbone looked at Hooper more carefully and noticed that he was standing in the witness box not entirely straight. One might have taken it for the awkwardness of a big man in a confined space, and perhaps taken by the tension of the experience. Now he could see it was truly the adjustment of weight of someone who was not entirely healed from an injury.

'I'm sorry to hear that,' Juster answered. 'I hope you are close to recovery.'

'Thank you, sir, very close,' Hooper acknowledged it.

'But nevertheless you went with Mr Monk to look for his wife, and attempt a rescue?'

'Yes, sir. Once Dr Rand gave us the address we reckoned there was no time to waste. If Mr Radnor died, then there'd be no reason to keep Mrs Monk alive. She could testify against him.'

Colbert shot to his feet. 'My lord! That is an extremely prejudicial remark. The witness has no knowledge whatsoever that Mr Rand would do anything of the sort! Indeed, as the court heard, Mrs Monk has considerable regard for Mr Rand's experiment. She even went so far as to say it may become a gift to all future medicine. I ask that you direct the jury to disregard the witness's remark, and caution him to make no more such observations.'

Patterson held his hand up to silence Juster's protest and turned to the witness stand. 'Mr Hooper, did you say that she "could" testify against him, or that she "would" do so? Please be exact, sir.'

'That she could, my lord,' Hooper answered levelly. 'She would be in a position to . . .'

Patterson nodded and turned to Colbert. 'That seems to be a fair observation. If Mr Radnor had died, Mrs Monk would undoubtedly have been in a position to testify. Please proceed, Mr Juster.'

'Thank you, my lord.' Juster turned to the witness stand again. 'How did you find this cottage, Mr Hooper?'

Hooper gave a simple and vivid account of what they had done, starting with obtaining a wagon suitable to the journey. Then he described – with frequent objections by Colbert – how they had overpowered the gardener and tied him up before going into the house, and discovering Adrienne Radnor in the kitchen, and Hester assisting Rand in ministering to Bryson Radnor. He included how Rand had reacted, his threat to Hester and how she had defeated it.

Colbert made only one serious attempt at defence when he rose to cross-question Hooper.

'I will not ask you, Mr Hooper, why you felt it necessary or appropriate to attack the gardener,' he said contemptuously. 'The poor man is still suffering the aftereffects of his experience and so is unable to testify today. Therefore the only other word we have regarding this sorry affair is yours, and that of your friends. But you might tell us whether Miss Radnor resisted your invasion? And please tell us why you omitted to say that she was just as much of assistance as she appeared to be? Her beloved father, her only living relative, was desperately ill, and without Mr Rand's help, certainly dying. Is it not natural that she would remain with him, even if only to tend to his needs and comfort him in his final days? Would not any daughter do as much?'

'Yes, she would,' Hooper replied with a very slight smile.

'But she is the only one I know of who kept a nurse and three children captive to do it.'

'Captive, Mr Hooper?' Colbert said with deceptive smoothness. 'Was Miss Radnor armed with some weapon? From your account of Mrs Monk, she is a formidable woman when it comes to combat. What was Miss Radnor's weapon? Surely none so deadly as the surgical knife Mrs Monk so expertly dealt with when Mr Rand had it at her throat?'

'Miss Radnor had a key,' Hooper replied. 'One that locks the door so you cannot get out. And of course the assistance of a gardener with a shotgun.'

Rathbone let his breath out in a long sigh, and smiled, feeling the pain of tension ease momentarily from his shoulders.

Juster did not even attempt to hide his jubilation. Nothing Colbert could do now would erase this from the jury's minds.

It was nearly five o'clock in the afternoon. Surely Patterson would adjourn any minute.

Patterson smiled. 'Gentlemen, I think that this is the ideal moment to—'

He got no further. The entrance doors to the courtroom crashed open, flung so wide that they let in the cool air and the buzz of voices from the outside hall. Everyone turned to stare at the violent interruption. An elderly man stood there, the silver in his wild hair gleaming, his dress immaculate. He was flanked on either side by the court ushers who had failed to prevent his entrance.

'Sir!' Patterson began.

The man strode forward firmly; his head high, face alight with vigour.

'This is the trial of Hamilton Rand and Adrienne Radnor?' he demanded, his voice ringing. 'On the charge of having conducted unlawful experiments in medicine, and the transfusion of human blood from one person to another? Yes?' He kept striding forwards, ignoring everyone else and addressing his questions only to the judge. 'Yes, I thought so. Well, I sir, am Bryson Radnor. And as you can see from my demeanour, I am in excellent health, rescued from the edge of the grave by the courage and the genius of Hamilton Rand. And of course the loyalty of my daughter, Adrienne, who never gave up the fight to save me from death of that terrible illness we know as the white blood disease – the cause of so many we cannot count them.' His voice was strong, resonant, commanding.

There was utter silence in the court. The jury could have been wax statues coloured to look like men. Even Patterson seemed frozen in mid-sentence.

Radnor turned at last and regarded the rest of the room. 'Ladies and gentlemen, Hamilton Rand is one of the heroes at whom future ages will gaze with awe. Soldiers on battle-fields we have not yet dreamed of, victims of all manner of appalling accidents, will live because of his work, his patience, his faith in the arts and sciences of medicine and the will to learn.'

A man in the gallery stood up and raised his arms in the air.

'Wonderful!' he cried out.

Another rose and did exactly the same. Then a third, a fourth, and finally the entire gallery.

Patterson commanded order, but his voice could barely be heard above the tumult.

Juster sat down as if his knees had buckled under him. He stared hopelessly at Rathbone and did not bother searching for words.

The jury sat baffled, but they were smiling.

Gradually the roar died down and Patterson was able to make himself heard.

'. . . Gentlemen! Ladies and gentlemen! Order, please!'

At last there was something approaching silence. Slowly people resumed their seats.

Colbert was elated, but he had the good sense to say nothing, and artfully to look as amazed as everyone else.

'Ladies and gentlemen,' Patterson began again, 'in view of the remarkable events that have just taken place, I wish to reconsider the entire matter, and take advice on the issues now involved. I am adjourning the trial of Hamilton Rand and Adrienne Radnor until then . . .'

That evening Monk and Hester sat at the kitchen table and ate dinner without tasting it. Scuff was present, as usual, but Worm was there also. He had asked to be, and when it was time to leave he came close to physically hanging on to Hester's skirts so no one could take him away. She put her arms around him and defied anyone to fight her.

'He was part of the rescue,' she said, staring at Monk defiantly.

Now the four of them sat at the table over plates only half empty. No one had the heart to eat with any pleasure. It was Worm who asked what they were all thinking.

'Wot 'appened?' he asked in one of several long silences.

Monk had not been in the court during most of the evidence. He looked at Hester to explain.

'I'm not sure,' she said honestly. 'It looked as if we were winning, easily. Mr Hooper was terrific. I think everybody knew that Mr Rand took us to Redditch and kept us there by force. Then Mr Radnor strode into the court and claimed that Rand had cured him of white blood disease, and was one of the great heroes of medicine.'

'Is 'e?' Worm asked, frowning. 'I thought 'e kept yer there an' wouldn't let you come 'ome. In't that wrong?'

'Yes, it is. But probably just about everyone there knew somebody who was sick one way or another, or could be one day. They want to believe that it could be true that there is a way for them to be healed. We all want to think so. They don't want to have Mr Rand put into prison.'

'But 'e done summink wicked,' Worm said again. He could not understand why that was not enough.

Hester put out her hand and touched him gently. 'If I were very sick, and there was just one doctor who could make me better, wouldn't you want him to stay out of prison and do that?'

Worm stared at her, worried. 'Yer not sick, are yer?' His voice trembled a bit in spite of his efforts to control it.

Hester blinked hard. She was tired and feeling thoroughly beaten, more vulnerable than she wanted him to know.

'No, I'm not. I'm fine, and I'm going to stay fine. But some people are sick, and we hope every one of them has somebody who loves them.'

Worm nodded slowly. 'I see.'

'Do you? Being ill is pretty frightening. We don't always think very clearly when we're afraid,' she answered.

'Then nothin' 'appens to 'im, even though 'e did that to you?' Worm persisted.

'Not at the moment,' she admitted.

'We aren't finished yet,' Monk interrupted. 'We'll have to think what to do.'

Worm's face lit up. 'Will yer? Can I 'elp?'

This time Scuff also looked at Monk, the questions in his face.

'When I think of what to do,' Monk replied. 'Tonight I'm too tired to have many ideas.'

Scuff was frowning. 'The Robertses sold their kids, didn't they?' he asked, looking from Hester to Monk.

'Yes,' Hester replied. 'They couldn't feed them. They thought the Rands would.'

Scuff gave her a disbelieving look.

'Sometimes we believe what we need to,' she said sadly. 'We can't bear to think anything else. Why? We can't charge them with kidnapping.'

'You reckon he bought all of 'em?' he asked. 'If we could find even one 'e didn't. Has 'e really got enough money to do that, and buy all the stuff for machines an' that?'

'I don't know,' Monk said thoughtfully. 'I'll go and see Rathbone tomorrow. He might have some idea.'

He turned to Scuff. 'Maybe you could take a day off school. Stay here.'

'Can I too?' Worm asked eagerly.

'You don't go to school,' Scuff pointed out.

'Yes, I do!' Worm said instantly, although they all knew he didn't.

'Then tomorrow you can,' Monk said immediately. 'Scuff will teach you.'

Worm's face lit up with pleasure. He turned to stare hopefully at Scuff.

Scuff knew when he was beaten and he shrugged ruefully. Perhaps actually it wouldn't be so bad. 'I'll make you work,' he warned.

Worm gave him a dazzling smile.

Chapter Twelve

HESTER WAS lying rigid on the bed, terrified, but she had no idea why, or what it was that paralysed her with such fear. She wanted to struggle, to reach out in the darkness, very slowly, and see what she touched, but she could not move.

She strained her ears and heard nothing but a faint dripping, slow and very small. There was no other sound at all, not even her own breathing.

She tried to move her feet, but a tightness around her ankles held her feet. She jerked her hand. That too was tied at the wrist. Then, like a horror taking shape in front of her, she realised she could not move because she was tied down, wrists, ankles, and a band around the chest.

She jerked at them roughly, and they grew even tighter. She could still see nothing; hear nothing but the very faint drip. And then that too stopped. She was weak. Her mouth tasted dry. There was a sore place on her left arm, just inside the crook of the elbow, where the veins were close to the surface . . . That was what she could smell! That faint, warm coppery odour in the air – blood!

Who was bleeding so much that she could taste it in the back of her throat? She must help them, before they bled to death! Again she tried to sit up, and moved barely an inch before the band around her chest tightened. It allowed her room to breathe no more.

Then a terrible realisation came to her. She tried to put it out of her mind, but it was there all around her in its reality. They wanted her to live, to supply blood. There was someone who needed it. Like the old legend of the vampire who died unless he drank from human veins. It was his food, his life.

Just like Maggie and Charlie, she was kept alive to supply blood for someone. Radnor? Had she taken the children's place, as a punishment for not saving them, for not seeing that Rand was stopped?

She tensed her muscles again, but there was no strength in her. She was fading; it was getting harder to keep conscious. The smell of blood was stronger, filling every breath she took, choking her.

Was she dying? Had he bled her to death? Of course. Why not? There were always more people. The world was full of people. What was one more or less, in the scheme of things? It mattered only to those who had loved the dead person; the rest of the world went on exactly as before.

What happened to the dead? They would bury her body, of course. You can't leave corpses lying around. People would ask questions. And they would rot and smell awful. But what would happen to her? Who was she inside? Would she go on into another world, like sleep? Were the ministers of the Church right, or was it just darkness, like this? No sound, no sight, no movement? An endless silence, alone. And getting colder. She could not feel her feet any more.

Was she dead now? She didn't feel real pain, just an aching – and a slowly growing knowledge of being utterly alone! That had been Radnor's terror, hadn't it? Ceasing to exist?

She had no idea how long it was before she was aware of something touching her arm, something warm. She drew in her breath in horror, and heard her own voice crying out.

She tried to wrench her arm away. The hand let go of its grip on her, and she moved. The restraints had gone.

There was light beyond her eyelids, and warmth. She opened her eyes very slowly, dreading what she would see.

'Hester!' It was Monk's voice, urgent, edged with fear.

She looked up at him. He was close to her, his hand near her arm as if he had just let go of her. She was in her own bedroom, in her own bed.

Very slowly she sat up, moving her feet, her legs. There was nothing holding her, no restraints at all, except where she had tangled herself in the sheets.

She looked at Monk again. He was fully dressed.

'What happened?' she asked huskily.

'You were so tired I let you sleep,' he replied. 'But you cried out. You must have been dreaming . . . something pretty bad, from the fear in your voice.' He touched her gently, brushing the tangled hair off her forehead. He did not ask what she had dreamed. Perhaps he thought that like most nightmares, it disappeared a moment or two after you were awake. But this one didn't. It was still very real, there in her body, in the smell of blood in her nose and throat.

She lay back on the pillow. 'I dreamed someone was bleeding me,' she said quietly, then told him exactly what it had felt like.

'Hester!' He took hold of her firmly, almost tightly enough to hurt. 'Stop it! It was a dream. I won't leave you alone again. Not when you're asleep. Sit up.' He pulled her forward a little and up. His hands were warm. 'I'll put the kettle back on and Scuff can bring you a cup of tea.'

'No!' she said, reaching out to hold on to him. 'Don't go . . . not just yet.'

He did not argue, just moved her gently across further to her own side of the bed. Then he lay down and put his arms around her.

'I understand why Radnor was so afraid of dying,' she said quietly, trying to explore the jungle of thoughts in her mind.

'Maybe most of us are. We just don't think about it because it would cripple us. I felt . . .' the horror came back to her vividly so her whole body clenched, '. . . I felt as if I were tied up so I couldn't move. And I was getting weaker all the time. Do you think Rand has any idea what he's doing to people? Maybe he only sees the ones he's helping?'

'That isn't an excuse,' Monk said grimly. 'It's a child's answer. I would take that from Worm. From Scuff I'd tell him he must do better.'

'I know.' She was silent for a few moments. She was warm now, comfortable. She remembered the room with the contraption that held the bottle of blood and very carefully fed it, a drop at a time to Radnor. Rand's machine was cleverly designed and made. 'It was exactly balanced, William,' she said aloud.

'Being a good engineer doesn't excuse anything,' he replied.

'That wasn't what I was thinking. How long do you suppose it took him to make it?'

'Why? What does it matter?'

'Months? Years, to get the design exactly right? All the weights and balances?'

He sat up slowly to look at her, his face filled with the darkness of his thoughts. 'Hester?'

'A long time,' she whispered. 'How many other people's blood did he try with? And what happened to them? Obviously he wasn't caught for it, or he'd not still be free.'

He stared at her. 'What are you saying, Hester? That he took other people to the cottage to experiment on them?'

She met his eyes. 'Yes, I think so. The place was all prepared and set up when we got there. I think he took us on the spur of the moment, when he realised you were looking into it all too closely. He bolted. It wasn't planned. He decided it right then when I was in his office. He put ether over my face. It was a sudden decision. The children said they were taken in a hurry, after I was already there. They couldn't remember much, but all of it was hurry, and secrecy. He didn't have time to plan.' She took a break and rushed on. 'It wasn't the same machine in the cottage as the one he used in the hospital. It was already there, set up and ready to use. William, he'd used it before! How many times? How long? And what happened to those people?'

For several seconds Monk did not answer.

Hester said nothing more, lapsing into thought herself. She allowed her mind to go back to the time in the cottage. Now, instead of fighting it, she was actively trying to remember.

'The room was ready for the children,' she said aloud. 'There were four beds there, not three, all made up with sheets and blankets. You can't do that in a short time. Either Rand was planning to go there anyway, but was pushed into it before he had intended, or . . . or it was a place he had used before.'

'You said the machine, the contraption, was complicated. Could they have made that quickly?'

'No. And the screws were tight, jammed, as if they'd been there for a long time. I know because I tried to undo one with a spanner, so I could adjust the arm. I couldn't budge it.'

'Then I think I have no alternative but to go out there again, maybe take Hooper, and see what we can find.'

Monk sat up again, moving his arm away from her. 'And before Patterson recalls the court and tries to get some order back into the trial. God knows how he'll do it. And I'll take Worm back to Claudine at the clinic. I think he's safe enough now.'

'Are you . . .?' Then she stopped. She had been going to ask if he were sure Worm would be all right at the clinic, but then she remembered how frantic Claudine would be without him. To her he was unique. Every child should be special to someone: needed, not just accepted.

'Good idea,' she agreed. 'I must get up. What would you like for breakfast? There's—'

He pushed the hair back off her brow again, smiling. 'How about lunch?' he asked.

'Is it that time?'

'Almost. By the time you're dressed it will be.'

When Scuff heard what Monk was going to do, he immediately volunteered to come along as well. 'We'll find twice as much if there are two of us,' he pointed out reasonably.

'You are quite right,' Monk agreed. 'Which is why I will take Hooper.'

'Hooper's still hurt,' Scuff argued.

'Have you thought about how Hester feels?' Monk said gently. 'She was locked up there for days. She saw pretty well everything he did.'

Scuff felt a hurt tighten inside him. He wished he were bigger and stronger, so he could personally hit Hamilton Rand, beat him till he bled, and make him really sorry for what he had done.

'Then we've got to see that they put him in prison,' he said with intense feeling. 'We must! However long we have to look. Why aren't we going straight away? What are we waiting for?'

'Lunch,' Monk answered.

'What does lunch matter?' Scuff said incredulously.

Monk stared at him. It was the first time since he had known him that Scuff had been uninterested in any kind of food.

Scuff blushed, but he was still annoyed.

'Actually,' Monk said gently. 'I want you to stay here and look after Hester. She's having some pretty bad nightmares about being captive in that house, about being tied down and bleeding to death herself. I don't want to leave her alone – in fact I can't. I could ask someone from the clinic, perhaps—'

'I'll do it,' Scuff interrupted. It made him almost sick, the thought of using a stranger for this, compared with him. 'You shouldn't get someone else. That'd be bad. She'd think we didn't care. What's wrong with you?'

Monk tried to hide his smile but Scuff saw it. 'You did that on purpose!' he accused Monk, feeling the colour burn up his face. It was a mixture of anger, fear, awareness of terrible responsibility, and also of at last being almost grown up . . . and still belonging.

'Be gentle with her,' Monk continued. 'She saw some pretty bad things. She knew he'd kill her and the children if Radnor died, and it looked once or twice as if he would. But make her eat. Don't listen to her if she says she's not hungry. Cups of tea, bread and butter, but cut it thin. Have you ever watched her butter the cut end of the loaf, and then slice it afterwards, so the butter holds it together and you can do it really thin?'

Scuff nodded. 'Yes. Is that what I should do?'

'Yes, if you can. If you can't, then get her to do it herself, even if you pretend it's for you. Just get her to eat, and talk to her. Don't leave her alone. I don't know when I'll be back. Depends on what we find. It could take all night, even the next day. Don't worry, just sit up with her, if I'm not back. Don't let her have nightmares and wake up in the dark alone.'

'I won't,' Scuff promised. 'I'll sit in the chair all night, I promise.'

'Thank you.'

Scuff took his new responsibility very seriously. The more he thought about it, the more he realised that Monk not only trusted him, but he had offered him an opportunity to repay a small part of all that Hester had done for him.

Even now he occasionally dreamed again of being locked into the bulges of Jericho Phillips' boat.

Did Hester feel like that? She was so strong and so clever it was hard to believe she could ever have felt as small and vulnerable as he had, or so easily beaten. Maybe he could even be more help to her than Monk himself? He knew what it felt like. He would always know, whatever else happened to him. Even if he grew to be as tall as Monk, learned how to fight, how to get a proper job and earn money, that memory would always be there somewhere inside him, behind a door he wouldn't open, unless he had to.

As soon as Monk was gone he stoked up the fire and put the kettle on. Hester was folding laundry in the back of the laundry room and where the deep tubs were that you could wash sheets in. He knew there was cake in the pantry. He fetched it out and put it on the table, then went to find her.

As soon as he opened the laundry room door he saw her. She was standing with a clean sheet in one hand, thinking, as if she were miles away, or had forgotten how to fold it.

He took it from her and gave her back one end. She smiled and took it. Together they folded all of them and put them in a pile. He loved the smell of clean cotton. It was warm and safe. It was sweet – not like sugar, but like the wind in the country that blows in off fields. He had only smelled that recently, just the other day, but it wasn't something you forgot.

'Thank you,' she said with a slight smile. She still looked very pale.

'I made some tea,' he told her. 'And I got the cake out. Maybe if we eat all that then we could make some more.'

'We?' She smiled, shaking her head, following him into the kitchen. She saw the cake and the teapot and cups on the table. Suddenly she blinked very hard and looked away, as if there were something interesting beyond the window.

He pretended not to have noticed. But that told him Hester was in a bad way. Other women cried quite often, but not Hester. Whatever happened, she dealt with it. She never cried.

He sat down at the table and poured the tea, one cup for her, one for himself. Then he cut the cake in half and put a piece on each of the plates. She would argue about eating so much, but Monk had said she needed to eat.

Scuff took a deep breath. He did not know what he should do, and he tried to remember what she had done when he had nightmares about Phillips' boat. She had made him talk about it, little by little, not keep it all locked up inside him, too dreadful for words.

'Your tea's getting cold,' he said. Then he thought that was silly. He had only just poured it.

She turned away from the window and sat down opposite him. He knew from her face that she was just being polite, but she started to eat the cake, just in small pieces, one at a time. She looked tired and, if such a thing were possible, afraid.

He must say something. That was what Monk had left him here for, not just to sit and watch. It was very strange. It was always she who had made him talk when he was scared and miserable, remembering bad things and frightened they would happen again. It had been as if he even just closed his eyes, maybe he would open them and find he was back there, and the reality was in fact the dream.

'I still dream about Jericho Phillips,' he said quietly.

She looked up at him, letting the cake fall. 'I know. I can't promise it will go away. I wish I could. But it will get less.'

'It's less now,' he answered. 'But you said it was all right to talk about it sometimes, and I wasn't a coward because it still scared me.'

'It is all right,' she said quickly. 'Do you want to talk about it?'

'No. But is it true, what you said, that it's not silly to talk about it sometimes, and not being a baby if it still feels real, and bad?'

'Of course it's not silly. Why would you ask that? Have the dreams got worse?' Now she looked so worried he was afraid he had gone too far.

'No, they haven't,' he said quickly. 'Hardly ever happens any more. But I know what it's like. I was thinking about them little kids. Are they going to have dreams too, d'yer reckon? Or did you stop that 'cos yer were there so they weren't never alone?'

Hester smiled a little hazily. 'I'd like to think so. At least most of the time. They'll be back with their mother and father soon. When they're stronger.'

'But was their mother really pleased to see them?' he pressed.

'Oh, yes.' Now her voice was definitely husky, as if she were fighting back intense emotion. 'Yes, she was. It was as if someone had turned on all the lights inside her.'

Scuff was quiet for a moment, tasting the happiness of it. Then he took a breath. 'You could talk about it, too. I can listen. You taught me how to do that. I wouldn't think you were silly. Sometimes it's silly not to be scared.'

She smiled properly this time, and the tears came to her eyes again. 'Thank you,' she said huskily.

'So tell me about it.' He kept his voice firm. 'I'm not going to leave you alone, not till Monk comes back. I'm going to sleep in the armchair in your room, so if you wake up in the night I'll be there.'

'You don't have to do that!' she protested.

'Yeah, I do. I remember how scared I was, and when I woke up in the night you were always there, until I was all right again.' He stared at her, meeting her eyes, and she did not look away. He saw that she had been badly hurt, because of the children she couldn't save, and because she thought she would die and not see Monk again, or him, or anyone she loved. He knew that was what he saw because it was what he would have felt.

'It'll get better,' he promised. 'Even if they don't hang Mr Rand, something'll happen to stop him, or we'll make it happen.' He had no idea if that was true, but he reckoned that was what she needed to believe. 'I promise,' he added.

She reached across and kissed him very gently on the cheek. 'Thank you,' she whispered. 'I would like it if you slept in the chair. That way I don't think the bad dreams will dare to come.'

He felt a rush of pleasure like a warmth inside him. This must be what belonging was, not here because people were sorry for you, but because you were worth something too.

That night Hester still dreamed, and it was of reunion, of families together. It was not Charlie, Maggie and Mike seeing their mother again and knowing they could go home, it was of Adrienne and the restored and vigorous Bryson Radnor.

Had Adrienne known he would make that dramatic entrance in the trial? That was what had saved her, and incidentally also Hamilton Rand. Had she known he would do that? The terror in her face suggested not. Was that so no one would suspect, or had Radnor not even thought of it until the moment when he acted?

She would rather have assumed that he had, but glimpses kept coming back to her of Adrienne and Radnor together both in the hospital, and later in the cottage. He was impatient with her, condescending, sometimes even dismissive. Had that been his illness speaking, his fear? Or his nature?

Did Adrienne understand him, and it did not matter?

Or did she depend on him too deeply even to fight back?

Hester slipped deeper into dreamless sleep without an answer.

Monk and Hooper took a far smaller cart to Redditch this time, and a horse that could keep up a pretty good pace. They called in very briefly at the local police station, to let them know they would be at the cottage, looking for further evidence to do with the case. It was not only a courtesy, but a necessary precaution in the circumstances. Another necessary precaution was to take a pistol each, just in case the gardener with the shotgun, and now with a very real cause for vengeance, might still be on the property, or in the woods nearby.

'If he decides to shoot at me, he could say he thought I was a rabbit,' Hooper said drily.

Monk looked Hooper up and down. 'And expect to be believed?' he said incredulously.

Hooper grinned. 'Maybe not, but it would be a bit late for me then,' he pointed out.

They arrived in the golden autumn morning. Many of the fields were already harvested and the stooks stood sharp in a bucolic kind of beauty. After rubbing the horse down and giving it shelter and water, which was plentiful in the old stables, Hooper gave it a small portion of the oats they had brought for it, and then they turned their attention to the house.

'The local police have already been right through it,' Monk said thoughtfully as they stood in the kitchen. 'What could we see that they missed?'

'Something we know is here and they didn't,' Hooper replied without hesitation.

Monk thought for a moment, turning round slowly, staring at the walls, cupboards, storage bins. 'Food,' he said. 'The local shop should be able to tell us what stores were bought, over the last few years. Let's look for laundry supplies. Sick people need a lot of laundry doing. They also need the place clean. You don't clean the house every day if there's no one living here. We'll see what there is, what sort, what amounts. Old cartons could tell us a lot. How much bed linen is there? Later we can look for a workshop and the tools where Rand made the machine that delivers the blood drip by drip.'

'Right,' Hooper agreed.

'And another thing,' Monk added. 'Maybe this one isn't his first machine. If we can find the remains of another, older one, that would be evidence of his trying this for a long time.'

'Not proof by itself,' Hooper pointed out ruefully.

'It is if there are traces of blood in it,' Monk retorted. 'Let's start looking for bits and pieces that would have been parts. Notice everything with that in mind. It might look like a hosepipe or part of the plumbing now.'

Hooper rolled his eyes, but he did it with a smile, albeit a wry one.

They worked until it was dark, then lit the oil lamps and did what little could be done in their light. They found enough bed linen to offer changes for eight beds. Some of it was very old, as if it had been there when Rand was a child. Similarly they found a few toys in the boxroom that could have belonged to anyone in the last half-century. There was even an old rocking horse.

There was not storage for more food than three or four people would need, but the gardener grew potatoes, carrots, green vegetables, onions, lots of beans and most of the herbs that were common. The orchard was laden with apples, pears and plums, and there were wild berries in the hedges. There was a milking space in the cow shed, although the cows had gone, but perhaps not so long ago.

'Perfect place,' Monk said with a touch of bitterness. 'But what the hell proof is there of anything? All the experiments could have happened here.'

Hooper pointed to a pile of odd pipe lengths, plumbing joints, valves and lengths of wood sitting in the corner. 'He certainly used his workshop. Could have made the machine in the downstairs bedroom in here easily. But I couldn't find proof that there was an earlier one, although I believe there was. Maybe several.'

'If he'd any sense he would have got rid of the bits,' Monk

agreed. 'Probably buried them. He's got acres to choose his spot. We'll get an early night. Can't search much with a lantern. Let's start questioning the villagers tomorrow; see who they remember being here.'

Hooper's face was bleak. 'See how many kids have gone missing that were never accounted for.'

'That too,' Monk agreed softly. 'If this is where he did earlier experiments then there's got to be something.'

But the villagers could tell them nothing that was definitive. Many were willing to stand in the street and recall all that Monk and Hooper would listen to. Yes, this person or that had gone missing, but usually it was easily explained. This one had gone on a drunken spree and returned home without any recollections of where he had been. These two had eloped. Heard to be living a few miles away. That one had joined a travelling fair, so they said. Of course there were those no one could account for, but that was always so. Maybe more of them than might be normal were young and healthy. This was always very sad, but such things happened. Was it more here than happened in any other village? Who could say?

Monk and Hooper had a stroke of luck at the local pub. Both were weary and by now also disheartened. Talking about it only made it worse.

Monk was considering returning home. He hated having to tell Hester that they had found a dozen things that were indicative, but even taken all together, they proved nothing. There was no witness who could testify to anything, and also no signs of the gardener. He had apparently gone to recuperate from his misadventures with a relative over a hundred miles away, they learned.

'Wish I'd known that when we arrived,' Hooper said unhappily, when he and Monk had returned to the cottage. 'I wouldn't have been looking over my shoulder half the time.'

'He'll come back,' Monk said, standing near the potting shed. 'These tools are worth a fair bit. And well kept. No dirt on any of this, all clean, practically polished.' He walked over to the rack where spades and forks were neatly arranged. 'Lot of them. He must do a fair bit of digging. This one's got a brand-new head on it.'

'Digging,' Hooper repeated the word thoughtfully. 'Lot of garden here, but only so much digging you can do. Mostly a weeding and raking sort of thing, except when you dig up the potatoes. I'd do that with a fork, myself, not a spade.'

A horrible thought crept into Monk's mind, making him cold in the pit of his belly. He looked at Hooper, and saw the same thought in his eyes.

'What do you suppose they intended to do with the bodies, if they had to kill the children, or Hester?' Monk said.

'Bury them,' Hooper replied without hesitation, as if saying the words were somehow drawing their venom.

'Where?' Monk looked around.

'Not here!' Hooper said quickly. 'Somewhere that no one would notice the disturbed earth. Somewhere that the grass would grow thick and green over it quickly, and where that wouldn't be noticed either. New green is easy to see.'

'Pretty thick grass in the orchard,' Monk said thoughtfully. 'But it's all a bit lush and untended in there. Some of the apple trees look as if they could do with pruning.'

'You know about that?' Hooper asked with surprise.

It must be somewhere in the lost part of Monk's memory, which was all his life up to the point of the accident. Bits of knowledge came now and then, unattached to any experience. He did not want to remind Hooper about his mysterious past just now, though. All that mattered was proving Rand's guilt.

'Apples grow near the sea,' Monk said with as much of a smile as he could manage. 'Let's take the spades and look for likely places. Not close to the roots. It would be much harder work. And if they cut a root the tree might show it. The gardener'd know that.'

'Reckon he was in on it?' Hooper asked, taking one of the spades and following him.

'Have to be,' Monk replied, leading the way to the orchard gate and opening it. 'Couldn't risk having him find out by accident. He would feel betrayed and could be dangerous. He'd see the spades, anyway, just as we did, and work out what they were for. Keep him implicated, and he'll be twice as good a guard. Never betray them, or he'd be betraying himself as well. Rand's quite clever enough to have thought of that.'

Hooper grunted his agreement.

Once in the orchard they walked on the grass between the trees, which were haphazardly planted. There were no straight rows. All the grass was deep, as if scythed no more than once a year, but entirely unevenly. If there were any undisturbed patches they would be hard to find.

It was quarter of an hour of steady searching before they found a place lush enough to raise a hope.

'Could be a dog,' Hooper said with a shrug. 'Lots of people would bury an animal in a place like this.'

'Didn't see any sign of their having had a dog.' Monk was determined to believe in success. 'If they had one, it would belong to the gardener, and he doesn't live in.' He started to dig, driving the blade deep into the soft earth, still damp in the shade of the trees.

Hooper started several feet away, still in the greener grass. They worked in silence, just digging a spade's depth, taking out the earth, then another. It was hard work, using muscles they did not normally exercise so hard. Hooper could not hide the fact that his arm still ached from the injury.

It was Hooper who struck something hard first. He stopped suddenly, his face pale in spite of the exertion. He stared at

Monk. Then they both put their spades down and bent to their knees to search with hands in the rich loam.

It was a thick bone, about a foot long, completely without flesh.

Hooper laid it on the grass. 'Could be an animal,' he said. His voice was soft, as if he were trying to keep the excitement out of it, the hope, but he still trembled very slightly.

'Could be,' Monk agreed, rising to his feet and picking up his spade again.

Be careful,' Hooper warned him unnecessarily. 'Don't want to break anything if there's more.'

It took them another hour, moving slowly, always finishing with hands now caked with soil. Eventually they found all the rest of the bones of an old, disintegrated skeleton. It was beyond question that of a child of about ten or eleven years old.

'Do you suppose it's the only one?' Hooper said, his face grim, and smeared with mud and sweat. He wiped his hand across his brow, making it worse.

'Probably not,' Monk said unhappily. He had wanted to find exactly this evidence, but now that he had, all he could think of was how the child died, whether he had been terrified, in pain, even if he had been killed quickly. Had his parents ever known, or was he simply lost, still grieved over, still a mystery? If it had been Scuff, or even Worm, would he ever forget? Hester wouldn't.

'I'll go on here,' said Monk. 'You go to the village and find the sexton from the local church. Tell him what we've discovered and bring him, and any other grave-digger he has.'

'You go to the sexton, sir,' Hooper responded. 'You've more authority than I. It'll be—'

'I also don't have a recent arm injury,' Monk said tartly. 'Do as you're told. Don't make me pull rank on you, Hooper.'

Hooper smiled broadly, straightening up his back. 'You just did – sir.'

'That's right, so don't stand arguing with me. Go and get the sexton.'

'Yes, sir!' Hooper gave a mock salute, and winced.

He returned a long half-hour later, bringing with him the sexton and another grave-digger, both carrying spades. Monk had spent the time searching the orchard for other spots out of the way of tree roots, and where the grass was greenest. He was filthy, his hands were bruised and his back ached.

They worked until the dusk was too deep to see any more. They found six further bodies; in all there were four children and three adults, so far as they could tell. The adults were young women, small in height, slender-boned, but – judging from the skulls and teeth – fully grown. They were in various stages of decay. Nature and insects had taken nearly all the flesh.

It took the men until after midnight to inform the parish minister and have the burial places marked. The bodies were taken to lie decently, crowding the small morgue, which had never before had more than two occupants at a time.

These bodies were evidence, but as soon as all notes and drawings had been made, the local Church would bury them decently, even if in graves no one could mark with a name.

They knew of no way to say how long they had been buried, how they had died, or who they had been in life. The farmhouse had been frequently unoccupied over the last hundred years. Even when someone had been living there, there was easy access from the road to the orchard without going through the garden. Everyone believed it was whoever lived in the farm that had buried the bodies so that they would lie undisturbed in land to which they had the right, but there was no way to prove it. Anyone could have come from the far side, at night, and buried their dead . . . their victims.

Monk and Hooper found accommodation at the local inn.

Early the next morning, as the sun was rising, they walked back to the farm, hitched the horse to the wagon again, and set out for home.

They arrived in the late morning to find Hester up and busy in the house, cooking. This was not an occupation she sought willingly, but it required attention to do it well and prevented thoughts of other things. As soon as she heard Monk's steps in the hall, she dropped the wooden spoon with which she had been stirring cake mixture and ran to the kitchen door to meet him, Scuff on her heels.

Monk did not need to ask if she were better; it was in her eyes, in the strength of her arms as she held on to him. He kissed her mouth, her face, held her even closer, then looked past her at Scuff and saw the pride in him, and the question.

Monk nodded and smiled back. He would say the words of thanks later, when Hester was not there.

She pushed away from him now, looking up. Suddenly she was grave.

'The judge has abandoned the trial of Hamilton Rand,' she said quietly. 'And Adrienne Radnor as well. Oliver said there is prejudice attached, which means they can't be tried again. I'm so sorry.'

Chapter Thirteen

HESTER MADE as little mention as she could of the fact that Hamilton Rand had been effectively found not guilty. People might think what they wished; he could not be tried again. It was not even as if he were a doctor and there was any privilege that could be taken from him. And what Magnus Rand had known, or how much he had been compliant, had not ever been mentioned. There was nothing more Monk could do, therefore raising the subject caused nothing but useless regret, even guilt. They had done the best they could. Oliver Rathbone had been right in his instinct not to prosecute the case. Not that he would be tactless enough to say so.

The terrible knowledge of the bodies in the orchard troubled all of them. But whatever they believed, there was no proof at all that they had been buried by Rand, or by his gardener. The Rand brothers owned the place, but had seldom visited it. Indeed, Magnus Rand had not been seen in the village since his childhood visits to the aunt, who had owned it then.

The bodies were examined thoroughly, but it was not possible to say how they had died, or when, except very roughly. The only thing for certain was that there were no clothes found. Presumably those had been burned in the large furnace where other waste was disposed of. There was very little flesh left because the bodies had been exposed to the insects, worms and so on in the ground. For certain there were no injuries on the bones. None was broken or marked, and there was no damage whatever to the skulls. Any defence lawyer would claim that there was no connection with two brothers who lived in London and seldom visited. None of the bodies was identifiable, nor could anyone say to the month or year how long they had lain there. The land was accessible to anyone.

The gardener did not return, nor could he be found.

Adrienne Radnor was a different matter. Hester thought more and more of the relationship between her and Radnor himself. She had not liked the young woman, and yet there was something in her turbulent emotions that she could not forget.

She remembered her own father more often since she'd encountered the Radnors, all the good things about him: his sudden, startling sense of humour; his love of butterflies and the enormous knowledge of them that he had acquired, for no reason other than the pleasure it gave him. He knew they served a purpose in the life and nature of plants, but they were also unnecessarily and almost frivolously beautiful.

Other memories came back to her with painful clarity. He had been so proud of her when she went off to the Crimea to nurse. She could see his face in her mind's eye, filled with pride. It was her mother who had been doubtful. He had been convinced she would succeed and find both hardship and happiness in the venture. Of course he was right.

While she was gone he had been deceived, ruined and so – as a matter of honour, as he saw it – had taken his own life. Her mother had not lived long after him. And Hester had not been anywhere near to help. There might have been nothing she could have done, but that was not the point – she would have tried.

Adrienne Radnor's situation was different. She had given up any chance of her own personal happiness in order to stay at her father's side, first in his loneliness when her mother died, then later to nurse him as his illness developed and he became dependent upon her for even simple things.

What had she given up? She was a handsome woman. She must have had opportunities of marriage, her own children, freedom to be separate from her father, both financially and socially. And yet she had chosen to stay. Why?

The sharp unease of Hester's dreams came back to her. Had that been out of love, or duty? Was it some guilt or flaw in Hester that she saw it as a mutual kind of emotional dependence? Radnor needed Adrienne to care for him, but he could have hired someone to do that. He had more than sufficient money. Rand had told her that Radnor provided funds for his research, and would continue to do.

It was Adrienne's love for him, her need of him, her passion and vitality of life that he needed to feel, even touch. He needed her emotional force to live through vicariously, as he needed the literal blood of Charlie and Maggie, and when they were worn out, of Mike.

She considered speaking of it to Monk, but there was nothing he could do. This was something she had seen in the days when she was at the cottage, watching and listening because she could not help it. If Radnor died Rand could not afford to let her live and she had seen the knowledge of that in Radnor's eyes, too. He understood it perfectly, and it amused him. Her life depended upon his. It was the ultimate irony.

She recalled the vigour in him as he burst into the court-room. That was over a month ago, and yet the shock of it still rippled through her like a cold wind on naked flesh. She would feel it again and again. It was a cry of the passion to live, to survive. He was, in that moment of supreme victory, the passionate, indulgent, fiercely alive man his nature had created, unencumbered by weakness or the fear of death. He had seen the darkness of annihilation and beaten it!

Did he really need Adrienne any more? With his health back, was she anything more than a shackle, to make him remain here and in some way look after her?

He could marry her off. She was heiress to whatever he did not spend on himself. Perhaps that would not be so very much. She was still young enough to bear children, though perhaps it might not be as easy as in her youth. But perhaps she did not wish to. He certainly owed her more than a match of convenience after the years she had given up to be with him. She had said she wished to travel with him to see all those great sights he had spoken of when he thought it impossible he would ever revisit them. Hester could remember vividly the longing in Adrienne's face. She loved his company. All other men would seem tame to her.

Did Radnor want to take her? He had let Hester know that included in his love of life was his love of women in particular. His physical appetites were intense, and he had no thought whatever of curbing them. Was Adrienne going to be part of that? A watcher, unneeded and unloved?

With a cold certainty Hester was sure that Adrienne was not. Maybe she would be forced into a marriage she did not want. Or if she became too clinging, too clingingly dependent upon him, might she meet with a fatal accident?

No, of course not. Hester was allowing something she thought she had seen in Radnor's eyes to create a picture of evil that was totally without foundation.

However, it was engraved in her mind so she could see it every time she closed her eyes and was momentarily back in the cottage, feeling the emotional bonds tightening around her, keeping her there. Of one thing she was certain: Radnor did not need his daughter any more.

Tomorrow, when Monk was on the river, she would go and visit Adrienne to talk to her alone.

She had considerable difficulty persuading Scuff to go with her.

'Yer didn't ought to go,' he said with conviction. 'She didn't help you when you were a prisoner and could 'ave been killed. In fact, if Radnor'd died, you would've been. An' she 'ad to know that! She in't in any danger 'cept of being used by 'er father, and that's going to 'appen whether you say so to 'er or not.' That was very reasonable, and he knew it. He was behaving like a man, not a boy. He was telling her why she shouldn't go, whereas a boy would just have asked her not to. He smiled very slightly.

Hester smiled back at him. 'Are you saying that because she didn't save me, then I shouldn't try to save her?' she asked.

For an instant he was wrong-footed. 'Summink like that,' he agreed.

'You think I should be like her?' Now she sounded surprised.

'No!' Of course that was not what he meant. 'But yer don't 'ave to go out of yer way to tell 'er what she prob'ly knows anyhow. She won't listen to you, because she don't want to hear it. Yer said so and yer said she in't got anyone 'cept 'er father, so if she wasn't with 'im, what'd she do?'

'Get married,' Hester replied. 'Have a family of her own.'

He thought about that for a moment or two. The only time he had seen Adrienne Radnor was when they had rescued Hester and the children. Adrienne had been frightened and angry, fighting all the way. Her hands had been tied behind her back with rope, her hair all over the place and her dress filthy from when she had been thrown on to the ground as they overpowered her. He had never thought of the possibility of anyone wanting to marry her. But then he didn't understand a lot of things about why and who people married. They just did. A fair few regretted it later, both men and women.

'Yer can't do that for 'er,' he said, pleased with the logic of that.

'No, of course I can't,' she agreed. 'All I might do is make her see her position a little more clearly.'

He frowned. 'Yer mean scare her? She'll get angry!'

'Yes, I suppose I do. Because she might.'

He had expected her to argue, and then he could have argued back. The fact that she had not robbed him of a response.

'Come with me?' she asked. 'She'll be a lot more careful about getting angry with two of us.'

Scuff knew the look in her eyes. She would go alone if she had to. It would be much better if he were there. He would at least protect her if Miss Radnor were to lose her temper.

He conceded with as much grace as he could manage.

Hester timed her visit for the mid-afternoon. It was a little early for the usual social call, but not so early as to clash with a late luncheon. It was also the time she thought it least likely for Bryson Radnor to be at home. He had been abundantly full of vigour at the trial; she judged he would escape the confines of the house, and the tedium of female company, as often as he could. If she saw him present, or any evidence that he was so, she would turn and leave again – she hoped unseen.

She knew his address from Magnus Rand's notes on Radnor when he first came to the hospital, but the house was far larger and more imposing than she had expected. It spoke very clearly of Radnor's considerable fortune, both from its size and the care with which it was maintained. It was set well back from the road, and the late summer garden was filled with bloom. The second flush of roses sent out a rich perfume that wrapped around her before she reached for the bell-pull beside the carved front door.

The house should not have surprised her; Radnor had made no secret of his love of all sensual beauty. And yet its beauty caught her oddly vulnerably all the same. There was an ease in it, an exuberance for life. It pulled her memory back to his gaunt face, filled with passion and fury when he was so afraid of dying, of losing all the great, rich world and the excitement in its own infinite vitality. She hated him, but she understood him.

Perhaps she should have shouted at him that Maggie, Charlie and Mike had the right to taste all these things too. Even if they never savoured them as he would have, it was not Radnor's right to deny them, or anyone. Who knows the colours someone else sees?

The bell was answered by a footman and Hester asked if she might see Miss Adrienne Radnor. It was a matter concerning the health of her father, and in some degree of confidence.

The footman showed her in, and she waited with trepidation in a great room facing on to the garden. It was full of light, and decorated mostly in soft greens. There were several bookshelves and at least a dozen artefacts that looked to be of ancient origin, perhaps from the Near East, such as Egypt or Palestine.

Scuff had gone into the garden, just around the corner, where he could hear her if she called out, but need not be party to the conversation, if indeed there was one.

Hester would gladly have looked at the artefacts, and also the books, but within a few minutes of her arrival the door to the hall opened and Adrienne came in. Even in the short while since the time in the cottage, she had changed so much that Hester was taken aback. Had they met in the street she would have been uncertain if she was the same woman. She walked uprightly, her head high. The sheen was back in her hair; indeed, it was quite beautiful. Her eyes were clear and there was colour in her skin. She was dressed in a pale green summer afternoon gown, which became her excellently. She looked almost like a woman in love.

Was that possible? Could she have had a relationship of such a nature that had had to be set aside during her father's illness, but would now be taken up again? Perhaps Hester had been totally mistaken in the whole nature of her love for her father, and his for her, and it was only the terror of death she had seen in his eyes, not the evil she imagined.

Of course it was wrong to kidnap, and the use of the children beyond wrong; it was monstrous. To do so out of terror, no matter how deep, was not an excuse.

'Good afternoon, Mrs Monk,' Adrienne said with a lift of curiosity in her voice. 'Bartlett said that you wished to inform me of something regarding my father's health. I can assure you, he has no problems. He is his old self again – except that perhaps he values everything even more, if such were possible. And I bear you no ill will for your testimony in court. You said what you had to say, in the circumstances.' She smiled bleakly, as if conscious of the irony of the situation, and her own equivocal role in it. 'I had no part in your kidnap, but I could have helped you escape, and I did not. I knew we needed your skill to keep my father alive long enough for the treatment to work. And, in my better moments, I also knew that you would not hurt him, even to save your own life.'

'It wouldn't have saved my life,' Hester replied with equal honesty. 'If your father had died, Mr Rand would have had no further use for me. Indeed, he could not afford for me to survive anyway. But you are right that I would not have hurt your father. He was my patient. To destroy him would have destroyed me too.'

Adrienne shook her head. 'You are a very strange woman, but in a way I admire you. Certainly I respect you. And I do not expect you to have the same regard for me.' She did not hide the sadness that it caused her.

Hester made a sudden decision. 'You are not entirely right.

I admire the way you set your own ambitions and desires aside to devote yourself to your father's needs.' She adjusted the truth a little, not to save herself but to save the memory of her father's limitations, which still hurt her with a deep, unbearable pain. 'When my father was ill I was in the Crimea, nursing soldiers. I did not even know he needed me. I had gone because I believed it was the right thing to do, but also because I wanted the freedom and the adventure. I wanted something far more than the sort of domestic life I would have become locked into if I had stayed here.'

She saw the sudden emotion in Adrienne's face: deep, complex and, to Hester, unreadable. There was both surprise and pain in it, and a gentleness towards Hester she had never seen before, as if Adrienne had suddenly seen something in her that she recognised.

Her own confusion mirrored it. This was a woman she had disliked. She had come out of duty and a desire to find some way that Bryson Radnor could be made to pay at least something for his crimes. To her surprise, she found she now meant what she was saying.

'I was not there for my father, or my mother, when they most needed me. By the time I came home from the Crimea, it was too late. They were both dead. You did better than that.'

The silence lasted so long Hester was afraid that Adrienne was not going to answer.

'Did you know he was ill when you went?' she asked at last.

'No.' That was completely honest. No one could have foreseen his ruin. The fraud that had brought it about was not even thought of at the time of Hester's departure.

'Then you are blaming yourself simply out of grief,' Adrienne told her. She said it gently.

For a moment they sat in the beautiful room in silent

companionship, then Hester forced her mind back to the reason she had come. Was there still any need for her to say the things she had planned? Maybe it was she who was wrong, not Adrienne. Maybe Radnor would not go off on adventures and leave Adrienne behind. And if he took her, perhaps that was what she wanted. She would share in whatever he did, even love it as much as he did. As long as it was her choice, it was really none of Hester's concern.

How could she decide whether she should say anything further, or simply wish Adrienne well, and leave? Radnor was still guilty of all that they had believed of him, but there was no proof. Would pursuing it damage the course of medical discovery, without obtaining justice for anyone? Vengeance was a bitter dish, and in the end helped no one.

The silence was stretching too long.

'I imagine your father will continue to travel,' Hester said as naturally as she could. 'He spoke at times of some marvellous places he had been to. It made me long to go too; see sights I can barely imagine, they were so beautiful. Tropical islands, skies of such exquisite shades they made the earth seem luxurious beneath them; seas the colours of jewels, and fish that could fly. He spoke of cities in the ancient world that were old a thousand years ago, places with magical names like Isfahan, Trebizond, Damascus . . . Palm trees against the evening sky, the sound of camel bells in the night, and the smell of the wind off a desert as old as time itself. I envy you that . . .'

She saw the sudden change in Adrienne's face and stopped. There was no need for words. Adrienne had seen none of those things, and she was sick with shame that she could not tell Hester so without admitting that her father had not asked her to go with him, not ever.

Hester was overwhelmed with a sense of pity that she could not express without making it worse. When someone was humiliated, pity added salt to the wound. Maybe it was not love for her father that had kept her at his side day and night during his illness, and that had driven her to connive at Hester's captivity, but the need for him to love her! To mitigate some of the years of her devotion since her mother's death, keeping her little more than a child still, with the devouring needs of such a man to fulfil. Please God, he had taken his physical needs somewhere else. From his words, Hester had formed the opinion that it had been so. Perhaps Adrienne knew little of that. She would surely have chosen to look the other way.

In her own way, Adrienne was a prisoner even more tightly bound than Hester had been. No one would come and free her, because no one else knew she was bound. The chains were invisible.

Hester must say something now. Perhaps the only merciful thing to do was to pretend she did not know. What could she say that was not hypocritical, and transparent? She must leave Adrienne some dignity.

'I said that I came to see you about your father's health.' She picked her words a little desperately. 'It was not entirely true. I came out of some concern for you. I can only guess what your ordeal can have been, watching him suffer and fearing the outcome. Everyone's concern was vested in him. None of us thought of you.'

Adrienne smiled ruefully, but she did not interrupt.

'Now that my own difficulty is past,' Hester went on, 'I have things a little more in proportion, and I wondered if anyone was caring for you. I'm happy to see that you look so well. The relief must be immense.'

Adrienne was staring at her as though she were struggling to believe what Hester was saying. After the trial, and Hester's testimony, that was hardly surprising. It was time to be less evasive.

'I understand what it is to fight with every weapon you

have to save those you love, and who have loved you, and trusted you,' Hester said quietly. 'I would fight with everything I have for my family and think of the consequences later. I hope your father understands how much of yourself you have given so he had the chance to recover. He must wish above all to repay you somehow.' As she said the words she knew they were false, not because she thought so ill of Radnor, but because the confirmation that she was right was in Adrienne's eyes.

'Thank you,' Adrienne said so softly Hester read the words in the movement of her lips rather than heard the sound of them.

Hester stood up. She did not wish Radnor to catch her here.

'It is time I left you to enjoy your beautiful garden. From what I have seen of it, it is a masterpiece. Thank you for receiving me.'

Adrienne seemed bereft of words for a moment or two, and then she put out her hand and grasped Hester's so hard it was difficult for her not to wince.

'It was my pleasure . . . Mrs Monk.'

Hester was seen out by the footman who had let her in. As she walked down the path past the roses she saw Scuff come through the taller bushes from the back and join her at the gate. He looked at her curiously, but did not ask her anything. Maybe he was not certain if he wanted to know what had transpired. On the other hand, he may have seen in her face that she did not wish to tell him anything, at least not yet, probably not at all.

Two days later Hester was at the breakfast table ready to give Monk a second cup of tea when Hooper came in through the back door. He had knocked, but so lightly that they saw his shadow as he stepped in rather than heard him.

Hester knew instantly that something was very badly wrong.

'What is it?' she asked, putting the teapot down as if it had suddenly become too heavy to hold.

Monk stared at Hooper, waiting.

Hooper's face was marked with sadness.

'I just heard from the local station that this morning, at daylight, they found the body of Adrienne Radnor. She was lying in a ditch about quarter of a mile from her home. She was strangled to death. They don't know anything else yet. The inspector will tell us when they do.'

Hester wanted to say that it could not be so, but she knew with cold, sick certainty that it could. She put her hands over her face and felt the hot tears prick through her eyelids. She did not even hear what Monk said, and barely felt his hand touch hers.

Chapter Fourteen

RATHBONE HAD felt certain from the beginning that there was only a slight chance of a successful prosecution of Hamilton Rand for kidnap. Even so, victory had seemed within their grasp until the moment Radnor strode into the court, vigorous, almost larger than life, and proclaimed his very obvious cure. Then, of course, the case had fallen apart. Lord Justice Patterson had had no choice. No jury would have convicted after that.

It had been a much more bitter defeat than Rathbone had thought it would be. In spite of the success of the experiment, and the huge leap forward for medicine that it represented, he was still certain that there had been a crime committed. He had had no conception of how great a crime until Monk told him about the bones dug up in the orchard. It struck him with a new and far deeper sense of defeat that there was no proof whatever that they were perhaps the bodies of people experimented on by Rand. And yet these bones fitted what was known of Rand and his research.

Who were they? Those who would not be missed, either because they lived alone and no one cared enough to report their absence, or those whose absence could be explained in some reasonable way?

The bones seemed to belong to bodies of all sizes, all ages. Who had been the patients receiving the treatment? Old rich men terrified to die, like Radnor? They would have gone to Rand willingly, even paid for the privilege. If they had lived, everyone would have heard about their cure, so presumably they had died and theirs would have been the larger corpses – unless they had died in the hospital, like so many others. That would require no explanation. The very ill were expected to die.

The smaller skeletons troubled him far more. Were they children from very poor families, like Charlie, Maggie and Mike? Why take children? Was it something about their blood? Or were they simply easier to manage? They would certainly be easily overpowered, and far easier to keep captive.

Whatever the benefits to medicine, Rathbone would dearly have liked to see Rand prosecuted for his crimes. Someone else could take over his research. If those bodies were what was left of children he had bled to death, then he should hang for it.

Then, the previous day, Monk had told him very briefly about the finding of the body of Adrienne Radnor. In a matter of a few minutes Rathbone was hurled from contempt for her almost to pity, and he felt a sense of outrage on her behalf. He had thought of her as devoted to her father blindly, to an unhealthy degree. She had seemed to be dependent upon him not only socially and financially, and perhaps for all her material comforts, but also emotionally in a way that was beyond normal.

Now he saw her as pitiful, her devotion abused, a woman denied her youth, and now denied her maturity also.

Who had killed her, strangled her and dumped her body in a ditch as if it were so much refuse? Her reticule was gone, so the attack on her appeared at a glance to be a robbery turned unnecessarily violent. But as he sat in his office the more he thought of that, the less sense it made. She lived in a very wealthy area where few people roamed around at night.

What was she doing out on the road in the dark, and alone? And what could possibly be in her reticule that would be worth stealing, or committing murder to take?

Could it really be coincidence, so hard on the heels of so much else?

He wanted to go and talk with Ardal Juster, and see what he thought of it, and if there were reasonable suspects from the case. Exactly what had happened? Was there at last a viable prosecution in this miserable affair?

First he would talk it over with Beata York. Her judgement was sound, and any reason to see her pleased him.

He considered whether he would go home and shave again and change his clothes before calling, or if that would be too obviously contrived. Yet if he went straight from his chambers at Lincoln's Inn he would look tired, since it was the end of the day, and as if he had not cared sufficiently to go home and prepare. He decided to go directly.

The door opened and the now familiar butler welcomed him in. He did not even ask why Rathbone had come.

'Good evening, Sir Oliver. How pleasant to see you. I hope you are well, sir?'

'Very, thank you,' Rathbone replied. 'I apologise for calling without asking if it is convenient, but I'm afraid there has been a tragic development in the Rand case; at least I think it is connected. I would deeply appreciate Lady York's opinion as to whether it may be, or not. It concerns a woman whom she knows at least as well as I do.' He was talking too much, and he was aware of it. The butler did not care why he was here, and he certainly did not need an explanation.

'Yes, sir. If you care to wait in the morning room I will see if Lady York is available.' He appeared about to add something more, then changed his mind, and left Rathbone to find his own way through the open door of the morning room to wait there.

It was only a few minutes later that Beata herself came to the door. She was dressed in a pale, neutral colour that would not have been flattering on anyone else, but it complemented the warmth of her beauty perfectly, reminding him of sunlight in a quiet corner of a garden.

'I heard about Adrienne Radnor's death,' she said sadly. 'Do you think it is part of this larger matter? From the very little I read in the newspapers . . . and don't raise your eyebrows like that, Oliver. I do read the newspapers, and now that I am alone in the house, I read whichever ones I please.' There was amusement and very slight defiance in her eyes, just for a moment.

It gave him an extraordinary feeling of warmth, as if she were letting him know that no matter how close they became, there were certain privileges she would keep, regardless.

He smiled back at her. 'Good. That means I will not have to explain to you what we know or what I am concerned about. Possibly not even why I feel so oddly grieved for a woman I did my best to prosecute as complicit in the kidnap of Hester and the three children.'

'Do you?' she asked, but the lift in her voice seemed as much hope as surprise. 'Do you feel grieved?'

He did not know how to answer easily. 'Yes . . . I do.'

She regarded him carefully, perhaps seeing his weariness at the end of the day, the fact that he had not been home to change. Now he was conscious of it. It was a mistake, a discourtesy.

'Would you care to stay for supper?' she asked.

'I would like to very much,' he accepted.

'I shall inform Cook.' She turned away and pulled the bell by the fireplace.

A moment later the butler appeared again.

'Madam?'

'Would you please tell Cook that Sir Oliver is staying for dinner? Will she do whatever is necessary?'

'Of course, madam.' He smiled as if it pleased him. As he

bowed and left, Beata led the way across the hall to the sitting room. The windows facing the garden were open and the perfume of the last roses drifted in, with the rustle of wind in the leaves of the birch trees.

'Before we plunge into the tragic death of Adrienne Radnor – and I do find myself thinking it is tragic – how are you?' he asked.

She gave a little laugh, which was self-deprecating and yet completely honest. 'You mean how is Ingram? One week he seems to be sinking, the next he rallies again – at least in physical health. He was always a strong man. He seldom ever caught a cold.'

Rathbone was not sure what to say. She had never told him whether she went to the hospital to see York or not. He did not like to ask. He wanted to give her a kind of comfort, even that of being able to speak frankly to someone, not pretending that she wished that Ingram were better. The newspapers reported it as a kind of seizure and no one was tactless enough to suggest otherwise.

Rathbone was the only person, apart from Beata, who had been present when York had a temper tantrum so serious he attacked Rathbone, striking at him with his walking cane. It had been a blow that, if it had struck his head as intended, could have injured him very seriously. As it was, York had fallen to the floor in some kind of fit, foaming at the mouth, eyes sunken back into his head, body convulsed and kicking, lashing out where he could.

No one else needed to know that. Certainly Rathbone had told no one exactly how it had been, how pathetic and repulsive, or how dangerous. Rathbone did not believe that York had gone to a place in his brain from which it was possible to return. But that was not something one said, even to Beata, who probably already knew it.

Beata was watching him, waiting for his response.

Rathbone chose his words with care.

'Perhaps it would be most merciful for him if he were to have a seizure which, at the least, ended his awareness of his situation.'

'I have often thought that,' she agreed. 'Thank you for giving me leave to share it. There were times when I did not like Ingram very much, but I would not wish this on anyone.' She looked away. 'I don't go to visit him any more. He doesn't know I am there. Is that cowardly of me? I hate the smell of the place, the voices, the—'

'No,' he said quickly, reaching out his hand to touch her arm lightly with his fingers. 'I imagine he would prefer that you did not see him in such a state. Whether he deserves it or not, it is a last gift you can give him: to keep a memory of him at his best.'

She met his eyes. 'You are kinder to him than he deserves. He would have ruined you, you know, if he could.'

'Yes, I know,' he agreed. 'It doesn't matter now.' He was surprised that he would say that and mean it. Ingram York was important only in that he existed, and as long as he was alive Rathbone could not ask Beata to marry him. There was no question in his mind that as soon as she was free, he would. Perhaps it was better that it was not quite so soon . . . and yet he ached for it!

He must put it out of his mind now. It was an ugly thing to wish for someone's death, and he did not want her to see it in his eyes, or hear it in his tone of voice.

'There is no question that Adrienne Radnor was murdered,' he said. 'It appears she was robbed, but her lady's maid said she carried nothing in her reticule but a handkerchief and a little perfume or ointment – nothing whatever worth taking at all, let alone killing for. And she was not . . .' He stopped, not wanting to be coarse, although how else could one describe what he wished to say?

'Raped,' she replied for him. 'Does anyone believe she was killed for a handkerchief and a little perfume? Really, Oliver . . .'

'I think Rand may have killed her in case she betrayed him in some way. She must know a great deal about what went on in that cottage.'

'He cannot be tried again for kidnapping Mrs Monk or the children,' she reminded him. 'What else is there that Miss Radnor might have known about him?'

'I can't think of anything,' he admitted. 'Perhaps far more about his medical experiment than he would wish made public yet? People can be very jealous in guarding their scientific discoveries.'

'Then he will have to kill Hester too,' Beata observed. 'She would understand what he was doing in much greater detail.'

'Are you saying that because you think Hester is in danger, or because you disagree?' he asked. It was an ugly thought that had not occurred to him before. Had Monk realised the possibility?

'You are getting to know me too well,' she said ruefully. 'It is because I do not agree with you. He will be only too happy to tell everyone, as soon as he has the formula perfected. He will no doubt wish it to be named "the Rand procedure", or some such.'

'Maybe she knew something that could still betray him, if not something for which he could be tried again, at least that could damage his reputation,' Rathbone suggested.

'Possibly. But why are you so certain her killer is Rand?'

'Who else? Don't tell me it was some passing vagabond killed her. According to the first police reports, she did not fight him. She was muddy and her hair tangled, but there was no sign of a woman fighting for her life.'

'So, someone she knew,' Beata said very softly. 'Someone

she was not afraid of, at least not physically. What about her father?'

Rathbone was startled, not so much by the idea itself, but that Beata, who had not met Radnor, should come to it so quickly.

'She looked after him all through his illness,' he replied. 'In fact, she has been his companion since her mother died. No one could have been more loyal. Now that he is in almost full health again, and, I gather, keen to resume his travels abroad, she has regained the freedom to have her own life. To marry, if she wishes.'

'You mean if she ever found someone suitable, of whom her father approved, and who was willing to accept a slightly older bride,' she said. 'And, of course, whom she found agreeable.'

He looked at her, uncertain of the quality of pain he heard in her voice. Was it sympathy for a young woman she had never met? Looking at her, he believed it was something far more personal, something she knew rather than was guessing at.

He waited for her to make light of it, dismiss the remark as only an idea, but she did not.

'Do you think he really would?' he asked. 'Why? She had been devoted to him. Hester said she sat up with him night after night, without once asking for relief for herself.' He shook his head. 'He would hardly kill her rather than let her go!'

'From the way you describe it, he is intending to travel without her,' she said, biting her lip a little, her eyes not moving from his face.

Was she thinking of Ingram? Had he been possessive, domineering, demanding attention from her all the time? Surely that was only his courtroom manner in latter years, and then only when he was challenged, or perhaps felt proceedings

269

slipping out of his control. Had his mind been failing slowly, a hair's breadth at a time, for years? That would terrify anyone. When people were deeply afraid they lashed out sometimes, did anything but acknowledge the truth they feared the most deeply.

Ingram York was an arrogant and selfish man, but for a moment Rathbone felt a whisper of pity for him. He had had so much, and the love of such a woman! The loss of it all would be beyond most men to bear with any attempt at grace.

But all this was an assumption. He couldn't know for certain.

Beata leaned forward a little. 'Oliver, you said Hester described him as a man of huge appetite for life, one who wanted every taste, every smell, and every touch of beauty he could grasp.'

Rathbone winced as he recalled Hester's exact words.

'Yes.'

'Would such a man wish to take his daughter with him into the new journeys he plans? She has done so much for him, been his constant companion through his hardest times. He owes her his companionship now, don't you think?'

'Most certainly,' he agreed.

'And do you think he is a man who pays his debts willingly?' Her fine brows arched and her eyes were shadowed, unfathomable beneath them.

Now he saw a picture far uglier, and he was afraid of how she knew such things. There was pain inside her. He could feel it because it was only just beyond his reach. Maybe he would never touch it. Maybe he shouldn't, but she had allowed him to know it was there. He must, above everything else in the world, be gentle, leave everything unsaid. He had to allow her to tell him, or not tell him, but let him understand without ever saying so.

'You think he could have killed her to free himself of every obligation to her?' he said carefully. 'Cancel the debt, now that he doesn't need her? That's monstrous!'

'Don't you believe in monsters, Oliver?' she asked. Now there was a shadow in her eyes that he knew perfectly well was doubt, and the memory of sadness, perhaps even disillusion.'

'Yes, I do,' he answered quickly. 'But I wish I didn't. I suppose especially this one, because I let him go.' That was more honest than he had intended to be.

She smiled, and then moved a little away again, only inches. 'You won't make a very good St George if you don't believe in dragons,' she said, something of a certain lightness coming back into her voice.

'I don't know how to get this one. And I have a strong feeling the police don't either.'

'I don't suppose it is Monk's case, is it?' she said doubtfully.

'No. But that doesn't mean I can't talk to him about it.'

'Good. I think dinner is nearly ready. Shall we go to the dining room?'

He rose and offered his arm, feeling a little self-conscious. There was no one else present, and it was her home. But it was a very nice feeling when she laid her hand on his sleeve, so lightly he saw it rather than felt it.

He visited Monk the following evening, convinced that Monk would by now know as much as the local police investigating the matter. He found him pacing the floor and Hester sitting in her usual chair. Her face was pale and he could even see, in the strange accents created by the lamplight, the marks of tears on her cheeks.

'Have you heard anything?' Monk asked as soon as Rathbone was inside the room. 'Are they going to prosecute Rand for this?'

Rathbone walked over to the fireplace and stood looking from one to the other of them. 'Do you think Rand killed her? Why?'

'No, I don't,' Monk answered sharply. 'But Runcorn tells me the local police do. The evidence seems to suggest she put up no fight, which doesn't sound like a robber. She trusted whoever it was.'

'Doesn't mean it was Rand,' Hester argued.

'Are you working for him again?' Rathbone said incredulously. How could she, after what he had done to her?

'I'm working for the hospital,' Hester told him, 'for the patients who still need someone to care for them. Oddly enough, some of the other nurses who might have done it have suddenly changed their minds.' There was sadness in her voice, and quite definitely anger as well.

'I'm sorry,' Rathbone said. He meant it. The trail of pain this wretched case was leaving behind it was far wider and deeper than he had imagined when he began. Perhaps most cases were like that; he had simply forgotten that in the time he had been away. Sometimes you freed an innocent man, which meant the guilty one was still loose somewhere. If you convicted a guilty one, the story was seldom as simple as the charge made it seem.

'I went to see her,' Hester said suddenly. 'Just before she was killed.'

'Did you?' Rathbone was startled. 'Why?'

'It started as duty, I suppose, because I thought she might be in danger. Not very effective, was I!' There was bitterness in her voice now, and self-blame. 'I didn't like her, but I felt I might give her some kind of warning. I ended up by seeing it a great deal more from her view than I had before, and being no use at all. She was a good daughter, devoted, selfless really. Radnor made her so she thought she couldn't live without him, even that she shouldn't want to. People can do that to each other – suck them dry. I think he took people's lifeblood more than just literally.'

'Do you think Rand killed her to keep her from making any of his work public, before he was ready?'

Hester stared at him. 'Why on earth would he do that?'

'To protect the secrets of his formula for storing blood. At the moment he's the only one who knows the exact proportions, unless you do?'

'I don't think he killed Adrienne to stop her revealing how he did it. And yes, I do know what proportions he used to stop it from clotting so it was unusable. That isn't the secret.'

'What is?'

'Why some people's blood, which looks exactly like any other, cures people, and other blood kills. Some people's blood always works, some seems never to, and others works some of the time and not at other times.'

'And what is the answer?'

'I have no idea, and neither has Hamilton Rand.' She looked at Rathbone, then at Monk. 'He isn't wicked; he's just oblivious to other people's needs. He wants to find the way to transfuse blood from one living person to another, and he doesn't care who pays the price for it. He doesn't particularly want wealth, or fame. He wants the cure for white blood disease. His brother Edward died of it when he was a child. I think, to Hamilton, it would be like defeating death itself. Almost as if . . . as if he could bring Edward back and undo that loss he can't forget.'

Monk thought about it for several moments before he replied. Rathbone waited. When Monk finally spoke it was to Hester.

'So you don't believe he would kill Adrienne to keep his process secret?'

'If he wanted it secret, he would kill me first,' she replied with a tiny shrug. 'Adrienne didn't know enough about it to understand. She was there only to help her father! I was there because I was taken, and then I was a prisoner both literally, because the door was locked, and morally, because I wouldn't leave the children.'

'And you understood his passion,' Monk added, but there was no blame in his voice.

'I came to,' Hester agreed.

Monk looked at her, then at Rathbone. 'She was found in the morning, fully clothed and lying in a ditch within a quarter-mile of her home. Her clothes were crumpled but not torn. She was half hidden by the long grass and undergrowth. Her body was cold, so she died some time quite early in the night, probably before midnight.'

Hester blinked rapidly and wiped her hand across her cheek.

Rathbone noticed the gesture. She had made him laugh, infuriated him, earned from him a fierce admiration, terrified and exasperated him at times during the years he had known her, but this was the side of her he cared for the most deeply. He had once thought he would never love anyone else so much. It gave him a deep feeling of peace to know that he had been wrong about that.

'If they try to prosecute Rand for this, I won't take part,' he said with conviction. 'It doesn't look as if anything about this is going to end well!'

'It's not finished yet,' Monk said grimly. 'We won't let it be!'

Chapter Fifteen

'GLAD TO see you back,' Sherryl O'Neill said with a smile when Hester returned to duty at the hospital the following evening. Then she frowned. 'You don't look so good. Trouble is we really can't do without you. Bad accident on one of the navy ships. Five men injured.' She peered forward, studying Hester's face, the tone and colour of her skin. 'That horrible Mr Rand didn't hurt you, did he? I mean . . .' She stopped, not wanting to put her thought into words.

Hester could not help laughing at the idea. Hamilton Rand had about as much sexual passion for her as for a bucket of mud. 'You have no cause to be concerned,' she said, still smiling widely. 'The very idea is the funniest thing I've heard in months. Please don't be offended. I needed to laugh.'

'What's wrong?' Sherryl was very direct. She was used to dealing with urgent and very personal matters. There was no room for prudishness or euphemisms in nursing.

'Someone murdered Adrienne Radnor,' Hester said quietly.

'I thought you didn't like her,' Sherryl observed, 'which I can heartily understand.'

'I didn't, at least not much. But I might have, if I'd known her better. Either way, I was sorry for her.'

Sherryl shook her head. 'Sometimes I think you've got more heart than brains. But I'm glad to see you. We've got enough to do for six of us.'

And so it proved. Doing whatever was possible for seriously injured men, dressing their wounds and listening to their camaraderie, bad jokes and laughter laced with pain, reminded her of the Crimea and the desperate courage needed there. Hester had no time even to remember her own feelings, let alone consider them important.

At the end of a long night, when the sun was already risen, she met Magnus Rand for the first time since she had been smothered with ether and taken to the cottage. She was walking along the corridor on her way towards the entrance, having handed over her notes to the day nurses. She encountered him coming out of his office. He stopped short at seeing her.

'Good morning, Mrs Monk,' he said quietly. There was no mistaking the embarrassment in his face, but he did not avoid meeting her eyes.

'Good morning, Dr Rand,' she replied. She was too tired to be evasive. She had seen too much suffering to speak in euphemisms. 'The patients are doing as well as men with such injuries can. We lost no one, but they are a long way from safe. All the notes will be on your desk.'

He was clearly unhappy, but he stood directly in front of her so she could not pass him without physically brushing by him. If she took even a step he could block her way.

'It was not about the patients I wanted to speak to you.' There was a definite flush in his cheeks. 'I am sure you will have done all that you could. I think we may save those that are left. It is not an easy task, and I am very grateful that you came back. I would hardly have blamed you if you had not.'

'It is not a question of what you think, Dr Rand,' she told him calmly, no anger in her voice. 'It is the patients' wellbeing that is important. Those men had no part in your brother's experiments.'

'They might benefit from them,' he pointed out. 'Or other

men in the future, once the technique is perfected. At least there is hope.'

She looked at his face. For a moment she wanted to agree with him, say that it had been worth it. Perhaps for those people it would be. Now she was still too raw, too bruised by fear and loss, to think of such a distant future.

'Not until you know why the Roberts children's blood always worked, and other people's does sometimes and not others,' she said. 'The rest I already know.' She made a move to pass him.

He still blocked her. 'I know. I owe you a debt I can't pay, and I am very aware of it. My brother Edward died of white blood disease.' His voice was thick with emotion. 'I never really knew him, but Hamilton loved him deeply. Hamilton gave up his own career to look after me, and then to see that I had the education that he had not.'

'I understand your loyalty to him, Dr Rand,' she said sincerely. 'Perhaps you can then understand my family's loyalty to me? The son I . . . I was going to say adopted, but that is not really true. I think he adopted us. The Roberts children were your patients too. I think Maggie wanted to save her brothers just as much as you wanted to save yours.'

His face was white. 'I know all the arguments, and you are right. I don't know why I imagined that saying anything would help. My conscience prompted me, I suppose. It was not so much anything to do with you. I don't expect you to pardon what happened or find excuse for it. I am grateful you returned. Accept that at least.'

'I do accept it, Dr Rand. As I said, I didn't come back for you, I came for the patients. I suppose even more I came back for myself.'

'For yourself?' He was momentarily confused.

'You must be whoever you want to be, Dr Rand. I will not let you choose who I will be. Whatever I do, it is my . . .

failure . . . if I let you dictate my actions.' She did not avert her eyes but stared straight at him.

He looked for a moment as if she had struck him, then he lifted his head a little. 'How easily you say that – as if the choices were always so clear. Is it so easy for you, Mrs Monk? Right and wrong! No shadows you can't escape, no debts of love or gratitude where you don't have to weigh one against another?'

Now it was she who was embarrassed. Her tiredness and her grief had made her far too quick to judge. 'I'm sorry. Of course there are. And I have made mistakes. We can all be wiser in hindsight, as well as on behalf of others. I suppose I should be more grateful that I have the chance to come back. You need not have offered it to me. Good morning. I'm going home to sleep.'

He smiled with a warmth she had not seen in him before. 'Good morning, Mrs Monk,' he replied.

Hester returned to work a little early that evening and went to report to Magnus Rand before going into the ward. She wished to hear directly from him what had happened during the day, rather than read it from notes she could not question, or hear only the opinion of the nurses going off duty.

She stopped in the corridor just outside his office. The door was not quite closed, but she would not push it open without knocking first. She had her hand up and had almost touched the wood when she heard Hamilton Rand's voice with its now highly familiar quiet sarcasm.

'Really, Magnus, the issue has been decided. You are fighting against the tide. I accept that my methods were unconventional, but—'

'Unconventional?' Magnus's voice rose in disbelief. 'We are incredibly fortunate that Mrs Monk has not attempted to sue us for the way you treated her.'

Hamilton's tone kept the same slightly patronising calmness. 'Magnus, you've worked with the woman for weeks now. Haven't you ever really looked at her? She understands. She may hate me, and be thoroughly sentimental about the children. I dare say she even loathes Radnor. God knows, he's an unlikeable man. He's selfish, greedy, and treated his daughter like a cross between a child and a servant.'

His voice rose a little, becoming smooth, more urgent. 'But Magnus, she understands! I saw it in her face, in the way she moved her hands on the machine, the way she knew what to do for Radnor when he was failing. She's a born nurse, whatever else she is. She knows what I'm doing, and she knows it can work. She wouldn't deliberately sabotage it because that would be a sin against the very practice of medicine. She couldn't do it, whatever she threatens. And what's more, Magnus, she knows that I know it. She might hate me for that, but she won't strike against me because it would destroy who she is as well.'

Hester froze. Her stomach was knotted and her hands were so tightly clenched they hurt. The arrogance of him was breathtaking. And the thing that made her want to curse him with every word she could think of was that he was right. Personally she loathed him, but professionally she understood what he was doing. Her vision of what it could achieve if he succeeded infinitely far outweighed any petty and self-indulgent ideas of vengeance, or whatever might be considered justified for what had caused her no more than fear, pity and a small degree of hardship. What was any of that, compared with saving countless lives?

For Maggie, Charlie and Mike it was different. But they were not dead. Whether he would have bled them until they were she did not know. He had not been put to that test. She thought he might have failed it, but she could be wrong.

'Did you kill Adrienne Radnor, Hamilton?' Magnus asked.

279

'What? What the devil are you talking about?' Hamilton sounded utterly confused.

Magnus was suddenly really angry. 'I'm talking about Adrienne Radnor. Don't pretend you didn't know she was dead. She was murdered, strangled. Three days ago. She was found in a ditch by the side of the road, half a mile from her home.'

'God in heaven, Magnus! Did you think I did that? Whatever for?'

Hester heard the disbelief in his voice and, much as she wished not to, she believed his amazement, even his sense of outrage. He could barely grasp what his brother thought of him.

'Because she threatened your continued work,' Magnus answered. 'What did she know that could possibly have got in your way? You're a help to all the people who matter! You're safe now. Just—'

'I never touched her!' Hamilton shouted back. 'For God's sake, Magnus, pull yourself together. I hadn't seen her since the case was dismissed, nor had I intended to. Now turn your attention to the present. We have work to do.'

'You hadn't seen Miss Radnor?'

'No, I hadn't. Now stop wasting time with something we can't alter or help. I want to use Mrs Monk again. She will save time because she already knows all she needs to be of use. It will take me weeks to train someone else to take her place, even if I can find someone with her intelligence. I haven't time or the patience to deal with a woman who's forever asking questions about everything and then making short-sighted judgements. And another thing: Mrs Monk doesn't need to be told what to do in an emergency. She just does it, and tells me later.'

'I thought you didn't like her,' Magnus said drily. 'You certainly gave that impression.'

Now Hamilton's voice sounded incredulous. 'For God's sake, Magnus! I neither like nor dislike her. She irritates me at times because she makes judgements that get in the way of my work. But that is the other side of the coin. You have to accept that if she has sufficient intelligence and strength of will to make her own decisions, and act on them, then she will at times make mine also. I must watch her carefully enough to prevent it. I require her. Please send her to the laboratory.'

Hester heard his footsteps on the floor and she turned and walked away as quickly as she could, without looking behind her.

Nevertheless, half an hour later Hester stood in front of Hamilton Rand's desk by the window of the laboratory and he sat looking up at her.

'I have no time for emotional games, Mrs Monk, and I hope we are beyond that now.' He regarded her quite candidly. For once his hazel-coloured eyes appeared to conceal nothing. 'This work's importance I do not need to explain to you. I think you are almost as well aware of it as I am. In some cases, such as death from the shock of blood loss in difficult births, you feel even more deeply than I do. I am quite aware that you disapprove of my use of the blood of children, even though it works. I, in turn, do not bear you any grudge for testifying so powerfully against me in court. You acted according to your conscience. It is childish to bear any ill will because of that.' If he saw her surprise, he gave no sign of it.

'I wish you to assist me in this continued work, from time to time, as I need you. If you need to haggle about pay, then do it with Magnus. He understands that kind of thing.'

She searched his face, but she could find no intention of insult in his face. He was speaking of practicalities, no more. Should she reply tartly that she had come back to work with patients who needed her skills, and only that? She was angry with herself for being complimented that he knew she understood what he was doing.

'It has nothing to do with money!' she said firmly. 'I came here to take the place of a friend, who is unfortunately still unwell. Who will you get to do that, if I don't?'

'For heaven's sake, woman, there was other nurses,' he said impatiently. 'Not of your experience, perhaps, but adequate. We'll make more funds available. People are falling over themselves to devote to the cause since Radnor's dramatic appearance.' He said it with a slightly twisted smile. It was the first time she had seen any sense of humour in him. She wondered if he had always been like that, or whether Edward's death, his parents' deaths and his own sacrifice of his medical career had erased all laughter inside him. Was his all-consuming obsession with his work his shield against painful memories, and the emptiness that would otherwise consume him?

That would not be difficult to understand.

'Mrs Monk!'

'Good,' she said decisively. 'Pay somebody else. In fact pay several people. It is often good nursing that saves lives. That takes time, care and practice. If you can make this blood transfusion work, then you will need many nurses skilled in the treatment of shock, negative reactions, fear, all the distress both physical and emotional that go with it.'

'And you'll help?' he said, moving forward a little, his face eager.

Before she could answer there was a sharp rap on the door behind her and then it was flung open. Two uniformed policemen came in, leaving the door swinging behind them. They walked purposefully, unsmiling, towards Rand. Neither of them spoke to Hester.

'Hamilton Rand?' the larger of the two said peremptorily.

'Who the devil are you to walk in here without a by-your-leave?' Rand demanded. 'Whatever you want, you can ask for it civilly.'

'Are you Hamilton Rand?' the man repeated. His colleague glanced at Hester, and then walked round her to stand on the other side of Rand.

'Yes, of course I am. What of it?' Rand snapped at him.

The larger policeman replied coldly, and with a bold stare. 'I am here to arrest you for the murder of Adrienne Radnor. I advise you to come with us without making trouble. It would be best for you not to oblige us to use force, which we will do if you make that necessary.'

Rand stared at him as if he had spoken in a foreign language.

Hester, too, was stunned, but not sufficiently to govern her anger.

'You haven't identified yourself,' she said with a fury that startled them. 'Who are you?' From what station? Where is your warrant for this? You can't just barge in here without even knocking, and arrest anybody.'

'Ma'am, this is none of your concern,' the larger man said to her sharply. 'This man has committed murder. He will be properly charged with it and tried before the courts. Now if you will move out of our way, we can do our duty. You wouldn't want to stand in the way of the police, would you?'

Hester did not move. 'I am Hester Monk. My husband is Commander of the Thames River Police. Who are you?'

'Art, I think she really is,' the other policeman said a bit nervously. 'I've seen her before.'

But Art was not to be deterred. 'That may be, ma'am, but I have—'

'What do you mean, "may be"?' she demanded. 'What charge have you against me that you openly suggest I am a liar, even as to my own name?'

This time Art did back away a step. 'It's just a manner of

283

speaking, ma'am,' he said more gently. 'I didn't mean to say as you are lying. But this man is charged with the brutal murder of a young woman—'

'Most murders are brutal,' she cut across him. 'I knew Adrienne Radnor. I hope very much that you catch whoever strangled her.'

Art looked at her narrowly. 'How do you know as she was strangled, ma'am? Didn't say so in the newspapers. Did he tell you that?' he gestured towards Rand.

'No, he didn't,' she responded, although she knew it was a losing battle. 'If you were listening to me at all, you would have heard me tell you that Commander Monk is my husband. He was informed of the crime by officers of the law. Where is your warrant for arresting Mr Rand?'

Art took it out of his pocket and showed her, keeping it far enough away that she could not reach for it.

As soon as she saw it she knew it was genuine. The man may have acted unprofessionally, but perhaps he had children himself, and was thinking of the three that Rand had used, and come close to destroying. Perhaps also he had never lost anyone to disease of the blood, or death from haemorrhage in giving birth, or from a violent injury. It all depended so much on what you felt bone-deep in personal terror or loss, and on what you understood.

Whatever Art had known, or not, he was right to arrest Rand, at least in the law, and that was all he was answerable to.

Rand knew it, too. Like a man moving in his sleep, he held out his wrists for the manacles. He walked away between the policemen with only one glance backwards at Hester. He looked confused, even frightened, as if he did not understand.

Was he guilty of having killed Adrienne Radnor, and had seen it as a necessary act, in order to protect his work? Therefore it was not a crime, in his own opinion.

Or was it not he who had killed her at all, but someone else?

Rathbone heard of Rand's arrest and charge with a sense of dismay. And yet he had every reason to be pleased. The man was guilty of having kidnapped Hester and imprisoning the three Roberts children, even if the law could not prove it. Rathbone had not for an instant doubted Hester's word, even if he was aware that she had a respect for Rand's work, if not for his methods. And in spite of all that had happened, she was back working at the hospital where she would probably see him every day.

That much he realised that he understood perfectly. A lawyer defended people accused of appalling crimes, whatever their own opinion of innocence or guilt. He had been wrong more than once, although had he been right every time that would not alter the principle.

Nevertheless, when Ardal Juster asked him to call at his chambers, Rathbone went only because he owed Juster that courtesy. After their disappointment over the previous prosecution, and the complete shambles in which it had ended, for Juster to call on Rathbone again was more than courteous, it was generous.

'Looks as if we have a second chance at it,' Juster said as Rathbone sat down in the comfortable chair opposite the desk in Juster's chambers. He smiled ruefully. 'Although I have a feeling you are going to tell me again that you don't think the case against Rand is a very good one.'

'I haven't heard it,' Rathbone replied. He clearly hoped that he was mistaken in his scepticism.

'We have motive, means and opportunity.' Juster leaned forward across the desk in his enthusiasm. 'He can't account for his whereabouts for most of the probable time of the murder.'

Rathbone began as devil's advocate immediately. 'Seems it was apparently the middle of the night; neither could I. Could you?'

'What?' Juster looked startled, as if Rathbone had accused him of something.

Rathbone smiled. 'Most men who do not sleep in the same bed as a wife cannot prove their whereabouts at two or three o'clock in the morning. Did anyone see Rand, or a man who could have been Rand, in the neighbourhood?'

'Not so far,' Juster conceded. 'No one at all has been seen, but quite clearly someone had been there. The woman didn't strangle herself.'

'You make a nice argument for a jury,' Rathbone agreed. 'Is there anything at all to indicate that it was Rand? Something he left there? Something found in his home, his office, his laboratory? Mud-stained clothes? A footprint in the ground? Mud on his boots?'

'Miss Radnor was found in the ditch beside the road,' Juster said impatiently. 'There would be no occasion for her killer to go off into the ditch himself. And he had the means. She was strangled. Any man of average strength with two hands could have done it. And before you ask for more than that, she put up no struggle. There is plenty of evidence of that in the state of her clothes, and her body. She did not run, and she did not fight until the last few moments, when she real- ised what he had already begun to do. It was no stranger who followed her or crept up on her. There is plenty of evidence, which, if properly presented, can lead to no other conclusion.'

'Could she have had a lover who quarrelled with her?' Rathbone was still testing the case, looking for the arguments the defence would use.

'I've looked for one, but found nothing at all to suggest she has had a suitor of any kind in the last three or four years. In fact, since her father's health began to fail, and he didn't travel so much but stayed at home, she has been constantly at his side.'

'A secret lover?' Rathbone persisted.

Juster gave a sharp little laugh. 'Secret from Bryson Radnor? What do you think are the chances of that? He controlled her life. That I can call abundant evidence to prove, if I have to.'

'It begins to look like a better case,' Rathbone agreed, and saw Juster's immediate satisfaction. 'Don't want it too much,' he warned, his voice gentler.

Juster faced him squarely, his dark eyes bright. 'And you are precisely the man to warn me about taking short cuts with the law, or allowing my own sense of what is right or wrong to guide my actions, ignoring the niceties of the legal system.'

Rathbone knew exactly what he meant, and the barb had been a long time in coming. Indeed, he was surprised, considering how harsh he had been with Juster, that it had been so long.

'Of course I am,' he agreed with painful honesty. 'I have done what I am warning you not to do, and paid the price for it. You, of all men, know that. Is it a pattern of behaviour you wish to emulate?'

Juster blushed. 'Actually, I would very much like to emulate both your skill and your passion,' he said with sudden humility. 'But if I don't learn from the price you paid for that, then I am a fool. I mean to prepare this case against Hamilton Rand with the utmost care, diligence not only in every detail, but in all the moral and emotional aspects as well. And I would be profoundly grateful if you would help me, for the sake of justice, if not for the excitement of the battle.'

He leaned across the desk again, keen face earnest. 'You and I know that Rand kidnapped Hester Monk because she was useful to him, and because if he left her behind, she would tell people what he was doing. But whether she wishes to press charges or not, there is no question what he did to those children.'

Rathbone started to speak.

Juster held up his hand. 'I know! I know . . . we could not prove that the money he gave the parents was payment to get himself off any subsequent charge of kidnapping the children. And the parents, poor devils, needed it far too badly to admit to knowing much. It stood between them and the starvation of their children. They would rather have food and be thought to sell their children than keep their reputation and watch the smallest ones cry from hunger until they haven't the strength to cry any more. God help me, so would I! My point, Sir Oliver, is that we know the man is evil. He escaped us before because of Radnor's dramatic entrance. After that even an eye witness couldn't have got us a conviction. People are terrified of disease or injury where a victim bleeds to death. He holds out the hope of a cure. You can't win over hope. But this is different. This is the wilful and deliberate murder of a young woman—'

'Why?' Rathbone interrupted again. 'Why did he kill her? You have to provide that motive! If you haven't got an eye witness and you haven't got physical evidence, then you must have an overpowering reason.'

'Because now that her father is well again, she doesn't need Rand any more,' Juster pointed out. 'We don't know what else she learned when she was in that cottage. She wasn't locked up like Hester. She was there of her own will, and when Rand and Hester were caring for Radnor, she had the run of the house. She had to. What did she learn when she was there, that now she could tell anyone?'

'Such as what?' Rathbone asked, but the idea was too powerful to dismiss.

'Where the bones came from that Monk and his man dug up in the orchard, for example,' Juster suggested quietly.

'They were human bones. Some were very small . . . the bones of children.'

'They could have been anybody.' Rathbone tried to keep his voice level, reasonable, but the horror and the pity strained him beyond control. They were somebody's children, whatever they died of. Why were they not in a churchyard, a grave in hallowed ground, like other dead children of the village?

Juster saw his face, and he did not waste words on answering. 'Will you help me?' His mouth twisted in that odd, wry smile of his. 'To keep me within the law, if nothing else!'

Rathbone sighed. 'I suppose I'd better do that. I owe you a debt of considerable gratitude. I would certainly like to see Rand put away, but fairly.'

Juster nodded. That was good enough.

The second trial of Hamilton Rand opened to a courtroom so packed that no one could move in the gallery without jostling his neighbour. People stared at the witness box or the judge, Patterson again, because there was no room to turn their backs to stare across at the jury. Still less was there room to crane their necks to look up at the dock where Hamilton Rand sat between two gaolers. He seemed to be looking beyond the court to some distant sight that only he could see.

He was charged this time with the murder of the woman who had been his co-defendant in the previous trial when both were charged with kidnap, and – by default – been found not guilty.

Juster began his prosecution very carefully, laying the scene piece by piece, as Rathbone had counselled him to do. He opened by calling as his first witness the man who had found the body while riding his horse early in the morning. The animal had smelled something that had disturbed it and had stopped in the middle of the road, unwilling to go on.

The man described his actions, and what he had found.

He had then ridden back at some speed to ask a neighbour's assistance to guard the body, and send for the police. He had not touched the dead woman, except to assure himself that she was cold, and beyond human help.

Counsel for the defence was a man named Lyons, who had fading red hair, and who was in fact far older and wiser than he looked. Rathbone knew him only by repute, but he had a considerable respect for him. He was not surprised when Lyons declined to distress the witness by asking him for any further and unnecessary details.

The police evidence was exactly what everyone expected. The surgeon was brief, as if he disliked describing the dead woman, now unable to defend herself, from the somewhat prurient interest of the public. He spoke of her with the slight euphemisms he might have used were he speaking of someone still alive.

Juster found it annoying. It blunted the edge of what had been done to her. Rathbone could see it clearly in his face.

'Don't,' he warned very quietly.

'He's making it almost as if she weren't really hurt!' Juster hissed the words between clenched teeth. 'She didn't lie down in the ditch and go to sleep. She fought for her life when she realised he was trying to kill her! I've got to make the jury see—'

Rathbone tightened his grip on Juster's arm until he winced.

'No you haven't! He's made her seem human! He's left her dignity intact rather than allowed you to speak of her as a piece of evidence in the case. He's inviting the jury to see a real woman, one to protect, not exploit. Use it, Juster. Use it!'

'Mr Juster?' Patterson asked politely. 'If you have no further questions for this witness, perhaps you would oblige me by allowing Mr Lyons to conclude?'

'Thank you, my lord,' Juster said with a slight nod. 'I think the police surgeon has given us an excellent medical account of the tragic death of this young woman, at the beginning of her own life, after her selfless devotion to her father in his long illness. I don't think we need disturb her peace with anything further.'

Lyons' face was a picture of distaste as he rose to his feet. He knew precisely what Juster had achieved and was not fool enough to earn the jury's disfavour by harassing the surgeon for more detail. He made his question brief.

'Was there anything in the poor woman's injuries to indicate the height or weight of her attacker, or anything else about him?' he asked.

'No, sir, except that he was far stronger than she was,' the surgeon replied. 'And he had the advantage of surprise,' he added.

'She was unaware of his approach?' Lyons asked, raising his eyebrows.

'No, sir. From the positioning of his hands on her throat, as I think I said before, she was facing him. She did not expect him to attack her.'

'So it would be reasonable to suppose that he was someone known to her, and trusted by her?'

'It would.'

'Thank you. I have nothing further.'

Other professional testimony such as that of the police, who had conducted various parts of the investigation so there could afterwards be no detail misinterpreted, took up the afternoon. The following morning when they continued, the courtroom was so crowded doors had to be closed half an hour before the trial recommenced.

Juster called Hester Monk. He intended keeping Radnor himself until last. Anything Hester failed to do to engage the jury's sympathy, Radnor was certain to do. Juster felt confident, which was clear from the grace of his step as he walked out into the open space and faced the witness stand. It was in the smooth ease of his voice when he spoke.

'I am sorry to have to put you through this ordeal again, Mrs Monk,' he said. 'This time I hope we will have a less unfortunate outcome.' He smiled very slightly, facing the witness stand and the jury, not the gallery. This might be a superb performance, but there was only one audience that mattered, those who would deliver the verdict. Rand's life depended upon this, and – in a larger sense – justice itself and the belief that in the end it prevailed.

'Mrs Monk,' Juster began, 'I know that you have given evidence before on a great many of the things that I will ask you, but remember that to this jury, it is all new. Have patience with me.'

It was not a question and she did not answer. Rathbone thought she looked pale, and very tired, even touched by grief. She might be the perfect witness, better even than Radnor, since he had to be emotional about his daughter's death. Indeed, it would be conspicuous if he were not.

'Mrs Monk,' Juster continued, 'will you tell the court briefly how you came to know Mr Rand, and Miss Radnor?'

Hester was very brief indeed, as if she had rehearsed it in her mind, but did not leave out anything essential.

'I took a temporary post as night nurse at the annexe of the Greenwich Royal Naval Hospital. A friend from my nursing days in the Crimea had to take leave because of illness. I said I would fill her place as long as necessary, if I was satisfactory to Dr Magnus Rand, who is in charge of the annexe. During my service there I had occasion to meet Mr Hamilton Rand, who is a research chemist. Miss Adrienne Radnor came in when her father was admitted as a patient.'

'And what was your duty?' Juster asked.

'To assist Mr Rand and Dr Rand in Mr Radnor's treatment.'

'Why you?' Juster affected interest, as if he did not already know.

Rathbone glanced at the jurors. Most of them were leaning a little forward, waiting for the reply.

Hester answered without the slightest change of expression in her face.

'Because I have more experience in serious injury involving great loss of blood than most nurses have.'

'Indeed? Why is that?'

Hester answered very briefly, describing her time in the Crimea as an army nurse, sometimes actually on the battlefield.

Juster did not have to pretend his admiration. The battles and their losses were still sharp in public memory, and the name of Florence Nightingale was known everywhere. Many people had family or friends who had fallen at Balaclava, Inkerman, or the Alma.

Rathbone had heard this before, but it still gave him a shiver of horror, pity, fury for the incompetence, pity for the terrible losses.

There was not a man in the jury who did not listen to Hester with awe now. Lyons would be a fool to attack her, whatever she said.

'Did you know what these treatments were going to be, before you began?' Juster asked.

'No.'

'And when you did?'

She hesitated for several moments.

In the body of the courtroom no one moved.

'I could see the enormous potential.' Hester chose her words with almost painful care. 'If it worked it would result in the saving of more lives in the future than we could ever guess. Thousands, tens of thousands of people. Not just soldiers in war but people in any kind of accident – industrial, railway trains – women with difficult births, and of course all sorts of diseases of the blood. There is no end to what could be achieved.' There was a very slight flush to her face and her knuckles were white where she gripped the rails of the witness stand.

Juster nodded slowly, not wanting to break the spell before he had to.

'So he is a hero?' he said at last.

'A flawed one,' she said quietly.

Now the jury were straining to catch every word.

'Why?' Juster pressed her.

'Because of the means he used to obtain the blood he gave to Mr Radnor.' She shook her head and lowered her eyes. 'There is always cost to experiment. Success is not certain, or it is no longer an experiment. But those who pay the price must do it knowingly, and willingly.

'Mr Radnor was willing?'

She stared at Juster. 'Of course he was. He had no choice: he would have died without the treatment. But the children whose blood Mr Rand used were too small to have choice. And their parents had no idea what was going to be done. It is beyond the imagination of most of us.'

'Of course it is,' Juster agreed. 'But Mr Rand has already been charged with kidnapping you, and been found not guilty of that. There was some question that you might have gone willingly, in the interest of the great experiment. You do admire him, do you not?'

She looked at him with patience. 'If I had gone willingly, Mr Juster, I would have informed my family, not left them to be frantic with worry for me, and no idea where I was, or even if I were still alive.'

'Of course,' Juster agreed.

Lyons rose to his feet. 'My lord, I am sure everyone in this court has undying admiration for Mrs Monk's past heroism, and can understand her interest in such a medical break-through, but I see no direct connection with the murder of Adrienne Radnor. Indeed, I would understand if Mrs Monk bore a considerable grudge against Miss Radnor for being complicit in her imprisonment and forced assistance in the whole affair. Surely my learned friend is not going to suggest that Mrs Monk had involvement also in Miss Radnor's death?'

There was a shout of protest from somewhere in the gallery, a glare from the judge, and considerable fidgeting of embarrassment and discomfort in the jury.

Juster smiled. 'My lord, Mr Lyons makes my point for me. Miss Radnor was indeed party to Mrs Monk being held prisoner during the experiment. Therefore if there was a crime in that, or in the treatment of the children whose blood was so often taken from them and used, then Miss Radnor could have testified to it, perhaps in more detail than we have heard so far. Provable detail, that is.'

Lyons swung around and faced Juster angrily.

'Mr Rand has already been charged with that offence, and found not guilty. Whatever your opinion of him, it is irrelevant. He cannot be charged again.'

'Not with that crime,' Juster agreed. 'But Miss Radnor spent many days in the cottage in Redditch, and, unlike Mrs Monk, she was free to wander wherever she wished. What else did she discover? Did she, perhaps, discover the secret of the mass graves the police have since found there . . . graves of other people, other children?'

A wave of horror spread through the court like a wind through dry trees.

Patterson called for order and was ignored until he shouted above the roar. 'I will have order! Or I will clear the court!'

Slowly the noise subsided and people standing took their seats again.

Lyons was still on his feet. 'My lord, Mr Juster's suggestion is monstrous! There is no evidence whatever to say when those bones were buried or whose they were, as he well knows. For God's sake, they could have been plague victims from the Middle Ages!'

'Rubbish!' Juster said fiercely. 'They cannot be dated, not exactly, but we know perfectly well they were centuries more recent than that.' He turned to face Patterson's glare. 'My lord, all I want to imply was that Miss Radnor was party to the imprisonment of the children whose blood was used. She may have had knowledge of further involvement of Mr Rand's keeping other . . . blood suppliers . . . against their will. Does this court really think he developed such extraordinary skill in the art of taking blood from one person and giving it to another at his first attempt? It is a marvellous thing he has done. Superb! It is a triumph of skill, science, art and persistence. It is not some lucky guess that nobody has tried to achieve before him.'

Patterson's face was still grim.

'Your point is taken, Mr Juster, but you are very close to being in contempt of this court, or even of earning a dismissal of the case and a retrial, in which you will not appear. Perhaps Mr Lyons will be able to question Mrs Monk and give her room either to substantiate your accusations or dismiss them. If that is not so, then I will consider whether to continue with this trial. Do you understand me, sir?'

Juster bowed. Perhaps it looked humble, to the body of the court, but Rathbone saw the satisfaction on his face. He had established a perfect motive in the eyes of everyone, most especially the jury. Imagination would do the rest.

Juster very wisely yielded to Lyons.

Rathbone was so tense he could feel his nails digging into his palms again as Juster sat down near him. He wanted to tell Juster exactly how dangerously he was behaving, that he had overplayed his hand and jeopardised the whole case. Patterson could declare a mistrial for the way Juster had introduced the subject of the bones from the orchard, which had no proven connection with Rand, or anyone else still alive. Ordering the jury to ignore it was pointless. How could anyone ignore such a thing? It would haunt the imagination of every person in the court, or who read of it from the newspapers afterwards.

Juster did not look at him, as if he felt Rathbone's fury. It was exactly the sort of chance that Rathbone had taken, and earned himself disbarment. Juster had been the one who had defended him. That was a debt of which he had never once reminded Rathbone, but Rathbone himself could not forget. No man of any honour whatever, would.

Lyons faced Hester and she looked back at him, stiff and pale. Was she afraid of Lyons, of making a slip that could not be retrieved, or simply haunted by the memory of what had happened at the cottage? Please heaven, Juster would make certain the jury believed it was the last of these, even if he had to do so in his final questioning of her.

'Mrs Monk,' Lyons began, his voice respectful, even gentle. 'Are those three children still alive, as far as you know? You do know, don't you? You have not forgotten them in the events that have happened since then?'

'They are recovering well,' she replied. 'At least as far as physical health is concerned. They still have nightmares. So do I.'

Lyons was annoyed, but he did his best to conceal it.

Juster did not. He was openly pleased.

Rathbone held his breath.

'Mrs Monk, please restrict yourself to answering my questions, without adding your own . . . diagnoses,' Lyons said tartly. He might have meant it to sound critical to the jurors. They did not see it that way. Rathbone saw one of the jurors frown. Lyons' manner with Hester displeased him.

Perhaps Lyons saw it. He hurried on.

'Will you describe for the court your relationship with Miss Radnor, during your acquaintance with her, before your stay in the cottage, during it, and since, if there was one.'

Hester looked a little puzzled. 'She was the daughter of the patient,' she began. 'Our only concern was to save his life, and to assure her that all the treatment was to that end. She helped a great deal with the general care, cooking, laundry and so forth. She helped nurse him, as she had done at home, seeing to his more personal needs.'

'I meant the relationship between her and you,' Lyons corrected her.

'She was devoted to her father. We spoke of nothing else but his needs, his treatment, what we could do to make him comfortable. Once or twice she asked me if I believed he would recover. I always referred her to Mr Rand.'

'And in the cottage? If you were there as reluctantly as you say you were – in effect a prisoner – did you not ask her to assist you in escaping?' he said incredulously.

'I thought about it—' Hester answered.

'Yes or no, Mrs Monk?' he cut across her words. 'You did, or you didn't?'

Hester looked at him wearily. 'It is impossible to answer so simply, Mr Lyons. Her only care was her father's survival. That was always quite plain—'

'So you did not!' His face lit with triumph for a moment. 'You do not know, beyond doubt, that she would not have helped you, were you to ask. May I suggest, Mrs Monk, that your medical knowledge and interest, your understanding of the dramatically beneficial effect of Mr Rand's work, was sufficient for you to wish to be part of it? You did not want to escape. You wanted to see it through. You wanted to be part of its success. You are a military nurse, you have seen dozens, perhaps hundreds of deaths in the battlefield, and you knew what this meant – didn't you?'

It was a question to which there was only one possible answer. No one would believe her were she to deny it.

She smiled with a sad twist to her lips. 'I wanted him to succeed,' she admitted. 'Of course I did. I imagine everyone here would do. But in my case it was very personally immediate. If he failed and Mr Radnor died, then he would be guilty of a crime he could not afford to pay for. I was a witness to it. He would have to kill me too—'

'My lord!' Lyons protested. 'That is the wildest speculation—'

Juster shot to his feet. 'My lord, my learned friend asked the witness a question regarding her wishes in the experiment. He cannot now complain if he does not like the answer. Whatever the actual outcome, Mrs Monk wished the experiment to succeed for the very personal reason that she feared for her life if it did not.'

Patterson smiled bleakly. 'Your point is well taken, Mr Juster. And yours also, Mr Lyons. Perhaps you would like to rephrase your question?'

Lyons faced Hester, thin-lipped and angry.

'Perhaps we would fare better if I stuck to facts. Mrs Monk, did Mr Rand ever harm you, physically? Did he lay hands upon you at all while you were in the cottage, or since? I think you might manage to answer that with a yes or no!'

'No,' she said.

'Did he ever threaten you with harm?'

'No, never.'

'Yet you expect the gentlemen of the jury to believe that you feared he would kill you, if the experiment failed? Again, yes or no will suffice.'

'Yes.' She looked across at the jury. 'They are gentlemen of position and intelligence. They understand how someone with sufficient knowledge to be useful could, as circumstances change, become someone with enough knowledge to be a liability, even a danger.'

Juster hid his smile by pretending to blow his nose. When Lyons gave up, he declined to question Hester any further.

After the luncheon adjournment Juster resumed with his final witness, Bryson Radnor. It was masterful. Rathbone watched it with professional admiration, and a growing feeling of unease.

At first his anxiety was only slight. Radnor stood in the witness stand facing the court. He was a handsome man, broad and strong, his head like that of an old lion made gaunt by grief. He had allowed his mane of hair to grow a trifle long. The light caught the white in it, drawing the eye to his head, with his dark eyes and powerful features.

Juster led him to describe Adrienne's care for him, and the devotion she had shown him since her mother had died. He said in hushed and dramatic tones how her dependence upon him in her grief had gradually turned to the strength as his health had failed. It began when it had been slight, only after some time did he realise that he was experiencing the onset of a fatal disease.

The entire courtroom listened to him with intense emotion. His grief was palpable. Some of the women in the gallery wept. Men sat stiff-faced, attempting to be stoic in the presence of such loyalty, and tragedy.

Juster could hardly lose.

Rathbone knew that the substance of the case was already over. There did not seem to be anything Lyons could do that would substantially change the conviction that was grasping the jury.

At Juster's prompting, Radnor described what he could remember of his treatment. Any answer that might be uncomfortable he simply said he did not recall. No one could blame him. Even Patterson appeared impressed.

Rathbone did not even know why he was so disconcerted. Could he be feeling anything as base as envy, because Juster had got away with it. The right man was going to be convicted at last.

Or was he? *Was* Rand the right man?

All the evidence said so – at least, it seemed to. There was no one else to suspect. The murderer was someone Adrienne had known. She had been too busy to form any other relationships. And why would anyone else wish her harm, let alone to kill her?

Hester had argued that she did not believe Rand had killed her. She thought Radnor had killed her himself, to reclaim his freedom to indulge the rest of his life as he would, alone, unencumbered, without criticism, or the additional expense of a daughter to whom he owed such a debt.

What could the defence produce, or even suggest, that would raise a reasonable doubt?

Rathbone learned the day after: doctors. Two brilliant and over-articulate doctors explained to the court just how many people died of shock and blood loss who could be saved if Hamilton Rand's procedure were to be proved successful. It would revolutionise medicine. They each described bleeding to death with sufficient horror to paralyse the jury with fear.

The second doctor reinforced everything the first had said.

Juster did not argue.

His final witness was Magnus Rand. He testified to his brother's dedication to medical research, since the time of Edward's death. He could not prove that Hamilton had not killed Adrienne, but he drew a vivid picture of a man obsessed with finding a cure for white blood disease. He was not likeable. He was frequently insensitive, dogmatic, thoughtlessly rude. He did not hate anyone, since he was not sufficiently emotionally involved to care. He had not the personal imagination to envisage such a thing.

This testimony did not affect the jury at all. To judge from their faces, they saw only that he was cold, dedicated to his science and impervious to the human cost to others.

They returned with a verdict of guilty.

Rathbone was disturbed by it. It was the verdict he had wanted and expected, but now he was unsatisfied. He went to see Monk, and more importantly, Hester.

'No,' she said quietly in answer to his question. 'Rand is blind to other people's pain, if it isn't connected with injury or white blood disease. He can't imagine any other kind of pain. But I don't believe he killed Adrienne. I think Radnor did it himself, to be rid of her dependence on him, to be free of the expense and the obligation of his debt to her.'

'Is that because yer knew 'im when he was sick?' Scuff asked seriously.

Hester was too tired to argue, but she was clearly uncomfortable.

Scuff looked down. 'Sorry . . .'

'Not just that,' she said quietly. 'I think Hamilton Rand has all kinds of faults, but he wasn't afraid of Adrienne. He didn't even see her as a threat. I don't think he thought of her at all after she left the cottage.'

'Her own father?' Monk bit his lip. 'I wanted Hamilton Rand to pay for what he did to the children, and for taking you – but not for something he didn't do.'

'We lost.' Rathbone said, looking from one to the other of them. 'Rand is going to hang for something he didn't do. We have no idea whose bodies were buried in the orchard. And Radnor is going to walk away! I can't think of anything we can do about it.'

Chapter Sixteen

THE WEEKS passed very slowly until Hamilton Rand was hanged. Hester continued to work at the hospital. There was no more experimental work, but she stayed out of a sense of loyalty to her patients, who were in as much desperate need as before. They required reassurance, and even a new insistence upon hope.

She also stayed with a certain loyalty to Magnus Rand. The brothers had never seemed very close in life, but watching Magnus now, she realised that there had been a silent affection between them taken for granted. Growing up, Magnus had always known Hamilton was in the background, taking care of the material things, believing in their purpose, always having the energy of mind to press forward, however difficult it might appear, or however exhausted he was. Even hopeless causes did not deter him. He might have seemed cold, but there was a unique determination in him that drove him to believe in the work, regardless of temporary failure, other people's disapproval, even derision.

It was a different kind of heart from most other people's. It was not comfortable or attractive. Sometimes it was frightening. But it was admirable.

Certainly he had bought the Roberts children to use them in his experiments, although they were now healthier than ever before. Their parents not only feared public opinion enough not to neglect them, but also had the means to care for them, thanks to Mr Roberts obtaining work. He did not dare fail at it.

Certainly Rand had kept Hester prisoner in order both to use her skills and prevent her telling anyone about his use of the children. But she was sure that he had not killed Adrienne Radnor. He had not been sufficiently afraid of her to care one way or the other, and had no belief she would attempt to harm him.

What about the bodies in the orchard? Hester did not doubt that Hamilton and the gardener had buried them. But they might have died of natural causes, such as white blood disease. Perhaps they were people whom he had tried to save, and failed. It was probably a crime to experiment on patients without their consent, but that was not the offence for which he had been tried, and not one for which he should hang. All doctors lose patients. Sometimes error or carelessness contribute, but usually doctors have done everything they could, and still failed. She knew that all too well. She had lost too many herself.

Now Hamilton had been dead two weeks, and Hester was nursing in the hospital, still waiting for Jenny Solway to return, and doing what she could to offer some kind of comfort to Magnus Rand.

As if seeing that she was one of the very few people who both understood Hamilton's manner, and believed he had not killed Adrienne, he sought her company when time allowed. She was actually standing in the corridor talking to him when one of the nurses came running towards them. This was against hospital rules, but there was such panic in her face that neither Rand nor Hester thought to criticise her.

'What is it?' Hester stepped forward and the woman almost stumbled into her. 'What's happened?' Hester demanded firmly.

'Mr Radnor . . .' she gasped. 'He's back an' he looks terrible. Bad as he ever did . . .'

'Where is he?' Hester asked, shock all but freezing her. Her calmness was the result only of the training of years.

'In the hall, by the front,' came the reply. 'I called the porter to get him to a bed before he passed out right where he stood. Dr Rand, I dunno what to do with him.'

Rand, too, was stunned. He fumbled for words. It was Radnor's whole case that had brought Hamilton to ruin.

And yet there was no proof. And even if there had been, could he now turn away and ruin a man whose life was in such jeopardy, and who had come to him for help?

'Take us to him,' Hester directed the nurse. 'We'll do what we can.'

Looking relieved and intensely grateful, the woman swivelled on her heel. She strode at a brisk pace back the way she had come, with Hester and Magnus a yard behind her. They looked neither to right nor left, as they rushed straight across the entrance hall and the room where Bryson Radnor lay on the bed, fully clothed. His face was ashen grey, his eyes sunken in their sockets, sweat on his skin. But ill as he was, he was fully conscious and he looked first at Magnus, then at Hester. His gaze remained on her, as if he considered her the one who was in charge, and would decide his fate.

Magnus turned to Hester. He looked as desperate as Radnor, as if posed on a cliff edge with the devil behind him and the long fall to the rocks below.

Hester looked at Radnor, meeting his eyes. He stared back at her without flinching. There was a terrible black laughter inside him, as if even in dying he had won a victory over her, his will over hers. In that moment the last doubt in Hester's mind vanished that he had killed Adrienne. She realised that he was quite aware that she knew it, and could do nothing. He was also perfectly sure that she would care for him now, whatever she felt. If she failed to do so, that would be his final victory over her. He would have destroyed what she believed in. It was not the defeat over death that he wanted, but it would be a defeat of the life he had to leave to others, and no longer share.

He smiled at her, past Magnus, as if he had not been there. 'I need another transfusion,' he said a little hoarsely. His voice was weak. 'You know how to do that, don't you, Mrs Monk? You've helped poor Hamilton often enough – you know it by heart. And I'm sure you will have children you can use somewhere in the hospital.

There was an aching timeless silence.

Thoughts flew through Hester's mind. Did she want to save Radnor? With Hamilton Rand dead, did she have the skills? She had watched, but never done it alone. What if she made an error?

The doctor's oath – first do no harm.

She thought of Orme bleeding to death, and Monk's grief, which he was trying so hard to conceal.

How do you learn for the future, except try with the unknown?

Some things you discover, like fire. Others you have to invent, like the wheel.

It was Magnus who spoke. 'I'm not as good as Hamilton was, but I'll try. And Mrs Monk will help me.' He turned to her. 'Won't you?' There was pleading naked in his eyes, urgency. Surely not to save Radnor's life. Was it to redeem the reputation of the hospital? And was he aware of the exquisite irony of using Hamilton's invention to save the man for whose crime he was hanged?

'Please?' Magnus said softly.

If she refused, and with whatever reason she gave, Radnor would have won, or he would believe he had. Perhaps in the future she would believe it too. Excuses would become weaker and weaker until she knew them for lies.

'Yes . . . yes, of course I will.' She turned to Magnus. 'We must be quick.'

'Good,' he accepted. 'Thank you. Have him brought to the room we used before. The machine is still there. I'll go and get the blood and prepare it. I know exactly what Hamilton did. Just . . . just take care of him.' Before she could reply Magnus turned sharply and left the room. They could hear his footsteps fade away down the corridor.

A moment later a porter appeared with a wheeled chair and together they helped Radnor into it and as carefully as possible, took him to the transfusion room.

They lifted him on to the bed. Hester was horrified at how light he was, as if half the substance had gone from the man who had cut such an impressive figure in the courtroom twice, to give shattering evidence that had altered the courses of two trials. One had freed Hamilton Rand and sent him rising to the peak of his career. And the other had condemned him to be hanged.

Alone with him, Hester made him as comfortable as she could. He was feverish; she knew it even before taking his temperature, or his light, erratic pulse. She bathed him in cool water before helping him into one of the hospital night-shirts. She did it carefully, very gently so as not to further bruise his body. Adrienne could not have been more tender.

It pleased him, as if he had made her do it.

'I travelled,' he told her hoarsely. 'I went to France, Mrs Monk. I stared up at the sun and watched through half-closed lids the coast of Normandy, great skies with the white clouds drifting across them like ships with gigantic sails set. I smelled the wind in the ripe grass, up to my thighs, tangled with wild flowers and scented sweet as heaven. I lay on the dry earth and made love under the trees, hearing their leaves whisper of eternity.'

She did not answer.

'You think I'm going to burn in hell, don't you?' he

challenged her. 'Some religious hell of infinite pain, no doubt. It will be a new adventure, because I've already been to heaven.' He strained to keep his concentration on her.

She looked him in the face, seeing the wasted flesh on it and the burning, challenging eyes.

'I think hell is the vision of heaven you can't taste or touch, Mr Radnor. A place where you gradually lose the ability to feel anything except anger and self-pity, and the infinite regret for what you could have had, but threw away. Eventually you will become an empty wraith, incapable of beholding heaven at all, even if you could imagine it, except as an old dream you can't hold on to any more. But you will never forget that you could have had it, only you let it go.'

He stared back at her. 'Damn you!' he hissed between his teeth. 'Damn you!' All the hatred in his soul was in the words, and in his eyes.

Magnus returned, looking from one to the other of them. 'Have you prepared him, Mrs Monk? We have no time to waste. It's nearly four o'clock already.'

'Yes, he's prepared,' she replied, facing Magnus and turning her back on Radnor.

Magnus nodded. It was some time since he had assisted Hamilton, far longer than since Hester had, so he was very careful and relied on Hester's help. He attached the bottle of fresh blood to the contraption, checked that all the pieces were connected and working, and then inserted the needle into the vein in the crook of Radnor's arm. He opened the valve and the transfusion began.

Radnor lay smiling, as if even watching the deep red blood enter his body brought him strength. Or perhaps it was his victory over Hester and Magnus Rand that seemed to invigorate him. After all he had done to Hamilton, it was Hamilton's invention that would save his life, yet again. And Hester and Magnus would watch it.

It was slow. Magnus was meticulous. Everything was right. He had Hester check and double check.

By midnight, the procedure was completed. Radnor was sleeping peacefully, a half-smile on his face. Magnus was so pale and tense Hester was afraid for him. She sent word for Sherryl, whom she trusted both for honour and for skill, to come and watch Radnor. Then Hester persuaded Magnus to go to one of the empty rooms and lie down. Sherryl would send for him if there were any change. She accepted his order that she go home. She longed to go home to Monk and creep into bed beside him, feel his arms around her. Perhaps she would tell him all that she had felt, the conflicting emotions inside her. But, on second thoughts, it would be better not to speak of it at all, simply to be beside him.

In the morning both she and Monk woke up late. Monk was in the kitchen making a cup of tea and she was coming down the stairs when there was a knock on the door. She went to answer it, expecting it to be Hooper enquiring where Monk was. But when she opened the door it was Magnus Rand standing on the step. He looked haggard, and so pale he could have been on the point of collapse.

'Come in,' she said immediately. 'Please . . .' She stepped back to allow him to pass her and walk unsteadily into the sitting room. He collapsed rather than sat down in the large chair beside the fire.

She followed him in, afraid he was seriously ill. He looked weaker and more exhausted than even long hours or the horror of his brother's death could account for. She looked at him gravely.

'I can get you a strong cup of tea, but you need more than that. Please tell me honestly what is wrong with you, and what I can do.'

He looked up at her. His eyes were red-rimmed, his skin totally without colour.

'Have you been up all night?' she asked quietly.

'Pretty well,' he replied. 'Bryson Radnor died at about four o'clock, or a little after. Horribly,' he added. 'I didn't think it would be as bad as it was.' He smiled with a faraway look, as if reliving what he had seen and which now was indelibly graven into his mind. 'It's a while since we lost a patient to the white blood disease.'

'We did all we could,' she told him, emphasising each word. 'He had many months more of life than he would have had without your treatment.'

Monk walked past them into the room and stopped beside Magnus. He looked down at him with intense pity.

'Hester, the kettle is about to boil. I think Dr Rand needs a mug of hot, sweet tea. You'd better make it as strong as you can, and put a good tablespoon of brandy into it.'

She hesitated only a moment then went to do as he asked. Rand must ache with grief and loss. Now he must feel defeat on top of that. He needed help; above all he needed some kind of friendship. Hamilton's death had taken from him all the family he had, a man who had been both brother and father to him.

Monk sat down on the chair opposite Magnus.

'What happened?' he asked gently. He needed to know, in case the answer jeopardised Hester in some way. Whatever his pity for Magnus, he could not allow that.

Magnus looked across at him, no artifice in his face at all.

'We gave him a blood transfusion,' he replied. 'Or more exactly, I did, and Mrs Monk helped me. She's an extremely good nurse. But I expect you know that.'

'You did it the same way your brother did?'

'Exactly. Your wife would tell you that. She was with me all the time.' He took a long, deep breath and let it out in a sigh. 'She did everything she could. She is in no way responsible for anything that happened. And no one could think it, I promise you.'

'Then how did Radnor die?' Monk pressed him.

Magnus smiled with exquisite irony. 'We did not have the Roberts children any more. They are doing well, I believe.'

'Yes, they are. So whose blood did you give to Radnor?'

'Two pints of it,' Magnus answered. 'I feel like hell . . .'

'Whose blood?' Monk repeated, watching Magnus's ashen face.

'Why, my own,' Magnus replied, his eyes unwavering from Monk's. 'I couldn't give him somebody else's, could I? Knowing what he was . . . without their permission . . .' He smiled very slowly. 'I am afraid he died a very hard death, even if it was comparatively quick. Not as quick as hanging, of course.'

'Did you know it would kill him?' Monk whispered.

'I was pretty sure.'

Monk was silent for several seconds – in fact, until he heard Hester's step along the passage, bringing the tea.

'I suppose he insisted?' he said at last.

'Oh, yes! Medical obligation to try,' Magnus agreed. 'But Hester didn't know. She really didn't.'

Hester came into the room carrying the tea, looking with concern at Magnus, then glancing at Monk.

'You had better give it to him a bit at a time,' Monk told her gently. It was completely unnecessary. She would do that anyway. Whoever he was, and whatever she knew or guessed, she would do that, always.

FOR MORE FROM ANNE PERRY, TRY
THE COMMANDER
THOMAS PITT SERIES

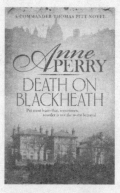

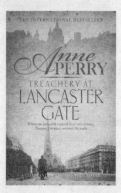

GO TO WWW.ANNEPERRY.CO.UK
TO FIND OUT MORE

headline

AND LOOK OUT FOR THE NEXT

COMMANDER THOMAS PITT

NOVEL

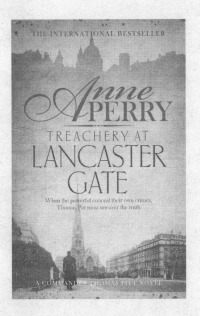

OUT NOW IN HARDBACK AND EBOOK

IF YOU ENJOYED THIS

COMMANDER WILLIAM MONK NOVEL

YOU'LL LOVE THE REST OF THE SERIES

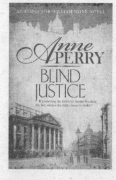

THE FACE OF A STRANGER

A DANGEROUS MOURNING

DEFEND AND BETRAY

A SUDDEN, FEARFUL DEATH

THE SINS OF THE WOLF

CAIN HIS BROTHER

WEIGHED IN THE BALANCE

THE SILENT CRY

THE WHITED SEPULCHRES

THE TWISTED ROOT

SLAVES AND OBSESSION

A FUNERAL IN BLUE

DEATH OF A STRANGER

THE SHIFTING TIDE

DARK ASSASSIN

EXECUTION DOCK

ACCEPTABLE LOSS

A SUNLESS SEA

BLIND JUSTICE

BLOOD ON THE WATER

CORRIDORS OF THE NIGHT

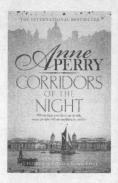

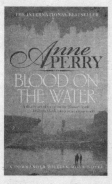

GO TO WWW.ANNEPERRY.CO.UK
TO FIND OUT MORE

__headline__